Pariah In the Mirror

Doug Booth

Pariah In the Mirror

©2017 RD Booth

Pariah In the Mirror

Part One
1

The unforeseen and incessant tempest blew in without warning to New Orleans midway through the dinner hour on June 28th while, peering from their dining room windows, Murielle de la Sorbonne sought comfort and courage from the young couples strolling hand in hand along the sandy shore or lazily paddling canoes in the calm and glistening waters of Lake Pontchartrain.

The black storm raged throughout the night, for two days worsening with threatening ferocity until at last abating the evening of July 01st as Murielle stood with her suitcase at the door of her parents' prestigious lakefront home.

"Madame," Monsieur de la Sorbonne vented, red-faced, "speak to this stupid child of yours! Clearly she has lost her mind!"

Murielle's mother embraced her tightly, warm tears dampening her daughter's cheeks. "Your father is right in what he says, ma petite. Please do not do this impetuous and terrible thing. You see this man through eyes too blurred to see clearly. You are swayed by his charm and his promises. He will not be good for you."

"He *is* good for me, maman, you will see. I am falling in love with him, from the very first day I felt something wonderful between us. He is a good man, a kind man."

"Écoute-moi, stupid one!" her father cut in. "He is a predator, tout simplement, as you are naïve and foolish. This is not simply a childish ploy you propose which will taunt and torment us. This very moment is the end of your youth."

"He is no such thing, papa. You are not listening to me. We are special together. Not once has he treated me unkindly. Not ever."

"Bah! Not once in five weeks or six," Monsieur de la Sorbonne scoffed. "You are the silly one who does not listen. He is thirty-three. You are barely twenty-one, an innocent amusement for him to play with until you are no longer fresh for him, no longer nubile enough for him, no longer appealing to his diseased mind."

"Your father is right, ma petite. This man, he does not love who and what you are. He desires what he sees of you. He will hurt you."

Her father inhaled a deep breath. He was done, exhausted. "Murielle, do as you wish. You are past the age of our interference. Whatever you choose to do with your body is your business alone, no longer ours. Though let us be very clear and to the point, mademoiselle, you and I. A passing and misguided dalliance is one thing, a pardonable thing. But this, what this corrupt and overbearing manipulator will do to you will tarnish your life forever. He will take from you the romantic dreams of a young woman and bring shame upon you and your family in return. Once he is finished with you only the basest of men will ever think to take on another's willingly soiled paramour. That is what he will give you."

Murielle blanched at the cold-hearted and even rebuke, her mother's steady flow of tears worsening the confrontation. Still, Monsieur de la Sorbonne was adamant.

"You will regain your senses at once, Murielle, and not

4

do this terrible thing to yourself or to us. He will tire of you in less than one year and put you onto the street, stupid one!"

"He will not," Murielle snapped. "I am in love with him, papa. We are in love together. You do not understand what we share."

De la Sorbonne had no anger left with which to lend him strength. "I know very well what you share with him. It is not merely a woman's brain, Murielle, which determines what she is or what she becomes. This you have not yet learned."

"I know what I am, papa. I am your daughter who loves you."

"A daughter does not shame her dear mother and her father."

She ignored him. "Maman, je t'aime." She kissed her mother's cheeks. Reaching for her suitcase she faced her father, horrifying her mother who knew better than to speak another word. "Papa, my dear papa, my taxi has come. I will see you on the fourth for maman's special celebration dinner when you will be more reasonable with me. I cannot talk with you when you are like this. Now kiss your daughter, my taxi is waiting." She leaned in to him, to kiss his cheeks, visibly shocked at the open hand halting her. "Papa? You will not kiss your daughter?"

"You have heard nothing these past seventy-two hours, Murielle." He stepped aside, extending an open palm. In a calm voice he said, "Your key, mademoiselle, your phone and your card. I will not support another man's coquette. My door is closed to you. You are a stranger whose unfortunate future is clear to me, if not to you. One year, you foolish girl. Believe what I tell you. One year, beyond which I wish you good fortune."

She fumbled in her purse, filling his hand with what he

wanted, unable to face him. She was trembling, fighting back tears. "You are the one who is wrong, papa, not me. You will see. What will your life become without your daughter?"

He stepped past her, reaching for the doorknob. Without another word he closed the door behind her.

2

JULY 08th, one year later, Murielle lay in bed dreamily contemplating her summer months, relishing her first taste of freedom from the never-ending demands of university life. So hectic were the previous twelve months that she seldom gave any thought whatsoever to her parents.

Ironically she spent much of the previous July alone in her parents' native France while multi-millionaire Kenneth Stonewall conducted business with his French counterparts who were captivated by her at dinner. Before returning home she vacationed with him in the Côte d'Azur, in Barcelona and Naples. At Christmas they cruised the pristine turquoise waters of the Bahamas, celebrating New Year's in a much more vibrant Miami. Her Spring Break getaway leading into Easter and her May 10th birthday was a Caribbean Cruise, in exchange for which he exacted a pledge that she would study intensely through to the end of her final semester and graduation.

Throughout their first year in New Orleans they dined often at fashionable restaurants, attending the theatre and operas alone or in the company of his urbane acquaintances. They were the quintessential happy couple. He was handsome and young at heart; she was youthful in every way, becoming more cultivated with each wide-eyed experience he brought to her.

One day soon she would have her dream job, her

success a certainty. She was at the top of her class with an honours degree and fully ready, her CV professionally produced by Stonewall's Southeast Industries publicity group while her envious peers were left to copy generic models from the web. God how she loved him, snuggling contentedly into the warmth of their bed for a final few minutes of peaceful dreaming. After all, she deserved. And that she frequently bartered her perfect body inclusive of her final year to ensure those superior grades did not in any way diminish her love or her loyalty.

She was being pragmatic, intent on pleasing Kenneth. She would never disappoint him, particularly since she knew what other delightful surprise he was planning for her.

Her father was so totally wrong.

*

Kenneth Stonewall stood on the balcony of his upscale third-floor pied-à-terre, owned by a little-known division of Southeast Industries so that he might come and go with complete anonymity.

He was appreciating the quiet, sipping an expresso and reflecting over his past year with Murielle. He was already dressed to go, his tailor-made Belmont shirt brilliantly white against his dark blue Belmont suit.

He was gazing across one of the Garden District's finest avenues, studying the District's daily parade of trendy nubile runners and trainers, all wearing designer gear, all drenched in sweat, bent over and grimacing against lampposts, catching their breath or stretching out tortured muscle groups. Not a single adherent to the cause was smiling, millennial high-fives reciprocated with nods acknowledging each other's intense devotion to self. Good for them, unlike Murielle whose idea of an intense self-motivated workout was pirouetting naked in front of her mirror and concurring with 'self' that she was indeed the most beautiful woman in New Orleans. Which she undeniably was for the time being.

Not so the twenty-something redhead in the red halter and mesmerizing hip-hugger boy shorts looking to get pulled into the bushes. She would have been a definite contender for the coming year if not for the fact he watched her intriguing routine faithfully each morning he was at the condo come rain or shine. Truly unfortunate. Truly. However that close was not a good thing.

The day was beginning splendidly, one the announcer's affected drawl was warning would degrade into thunderous dark skies, torrential rains and record-level oppressive heat. He glanced at his Cartier: 09:15. Two hours since his shower; thirty minutes since brewing his third expresso and she remained lounging in bed.

He gave the redhead a final glance, stepping from the balcony into the condo, murmuring. He ought to have been honest, he should have told her one month earlier, returned her to reality and given her time to adapt. Instead he allowed her the benefit of doubt that telling her then might have ruined her supposedly most important day, eclipsing the excitement of her graduation ceremony. More importantly their intimate celebration the previous Friday would not have materialised.

The uncharacteristic and impulsive beneficence had put him a full month behind schedule, causing awkward moments with his incoming companion and the needless expense of suitably housing her elsewhere in the meantime, and that Murielle remained in bed while others her age were making good use of a splendid morning annoyed him greatly.

He jabbed a fingertip hard against the radio, when what he truly wanted was to puncture the man's throat. Silence. What did he care about another damp and muggy Saturday in the nation's worst urban swamp?

He put his attaché case by the front door and strode into the bedroom where he studied her with no particular expression or feeling of regret, wondering instead how anyone could possibly fall into such a deep sleep that quickly in daylight. He was devoid of sentiment, a personality disorder he readily accepted as normal. He was concerned with practical results and never given to emotion, adept at conveying the opposite of whom and what he was when need be. He rarely smiled and laughter was as foreign to his character as compassion.

Mutual gain, he mused. Win-win. She lay on her side naked and purring, her body twisted into silk sheets. She was twenty-two, a year and several weeks older than when he first captivated her with practiced charm, sangfroid poise and genteel manners. He was elegant, tall and dark, inherently remote, his attentiveness purely the illusion of an awestruck girl.

His tanned and lean physique belied the encroaching midway point in his life; his sense of self too entrenched, too focused on wealth and achievement to ever lend credence to the existence of the proverbial male crisis. Better she should pout and whimper sniffles into her pillow until hate and loathing would for a while supplant all memories of a glorious and gainful fourteen months.

She was without question stunningly beautiful. She was eager, if not completely unrestrained in matters of the bedroom, generously remunerated for her love and devotion with extravagant gifts and exotic travel, her four-year university debt paid in full with the stroke of his Montblanc one week earlier. A staggering price to pay for nubile affection, indeed, albeit quite affordable. She was without question a justifiable and deserved expenditure considering the impoverished state of his many divorced executives.

Win-win. She did well for herself. In spite of which feelings of desertion and failure would certainly and very soon invade and destroy her sense of worth: The female condition, which was not his to worry over.

The electric blue by her pillow glowed 9:18.

He cupped a hand over her shoulder, firmly squeezing into soft and warm flesh, provoking a guttural groan. Then nothing, Stonewall shaking her with intentional brusqueness. He had no tolerance for indolence, irritated by her continued reluctance to free herself from the languor of university life. He had spoiled her excessively; the real world would not by any measure, she was about to discover. Certainly no longer his issue.

"Open your eyes, Murielle. I must leave you now." He tugged abruptly at the sheets, frustrated. He dared not touch her more than he had, despite the mounting temptation to savour her charms one last time. "For pity sake, would you *please* open your eyes?"

She moaned, stretching, contorting her body into a fluid and erotic oeuvre. She was the quintessential companion, Stonewall recalling his earlier misgivings: She was indeed a difficult one to replace.

Reaching out to pull him closer her dreamy smile evaporated into pursed lips and a furrowed brow. "Kenneth, darling, you're dressed. Why are you dressed? It's Saturday."

Precisely at 9:20 her world imploded.

"Indeed I am, Murielle, with a view to facilitating the overdue termination of your year with me in order that you might forge a new and better path for yourself without me by your side."

Her eyes were instantly clear and alert, her face masked with shock and disbelief. "What!"

He stood. "Thank you, Murielle. I did very much enjoy

11

and greatly appreciate the impact and influence you had on my life. I am extremely grateful and shall forever value the many vivid memories we created together. I trust you will likewise remember me fondly in the years to come."

"No!" Murielle de la Sorbonne struggled to free herself from her silk shroud, lunging onto her hands and her knees, frozen in time and place by a commanding finger. She looked more wretched than ridiculous. "Kenneth, no! Is this some sort of cruel joke? Are you teasing me?"

"Hardly, my dear. Simply requisite, with nothing to be gained by further mournful pleas. Please be gone by month's end with your belongings. Adequate time I believe to relocate given your abundantly free schedule. The thirty-first, Murielle, by end of business when the lock will be changed."

What! She was too horrified to cry or scream out her anguish, believing her heart would stop beating. She felt nauseous and disoriented, as though savagely and relentlessly beaten. She was devastated.

"Do not do this, Kenneth," was her desperate plea. She gulped air. "What have I done? Tell me. Please. We'll have breakfast, we'll talk this through. This cannot be happening to us."

"Nothing is happening to us, Murielle. Nor is there anything to tell or for you to lament once your shock subsides. You have done everything exceptionally well, far beyond my highest expectations and fanciful dreams. I did however leave a cheque on the sofa table, my thank-you for an entirely satisfactory year and sufficient to sustain you through to the commencement of your forthcoming career."

"Kenneth, no. Last week, all the things you said. A great surprise. You said I'm in for a great surprise. I thought…"

"I know what you thought, which sadly speaks volumes."

"I love you, Kenneth. Why are you being so incredibly cruel?"

"Clearly you do not. You love the thought of me. You love travel; you love fine living and designer fashions. You love being seen. What I have come to see and believe, Murielle, is that you are as shallow and as devoid of love's prerequisites as I. Sad to say for someone your age. The surprise I was alluding to is the real world that awaits you, to the stark reality you will face if you choose to remain indolent all day while your competition is aggressively expanding their networks, seeking as they should to advance themselves. Something you have shamefully and manifestly ignored for an entire week."

She sat back like a scolded child. Her eyes were fixed on the floor with her hands clasped in her lap, her lips quivering, her cheeks flushed a deep pink.

"I would counsel you to act more responsibly, to become as sought-after a lobbyist as you are a desirable and thoroughly delectable woman, which I suspect played no small part in your four years of notable scholastic achievement. Bravo. One must always make the best use one's finely honed assets. Apart from which you have achieved nothing remarkable in your life. Goodbye, Murielle."

He spun on his heels, disappearing into the living room.

The door closed with a sharp click. Kenneth Stonewall was not given to drama. She would cry, yell, scream, and get on with life…hers. Or, as was more likely the case, she would not.

He skipped down three flights of stairs, stepping into the historic Garden District, pausing.

As much as he enjoyed the freedom of driving himself most weekends, he did not appreciate the discomfort of waiting for the AC to neutralize the suffocating heat trapped in the car, nor did he appreciate valet service in a city with no parking when subsequent to each event he would perforce sanitize the steering wheel.

Inhaling a deep breath he strode to his Bentley and forgot her.

3

Murielle de la Sorbonne fell onto her side, hugging her knees to her chest and staring at the door. She was numb; she wanted to be sick.

What had just happened...to her life, her plans, to him? He was her man, her lover and her mentor. She utterly adored him, longing for the day she would be his wife and no longer his companion. A week earlier she had wakened in his arms, his caressing fingertips strumming soundless chords across her back in a Madison Avenue hotel suite, her mind reeling from the excitement of the previous day.

Her B.A. in Public Relations brought to an end four years of studies in journalism and writing, campaigns and the law, and three difficult summers of menial internships without pay because they knew she lived at home with mommy and daddy and had no choice. Until Kenneth. His bank draft a week earlier, what he long ago promised during their second dinner together, that she never truly believed, had instantly eradicated her financial woes. The flight to New York for a Broadway performance and what she now realized was their last dinner was almost surreal.

She was catching her breath. What was the big deal taking a week to pamper herself with late mornings and doing nothing? She deserved. She was overwhelmed. *He* overwhelmed her.

He had insisted on attending the ceremony, proudly

standing and applauding as she flung her bachelor's cap and tassel into the air. Later he surprised her even more en route to the airport in his corporate limo, giving her a designer gown she would wear to the theatre when other grads were renting limos and wearing altered tuxes and gowns to their uninspired pedestrian celebrations.

Making her mind whirl all the more, the following morning his tender strokes evolved quickly into the unbridled urgency of heated passion before a sumptuous in-room breakfast and flying her home in a dreamlike state. Who would do all that and simply leave?

What did she do, what could she have done? Murielle realizing with a sorrowful grunt that he hadn't once been to the condo throughout the entire week except for the previous evening, arriving late for dinner without an apology, not even an "I missed you." She didn't do anything wrong. The frigging bastard. He could have told her the moment he walked in, yet he didn't because he needed to get seriously laid one last time, using and deluding her one last time.

She hurled a pillow across the room. For an entire year she wasn't his girlfriend, never a true lover; she'd been stupid and blind, a well-paid live-in whore. She inhaled deeply, blowing a long breath. A whore? Big deal. What girl in her classes didn't freely put herself out there, fucking how many brain-dead troglodytes and amenable professors? At least she was a debt-free whore.

So who would be his next whore? Who would take her place? Her mind went blank, blurting a sudden cough realizing her eyes were dry, that her mouth and lips were moist, that her heart was not about to stop beating anytime soon. She was royally pissed, furious with herself for not thinking to hurt him. She wanted him back, she wanted to…she didn't know, do something bad.

Then, "Shit!" Evicted from two homes in a single year with three weeks left to get out and start over. Again.

She squirmed her way to the edge of the bed, sitting huddled into herself, pondering where and how she would ever find a decent place to live, a place as stylish and chic as his condo. Her parents were out of the question, her father had made that abundantly clear.

She pursed her lips, snorting. Her father was right; she should have known. He knew from the beginning what she had moments earlier discovered, his terse and explosive rant the very last words he spoke to her. Yet not as harsh nor as bitter as the door of her childhood home closing noiselessly behind her, she remembered. The most horrible sound she could imagine, until now.

She pushed her weight from the duvet and went to the table. Her father *was* right without saying the word. She *was* a whore, her single most life experience which she thought to capitalize on while running errands between offices at the state capitol throughout those three summers. Not one of them willing or able to pay the hoped-for dividend of a promotion to a higher paygrade the following year, not one of them yet responding to her CVs.

She ascribed all of them to practical experience, a learning curve. Nothing she would ever lose sleep over.

She nodded. Ten grand. A highlighted note warning her of the cheque's August 01st cancellation date. Possibly enough to live well until her entry-level income kicked in. She didn't know. She had no idea how long the money would last. She hadn't once in her life paid for groceries, or wine, or clothes; never checked her receipts. He simply gave her a generous weekly allowance which she spent freely and maintenance money with appropriate instructions. She had never paid rent or bought appliances, her financial savvy limited to bus tickets, campus cafeteria lunches, additions to her wardrobe and school books.

Although three months did seem reasonable, given that prospective employers would soon begin inviting her to consider their offers. Satisfied, she took the cheque, that same morning adding the gift to the $495 in her chequing account, returning to the condo to enhance who she was on social media and begin lobbying prospective employers on the virtues of one Murielle de la Sorbonne.

Her first night alone she ordered pizza, feeling absolutely vindictive. She really needed to damage Kenneth Stonewall if only in her mind, prepping herself throughout the day, rehearsing as she would for a job interview and no less pleased with what she viewed in the mirror.

Standing on her balcony thirty minutes later wrapped in a silk shawl, she watched him arrive. Nodding her approval she buzzed him in, nonchalantly answering the knock on the door in a lace thong and bright smile. Taking the box matter-of-factly she turned her back, sauntering to the sofa table for her purse, asking the kid his name and how much.

"Zackary, ma'am. Fifteen even."

She took a deep breath, feeling exhilarated. She was in her element, being adored. A moment later she was framing herself in the doorway inches closer to him with a crisp twenty in her hand.

"So here's the thing, Zach. Your choice. You keep the twenty…or you come in for a slice of pizza, me, and some sixty-dollar grand cru. That's wine, Zach, very good wine."

"Ma'am, you're inviting me inside?"

She stepped back. "I am, if you want to play a little. Your choice, though. This *is* your last delivery after all." She parted her feet, placing her hands on her hips. "Got anything better to do than this…Zachary?"

His mind was racing. He was nineteen at most, 6'2", his

freshman jacket denoting him as the school's basketball hero with Louisiana manners well instilled.

"No, ma'am. I don't. Not really, I suppose."

She signalled him in. "Good answer. The pizza can wait."

Zachary left four hours later, showered and energized while Murielle sat on the bed naked, swirling her wine, smiling contentedly at the empty bottles with a definite craving for more pizza. The kid wasn't bad, not once he was naked with no clothes left to trip and stumble over.

Three weeks later she moved out with a fashionable wardrobe, what remained of Stonewall's French wines, and her Nikon whose memory card was free of him. What she did leave him were numerous artistic prints pinned to the walls, a vivid exposé capturing the best of four Saturday nights with her very keen pizza stud from her increasingly unabashed greetings through to the kitchen, the bedroom, living room and bath.

With Stonewall and his luxury gone, and Zachary behind her, she sank from one day to the next to a dismal depth she could not believe was possible. The furnished basement flat squeezed between a laundry room and stairwell in a non-descript four-storey box in Chinatown at $950 monthly was close enough to the underbelly of the I-10 to worry that, if her situation didn't soon change for the better, she would eventually metamorphose into a troll.

On the first she bought a stereo, a flat screen, a phone plan, a toilet seat, kitchenware, bedding, food for a week, and a six-month gym membership. Either unwittingly down to a paltry $6900, or lost in her naïve disconnect with real life.

More importantly her mind continued festering with resentment and loathing. For an entire year she was a superb lover and attentive companion, not once refusing him, never questioning his appetite for novelty. Nor was her father any better, acting as though throughout her entire lifetime she was not the most wonderful daughter. And what? Rejected by both. Spurned by her father for being deeply in love and heartlessly cast by Stonewall into a miserable existence, because why? She didn't understand. She was young and she was beautiful, alluring and smart. What was his problem?

She knew better than to call him, to grovel. And the few times she called her father she pressed END at hearing the drawn out beep.

4

One month later her situation had deteriorated along with her bank account, the last Saturday of August Murielle realizing she hadn't gone clubbing since first sleeping with Stonewall and that she was bored to tears.

Zachary did serve his purpose with undying devotion to the task at hand, in spite of which Murielle reluctantly sent him home to his mother their last night together with false hopes of yet another delivery. He was a freshman and broke, albeit polite, becoming too attached to her and the good life. She needed someone to rock her world, to make her feel like a woman the way she did with Stonewall and not a convenient receptacle for the excess testosterone of sophomoric college boys and amoral professors.

She stood 5'9" in her stockings with straight shoulder-length auburn hair framing a flawless Mediterranean olive complexion and liquid brown eyes, the several hundred she paid out for six months of intense private workouts a worthwhile investment. She wasn't slim; she was shapely, everything in the right place and proportioned. In cut-offs, runners and a tank top she could pass for eighteen; in dresses that were short even by shameless New Orleans standards, and skirts made more alluring with sheer blouses and push-up bras, anyone would believe late twenties.

She craved men admiring her, eyeing her, imagining the little of her they could not see. The gym was quite another matter. Wearing her favourite microfibre low-rise short shorts and décolleté crop tops, imagination was simply not requisite. She deliberately stirred wishful thinking in the men as though punishing them, revelling in their undisguised yearning while manipulating the very clear envy and disapproving stares of other women who were nowhere near her equal.

Clubbing was an after-nine thing with a narrow window allowing for an even narrower range of selective hook-ups. Any earlier and she would sit alone like a hooker on the prowl, any later and why would she bother? Timing was crucial.

She arrived at five minutes past, prancing across the street in line with the bouncer. She was beaming, first scanning the long queue before facing the steroid mountain with her shoulders drooping and a pitiful frown articulating her ruined evening. The doorman commiserated, not immune to her sorrow or the strapless tube dress and stilettos that were her free pass into the posh and sophisticated club. He unhooked the red velvet cordon, sweeping her through with a quick nod and approving grin. He ignored the jeers and the jibes, he had a mandate to uphold.

At the bar she ordered a Silent Sam with a splash, running a tab since throughout her years on campus and with Stonewall she hadn't once paid for a drink. So why would that evening be any different when one particular breed of man would likely approach her before all others? He would be either side of thirty with money or expenses, well-dressed, able to afford her and hopeful of a return on his investment whether single or divorced. Or an unhappy liar needing something more exciting and prettier than what he had waiting at home or out doing likewise for the same reasons. She didn't wait long, and he didn't hesitate to sit beside her.

He was early thirties with an easy smile. He was attractive, tanned, 5'10" in a black tailored suit and crisp white button-down. Definitely a good beginning. He was relocating to New Orleans from Atlanta, taking a breather from house-hunting and he was single. She believed him, acknowledging his bare and tanned fingers. He was also a terrible dancer, he confessed. Thing is, he abhorred jazz and sitting alone in even the finest cabaret made any man look and feel desperate.

"That said, I'm Todd. May I offer you another cocktail?"

"Thank you, Todd. I am Murielle. And I am here for the same reason, you know. Being alone, it is not good. Also, I am almost there myself, approaching thirty years too quickly to be very happy with myself," she lamented. "Misère."

"That is impossible to believe. Should I be asking to see your ID?" He chuckled, planting an elbow on the bar, bracing his chin on a clenched fist. He was fascinated, immediately spellbound by her throaty accent and disarming eyes. "You're ravishing, Murielle. Incredibly beautiful. Am I right in assuming from somewhere in France?"

"Thank you for saying so. You are very gracious." She sipped her vodka. "I am here recently from Paris to teach French at Tulane."

"No kidding. You're a professor, Murielle."

"I am, yes. Here because Paris has become too painful a place for me after the deaths of my mother and my father not many months ago."

He pressed an open palm to her shoulder. "Murielle, I'm very sorry for you. How terrible."

"Thank you. However, I am slowly beginning to heal.

Tonight is the first time in a long while that I am enjoying myself." She touched his elbow. "Thank you for sitting with me, Todd."

By 10:30 the decision was easy and mutual. More drinks would blur the evening. A late-night snack at his hotel a few blocks away seemed fitting since her condo in the Garden District was being painted and much of her furniture had not yet arrived from Paris. Besides, his en suite sitting room boasted garden doors onto a wrap-around courtyard balcony overlooking a lush garden. What better way to end a wonderful evening, he suggested? She answered the rhetorical question with a demure smile, taking his hand.

They strolled arm in arm, quietly meandering their way through a thick tourist horde of wide-eyed gawkers, hawkers and street performers. Murielle was oblivious to the habitual raucousness and blitz of bare breasts whose out-of-town owners sought to garner the greatest number of authentic Mardi Gras beads imported from China; whereas Todd considered the tolerated custom quite delightful, tactfully refraining from any potentially damaging comment. He was after all a Southern gentleman.

At the hotel Murielle wavered not at all, striding through the lobby to the elevator mildly curious. Stepping into the second-floor eighteenth century hallway, she was impressed. Not yet thinking to disentangle her arm from his. Neither was Todd in any great hurry.

The suite was spacious, the sitting room overlooking a private and deserted garden, the pool's turquoise lighting eerily illuminating manicured flora and trees while somehow making the wrought iron tables and chairs appear incongruous. He displayed the distinctive blue bottle as he would a valuable objet d'art. All he had was Cîroc, French. Did she know it? She did, she lied. Did she approve? She did very much and Todd hurried into the hall for ice.

Murielle remained on the balcony. She was pensive. What was stopping her? Eventually she would hook-up with someone and eventually Todd would need a girlfriend. So why not her? He was single and successful, good-looking and was without question a good fit. She liked him. He absolutely adored her and she was positively going to bed with him. Over time, a couple of months, possibly something more. Her lie didn't matter, she would simply tire of teaching at Tulane in favour of a more fulfilling career. By then she would be employed, renting for the short-term in the Garden District she was accustomed to, that she deserved. So why not? No way once in bed with her, once seeing her naked, would he want to lose her.

Moments later he startled her, passing her a crystal old-fashioned filled two-fingers deep with a single large cube crackling in the warm liquid.

"Murielle, this is too weird for words. God, you are an angel. Not in my wildest dreams did I ever imagine meeting anyone like you this evening. You are divine. Really, most times I sit out here feeling sorry for myself. Tomorrow will be a total downer for me without your company, an evening of unbearable torment after my time with you this evening."

She clinked her glass to his. "Then you must call me tomorrow, Todd. I would like very much that you do." She touched his cheek. "How cruel would I be to make you," she furrowed her brow, "down, to cause you this torment?"

"God, I love your accent. Do all French girls have such sweet voices?"

You're about to love more than my accent, Todd. "I suppose many do, yes. However, not all Frenchmen are as charming as you." She sipped her vodka, searching his eyes. "Alors, qu'est-ce qu'il y a, Todd? What is it?"

"Nothing. A thought. A crazy dream. Really, it's nothing."

"Tell me." She could see the worry in his eyes. He was afraid. "What is nothing?"

"Okay." He put down his glass, filling his lungs with the warm midnight air, stroking her hair. Cupping her head in his hands he kissed her, stealing her breath. "Stay the night with me, Murielle. Stay with me all day tomorrow. And yes, I am definitely calling you…every night."

She put her hands gently over his, hesitating. "I will stay with you, Todd. Yes, I will. Not because I am French or a," she faltered, "comment dirais-je…a cheap woman? I do not want that you think badly of French girls. Never have I done such a thing before. It is because I feel good with you, you know. Je ne sais pas pourquoi, yet I do very much know why. I am enchanted by you. I am also very nervous to be here with you."

"You're the enchanting one, Murielle. And we're both nervous." He reached for the chilled Cîroc resting on the railing, grinning. "What do you think we should do about that?"

"I believe you already know what, monsieur." She took his hand. "Come."

She led him through the double doors, not bothering to close them. She put her old-fashioned on the bedside table, pulling back the duvet and sheets while Todd dimmed the room into darkness, the garden's luminescence at once transforming their eager bodies into impassioned silhouettes as their lips pressed urgently together.

Murielle's dress came away from her body in a single unhurried manoeuvre leaving her standing backlit in her thong and stilettos while Todd stared at her with visible disbelief, as though he had never in his life beheld such flawless beauty. She expected nothing less from any man, stepping in, pushing his jacket from his shoulders, making her fingers work less deftly at his buttons than she wanted.

26

His buckle was next, tugging away his shirt, guiding him gently backward onto the bed, first tugging at his socks, then his zipper before pulling away his slacks.

"What you see is what you get, Murielle. Final sale, no refunds."

"What I see is what I do desire very much, Todd." She gulped. "Very much."

He stood facing her, taking her in. Murielle was equally pleased. He was confident; she liked that, his body lightly tanned, trim and toned. Kneeling to unstrap her sandals, she acknowledged with a coquettish "hmmm" that Todd was hers.

Standing, she kicked them away, in the same fluid motion guiding her panties with tormenting insouciance to the floor. In bare feet she became enticingly more petite; naked, she was inexplicably younger and more vulnerable. She placed her hands on her hips, ardour sparkling in her liquid eyes, turning a full circle with tauntingly precise steps.

"And this is all of me, Todd. I hope that you do like what you see."

"Wow, Murielle. Exquisite."

"Also a little more naked than you are, monsieur."

"Touché." He stepped in to resolve the matter, cupping her head between his hands, kissing her, sweeping her into his arms and laying her on the bed before pushing his straightbacks to the floor.

No wonder he was confident, she mused, reaching out to him. They were a superb match, both of them striking and desirable. He would definitely stay around.

Tentative touching wasn't on the menu. She was and Todd satiated his appetite to the fullest; Murielle no less ravenous. By sunrise every part of her pulsated as she eased from the bed, promising to hurry, padding naked to the bathroom where she stood leering into the mirror. She was shocked. Her lips were smudged a glossy mahogany and numb, her cheeks smeared with light and dark shades of copper. Her once shimmering hair was damp and matted, plastered to her forehead and shoulders. She grimaced at what the night had done to her, what Todd had done to her. God! Did she say she loved him, actually say the words? Shit! Did she? And Todd, did he call her babe?

He was a tireless lover, his expert fingers not once ceasing to probe and titillate every part of her, a complete stranger more familiar with her body than any privileged doctor. She blew a long breath. Whew! She could scarcely stand. Worse, she reeked of melded sweat and the thin glaze coating her belly and thighs.

She dropped onto the seat, at once slapping her legs together, her face contorting in concert with the first stinging hiss of warm pee.

Finished, she stepped into the shower where she stood weak-kneed under a steaming torrent, bracing herself against the wall, her feet wide apart, groaning as the soothing rivulets began healing her wounds most in need of repair. Lost in time and reverie, her heart pounding, she stepped out as her skin began prickling. She coated her body with the hotel's perfumed cream, combed her hair into a straight curtain, admired the results and tread softly into the bedroom wrapped in fleece. Smiling innocently, she went to him on the balcony.

"You okay, Murielle? I was worried."

"I did need to shower very badly." She hugged him tightly, making a face "As you must also shower, monsieur."

He chortled. "What I need is more of you tonight after dinner, Murielle. I'm floating in a magnificent dream that I don't want to end. I don't want to wake up."

"You called me babe."

"Because you said you love me. Babe seemed more appropriate than Murielle."

"So this was not a one-nighter as you Americans say?"

"Not a chance, chérie." He kissed her. "I think we have a lot to talk about, you and I."

She couldn't agree more, pleased with her choice. "I am so happy."

"I'm hooked. What else can I say? I can't possibly think of letting you go."

She giggled. "I do like the sound of chérie very much. I must also find a special name for you." She scanned the courtyard. "But, Todd, you are outside in your underwear."

He shrugged. "So what? You're in New Orleans and you're French. The doors were open all night and you're in a towel. What's your point?"

"That you stink very badly, monsieur. You must go to clean yourself at once."

He did, first pinching her chin and kissing her, whipping away her towel, believing she would scurry past him. But she didn't. She remained where she was tousling her hair, in fact posing for him until he finally got the message.

He ordered room service when Murielle refused to wear her evening dress to breakfast. Near 11:00 he gave her a key card and taxi money. They clung to each other, Todd refusing to let her go, ardently pressing his lips to hers. He expected her anytime that afternoon, the earlier the better with a suitcase and bikinis. Tiny French bikinis in particular. He wanted to spend the entire week with her.

By noon Murielle was in her flat despising the place. Todd wasn't the only one floating in a dream. She had found a way out, a man more her age, a better man who would love and adore her for as long as she wished, who already loved and adored her. She was thrilled, exhilarated, stripping and bathing in scented water with her legs wide apart to let the deep heat soothe her swollen lips, dreamily towelling herself and smearing cool salve onto the tender folds.

Of course she didn't love him; she probably never would and she sure as hell did not want his kids. But he was single, moving to the city, and by week's end he would be addicted to her. So why not shack up in the short-term and make things work?

By 2:00 her suitcase was packed with designer fashions and her French bikinis proudly made in Florida. Thirty minutes later she was inserting the electronic key into Todd's hotel door, exasperated. She knocked twice, calling his name in a strong whisper, her palms and forehead pressed against the door. She was becoming angry, finally realizing he was at the pool waiting for her. Of course he was. Angry with herself for being silly, for wasting time, she hurried to the Reception Desk to put aside her suitcase and have the card magnetized.

The clerk remembered her, taking the key and dropping it into a slot. "Madam, the guest in 216 checked out this morning. Not very long after your own departure."

"You mean he's gone out."

"The gentleman has left us, madam. However he did leave you an envelope, possibly an explanation."

"That's not possible. His name is Todd. Please check again."

"I cannot divulge his name, madam. However the name is not Todd, I assure you." He passed her the envelope. "Good day, madam."

Murielle hurried onto the street mortified, on the verge of tears. She needed to read his letter privately, had he written one. Instead she stared at the twin 100-dollar bills that sent a clearer message than any letter would. She

wanted to scream.
*

Near 3:00 that afternoon forty-year-old Jason Black was halfway to his home in Tampa, his wife and a couple of kids after a week-long sales meeting in New Orleans that ostensibly ended late Saturday with dinner and drinks. Not entirely a lie.

Murielle was stunning, worth every penny. She was captivating, out for a good time and she found one. She was a sensationally good lay, a semi-annual and harmless revival of his bachelor days and far less costly than a messy divorce and child support. If not her, someone else. There was always someone else. They didn't call the place the Big Easy for nothing and she was about as easy as they come.

He snickered, clicking through her morning performance on his cell. "You were consummate, kid; no doubt about that. My best ever and, 'Not because I am French or a,' he mocked in a Parisienne accent better than hers, his eyes blurring from laughter, 'comment dirais-je…a cheap woman? I do not want that you think badly of French girls. Never have I done such a thing before. It is because I feel good with you, you know.' Bullshit, darling."

Thing was, his supercilious bitch of a wife was Parisienne. Murielle was not. Neither was she a professor closing in on thirty, not according to the student ID in her purse. Whatever else she might eventually become wouldn't much matter.

"We are what we are, kid."

5

September was long and tedious. No one was responding to her CVs despite her references penned by appreciative professors and the enviable A Grade Point Average denoting outstanding achievement which, in the strictest sense, was appropriate.

She didn't understand why no one wanted her. Worse, by October 01st she was at $4350 and she hadn't bought food for the week. She felt trapped, still livid over the stranger actually paying her for sex that was a thousand times more humiliating than simply disappearing. That she would have understood. Sex at university was strictly a social thing, for her and everyone else, an integral part of being connected. No big deal. No one that young expected or wanted lifetime guarantees.

In fact none of her boyfriends were aware of her keen desire to ensure good grades by regularly assuaging her professors' sense of obligation to academia. Truth be told, what did they care about her long-term goals, a full A or a B-plus? They didn't. What they wanted was her naked, doing as much or more with her in bed and over their desks as they were in the classroom to prepare her for lobbying.

That was all different, no one got hurt. But that the Todd guy paid her was cruel. She didn't deserve such an insensitive disregard for her feelings.

Monday, October 02nd, began as a job search that

quickly deteriorated into an afternoon nap on her couch. Near the close of business her phone's piercing beep startled her, her legs and arms flailing. Seeing the Caller ID, she blurted a high-pitched "Holy shit! No way!"

Rubbing her face hard, she pressed SEND. A woman from The Gilmore Group was asking her to hold, the head of HR needed to speak with her. The Gilmore Group. No way! Her entire body shuddered. They were the largest lobby group proactively representing pharma-care and health.

They were interviewing several candidates, he told her, keenly interested in interviewing with her the following Monday regarding a junior research position with a commencement date of October 30th providing she hadn't yet signed on with another firm and was prepared for a good deal of menial work and learning.

She pressed END, shrieking, delirious with no one to call. She had no friends, no one special in her life to skip and dance and jump up and down with. She was alone with no one to help her with roleplay or her outfit, realizing her wardrobe was either trendy evening wear or a collection of short, tight and sheer, each piece meant to provoke desire and envy. She had no appropriate business attire. Shit! Why hadn't she thought of that?

The next day she went shopping for practical dark-blue pumps, a dark-blue pantsuit, a modest silk blouse, a silk scarf and camisole. She bought a leather briefcase, a leather-bound agenda and purse from a specialty store, a sterling pen set and digital recorder. She was good to go and abysmally close to penury, buying newspapers every morning and afternoon to make herself current and marketable, each evening spending hours responding to likely questions she had found on a website and had dictated into her microcassette. Sunday, as a special favour, her hairdresser styled her auburn curtain into a classic French braid, her fingernails into the white-tipped French style.

Monday she was ready; she was all business. Or she would know soon enough that she was not. With the local morning paper added to her briefcase, she called for a cab.

The Gilmore Group was a leading firm. Even bottom-rung entry-level was a laudable accomplishment, a catalyst to a secure and lucrative future. The appointment was for 10:00 AM, the department head introducing himself at 9:58. Lobbying was all about timing, respect and reputation.

Moments after introductions and Louisiana requisite pleasantries, Miss Murielle thought she would perish on the spot, praying her cheeks were not as flushed as the searing heat infusing her. The interview, he explained, opening the door, was scheduled to last ninety minutes. If all progressed well she would have ample time to refresh herself before interviewing with him personally over lunch. He then presented her to the four-person panel and left her.

The lead inquisitor made clear that what was to follow was intended to evaluate her competencies, her relative experience, and her composure under stress since the successful applicant would be expected to advance rapidly and would at some point interact not always agreeably with very intimidating people. If successful, she was to expect long days and late nights.

She understood. She was ready.

The barrage of probing questions and hypothetical scenarios that followed were brutal, at one point Murielle taking a breath to ponder why she hadn't become that French professor. At 11:30 they left her matter-of-factly without the slightest encouragement, her mind flooding with apprehension. Fifteen minutes later, refreshed and no less apprehensive, she was experiencing déjà vu being driven to a luncheon in the back of a corporate limousine.

At 1:00 the head of HR offered to drive her home without any indication that she was either short-listed or incompatible in their view. She politely refused, forcing a thin smile. In which case by Monday next she would hear the good news or their best wishes for a prosperous career elsewhere. He wished her a wonderful day, waiting as the chauffeur assisted her onto the corner of Canal and Bourbon.

Tuesday morning Murielle woke feeling nauseous, blaming the anxiety of the previous day, grudgingly admitting that her last glass of wine the previous evening wasn't absolutely needed. Though by the weekend her mood had darkened considerably; she felt miserable, worrying over her near empty bank account until midmorning the following Monday when her phone once again jolted her from her wretchedness.

She was quivering, damp with sweat, her skin clammy and abnormally pale. She cursed the thing, whipping back her covers and sitting straight, scarcely believing what she was hearing. The Gilmore Group was inviting her into their fold, a world of high-level diplomacy, of favours given and favours owing.

Disconnecting she stared at the phone, bursting into a torrent of tears. She felt entirely alone, abandoned. She hadn't spoken to her parents in fifteen months, nor Stonewall in almost as many weeks, her persistent memories of the Todd guy's tactile and olfactory imprint on her pervading her mind like rot.

She forced herself from the bed, making her way into the kitchen where, at the first whiff of ground coffee, she vomited violently into the sink. She should have been jubilant, instead she felt incurably morose. Her life was total shit.

She showered until the steaming water tinged her flawless skin, shampooing her hair and fighting back more tears. She needed to focus. She had $2500 left with a full month to survive until her first payday. She no longer owned a credit card with rent to pay, an empty fridge, a bus pass that would expire on her first day working and at least four new outfits to coordinate.

Dressed in suede boots, jeans, a tee and leather bomber, she splurged on a taxi and went to the closest Emergency Room complaining of feeling like shit, annoyed by the ensuing inquisition when all she wanted was a quick fix that was not going to happen. First though: Did she have insurance, the ER nurse enquired? Murielle didn't think so, in which case she should have gone to a less costly Urgent Care facility.

Then came the forms, the cheap cotton gown, the equable doctor, the poking and the prodding.

"Miss de la Sorbonne, I will not waste our time or your money doing urine or blood analyses this afternoon. Visit a pharmacy if you wish. Do your own test which is much less costly and equally accurate. Though, really, you need not bother."

"I don't need a test to tell me I'm very sick, Doctor."

"You are not sick. You're perfectly fine. What you are is very pregnant, Miss de la Sorbonne. Thirteen weeks give or take, which I see by your expression is not quite a blessing. In spite of which you do require a physician and close scrutiny. You will not be doing this on your own." He handed her a pamphlet. "Pregnancy 101: The do's and don'ts. The first of which is to stop drinking, the second is finding an obstetrician."

"You cannot be serious. I cannot be having a baby. Do I look like I want a frigging baby?"

The lecture was terse, he didn't have time; Murielle

retorting that her long-time boyfriend had a procedure, that...Her frozen expression and unblinking eyes told the entire story. He didn't care, he wasn't a social worker. He wished her well and left her to dress.

Early Monday evening with dinner she allowed herself a glass of wine, justifying that she might have gone to the ER later in the week. Anyway, what was the big deal? She didn't care and halfway through her meal, slamming shut her computer, she poured a second generous glass.

If she felt confused and disoriented at the hospital, she wasn't any longer. She was clear-headed and determined.

Without insurance she could never afford the nearly twenty grand for a delivery, worse if they had to cut into her. Nor was giving the thing away a real option, not when she would inevitably endure six more months of absolute agony that would leave her body considerably less stunning with scars impossible to disguise or explain.

She would not on her life go to her father begging for help, not with news of Stonewall or that she had deliberately and unashamedly fucked a pizza delivery boy. He was French to the core. She was merely fluent and could not imagine the rage, or her mother's overreaction to an abortion. No. She would go to the condo, to Stonewall's retreat.

She went to bed early. Children never crossed her mind. Not hers, not anyone's, seldom encountering one she didn't consider obnoxious. They were demanding, loud and messy, costly and disruptive. There were too many negatives, not the least of which was permanently disfiguring her body. And that's if it came out normal. What were the odds? What if the thing wasn't normal? What then?

She tried to imagine a single positive that didn't exist, not for a beautiful twenty-two-year-old beginning a career.

Not for any woman whose body was at its most perfect, envied by most women and certainly the erotic fantasy of any man seeing her.

She didn't suffer from the Mom Syndrome, not once entertaining the irrationality of doing something that would forever disrupt her life. The risks were too great to her body and her future. She had nothing to prove. The thing was an accident she had no connection with.

Simply being Murielle de la Sorbonne proved everything.

She curled onto her side, adamant she would never be a mother and that Kenneth Stonewall would pay dearly one day for what he had done to her.

Dressing late the next morning for her shopping spree was a challenge. Yet she forced herself, certain that after the next day's abortion she would require complete bedrest leading to the thirtieth.

She bought four outfits with shoes, blouses, and requisite accessories, pausing midway for a green salad and Chardonnay lunch. She was pleased with close to $900 remaining for food and essentials until payday. She didn't believe rent was a big issue. The janitor was always smiling at her, he would understand and certainly give her a small two-week extension.

6

Murielle went to the closest clinic early Wednesday morning. She was neither excited nor anxious; she was resolute. She was beginning to show and just wanted the thing gone. She needed to forget the whole ordeal; she needed to forget the three worst mistakes of her life.

An hour into her fifty-dollar Consent Session she was stunned into silence. She was a week into her second trimester and too far along for the Morning After pill. Worse yet, she was ineligible for assistance since she was about to earn sixty-five K and the upfront fee for the procedure was an inflexible $800 with a mandatory twenty-four hour wait time. That reality was devastating enough to process, what he said next put her instantly into a state of near panic.

"What!"

"That's right, Murielle. Twins."

Silence.

"Holy shit! No!"

"Twin girls." He nodded with grim detachment. The script never changed.

She wanted to vomit. "I'm twenty-two walking into a dream job. What do I need with two frigging kids?" He saw the alarm, the colour draining from her face. "Listen, I'm good for the money. I am, I promise. I can give you a couple of hundred now, the rest with my very first paycheque. I swear. I cannot be a mother. I do not want to be a mother and I sure as hell don't want anything growing inside me. So please," she implored, "help me out here. We're talking four weeks, tops."

"I understand your predicament, Murielle. Of course I do. Unfortunately the clinic reports to shareholders who are more business-minded than humanitarian. Perhaps your employer would advance you the funds...as a goodwill gesture."

"Yeah, right. They're pro-life advocates and if I don't get these things out of me I won't last five minutes the first day, let alone expect maternity leave. They don't want whining mothers, they want eighteen-hour days and seven-day weeks." She squeezed her eyes shut, groaning a guttural scream. "I am so totally screwed. I mean totally."

"What about the father or your family? You haven't spoken about them. Surely the funds are within their combined reach."

"I have no family and the guy doesn't know. He was a good time and a bad mistake. Enough said."

"In which case one other possibility is available to you, Murielle. Not ideal perhaps, given that you're here and understandably disinclined to endure the coming months. I'm talking about private adoption. In return for your labour, as it were, and for matching infant girls, you could easily expect a reasonable twenty-five thousand with no cost to you, no maternity leave to jeopardize your career, and complete anonymity. At most a week of uncomfortable post-delivery days."

"Great. I'll get twenty-five K for six months of puking, probably a ruined vagina or worse, and be unemployed. I told you they want dedication, not mothers, and certainly not female pods plodding around the office."

"Things happen. Be forthright with them. Or, for what it matters to anyone, explain that you're acting as a surrogate. You simply forgot to tell them in your excitement, which is not a misrepresentation by any means. Isn't part of being a lobbyist being creative? They may be pro-life, yet they do understand the human condition. In a very real way you'll be doing a good deed. Who would deliberately fault that, particularly   a   pro-lifer?"

She wasn't convinced. "It's illegal, like trafficking."

"It's no such thing and entirely legal, far better than babies raising babies with predictably disastrous consequences both social and financial." He scribbled a name and number on his note pad, tearing off the sheet. "His services are free for the donor and strictly confidential, Murielle. The adoptive parents bear the entire cost including all matters prenatal. Give this some thought, and call your employer. I have no doubt they will appreciate your honesty." He stood. "I'm afraid that concludes your consult, Murielle. I wish I could do more."

"You and me both." Murielle took the paper. "What if I do get you the money, Doctor? How much time do I have?"

"Two weeks, after that another consult session." He stopped at the door. "Murielle, if we're talking about something less virtuous than a little white lie to your employer I strongly advise that you stay the course. Take the tax-free twenty-five, avoid a guilt trip and re-evaluate the correlation between your good times and bad mistakes. Believe me, you'll be beach-ready by June with not a single battle scar to cause undue distress." He put a hand on her shoulder. "A little paternal advice, if I may: This will be over very soon. Please don't do anything that will needlessly complicate your life."

7

She didn't believe him. She knew better. Gilmore would positively distance themselves from a female perceived to be promiscuous. Every woman she passed or had met at the office was photo-grade with not a hair out of place, wearing their vanity with as little diffidence as their designer fashions. Every man was urbane and fit, dressed in quality suits. Not one she saw carried extra weight or wore facial hair. She would fit right in, just not in dowdy maternity outfits emphasising her distended belly.

Once in her flat she crawled onto her bed, crossing legs, hugging her pillow and staring at the phone clutched in her trembling hands. She needed that procedure desperately, loathing herself for what she was contemplating. Before she could think to smash the thing against the wall she steeled herself against a worse shockwave and pressed PAPA in her contacts, not breathing, waiting as though for some invisible executioner to throw the switch.

"Yes?"

"C'est moi, papa, C'est ta fille, Murielle. I am sorry, papa. I am. I am sorry that I hurt you and maman."

"What do you want, mademoiselle? What do you need?"

"You were right, papa. Kenneth, he did leave me the way that you said that he would. Three months ago. I have been alone for three months, papa."

"Mademoiselle, what is it that you want?"

"I am not that stupid girl, papa. I am not, not any longer. I graduated with honours and very soon I will begin work at Gilmore. They called me, papa. In my dreams I could not have wished for such incredible good fortune."

"And now you are calling me. Answer my question."

"To be your daughter once more, papa, for you and maman to love me once more. I need you, papa. I need maman."

"For what, exactly, after more than one year?"

"I am pregnant, papa."

She stopped breathing, the one sound amid the nerve-wracking quiet came from her pounding heart.

"I presume it belongs to Stonewall?"

"What does that matter? I cannot do this. Gilmore will not want me. Comprends-tu, papa? I cannot do this thing. But the clinic, they want 1000 dollars or they will do nothing to help me. Nothing. And Kenneth, he will not help me. I am lost, papa."

"What is lost are your senses. An abortion, and you dare to tell me that you are not stupid? The mother you so heartlessly discarded behind a closed door would perish to hear of this."

"And I will die if I do not, papa. My future will be ruined. Gilmore will shut me out. I will be alone in this horrible room. Is that what you wish for your daughter who loves you?"

"Who did this, if not Stonewall?"

"He does not matter, papa. He is gone. I was vulnerable because of Kenneth. He was a terrible mistake…my last mistake. Je jure. I swear, papa."

"Indeed your last, since what you propose is despicable beyond words, far worse than daring to believe we would for a moment condone your debaucheries or these men. Or whatever sordid convenience you will invite to share or worsen your soiled life. You *will* be a mother, mademoiselle. I warned you, did I not? I warned you when once you did have a loving mother and father. Goodbye, mademoiselle."

She sat devastated, tears welling in her eyes, her breathing erupting into uncontrollable sobs.

She was too distraught to think, to imagine that her papa no longer loved her, or that she was alone to find her way, without warning jolted into her unexplored and solitary world with a seething "Go to hell, papa."

She pressed her palms across her cheeks, smearing her tears. Crying would resolve nothing. She needed to clear her mind, to forget them, to devise serious damage control strategies. She heaved herself from the bed, padding into the bathroom, leaving a trail of clothes.

She stood under jets of steaming water until her body blossomed to a deep pink and began prickling, towelling herself before soothing her irritated skin with creams and her red eyes with drops. She dressed in a fleecy robe, styling her hair for something to do, all the while creating vivid and workable possibilities with renewed vigour and determination.

Plan A would be the janitor that very night; Plan B was meeting with Kenneth Stonewall at the condo the next evening if Plan A failed. Stonewall's downtown office was off-limits; she wouldn't get past security. His real home was a well-guarded secret she had never asked about. She was waiting, curbing her curiosity for a year until her graduation day. She had wanted, she dreamed of, the full impact of her engagement, her wedding, and Stonewall carrying her as mistress of the household over the threshold of her stately home.

Plan C, if need be, was not at all the worst case scenario. She wasn't in the least frightened by the prospect thanks to how easily she had met Todd. Sex with one man all the time, or with a few men some of the time for a good reason, what was the difference other than social stigma propagated by hypocrites pointing fingers from inside glass houses? In fact Jake was the worst case, with hopefully the most to give in return for the least effort.

Jake the janitor lived across the hall, bordered by the utility and garbage rooms, a pigeonhole no better than hers. He was late-forties, maybe early fifties, and understandably unattached. He chain-smoked and seemed perpetually infused with Jack Daniel's; he seldom wore a shirt over his singlet, his wardrobe apparently consisting of one set of fatigues and a single pair of GI boots.

He clearly had issues she didn't care about, possibly a PTSD causality of war or a woman, probably believing the grungy dress code made him appear virile. Either way he was wrong. He was a loser, a ne'er-do-well creature of the urban swamp. He was 5'8" and balding with mushy arms and a paunch of sufficient weight and magnitude to completely conceal his belt buckle. Still, he did drive a vintage Corvette convertible.

With that faint glimmer of hope, later that evening after a light meal she could scarcely keep down, she eased her anxiety with a few Silent Sam she could scarcely afford as she dressed in low-rise cut-offs she modified to ensure success and a raglan three-quarter sweater. She didn't bother with panties or a bra, anticipating the worst possible outcome in her favour with no intention of enhancing his experience.

She was not stripping for him, not leading him on. This was a one-time thing, something for him to remember and drool over, if he agreed to the terms. She would get in and get out, and so would he: Basic sex in exchange for an extension on her rent. If not, she would negotiate the best he's ever had for a meagre few hundred. Cash up front. This was purely business. No freebies and no seconds.

At 8:55 she knocked on his door, her bare feet as essential to her successful evening as her ensemble, instantly feeling her throat constrict. "Hi, Jake. Got a minute?"

The cargo shorts and singlet gave him at once a sickly and comical appearance. His legs were spindly and bowed, as pasty as his mushy arms, his purplish bare feet adorned with stubby toes and yellowed nails he could possibly use as impromptu weapons.

He absorbed her from head to toe, lingering at the swell of her breasts shimmering with gold body dust, her bare midriff and curled 'V' at the snap she had undone at the belly she was doing her best to make tighter. In a word, she was light-years beyond his sickest dreams.

"You got a problem or somethin', Murielle?"

"Yeah. A small one, Jake. I need two weeks on November's rent. Things are a little tight. I do have a job, though, a good one. I start in two weeks. I just need a little time."

"No can do, sweetie. The boss, he'd eat me out big time. Kick my ass outta here."

"Two weeks, Jake. I swear."

He shook his head. "Not even two days. Sorry."

She couldn't waste the energy affecting a smile. "You're certain? Not even for your favourite tenant?"

He shrugged. "Nope. Sorry."

She wouldn't beg. She stood back scanning the dank and ill-lit hallway. The stairway and laundry room were quiet. They were alone, Murielle calm and collected. She was determined. Not all her professors were thirty-something prime specimens either.

"Jake, I'm in totally deep shit. So here's the thing. How

about you get me for one hour? Nothing kinky, nothing oral, and sight unseen. No free peepshow, but you will not be sorry."

"Say what?" He coughed a coarse laugh. "You serious?"

Good. "Yes, I am. Either for the time I need or for two-hundred, cash up front. Very serious. Like I said, I'm in the deepest shit."

He slouched against the doorframe, studying her. "One hundred. Best I can manage."

"Are you kidding? That won't get you a grope." She turned toward her door, confident. He was a loser and a pig. "Sorry we couldn't do business, Jake. Enjoy those wet dreams tonight."

The bottom edges of her cut-offs were cut extra high and frayed, her lightly tinged and smooth flesh peeking out tauntingly irresistible.

"Okay, sweetie. We got us a deal. Two-hundred. I got the cash. But I gotta ask. You do this often?"

She spun, walking past him. 9:00 PM. She'd be gone by 10:00. "No, I do not. This is a short-term fix for me and a lifetime of jerking off for you and don't be in a hurry. One hour, Jake, and one time. I'm not a sewer. I'm on top with no mouth-to-mouth, no mouth anywhere, no pictures, and when he shoots he scores. Which means make it last. Got it. And if you've got something to drink that would be good too."

He understood. No problem.

Inside, once the money changed hands, Murielle tugged away her sweater and pushed her personalised cut-offs past her ankles as if she were alone. No way did she want him in her bed or in her flat. She walked into his bedroom matter-of-factly, casually throwing back the covers. Not the least surprised, she asked where he kept the fresh linen, or whether he had any, and went about changing the bed. All the while naked, killing time, killing the janitor.

In the kitchen he poured her a cheap shot of Jack Daniel's, Murielle tipping the neck of the bottle deeper into her glass that she determined was clean enough. Three shots would barely prevent her from puking. He was years older than her father, Murielle allowing that he might possibly have bathed several days earlier which was nowhere good enough.

She ordered him into the shower stall with forty minutes remaining, declining his invitation to join him. She told him to be thorough and when he was gone she quickly gulped what remained in her glass, gagging.

She added another half-inch before walking into the bedroom where she tossed a single condom onto his pillow before standing on the mattress to sit side-saddle against the gaudy headboard upholstered in purple velveteen. She wasn't posing, she had no need to. She was setting the scene in her mind, directing the players. She knew she had a killer bod, the most beautiful female he would ever see naked outside of a magazine. Good for him. However of utmost importance was ensuring the least possible contact. Of utmost concern was her $1300 shortfall.

Jake trudged into the bedroom, gripping a threadbare towel at his waist. He was a man on a mission, faltering at seeing her poised and ready. Grinning dumbly he let the rag fall to the floor. His stringy comb-over was swept back, greasier than wet, his damp body hair looking coarse and prickly. His chest was concaved and droopy, his shoulders rounded. His flat buttocks were pot-marked and scratched, sparsely carpeted with dark whisker-like sprouts, though what most appalled her was the requisite appendage buried beneath a dark shrub of wiry curls and the fleshy overhang. The man had bigger thumbs.

She downed the harsh Tennessee whiskey, tossing him

the glass.

"Guess a man never knows what to expect, sweetie. Can't say I haven't done some creative thinkin' along these lines these past weeks. Tell you what though, I'll be pickin' things up a notch from here on in. That's the God's honest truth."

"You're closing in on half-time, Jake. Get on the bed."

He did, quickly, clambering onto his knees inches from hers. The sensation of his rough hand squeezing the tender flesh between her thighs made her ill, the indelicate fingers pressing into her scented auburn curls made her quiver. He looked ridiculous.

She had never seen such desperation, each beefy mitt working at cross purposes and very different tempos toward the same objective.

He was gruff and clumsy, compensating for lost years or accustomed to twenty-dollar BJs in some dark alley with some equally repugnant female he could never drink pretty. She parted her legs wider, giving him better access and more reason to salivate. She didn't need bruises, she needed to finish up and leave, to get out, thinking to cup her breasts for the added stimulus while shielding them against his careless mauling.

She flicked the condom with her toes when she determined he couldn't be much better than he was; she didn't need or want the thing falling off. God, no! "One size fits all, Jake. Make it work."

He did, fumbling, blurting an excited "ho-ho" when Murielle pushed him backward with a petite foot.

She stood over him, absently teasing or provoking. She didn't care which. The best he ever had wasn't going to work for her. Just her being there, standing naked over him, was the best he ever had. With the pizza guy, even Stonewall, she would come away each time glistening with sweat. Not with the janitor. Not a chance. The man was a dreg, Murielle accepting as she sank as low as she dared that she had hit rock bottom for one simple reason: Kenneth Stonewall.

Straddling him, her feet as wide apart as she could manage without losing her balance, she closed her eyes and ordered him in. She was focused. Already soiled by him she would contain the contamination. She had no intention of touching him anywhere with her pristine hands. She wanted no memory of him.

Connected, she supposed, though not completely convinced that she was, she squatted with her arms crossed, her elbows planted firmly on her knees, doing the impossible and feeling more like a porno queen than a neophyte whore. Losing count near 150 slow thrusts her legs were burning, her abs cramping into knots when the janitor at last twitched and jerked, the sound of his grunts and groans making her nauseous.

She instinctively plucked herself free, wincing. Her calves and thighs were aching, barely able to support her, causing her to stumble backward against the headboard and wall. She rubbed heat into them, worsening the pain, her breathing strangely even; while he remained spread-eagle, panting and grinning stupidly as though he might somehow have metamorphosed into a far less hideous creature.

"Damn, Murielle, that went kinda quick. Didn't get to those little puppies you're keeping to yourself." He checked his watch. "Seems to me we got a good quarter-hour left to us."

"He shoots, he scores. That's the deal, Jake. Want to rethink that extension? Maybe then we'll talk."

He rolled onto his side, swinging his feet onto the floor. Standing, he snapped off the latex. "Not likely to happen, sweetie. And I gotta say though, two-hundred's a bit stiff for a couple of minutes of straight pokin'. Won't be doin' that again, not till the price comes down sufficient to fit a workin' man's wallet."

"The price goes up next time, Jake. Tonight you got a real bargain, a low-cost sample."

She eased onto her knees, planting one foot on the floor and twisting, deliberately planting the other and fully aware he was ogling her. He was transposing each enticing movement and curve into his sick mind.

"Stay for a drink? Least you can do is linger a short while."

She nodded, smiling. "Ten minutes, Jake. Sorry I can't and won't give you an extension. You've got ten minutes. Make the most of it because tomorrow we're back to status quo."

"Meaning what?"

"Meaning look and remember without touching. And please put on your shorts."

She sauntered from the room feeling dirty, her legs slick and stained. She would wait. No way would she spend a second of private time naked in his contaminated bathroom. In the kitchen she hurried to pour herself a whiskey, pulling her weight onto the counter and crossing her legs. Sipping quietly she limited herself to an occasional "uh-huh," when truly she was wondering how she had sunk so low as to literally pollute herself with the village idiot. In fact, she knew very well.

What could she say, that he was great...breathtaking? Not frigging likely, not when any horny dog would have done a better job on her leg. More to the point, she had her money and he had a memory that would fade or exaggerate with time. More likely to fade, she believed, checking her watch with each sip.

At 10:00 precisely, anxious to leave with her modesty

somewhat of a non-issue, she gulped what was left in her tumbler, uncrossed her legs, and shoved herself forward onto the linoleum flooring with taunting indifference. She strode past him into the living room, ignoring him, stooping to gather the clothes she would never wear again. Could never wear again without being arrested for soliciting, and certainly never to the laundry room.

She thanked him for the drinks without smiling or a sideward glance, reaching into a pocket for her keys and stepping into the hallway naked. The basement was always deserted at night and she wasn't about to give him more to ogle and remember by squirming and twisting into her cut-offs and sweater. Who cared if someone saw her? Good for them. Anyway, she would soon be moving. She didn't belong with social misfits and sickly blue-hairs. Nor did she deserve to live in a tenement basement beside a janitor she knew was framed in his doorway doing his best not to blink, getting the most he could for his money well-spent.

Once inside she wasted no time adding the soiled costume into the next day's garbage before running a bath and shower. She took two kits from her travel bag and stood under the warm cascade, intently douching twice, vigorously shampooing her hair until satisfied she had fully cleansed her body of him. Craving no less for the purity of her mind, she immersed herself in the bath of steaming water that was deep and penetrating.

Stepping from the tub lost in time, her entire body tingling, she patted herself dry.

Standing by the mirror she caressed her body with cream before wrapping herself in a thick fleecy robe, pleased she had neutralized any and all noxious contaminants. Then she poured a Silent Sam neat, deep enough to bring on sleep when she was ready and sat in bed pondering who was sleeping in her rightful bed with

Kenneth Stonewall, wondering who would answer the door the next evening.

Part Two
8

The year Madame de la Sorbonne first accompanied her husband to the diametrically different and curious world that was New Orleans, she brought with her more than a suitcase, uncertainty, and fond memories of her beloved France.

Not many months later she presented a tiny pink and wrinkled Murielle to the girl's new papa whose heart was bursting with pride and joy. He doted over the child from the very first moment, rushing home each day with some little thing for her to wonder about with wide sparkling eyes while not quite understanding the silly sounds he was making as together father and daughter planned her bright future.

Little Murielle would not for several years come to know or comprehend the eccentricities that made New Orleans the Big Easy. Nor would she understand or appreciate her beautiful home with a garden or her father's fancy car. Her world was a simpler place shared with her adoring maman and papa, her dolls and her toys.

Which wasn't quite the case for Jackson Belmont, Jr. whose life changed forever one frosty January day five years earlier when loving parents went to the Mobile Infirmary from Tennessee to take home their newly born Nathanial Thompson.

*

Bette-Mae Carter was fifteen in grade ten at Louisville High. She was a good and decent girl; she was tall with long obsidian tresses, a pretty smile, and was well ahead of the other girls in her development. She was good at school and sang each Sunday in the church choir. She loved her mother and obeyed her strict Baptist father. She wore decent clothes, had never kissed a boy, and never dillydallied on her way home from dances at the school and church. Not until her next-door neighbours moved away the first day of that year's summer break.

One day later Rad Harken moved in with his parents. Bette-Mae, rushing to finish her breakfast, was sitting in her bedroom window as the cartage truck arrived, making certain she would not miss a single thing that was happening, too engrossed in her spying to see that he was looking up at her.

"Hey! You up there in the window. What's your name, little girl?"

She was mortified, practically leaping backward to the floor, stumbling onto her backside. How tactlessly ill-mannered of him! She hated him immediately.

Not five minutes later, with her dignity somewhat revived, the pink ribbon in her hair gone and her tresses freshly brushed into lustrous curls, she stomped down the steps of her back porch and marched to the fence where the new boy was standing idle while the real men were damp with sweat. She wanted to smack the silly grin from his face and tell him how horrible he was.

"Do I look like a little girl to you?" she challenged, scowling. "Well, do I? And why are you grinning like a complete idiot." Somehow he was making her furious. "Are you deaf and dumb as well?" Infuriating silence. "Well are you?"

"My little sister's seven. She wears ribbons in her hair. Where I come from real women don't do that. They're more refined and wear dresses."

She was appalled. "You are incredibly rude, and for your information I do wear dresses and I'll be sixteen in a couple of days."

He leaned over the fence, eyeing her from her sneakers and bobby socks to her scathing green eyes. "Well I suppose you do look older close-up. More mature, I have to admit. Did you do that for me, Bette-Mae…taking off you ribbon?"

"You know my name?"

"Bette-Mae Carter, yes I do. Your old neighbours told me some time back. They said you were pretty, but didn't mention you're a bit sensitive about your looks." His grin widened. "Also, where I come from, we call this a smile. It's what we do when we're speaking with a beautiful woman." He held out a hand, Bette-Mae too gracious not to react appropriately. "I'm Rad, Radcliffe Harken for short. But you know that…and I am sixteen. I bet you know that also."

Bette-Mae Carter melted, her core temperature soaring. His grip warm and gentle, his dark brown eyes piercing hers as though probing her very soul. She was flustered; she needed her bedroom. She needed to breathe, to stop her heart from exploding, to splash cold water on her face that she knew was glowing a deep pink. She pulled away.

"I don't care who you are, or how you know my name." She spun around, marching away. When she chanced to glance over her shoulder from her steps he hadn't moved from the fence, his chin resting on his arms, his smile completely captivating. "I don't care at all whether you come or not, really I do not. Anyway, I always take my lemonade at four here on the veranda if you're remotely interested. Which I very much doubt."

He shrugged without answering. She scrunched her face and hurried inside. How more ill-mannered could any man possibly be, she hissed aloud.

Bette-Mae spent her morning rummaging through her wardrobe, searching for something that didn't scream prissy daughter of a Baptist preacher. She settled on her least frilly blouse, a pleated skirt her father had required some convincing to buy, nylons, and her best Sunday pumps. In the afternoon she made a pitcher of fresh lemonade, carefully selecting biscuits that would not stain her fingers with chocolate or marzipan or crumple onto her lap. Near 3:00 she cooled herself in a shallow bath; she styled her hair in a mature teenage pageboy, strictly following the magazine's instructions. By 4:00 her table was set, the shades were drawn against the glaring late-day sun and Bette-Mae sat staring blankly into her book. She couldn't care less whether or not he came to sit with her.

Five minutes later she hated him entirely, filling her own glass. "What a despicable boy!"

From behind the voice startled her. "Uh-oh. I think she means me, Mrs. Carter."

"Bette, my dear. You have a gentleman caller. Mister Radcliffe Harken from next door has come to join you for lemonade and biscuits. And he's brought us both such delightfully lavish posies. Really, Mister Harken, a truly lovely gift."

"For two lovely ladies, Mrs. Carter."

Bette-Mae twisted in her seat, heat once again rushing to her face. How did he know she loved long-stemmed white roses, or that her mother adored carnations?

"You came?"

He put three flawless roses tied with a pink ribbon into her hands, the colour she wore that morning. "I did, for a glass of delicious lemonade. Unless I'm still a despicable boy."

Mrs. Carter giggled, suggesting her daughter was most certainly condemning another young gentleman. She graciously acknowledged her flowers once more, suggesting to her daughter that perhaps her guest would be more comfortable seated.

Bette-Mae breathed in the petals' subtle fragrance, giving them into the care of her mother.

When they were alone, "That was very thoughtful of you. I didn't believe you were coming."

"I was teasing you this morning. Thank you for inviting me, and for making yourself even lovelier for me. I suppose I should have dressed a little better. I will next time."

As though he hadn't. He must have spent an hour shining his boots, she thought. His jeans were belted with a rich oxblood leather, his impossibly white button-down open at the neck with his sleeves rolled neatly midway to his elbows with razor-sharp creases to his shoulders. He was impeccable. And gorgeous.

She reached for the pitcher, filling his glass. "So now I'm a lovely lady and not a little girl?"

"You were wonderful this morning, Bette-Mae. I was testing you because I want a girlfriend who's as beautiful as you are *and* has a sense of humour. I was pretty sure when I saw you in your window that you would like me. The good thing is, you really convinced me when you hurried to the fence to stake your claim. Pretending you were angry, that was pretty funny. Beautiful and funny, that's cool."

She truly believed her heart would burst from her chest. "What! Excuse me! I am not your girlfriend! Nor do I ever want to be your girlfriend."

"I disagree. I believe you will be very soon. I do. You like me, I can tell. That's why you were sitting in your window, hoping you would like me." He sipped his lemonade. "Hmmm, delicious."

"You're very brash, Radcliffe Harken. Whatever were you thinking to peek in a young lady's bedroom window?"

He chuckled. "I prefer Rad, Bette-Mae. Much less haughty than Radcliffe, and you were the one on the second floor. I wasn't peeking, you were."

"You're very incorrigible"

"Which is why I'm inviting you to the lake tomorrow for a picnic. Your mother gave me permission. I'm late because we were talking. She likes me as much as you do. I really can't take a chance on some inbred Kentucky hillbilly getting to you first. You deserve better."

"Really? I deserve you? That's what you're telling me? You don't even know me."

"That is what I'm telling you because you're very particular. Or else you'd already have a boyfriend, which is why you have to come swimming with me. You do have a bikini, don't you?"

"Of course I have a bikini," she blurted.

"Is that a yes?"

She swirled her lemonade, not at all pleased that he was sitting completely composed, as though he hadn't utterly flustered and frustrated her. How could she possibly appear poised and unruffled when her heart was beating so wildly?

He beamed. "I think that is a yes, Bette-Mae. I'm pretty sure."

"You're very annoying, Rad Harken. Although I do suppose if mother likes you I can at least try, especially since we're neighbours and I can see that you'll become a thorough nuisance if I don't." She sipped her lemonade. "So yes, you may accompany me to the lake for a picnic, which does not mean I'm your girlfriend. Do we understand each other?"

They sat together until Bette-Mae was called to dinner by her father who came to see for himself the young man who brought his wife flowers, to ascertain without his wife's biased appraisal that the Harken boy was suitable company for his young daughter.

He was reluctantly pleased. Rad did all the right things. He stood and he shook the father's hand, he respectfully declined Mister Carter's invitation to dine with them and thanked Bette-Mae for her kind attention and refreshments. In the parlour he thanked Mrs. Carter for allowing him to visit with her daughter and wished them all a pleasant evening.

*

Although Bette-Mae's evening was far from agreeable. Her father spent the entire dinner hour teasing her that, with her new boyfriend so conveniently at hand, he would certainly be keeping a watchful eye on their shenanigans. She was, after all, at a curious age with her young woman's heart all aflutter; Mrs. Carter compounding the playful torment by blessing the young man in her unusually gleeful dinner prayer. Bette-Mae asserting adamantly that Rad Harken was entirely too infatuated with himself to ever care as deeply for anyone else and that perhaps God's good work would be better spent instilling the irritating boy with even the faintest hint of humility.

Later in her bed she lay awake inventing reasons to worry. For some time she had wondered about kissing a boy, never finding anyone worth the effort. She was taller than most boys in her class who were often more interested in poking fun at the girls or showing-off by pushing and shoving each other whenever the girls chose to ignore them, acting like little children. They were awkward and chubby, always wearing heavy boots and caps on backward, baggy jeans and chequered shirts like sweaters over shapeless singlets.

The boys in the choir were no better in their gowns and bows, acting in front of her father as though they might at any moment sprout wings and metamorphose into His most virtuous angels.

Rad wasn't like any of those boys. He was as tall as her and slim with gorgeous black hair like hers and the most beautiful eyes. She saw at the fence that he was strong and would never be afraid of anyone. His jeans were fitted and his shirt was tapered with darts like the ones she had seen many times in her magazines. Nor would he ever for a moment think to wear work boots. Not Rad.

His bedroom window was a stone's throw from hers and in a couple of hours she would be with him again at the lake, wearing an ugly thick one-piece that she hated. She never went to the lake, not since high school; not when other girls were wearing cute two-pieces and string bikinis. That was wholly on her father. She loved him dearly but, God, was he an old-fashioned prude.

Now what would she do if her day with Rad wasn't impossibly perfect? She could never face him again. They would be a complete laughingstock because of her and he would always hate her, the most terrible thought striking her like lightning.

God, the backyard! The previous neighbours were old and childless, the husband practically blind. How could she ever spend her days reading and sunning in the backyard knowing that from over the fence Rad and some other girl would see her wearing the hideous rag and laugh at her?

She wanted to die. She absolutely wanted to die, adamant that she would then tell God she passed away in her sleep because of her father.

9

Bette-Mae woke Friday morning very much alive to her mother tapping on her door, not at all pleased when realizing that God hadn't clued-in to her personal dilemma, her glum state not in the least way brightened by hearing, "Rise and shine, dear. The day is sunny and wonderfully warm. Such a splendid day for a picnic with Rad."

Managing with no little effort to leave her bed, she spent a half-hour in the bathroom doing her makeup, styling her hair and coating her body with Hawaiian coconut oil. She spent another thirty minutes tormenting over what would best conceal the Victorian one-piece nightmare. Deciding on a denim skirt and floppy tee when other girls would be wearing bikini tops, she trudged into the kitchen.

Rad would come for her at 10:00, ample time to create a picnic lunch and convince God that she wasn't kidding. She wanted to die. However much she would have preferred crossing over in her sleep, she was truly ready.

"What's wrong, dear? Why the long face? The day could not be any more fabulous for your picnic."

"Rad is wrong, mother. His picnic idea is terrible."

Mrs. Carter smiled lovingly. She went to her daughter fully grasping the situation, wrapping the girl in her arms. Of course she understood. Bette-Mae had never before shown interest in boys and now Rad was calling on her.

"He's a fine boy, Bette. I'm sure he's as nervous as you,

dear."

"He isn't nervous about anything, mother. It's me…this stupid bathing suit."

"Your swimsuit is delightful and flattering. It's very pretty on you."

Bette-Mae tugged her top over her head. "Really, mother? I'll be sixteen in a couple of days, I got this when I was fourteen. I look ridiculous. All the other girls have strings. If I'm this embarrassed, imagine what he'll think of me."

"Your father's a preacher, dear. We're expected to present ourselves with a little more reserve and decorum than many of his congregation. Rad will see you for what you are, a very pretty girl."

"Father's thirty-eight, mother. You're scarcely thirty-five. How many of his congregation know about that not very reserved decorum?"

Mrs. Carter patted her daughter's cheek. "That was by no means a mistake and the second best day of our lives. Holding you for the first time was our first."

"Yes, and the third was running here from Missouri before *your* father could kill mine."

"We didn't run anywhere, missy. We eloped and were married almost immediately."

"Yes, while standing at the altar in a mini-dress…very mini, mother. Shorter than anything you let me wear."

Mrs. Carter smiled dreamily. "I suppose it was a tad scandalous. He bought it for me when we could barely afford our rent."

"You were in a church of all places. I'm talking about a beach. These kids aren't hypocritical adults, mother. They're worse. They already think I'm weird for not having a boyfriend. I know they talk about me. I know what they say, mother. Which is why when they see me wearing this

63

thing with Rad I will absolutely die."

Mrs. Carter smoothed her apron, her expression transmuting from pleasant to shadowed pensiveness, expelling a faint "Oh dear" with a long breath.

"What, mother? What is it?"

Mrs. Carter took her daughter's arm, leading her into the parlour. "Your father will require some very proactive pacifying from both of us this evening, Bette. We'll be extra attentive toward him without being overly effusive." She took two fifties from her pocketbook. "I trust you to buy something nice, dear. Something for a young lady your age, something a little nicer than the other girls' and perhaps an accessory. I'll take charge of your picnic and Rad if you need more time."

Bette-Mae lunged at her mother, squealing, squeezing and kissing her. Her mother was the greatest ever. She knew exactly where she would go at the mall and what she would buy. She would also leave the rag in one of the public trash cans.

Rad Harken stepped onto the front porch on time with a duffle bag slung over his shoulder, Mrs. Carter apologizing for sending her daughter to the store for an ingredient essential to the evening meal, Bette-Mae arriving home by the time the picnic basket was ready. She told her date she needed a few moments more, pulling her mother up the stairs to her room. Once inside she put on a one-lady fashion show to her mother's quiet applause. Her daughter was lovely in the navy blue Brazilian-cut tied at the sides with bright red strings, the matching triangle top and red Serengeti knock-offs. She would positively outdo the other girls. What's more, she whispered with a girlish giggle, her daughter's date was the absolute hottest. Not to say rules weren't in place, Bette-Mae promising they would be home by 4:00.

*

At the lake most kids had laid out their bedsheets or bamboo mats on the coarse sand, or unfolded their sleeping bags in age-defined cliques of four and six near the main entrance.

Rad Harken didn't know them. He didn't care about them, wondering aloud why anyone would bring part of their bed to the beach, or a straw mat that later in the day would smell like cat piss.

He strolled past them hand in hand with his girlfriend, exuding a nonchalance beyond his years, to the far end where the water's edge was framed by a cliff sculpted by erosion and decorated with all manner of rock formations.

Bette-Mae chose a spot where they would be seen. What was the point of being with a hot guy in nylon sweats and a compression tee if no one could see her, especially in her very au courant bikini?

He spread out a beach blanket lined with soft fleece for his lady, once again taking her hand to help her sit gracefully. Rummaging blindly in the canvas bag for his SLR and tripod, the radio and his towel, he finally stripped away his sweats and tee, casually stretching out beside her in a Speedo she was hoping for.

The other boys were nowhere near as manly, wearing denim cut-offs or trunks no different from her father's boxers that would stick to their legs and look ridiculous. Nor were the girls any better in their plastic drugstore sunglasses, Bette-Mae realizing as she passed them that their bikinis were actually quite ordinary. They weren't particularly cute or sexy or daring after all.

Hers was. She couldn't be more excited, elated that God understood she was being silly. Or that His guiding hand had given her mother a little nudge.

"Thank you, Rad."

"For what, Bette-Mae?"

"For holding my hand before they saw us."

"Truth is, I did that for me." He reached for her hands. "I want to hold them all day."

"I haven't come here for years…and never with a boy. That's why they're all gawking at us. They're talking about me, about you."

He chuckled. "Then I'm glad you waited for me and they don't matter. Only you do."

"That's very sweet, Rad. Thank you." She gazed into her lap, squeezing his hands. "Mother really didn't need anything at the store. I went shopping for a bikini, I never liked the old one. I had no idea you would happen yesterday, or that this would happen today. Anyway, I'm glad. And you're right, they don't matter."

Bette-Mae scrambled to her feet, nervous and exhilarated. First into the air was the off-the-shoulder loose-knit sweater her mother suggested would be more suitable to the occasion than a faded tee. Second was the denim skirt she pushed to her knees and let fall to the sand, standing with her back to distant and curious eyes, feeling more exposed than ever in her life in front of a boy she had known a mere twenty-four hours.

"Wow! That is…I don't know. That is wow."

She turned a half circle, stopping for the fullest effect, relishing the girls' clear envy and the jealous prattle she could practically read on their lips; the boys seemingly believing they would see more of her by straining their neck muscles to the point of rupture.

Completing the circle, seeing Rad visibly delighted with her, she also realized she wasn't the least bit bashful. She was thrilled the other girls were jealous, their boyfriends dreaming the impossible, all of them guessing whether she had already gone all the way with Rad. Not knowing would make them crazy. She was a virgin, most in her ninth grade were not. So let them gossip all they want.

"What's in that little head, Bette-Mae? Something's happening in there, I can tell."

She knelt beside him. "You'll be at school with me in September, Rad. Some of those girls are…you know, very easy to like."

"Not interested in some other guy's hand-me-downs. I told you yesterday, you should be my girlfriend. I knew the moment I saw you spying on me from your window and from where I'm sitting it's a no-brainer. I'm really what every girl wants, you most of all."

"That's it, I should be your girlfriend?" She planted her hands on her hips. "You are unbelievably smug, Rad Harken."

"I would have preferred balanced. But thanks anyway. I guess anything you say sounds wonderful." He glanced past her to the others, smirking. "I don't see anything over there for either of us, Bette-Mae. Makes me think we don't have a choice. We need each other." He jerked sideways, instinctively avoiding the clenched fist aimed at his shoulder, springing to his feet. "Okay, we *want* each other. Now let's get wet." He held out a steady hand. "I won't let you go, little girl. I promise."

Her eyes flared open, her hands catapulting her from her knees to her feet. "Little girl, really? I thought we got past that you insufferable egomaniac."

"We did. I just needed you standing." He swept her into his arms, stifling her shriek with the soft heat of his lips on hers. "This is sort of where you wrap your arms around my neck, Bette-Mae, to help me out a little. You're not the lightest thing I've ever carried."

She did, after she smacked him, floating on air until he eased her waist-deep into the cool and pristine water and kissed her again.

"This feels very strange, Rad. They must really be stunned over there seeing me like this, with you. I know I am."

"They're not stunned, they're jealous hillbillies going nowhere and don't know any better.
They'll probably marry each other, make more hillbillies and spend their lives working at the mill or wearing aprons. They'll never know more than their trucks and guns, bourbon and hunting season. You and me, Bette-Mae, we're better than them. We're going places, we are not staying here."

"Really? We aren't? And where exactly are we going, you and I, Rad Harken?" she asked, twirling and wading into deeper water, figuring she had a right to know.

"To the ocean, either one after we graduate from college."

She fell backward, disappearing, surfacing, her hair a glistening black skullcap. "I haven't thought about college, not yet." She signalled him closer. "Can you swim?"

"Of course I can. Can you?" He disappeared with barely a ripple, Bette-Mae's knees pushed gently apart, her body abruptly launched from the water. "I didn't hear you. Say again?"

She was clutching his head, straddling his shoulders, teetering from side to side, too elated to feel embarrassed. "Rad Harken, you put me down," she threatened. "You're making us a spectacle."

"Well I suppose I could if your legs weren't digging into me so hard, little girl."

"What!" She leaned forward, pounding his chest with her fists. "Put me down! You are completely horrible!"

He shrugged, shifting her weight, moving his hands from her thighs to her ankles, Bette-Mae's mouth and eyes gaping at seeing her feet spread wide against the blue sky for the fleeting instant her screech pierced the still air. Then came silence, Rad's sincere concern masked with a wide grin as she struggled to plant her feet on the silty bottom, twisting and flailing, at last surfacing to catch her breath, sputtering and coughing, her thick hair plastered across her forehead and eyes.

"Hey, that was so much fun."

"No, that was not fun." She punched him. She didn't know what else to do with him. She was afraid to wrap her arms around him, even more afraid to kiss him. "Idiot."

Rad stepped in closer, pressing his hands into her waist, staring into her beautifully dreamy eyes as he spun her in a tight half-circle. "Okay, that's cool. But, better than that, I'm your idiot and they're all seriously gawking. Check them out. Funny thing is, the jerks don't know at what."

"I know at what. At us, at me, wondering how I got such a fabulous boyfriend. Let them call me a stupid dyke now."

Bette-Mae at once pressed a flushed cheek to his; she needed to hide from him.

"Maybe they are. Seems reasonable to me. I mean, think about it. Hillbilly boyfriends or trailer trash girlfriends. But you, not a chance. What they're really seeing is next year's hottest school couple. You and me." He kissed her. "Fabulous, I like that."

"I'm sure you do." This time she kissed him, testing herself, partly believing him, partly believing she might have died in her sleep, transported by adoring cupids to some magical dreamland. "Or maybe you should date yourself and be your own hottest couple."

"I could never do that to you. You'd miss me the way you did last night."

Bette-Mae shook her head, rolling her eyes. She pushed him aside, wading toward shore, seconds later taking his hand.

They ate Mrs. Carter's lunch, listening to the radio without hearing the music. They lay in the sun and frolicked again in the water, Bette-Mae threatening violence if he even thought to drown her again. She posed for his lens, breaming and pouting, snarling and scratching the air. The final shot, one she would cherish forever, captured Rad Harken framed in his girlfriend's legs and wrapped in her arms.

At dinner that evening, Mrs. Carter was delighted by the sparkle in her daughter's eyes and the contagious excitement permeating the entire house, whereas Pastor Carter was silently wishing throughout the meal that his wife had borne him a magnificent son no less gorgeous and strong, fearless and manly and as incredibly perfect as Rad Harken.

10

By summer's end Bette-Mae's black hair was longer, her skin was more deeply tanned for the first day of classes from her days at the lake with Rad, and her latest wardrobe left no doubt whatsoever that she was no longer a little girl...except Rad's. As much as a pastor's daughter was permitted by paternal law.

They went everywhere and did everything together, missing each other those times when family vacations and occasions drove them apart. They were each other's best friend, each other's only friend.

That the other girls invented more cruel things to say about her came as no surprise, since she was clearly no longer a disgruntled lesbian. At least not since Rad who was the root of their innuendos and no less a victim. Not that he or she cared. He outshone the other boys physically and in the classroom, as much as she did the girls, proving himself superior in all pre-season tryouts before insouciantly quitting the team the day he was appointed captain. In the classroom he and Bette-Mae were the brightest stars, each other's closest rival earning the highest marks.

Then not soon enough for Bette-Mae the school year was over. Summer had scarcely begun and she was thrilled about being seventeen, about becoming more mature and feminine for Rad. She was excited about her first summer job working near her heart's delight at his father's car dealership as office girl and stand-in receptionist while he changed tires, jockeyed and washed cars. Both girlfriend and boyfriend quietly grateful that their respective parents were remaining amicable neighbours on their respective sides of the fence.

Afternoons at the lake were rare occasions, too few private hours after Saturday chores and Sunday dinners at which Rad was a frequent guest all the more precious. They made up for time lost by talking on the phone from their bedroom windows since the local drive-in in Rad's newly acquired ten-year-old Buick was not up for discussion, which Bette-Mae didn't care about because drive-ins were too public. She wanted Rad to herself, the next school year nevertheless arriving with predictable indifference despite her deep feelings.

Two boys in the homeroom were conspicuously absent the first day. Neither one had enjoyed his summer, nor was either one enjoying his marriage. One had found employment in the coffee shop, the other at a corner gas station. Each one convinced Rad Harken had maliciously blocked their job applications at the dealership, thus ruining their present and future prospects. Their comfortable homes, beds, and home-cooked meals were gone. To make ends meet they and their wives shared a two-bedroom flat furnished with whatever they could afford at the local thrift shop.

The fledgling brides, unemployable for years to come, were sitting together at the rear of the class. They were no longer envied or emulated by the other girls. They were no longer cool; they were lepers, school sluts who would be mothers by Christmas. They were yesterday's news, the novelty had worn off. The other girls not nearly as righteous as they were resentful for the loss of freedoms strictly imposed by cautious and worried parents, nightly inquisitions and lectures at the dinner table becoming the norm despite unconvincing theatrical tirades and tantrums asserting their innocence and highly prized purity.

As for the other boys, some of whom might well have been called upon to marry those same girls if not for the luck of the after-school draw, each one counted himself lucky. They saw the girls as unashamed and stupid whores to talk about, equally resentful toward them for making some of their current girlfriends afraid for no good reason.

Rad Harken viewed both sides differently. He knew the 'in' girls were getting laid on a regular basis, that the least attractive students went without because, male or female, they believed they deserved better.

Bette-Mae let him go, the entire class looking on. Blocking the husbands' chances of better paying jobs and reasonable futures didn't mean he was finished with them. He sat side-saddle on a desk in front of the girls, smirking, loving the moment.

"Wow. Haven't seen you girls for a while. You look totally different. You look, I'm not sure, like mothers on welfare. I suppose. Can't really say I know any mothers on welfare." He leaned closer. "How's that exclusive condo working for you? Must be super cozy, you and the guys." He shook his head, snorting. "Then again, I guess shacking up is no big deal since you did get laid together. How did that work, exactly?"

"Screw off, Harken," one girl said.

"Yeah, screw off."

He winced. "Well that hurt. I have to tell you though, the thought dawning on me while driving Bette-Mae to school this morning, we really should have stopped for gas and a coffee. Not that I can't get both at my father's dealership for free. You know, to support your husbands in their privileged careers." He stood, grinning. "Better yet, what occurred to Bette-Mae was that you probably would have graduated next year if you two were lesbians. You know, real lesbians, since you seem to recognize who is and who isn't one. Really makes a guy wonder. Thing is, instead of being with each other, which personally works for me, you're quitting school at Christmas. Going nowhere fast with loser husbands you don't want and screaming brats you don't want. Not to mention what they'll do to your bodies. So good luck with that. You are royally screwed."

The door opened and closed. The "Mister Harken, take your seat" was not a request.

"You are such an asshole," the first girl snarled.

"Like you're not doing your bitch girlfriend."

"How can I? She's a lesbian, remember?" He coughed a loud laugh. "I wish."

"Mister Harken, front and centre. Stand here and tell us all what's more interesting this morning than me."

Rad swaggered confidently to the front of the class, standing shoulder to shoulder with the teacher.

"I was counselling the inexperienced wives and expectant mothers, sir, letting them know they have options when things don't work out because they won't be graduating. A real tragedy we should all learn from, sir. I was being concerned. We should all…"

"Mister Harken, I believe many here believe *you're* somewhat of a tragedy, not the least of whom I imagine is Miss Carter. Now take your seat."

Rad did take his seat beside a giggling Miss Carter, aware the entire class was staring at him. When the school day ended he drove Bette-Mae home through a torrential downpour, both of them scurrying onto her front porch where a note laying on the chesterfield detailed what she was to take out for dinner. Since Bette-Mae would soon leave home for college, Mrs. Carter, facing a lonely existence, had weeks earlier begun a career as a secretary in a law firm.

In all their fifteen months together they hadn't once been caught in the rain, hadn't once been alone inside their homes, Bette-Mae insisting that she dry Rad's hair before beginning their homework. He hadn't once been alone in her bedroom peering from her window; nor had he ever kissed her as ardently, nor laid on her bed warding off the demons of a teenage mind as he watched her care for her own wet tresses.

*

Christmas Eve day two girls still in their teens were screaming and straining their way hours apart into motherhood as their husbands sat together in the lounge drinking watered-down coffee, repeatedly asserting in mournfully low voices that they would rather be dead than fathers.

The four were alone, dispossessed months earlier by family and friends. For the first time in their lost lives they would have no tree, no gifts to open, no family homes or turkey dinners to gorge on. Their lives going forward into bleak futures would be devoid of parties and merriment, those youthful pleasures abruptly exchanged for shared misery and desperation. And no one cared.

Bette-Mae and Rad spent Christmas morning with their families, exchanging gifts later in the day when, for the first time, the Carters invited the Harkens and their children to a festive dinner. Which didn't sit well with two of the children whose secretive afternoon study sessions in the living room were then very much the norm.

By Valentine's those cherished afternoons of learning and growing closer were all the more precious, their long-awaited summer together coming too quickly. Days earlier

Rad received an invitation from a university in Mobile, Bette-Mae learning a day later that she would be earning a four-year degree in Louisville six hundred miles apart from the man she deeply and truly loved.

They graduated together at the top of their class a month before Bette-Mae's eighteenth birthday, making the most of a week of freedom before Rad, inexperienced at selling cars, would once again jockey and prep them while she booked appointments and greeted customers with a bright smile.

June 26th was a Monday, a day Bette-Mae would always remember and be thankful for. They would leave the lake to the high school kids, she told him. She wanted to spend their special day, the entire week alone with him. From then on they would have no privacy, no tender moments until they would no longer have each other.

They lay in the sun on her veranda, drinking lemonade and dreaming aloud, Bette-Mae more sombre with each passing hour. She adored his gentle touch, the way he kneaded SPF into her warm flesh, the way he cupped and kissed her breasts, the way he trailed kisses from her shoulders to the small of her back, tugging at the loosely knotted ties at her waist.

By early afternoon neither one was hungry. Eating seemed ridiculous given her serene mood and his adoring attentiveness. Instead she rolled onto her back, swung her feet lazily onto the wooden floor and stood, reaching for her bikini and taking his hand.

An hour later, stepping from a cool shower, her body tingling, her smile was thin.

"You are incredibly beautiful. And wow, finally a smile…sort of. I think."

"Thank you, sweetheart."

"For what?"

"For being an idiot that first day. I can't imagine not being with you. And for my bracelet, I love my bracelet."

"Thank you for mine. Can you believe two years already?"

He passed her a towel, stepping back to watch her bend and stretch.

"Two incredible years."

"Then why so glum all day?"

"I didn't want our day to end. That's all."

"I meant what I said, Bette-Mae, in bed. I do love you, very much. The next four years will go quickly. You'll see. And we'll have all sorts of time together. I promise. Especially when you marry me."

"Marry you?"

"That's right, marry me. As soon as we graduate. Four years tops. Thought you should know, if you didn't already." He stepped in, taking the towel, turning her by her shoulders, patting her back dry. "I think this is where you jump up and down and scream something cutesy."

She was in shock, her mind paralyzed, suspended between the best and worst day of her life. She twirled, kissing him, welled-up tears trickling down her cheeks.

He held her at arm's length. "Hey, are you okay? Is this a girl-thing happening here?"

"We never talked about marriage, not once. But I do love you, sweetheart. I do. I always will, no matter what."

"Some things we don't have to say. We feel them. Besides, who deserves me more than you? And what do you mean, no matter what?"

Bette-Mae stepped back suddenly feeling vulnerable and uncertain. She needed to see his eyes, to see the absolute horror and read his worst thoughts when she whispered, "Our baby."

11

Baby? Rad Harken was certain he understood the word synonymous with life's worst possible negatives. Frozen in time he stood staring at his naked girlfriend, thankful he was dressed despite the ominous revelation.

"Baby?" he replied. "As in…sooner than later? Are you sure, Bette?"

"I went to Doc Jenkins on Friday. I wasn't feeling well, Rad. He gave me some tests…and a really long lecture. He promised he wouldn't tell my parents."

"You should have told me. I should have gone with you, to be with you."

"I didn't know. I thought…I don't know what I thought. Certainly not this."

He blew a thin stream of warm air between his lips; Bette-Mae standing silently, her anxiety palpable.

"Okay, first things first. Let's not panic for no reason." He draped the towel around her slumped shoulders, pulling her closer, hugging and kissing her. "I can't think straight when I see you like this. Get yourself dressed. We're going to the park and we are not telling our parents until we figure out a couple of things for ourselves. Either way, they'll scream and shout, Bette. That's a given: Parenting 101. It's what they do, which doesn't mean we will."

"You mean we're good, Rad? You still love me?"

He spun her sideways, smacking her bum. "Put on

something pretty. I'll make the bed and start thinking things through."

Bette-Mae scurried from the bathroom into her bedroom, Rad following close behind. She dressed in a hurry into a chic summer wardrobe, since her father was grudgingly coming to terms with her transition from adolescence to the maturity requisite to her approaching autonomy. The truth being, he had no choice.

The park was deserted apart from some old men hunched over in sneakers and shapeless sweat suits feeding the pigeons while their wives in bright polyester suits were entertaining babies and toddlers that their sons and daughters couldn't properly care for without help.

The conversation was fragmented, peppered with uncertainty and long moments of silence.
Yet walking home minutes before the dinner hour Bette-Mae's mood was lighter if not cheerful. She knew the truth deep in her heart, loathing herself throughout the entire weekend for even thinking he would abandon her.

After dinner she sat in her window with her door closed ready for bed, thinking more of Rad than her mother and father. They agreed in the park to spend their evenings away from each other, to view what was happening from different perspectives without each other's influence and that simply agreeing with each other would inevitably lead to the easiest and worst solution.

They did nothing illegal. They were past the age of consent and mature for their age, the most terrible consequence would undoubtedly be their educations. Rad's dream was to become a marine biologist, hers was to become a high-profile lawyer that would require a skillset she would definitely put to the test Saturday evening assuming all went well.

She climbed into bed near midnight, hugging her pillow,

falling asleep contented. She knew what she wanted. She wanted Rad. What she needed was for him to agree with her and for his strength of character to withstand her father's predictable and pious outrage.

She woke Tuesday morning, declining breakfast with her parents. She sat on the veranda sipping fruit juice, putting Saturday from her mind while pondering the previous day and evening, absently wishing her parents a nice day without seeing them walk past her.

Rad came through the back gate at 9:30 in his swimsuit, acting as though Monday wasn't the worst day of his life. She kissed and hugged him and went to change. When she stepped onto the porch minutes later in a silk one-piece décolleté thong that was not a swimsuit he practically toppled forward from the railing…completely in accordance with her plan.

She wanted to smile, failing miserably. "I bought this a while ago, for you. This is what you'll see a year from now, Rad, if you can tell me this very minute that you really want to marry me. If you don't, I need you to tell me right now."

"I do, and I will. You know I do. I also have a reasonably simple solution to our situation."

"Good. Now we have three plans."

Bette-Mae sat with him and listened. When he finished, her piercing eyes and pursed lips were sufficient comment.

"That will not happen, sweetheart. You are not delaying your freshman year because, if you do send that letter, I'll abort before the weekend. That's my second plan. I'll abort in Lexington and find another boyfriend at college who isn't a complete idiot, who I may or may not keep for four years. I've already spoken with the clinic. Is that simple enough for you?"

"You're joking, right?

"No. I'm not. You are."

"Listen, I can make good money with my father, Bette. He's done alright with grade twelve."

"You're not listening to me. Promise me."

He inhaled a deep breath, expelling a long sigh. "Okay, I promise...maybe. Once I hear the real plan."

"We're legal. Or I will be this weekend. You and I are driving to Lexington. We're getting married, we're coming home to very irate parents and you're going to college in the fall. Mother's father left me a very considerable endowment when he passed away to punish my father, held in trust until Saturday. I do not need father's help for college, neither do you because he never forgave father for what he did to mother. They never spoke after what happened, not a word. Nevertheless, he did love me."

"I can't take your money, Bette. That's not a way to start a life."

"You can and you will. It's our money and Monday we're driving to Mobile to find an apartment. Case closed...or do I get myself another boyfriend?"

The rest of Tuesday and the week mirrored Monday, their mornings spent basking in warm sunshine, their afternoons beginning tenderly and ending with hands tightly clasped together as they strolled and talked in the park.

Rad learned about the endowment, Bette-Mae called her grandfather's attorney for an early Saturday appointment and a Presbyterian minister in Lexington who was not acquainted with her father. For his part, her fiancé booked a five-star in Louisville for their wedding night and Sunday and a full week at a Biloxi casino resort an easy hour's drive from Mobile. She also made very clear that she would attend the University of Mobile with him, completing her freshman year as a distant student, and that she had no great desire to become a mother. They were too young, the world was too big, and she wanted a career. She had no intention of being as unfulfilled as her mother.

Friday afternoon, after a late lunch, Bette-Mae called her mother from an upscale downtown boutique. Rad was taking her to dinner and a movie. Then with help she put together an elegant ensemble for her wedding day. Rad walked out with a black suit and upbeat accessories. At the jewellers she chose a titanium band with a diamond he could afford and she could see. His was a simple gold band.

Then driving home with an hour to spare before the movie would end, they sat in the park talking and dreaming, enraptured when they might have been afraid. Within a few hours they would be adults surviving on their own, which made leaving him to spend a sleepless night alone in her room the hardest part of her week.

Saturday morning she woke early and showered, too excited to eat. She positively adored her birthday present. The pendant would go beautifully with her new dress, she told them, causing their brows to furrow in unison. She kissed them both, telling them not to worry. She was spending the day with Rad who had a special gift for her and they would be home for dinner with the Harkens.

Stopping at the door, she said "I love you both very much," very much aware she would devastate them that evening. Equally aware she had her own life to live.

They were gone from the lawyer's by 9:30, finished at the bank thirty minutes later and her hairdresser by noon. They drove eighty miles to Lexington where they ate a quick lunch and paid for one hotel night they wouldn't use to the fullest, taking an hour to breathe and change for the wedding.

They arrived at the church at 3:00. At 3:30 Bette-Mae was Mrs. Bette-Mae Harken and by four she was making love to her proud husband at the hotel. Checking out at 5:30, surprising no one at the front desk, they arrived at the

Carter home on time at 7:00.

The stunning bride portrayed a graceful and modern young lady striding through the front entrance in a short mauve satin dress and bolero jacket, in heels and nylons, her coiffed hair swept into a cute updo and her lips painted a glossy violet. The dashing groom, looking formal in his black suit, smoky-grey shirt, silk tie and pocket hanky complemented the completely absurd image.

Her mother and father sat dumbstruck by the striking transformation, seeing their innocent daughter unexpectedly transformed into an unfamiliar woman without their knowledge or consent. The four parents at once exchanged questioning glances, their brows creased. Mister Harken, seeing his son holding her hand, took his wife's hand. Nothing good was about to take place.

Rad broke the uneasy silence with calm assurance. "We were married in Lexington this afternoon, people. We decided after a lot of talking things over that living four years and six hundred miles apart wasn't going to happen."

The questioning glances transmuted instantly into the fathers' faces washed red with rage and the mothers' horrified gasps.

"That is utterly ridiculous," Pastor Carter said first, snorting, scoffing at the words as though what he heard was a humourless joke. "Looking mature in those fancy clothes doesn't make you mature, boy. This thing you've done can be undone and will be undone."

"Indeed it will. A truly rash decision," Mister Harken concurred. "This puppy love of yours isn't a marriage, Rad. How stupid of both of you."

"Father, you have no say whatsoever in the matter. Not a word," Bette-Mae broke in. "We did what was right for us. At least we didn't run away the way you did with mother. Neither do you, Bill." The stunned reactions were unanimous. "That's right, Bill and Laura. And for Rad, it's John and Julie."

Julie Carter could scarcely find words, her eyes beginning to water "Bette, you cannot possibly be serious. And please show us due respect. We are your parents."

"We are respectful, mother. We're adults speaking intelligently with adults. Or we hope to."

"I can't for the world imagine what possessed you, doing this behind our backs, choosing to ruin a mother's proudest day for me. How very selfish and unkind of you. You know how I've dreamed of this moment, of your father hearing your vows."

"Gee, mother. I thought your proudest moment was having me. And what about your mother, how proud was her moment?"

"Don't be glib. You deliberately deceived us," John scolded. "Spending the day with Rad...a special gift. An unimaginable perversion of the truth, daring in the same breath to say you love us. Unequivocally shameful behavior. The antics of a spoiled child."

"We do love you."

Rad put a reassuring arm around her waist. "We did this for practical and legal reasons, Julie. Not to make anyone prouder than you should be already. If this is anyone's proudest day, it's mine."

"Teenage rhetoric. What we want to hear is how you plan to live." blurted her father. "Tell us that. And what about your education? Your tuition is one thing. However we will not, we cannot support immoral living arrangements."

Bette-Mae led her husband to the chesterfield, sitting by his side. "Reasonable questions, father, if not a tad ironic. I went to granddad's lawyer this morning, taking charge of my endowment. We're both attending college together in

Mobile where we'll be living. We no longer expect, require, or want your financial assistance. We'll be very comfortable and there's nothing immoral about us. We're married."

The air was thick with tension. John Carter stood. Wine wasn't strong enough, a likeminded Bill Harken suggesting that he not bother measuring either glass.

"And I'll take a beer, John. Thanks."

"The hell you will, boy. Not in this house."

"No, father. We are in your house as invited guests for dinner. My husband is asking for a beer and you *will* bring him one. Thank you."

"Please don't be rude to your father, Bette. You and Rad are not guests, you're our children."

"Adult children invited to dinner, Julie. Bette and I have made other arrangements for later this evening and tomorrow. Then were taking a week for a honeymoon before hunting for a place to live near the university." Rad turned to his father. "Sorry for the late notice, dad. We won't be working for you this summer."

Laura Harken looked to her hostess. "Julie, I'm sorry. I have no appetite at all for dinner. I'm feeling sick to my stomach."

Julie nodded. Their children had abruptly and manifestly soured the evening's cheerful mood.

Bill took the old-fashioned filled three inches deep with whiskey and ice, watching Rad take his beer. "Always thought I'd be pouring your first beer, son. Now your job? You're full of surprises this evening, the two of you."

"And what do you know about being on your own. You know nothing at all about life," John ranted. "What I demand to know is the name of the preacher who performed this atrocity. I'll have him severally reprimanded."

"Not a preacher, father, a Presbyterian minister for that very reason."

"What!" John Carter's whiskey gurgled in his throat, his face instantly a deep purple. "You did what?"

"You heard me, father. As for life, what did you and mother know, other than the obvious?"

"People, to be clear about all this," Rad broke in, "we are moving to Mobile and we are graduating in four years. You're incensed and disappointed over a matter that is not your concern. Your feelings are hurt because we excluded you with good reason. You think we'll be lost without you, and we get that. Nevertheless the truth is, we are not lost and you will get over this." He sipped his beer, putting the glass aside. He stood, smirking, reaching out for Bette-Mae's steady hand. "We're leaving. There's no need to stay longer since dinner is cancelled and no one seems ready to congratulate a stunning bride."

John put up a hand. "We're not done here, boy."

"We are done. This is good night, people. Once we're settled we'll drive back for what's left of our personal items. What we'll need in the meantime is in the car. We packed yesterday, suspecting this evening might prove a little awkward."

"Then what, Rad?" Laura wanted to know, her tone more angry than mournful. "Special occasions like Julie's birthday or mine? Tell us exactly what."

"We'll visit when we can, Laura. And we hope you will, at Christmas or any other time," Bette-Mae replied. "Except this Christmas because I'm pregnant. A couple of months, which is not the reason for us marrying." The room went deadly quiet. "Yes, mother. I'm pregnant. Fate, karma, call it whatever. Regardless of which I have no intention of being a mother, of ruining my life and two others. I'm giving it away. And that is my decision, not Rad's."

Laura Harken smothered a loud gasp; Julie Carter expelled a loud wail, clutching her chest.

"You will not! No daughter of mine could ever be that sinful." John snapped, furious. "What in Hell's damnation has happened to you, girl? You're no better than those other girls. And you," jabbing a finger at Rad, "worse than the ones who despoiled them!"

Julie was crying, devastated by her daughter's cold demeanour. "Bette, your father's right. What you're thinking is a sin. *We* will take and legally adopt your baby. What can ever be more important than family?"

"No, you will not. I will not be a sister to whatever comes out. That is really sick, mother."

Bill stood, facing his son. "Is that it, Rad? Can you possibly have more to overwhelm us with?"

"Just that we're leaving, that I'm taking my wife to dinner. You four have acted worse than we thought possible. We have nothing to apologize for, you do. All four of you. You're invited to visit whenever you want. Hey, we'll even serve dinner...once you mellow out. Because we do not need the grief."

"Then send us your address, Rad, when you get one. We'll ship your personal belongings. Frankly I don't believe the damage you two caused this evening will be assuaged in such a short time. Thank goodness your sister is at home untainted by this double atrocity. We believed she would be bored with no one her age to play with. Now what must we tell her? Shame on you for this disgraceful behavior. To say your mother and I are ashamed says nothing."

"Actually it says everything, dad. And really, there is nothing in the house I need."

Bill reached out for Laura' hand, facing Julie. "He's right. Staying longer is pointless. We'll talk later, the four of us."

The Harkens walked out deflated without another word

or backward glance.

"Okay. Let's get something straight here," Rad said coolly, staring down John. "There is no shame in what we did. Those other girls were class nymphos. They were sluts who started screwing in grade eight, big time. The hillbillies they married were not boyfriends, not by a long shot. They were last in line, screwing behind some bushes. Real classy." He snorted. "Or not the last. Could be they're bored or broke, doing what it takes. Who cares? But do not compare Bette with those sluts or me with the hillbillies. Or you and I, we've got a big issue, Pastor."

Pastor Carter faced his daughter. "Leave and take your husband with you. You need not concern yourself with future visits. This is no longer your home. We may have seen fit to pardon your shameful behaviour, however what you're contemplating is vile...contemptible beyond forgiveness."

"Now that *is* ironic. How hypocritically Christian of you, father. In which case nothing in the room upstairs is mine either," she replied calmly, reaching for the clasp on her pendant. "Or this. I have a beautiful ring to remember that I married on my birthday." She dropped the pendant into her mother's lap. "That you have nothing to say, mother, proves that I'm right."

The young Mister Harken and his bride walked out hand in hand, not the least apologetic or ashamed, believing their indignant parents would one day get real. They hadn't done anything immoral or illegal. They were not eloping, nor were they running. They were husband and wife, leaving on their honeymoon. Despite which, they were wrong. Neither one would ever see their parents again.

With no reason to remain in Louisville another night they drove to their Biloxi honeymoon the next morning, lazing by the pool by day and being newlyweds in their suite at night.

A week later they rented a comfortable condo near the campus, ending their first semester at Christmas with impressive grades. One month later, in the presence of a lawyer, a newborn without a name was taken unemotionally from them. They never saw the face or touched the baby's body.

The next day Nathanial Thompson was carried away wrapped in a blanket by his elated parents. Bette-Mae and Rad left the hospital twelve thousand to the good, relieved their ordeal was over.

Four years later Rad and Bette-Mae Harken moved to the East Coast to begin fulfilling and sharing their dreams.

12

January 31ˢᵗ in Mobile was unusually frigid and damp with blustery winds blowing off Mobile Bay.

The Thompsons left their hotel late in the morning, baby Nathanial blissfully unaware he'd been purchased by the strange creatures staring at him, passing him from one to the other, rocking and bouncing him for whatever reason and making noises he had no idea about; his mood instantly confrontational when the huge creatures jostled him rudely into what he didn't know was bright daylight and winter's cold.

Why were they not listening to him? Before, whenever before was, they made him feel happy and warm; now he was decidedly unhappy. He didn't like the way his face was feeling, he didn't like feeling trapped. He was already bound and defenseless. What was happening to him? Why were they locking him into something so much worse that he had no idea about? How could they not hear his screams? How could they not see his panic?

Thirty-five-year-old Matt Thompson strapped his new son into the backseat of his SUV while his wife Carrie loaded their suitcases eagerly into the rear cargo space. She was taking home her baby.

Shutting Nathanial in, Matt held the door for his wife. He put a finger to her lips with a wide smile, silencing the question. "Yes, again. I'm good to go. We'll drive straight through ahead of the system and we *will* be home for dinner with all of them," he told her. "Our moms are excited and waiting. I know that. Believe me, I do."

Sliding into her seat she was beaming. "They are, Matt. Really though, I think our dads are the worst."

He chuckled, leaning in to kiss her, closing her door and hurrying to his side "Yeah, no kidding. I paid the hotel phone bill. Whoever said talk was cheap?"

Carrie turned, reaching to gently touch the baby's head. "The lawyer said that girl didn't even look at Nathanial, that she kept her eyes shut tight the entire time. How cold is that, Matt?"

"Not cold at all. I don't believe so. She did what was best for them...for Nathanial and for us. They're bright kids. They have plans, a good a future ahead of them. Nathanial would have severely altered that future. They did the right thing. We're grateful for Nathanial, Carrie. We should also be grateful to the girl and her husband. Apparently she was steadfast in her decision. She did the right thing. She could as easily done something much worse."

"I suppose you're right."

He coughed a laugh. "God, I love those words almost as much as I love you."

Carrie giggled. She would have giggled at anything. She was in another world. She had her baby. Not once in the countless years ahead of her would she ever give the love of her life a more profound expression of that undying love than finding little Nathanial.

The first half of the road trip on I-65 to their home south of Nashville brought them to Birmingham under darkening skies. Neither was hungry and Nathanial was sleeping. Though by Huntsville, still ninety minutes from home, the SUV needed gas and Nathanial was in need of parental care better suited to his mother.

Matt turned off the highway to a diner promising cheap gas and Alabama's finest coffee. He knew the place well from his business travels, suggesting quick coffees and sandwiches since the worsening weather conditions would likely prolong their travel time.

Within thirty minutes the weather was abruptly turning foul, a mix of driving rain and sleet incessantly pelting the diner's windows. Matt wanted on the road; the storm arrived earlier than expected and the threat of unfamiliar snow was in the forecast. Carrie agreed, not wanting to waste precious time on the phone with her parents.

The parking lot was a dark maelstrom. The short distance from the diner to the SUV was a relentless gauntlet of furious winds and biting ice pellets, the access road four miles from the highway black as pitch and greasy.

"I don't like this, Matt. It's creepy."

He chuckled, reassuring her. "Not a big deal. We're three minutes from the highway. At most this'll add an hour." He reached for his coffee. "I've driven in a lot worse. Nothing at all to worry about."

Seconds later, "What an idiot, Matt. He's blinding us."

"The jerk behind isn't any better. Odds on them bein' hillbillies, missus," he joked. "Best shield yer eyes is all, ma'am."

Carrie did exactly that, both eyes flashing open at Matt's piercing scream. The last thing his wife saw was Matt uselessly twisting to shield her from death; the last thing Matt saw was the absolute terror in her wide-open eyes.

The impact welded the truck and SUV into a macabre sculpture. Carrie and Matt Thompson died instantly, their future stolen from them. The truck's single occupant lay splayed grotesquely between the two windshields, dead, the body shredded and bloody.

A rusted-out Cadillac Seville with Mississippi plates slowed to a stop on the opposite soft shoulder, the four-way flashers eerily illuminating tall black trees into dull yellows and reds.

The driver lowered his window. "Well screw the dog a good one if they ain't deader than yesterday's shit, Vera. The dumb bugger layin' in the rain sure as hell be dead."

He grabbed for his flashlight and ball cap, pushing open his door. He ambled across the road, pressing in to the slashing rain, peering first into the truck's passenger-side window. The driver's twisted legs framed the steering wheel, the space beside them littered with girlie magazines, paper cups and an open bottle of whiskey. Shining a beam on the tattered corpse, the gaping eyes and mouth negated any concern.

He peered into the SUV's front side window, shaking his head at the damaged bodies slumped behind their belts. He side-stepped to the rear window, freezing his throat with a sudden gasp, trying the crumpled door. Impossible. Not a chance. Instinctively he hurried to his trunk for a wrench, waving and shouting to the wife as he ran.

"Vera git yer butt over to the carnage. Be quick about it."

She didn't want to. She didn't like moving. She was rotund and warm, eager for a meal of beef stew and cornbread at the diner. "If they all be dead, what's the fuss about?" she yelled back. "They be dead, ain't they?"

He stuck his head into his half-open window. "Git yer fat butt out here. There be an infant in the car. I swear the thing be alive, screamin' and hollerin'."

She struggled from the car cursing, dressed in a heavy woolen shirt over her housedress, thick boots and thick woolen socks, pulling a headband over her ears.

He didn't wait for her, hurrying to smash the window.

Little Nathanial was alive, wailing. He reached in, tugging and straining, frantically working against time to free the tiny body from its car seat.

"Gracious be the good Lord, Wilbur. How's the thing alive through all this terrible mess?"

He passed her the baby. "What's fer us to know or care a whit." He grinned. "Now git to the car with it. Put it on the floor in the back while I work quick afore some other body comes snoopin' and spoilin' what it is I got brewin' in my head."

"Rich folk by the looks. Must somewheres be a bag for it," she yelled over the storm, hobbling back across the road. "Bring it. I knows good'n well what be brewin' in that simple head."

She laid Nathanial clumsily with one hand behind the driver's seat on the floor, bracing the door open with her other. Slamming the door shut without a second glance she hurried to the comfort of her own seat to wait for the husband who wasted no time claiming his rewards.

The SUV's tailgate opened easily to matching suitcases and a pale blue padded backpack that must be what the wife intended. He took all three, rushing to his trunk and back, crawling into the SUV.

He first reached over the seatback behind the woman, grabbing her handbag, taking several twenties and fifties from her wallet. He pushed the seatback forward crawling toward the couple. Reaching into the man's jacket, even more pleased with himself at seeing a few hundred or more in that wallet.

The woman was wearing a fine leather coat. He tried one pocket, straining to reach into the other. "Ya musta bin a real pretty one afore the wreck, darlin'" he mumbled "Real pretty." Pushing his hand inside the heat from her body was irresistibly compelling. Inside her blouse her breasts were soft and smooth, well worth his time and attention considering what was waiting in the car, wishing he was alone and not as close to the highway.

Making his way backward onto the road, he slammed the gate shut, hurrying with his wrench to the driver's side of the truck where he smashed what was left of the window, reaching over to the dead man's right back pocket. Glad that he did, counting another two hundred and change.

In all he hadn't taken five minutes. Within another five he was on the southbound I-65 headed for the I-20 and the backwoods of Mississippi where he knew some folks, promising the wife she would have her beef stew "somewheres" farther south.

*

By dinnertime the Thompsons and Carrie's parents were anxious about the weather, expecting the call. Their children were too thoughtful of each other to needlessly endanger themselves and little Nathanial. Of course they would be late.

Mister Thompson was the one to answer the phone. Recognizing the area code he smiled before putting his ear to the receiver, telling the others "Good, they must have taken a room." A moment later he wailed, clutching his chest and crumbling to his knees. "They're dead! They're all dead!"

Mrs. Thompson ran to her husband; Carrie's father ran to the phone to hear the Alabama State Trooper discreetly recounting the tragedy. The collision was not Matt's fault. The other driver, known for DUIs, crossed the line.

"Sir, I'm sorry. I have to ask. We found a hotel bill in the vehicle for two nights in Mobile. We also found Matt's and Carrie's wallets discarded. What we didn't find was luggage. I also must ask, sir, were Matt and Carrie travelling with a baby?"

*

Vera Keller got her hot stew three hours later at a 24/7 outside Tuscaloosa. Wilbur Keller wolfed a half-bucket of chicken wings and a couple of beers while Nathanial Thompson waited at the far end of the nearly deserted parking lot. Three hours and more later he drove into the mile-long lane leading to their one-bedroom broken-down Mississippi home some twenty miles from the Alabama border.

Nathanial spent his night on the floor bundled in his mother's blanket. The next day and for a week he was fed milk through an eye dropper, bananas and cream from Vera's homemade pies.

They used everything from Carrie's bag, after which he was seldom clean until at last Wilbur came home late one evening with cause for more jubilation. The crash had brought them close to a grand in cash, in addition to which the brat would bring an additional five thousand. That's what the man promised.

Babies were an easy thing to sell in the Deep South, what with backwoods girls so quick to part their legs for the attentions of eager boyfriends, curious brothers and desperate fathers whose wives had long ago lost any hope of recapturing their once youthful allure. The unhappy results were often a welcome source of family income, all the more beneficial when traded to rich city folk at a premium.

Forty-year-old Jackson Belmont presided over haberdasher shops in several Southeast cities, catering to those cities' well-heeled men who paid dearly for pampering and prestige. His thirty-something wife Melinda owned and managed an exclusive New Orleans hair salon.

They were well-to-do, managing to remain completely unpretentious while surrounded by pomposity and false

96

pride, and they were childless. In spite of which they didn't want, could never take, a hillbilly's inbred misfortune; they wanted brand new, a genetically and physically correct male child from a good bloodline and striking parents. They would wait, pray each day and pay whatever fee was appropriate.

When through a child welfare lawyer, who was a friend of a friend, Belmont heard of Mister Kellers' awful predicament he at once called his wife. The Kellers were a handsome and loving couple, the adoring parents of three lovely girls. The boy was an unintended blessing to the family, though with his wife tragically passing during childbirth the distraught father realized he could never possibly raise four children as he and his dear wife truly desired. He parcelled the girls out to family and the infant boy into the care of a foster home.

The Belmonts went that afternoon to the lawyer who in the coming days would complete the transaction and arrange for a birth certificate that would make Jackson Belmont, Jr. their very own. They saw the family portrait taken weeks before the young mother's heart-breaking death. She was beautiful and happy, her husband handsome and proud, their bright smiles sparkling with clear blue eyes and perfect teeth.

If the girls were any indication of what they should expect of the boy, fifteen thousand was indeed a reasonable price to pay for the best possible results, Belmont assured the lawyer with a handshake and ten grand in cash up front.

Four days after Carrie and Matt Thompson were buried by grieving their parents, little Jackson Junior was at long last at home with his.

Part Three

13

Murielle was done with Jake. He had probably sacrificed his whiskey money for the month to groan and grind his way into her. Which said a lot, she supposed. If a pathetic loser would spend most of his week's pay, why wouldn't someone who did have money pay to enjoy her? She had the clothes to meet any occasion: sultry slut or refined lady. At least Stonewall had given her that much in return, still not certain what she would say to him.

If he wasn't there or being a total prick, she would be left with nine days to fund and abort the nuisances growing inside her, assuming two or possibly three men that would leave her the final weekend to recover.

Thursday she decided on simple elegance for Stonewall. Her silk blouse was pale green and sheer, left unbuttoned to the lace of her emerald camisole; her belted black A-line skirt fell to a hand width above her knees, slit on one side to mid-thigh, inches from the delicate clasps and silk ribbons of her garters. The sheer nylons and stilettos together were as much a part of her strategy as style.

After a shower and a Silent Sam as deep as she dared, she called for a cab, hoping Jake wasn't at his door waiting. He wasn't good enough to see her looking so appealing; he didn't deserve the added dream. Though he wasn't, Murielle fairly certain he was in the can jerking his way down memory lane.

The ride to the Garden District deprived her of forty dollars. Stepping out the air was still and unseasonably warm. Looking to the third floor, the lights were on. He was there and she wasn't the least bit worried stepping into the main entrance. She was pragmatic. He would either show her deserved compassion for all they had shared, or she would later top any whore in the Quarter.

Pressing the buzzer, she didn't have to imagine the woman. She imagined herself.

"Yes, who is it?"

"I am Murielle de la Sorbonne. I would like to speak with Kenneth Stonewall."

The silence lasted what seemed like hours.

"Murielle, this is extremely inappropriate and unwelcomed. We had an agreement."

"No, we did not. You said I didn't love you. You were wrong. I did, and I do, Kenneth. May I come up, or will you come down? It's a lovely evening for a walk and I really would prefer not to meet my replacement."

The stream of air whistling past his lips into the intercom echoed in the narrow entrance. She heard the soft click of Stonewall disconnecting. Through the wrought iron barrier she heard his door opening and closing, his heavy footfalls stomping on century-old steps until he stood towering over her from the first landing. His mood and his eyes were dark. He was not pleased.

"Good evening, Murielle. Why are you here, precisely?"

"Kenneth, I think a short stroll around the block would be a little more dignified and private, rather than talking between bars and entertaining your neighbours."

He closed the space between them with measured steps, entering his code to open the gate. "I will walk with you, of course, as long as I feel inclined to listen. After you."

On the sidewalk she didn't bother taking his arm as she often did in friendlier times. "You hurt me, Kenneth. I cannot begin to tell you how much."

"Murielle, we had a simple arrangement convenient to our mutual self-interests: One year. And, for lack of any better phrase, all expenses paid. I am not inclined toward marriage or long-term involvement. I don't understand the need, nor do I harbour any desire to endure the intrinsic complications such as the one I am currently experiencing with you. What I do desire and can well afford is renewed novelty and youthful passion. I told you that. I said one year." He pointed over his shoulder. "I told her the same, as I explicitly told all your equally attractive predecessors. It's what I do, it is who I am."

"They didn't love you. She doesn't love you. I still do."

"No. You do not. You loved the idea of me, as I for the past year took pleasure in you. Let us not pretend otherwise."

"You never loved me? That's what you're saying?"

"Don't be naïve. You served a purpose, as I did for you. How could I possibly love a child twenty years younger in mind and body?"

She stopped walking, visibly shocked. "What!"

"Forty-two the week we parted. Now why are you here, Murielle?" He paused, snickering for affect. "Oh, let me guess. You're pregnant."

"Yes, I am. By the man I adore. Sixteen weeks. Or don't you remember New York?"

"I do, clearly. As I cherish all special occasions with my former ladies and long for many more in the future. However I would suggest fifteen weeks more precisely, my dear Miss de la Sorbonne. That *is* when you ordered out for pizza. That *is* when you invited the eager fellow in to share a slice with my exquisite wines before rewarding his prompt service with your own, a process you rehearsed throughout the day in my bedroom at the mirror striving for perfection. Your histrionics were entertaining in the extreme, my dear girl. You see the condo is wired for audio-visual, always was and always will be for obvious reasons. I witnessed most of your day with great delight. I heard your every peep and whimper, as I did throughout the entire year when business kept us apart." His brow creased pensively. "Zachary, as I recall. Yes. He was infatuated with you from the very instant you opened the door in your daring little thong. Dare I say lovesick? You see he was aware of your intention to invite him in, and for what purpose. I must say the two of you put on quite a theatrical event. Well worth the cost of a few bottles." He put a hand to her shoulder. "My chauffeur was outside waiting for him, instructed to pay the kid five-hundred not to disappoint you. You see I was correctly convinced you would do some foolish thing…and you chose not to disappoint me. What did, however, were the three subsequent deliveries and equally playful servings. In truth one might understandably wonder who was actually serving who. All witnessed and duly recorded as a matter of course."

"Bullshit. I don't believe you." She shrugged off his hand. "I need a thousand dollars, Kenneth. I am not keeping what is yours if you don't want me. You owe me that much. Or would you prefer a paternity suit?"

"Ah, then comes the threat. Yes. Actually no. You see what any DNA would substantiate, or expose, my enchanting Murielle, is that I need never worry about fathering any woman's child. The condoms were a matter of my personal hygiene, never intended as an alternative. Not that I didn't implicitly trust you at the time, although you must understand my current doubts. Simply put. And I owe you nothing, Murielle. You were well recompensed for your time with me, as was the kid for your début performance with him. A definite win-win. In addition to which, what judge would believe you once seeing you, how shall I put this…royally and repeatedly satiating a pizza kid for his tip?" He snorted. "That's right. And let us not forget the video of you plastering my walls with so-called selfies of you and our Zachary frolicking throughout the condo. Very creative indeed. A more suspicious mind might well believe that he was in fact paying you for your highly developed attentions."

"I don't believe you. This problem is yours, Kenneth. Please. I'm running out of time."

"Yes, of course, the job. They contacted me for references, greatly impressed by my highest regard for you. Congratulations."

"I need the abortion, Kenneth. You know Gilmore. Please. They cannot see me this way."

"Our bed was still warm, Murielle. I must have truly distressed you that you so quickly and urgently sought comfort from a maladroit boy. In any event, what is done is done."

"I cannot do this, Kenneth. You're ruining my future."

"Murielle, grow up. We as humans, particularly womankind, are simply convenient vehicles temporarily available at a cost to satisfy our most basic needs and pleasures, never the exclusive property of the driver. The more privileged of us, naturally, are able to afford the higher cost of more enviable luxury. And that would be you, Murielle. So go, before the restrictions of your predicament impede you. Rent yourself out at an appropriate cost. Spread those inviting legs of yours. Exploit your assets and remarkable skills to your very best advantage as willingly as you did with me and the boy. And how many others before me I cannot possibly imagine."

"You were my first, Kenneth. You know that. Zachary was just a very big mistake because you hurt me."

"I very much doubt that you were and the kid was by no means a mistake. He was quite possibly your defining moment, your realization of whom and what you are. A mere one thousand, Murielle, with several nights remaining should cause you no concern whatsoever. Not considering your instant success with Zachary. Imagine the limitless possibilities, although I would vigorously recommend that you direct your energies toward a less pedestrian clientele. Simply be mindful that spitefulness pays no dividends, as I'm certain you are beginning to comprehend. You clearly have the better part of two weeks. Do what you must, for the right reason. Understand your true nature, what you desire above all things. In a real sense I believe your four years spent achieving a higher education might well have been wasted."

"You're telling me I'm a whore?"

"I'm simply counselling you on how best to correct your situation, given your natural proclivity and compelling features."

"Fuck you. I mean really, fuck you."

"Precisely my point. Those enduring memories are very real, Murielle. You set the bar to its uppermost point. You were truly a difficult one to replace." Reaching into his pocket, snapping a fifty from a clip holding her thousand and more, he folded the bill into her fist. "For a taxi, and let us not do this again. Goodbye, Murielle. We are done, you and I."

"I will get back at you for this, Kenneth. I am not a whore. I'm not. However long it takes, I *will* get back at you!"

She was yelling at his back, standing in the dark watching him march toward his latest whore.

*

She studied the fifty, inhaling a deep breath as though bracing herself against some invisible force, teetering between tears and hysterical laughter. Tears for her desperation, laughter for being stupid enough to use her beautiful body for no better reason than pure spite. Stonewall was right; he was always right.

She walked several blocks in a daze before hailing a cab, pondering who, how much, and where? She had no place to take him and no guy seeing where she lived would ever pay what she was worth. If he didn't have a hotel room, she would find someone who did for nothing less than three hundred and without Todd's bullshit.

On a whim she tried the driver, figuring what the hell. She had nothing to lose, the backseat was no worse than her flat.

"...or right here for half. I guarantee you will not be disappointed."

He showed no surprise. "Miss, if I had that kinda money to spare I'd convince myself I'm ten years younger and we'd both be lookin' for a quiet place to park. Not much to pay for a frequent dream come true, and reasonable judgin' from what I saw standin' on the curb back there. Just a little steep for a guy workin' double shifts, tryin' to keep up with an unhappy wife and a litter of spoiled brats. I do thank you though. You know, twenty years ago, give or take, she was about as pretty as you. Seems a real long time ago. Sorry to say that these days she's kinda easy to leave at home. Real sorry."

"Yeah, me too."

"I'm curious though, given the generous offer. Where's all the boyfriends for someone as pretty as you. You don't talk or act like a hooker thinkin' to put out in the back of a cab. I've seen my fair share. You are definitely several notches above."

"He's gone. He left me with a gift I don't need or want. And I'm not a hooker. I'm a little pregnant and a little out of options, hoping to use what got me into a mess out of a mess. Seems logical, don't you think?" She paused a moment, musing. She wasn't at all embarrassed. "Guess I flagged the wrong cab."

"I truly wish I could help. But the wife…well, truth is I'm servin' a life sentence." He sighed. "Like I said, if only."

Too bad, she thought. The guy was groomed and clean, younger than Stonewall. They might have enjoyed each other. "How many times have I said that?"

"I suppose. Here's the thing though, miss, if you're goin' through with this. Decent hotel lounges are way out of bounds. They'll get you arrested. Understand that. Off duty cops workin' security won't share your sense of urgency and their guests won't likely want to be seen doin' business with a pretty young girl. And the not-so-good ones…well, just stay away from them. Do not go where you do not belong."

"Any suggestions?"

"I shouldn't be sayin' so considerin' all the daughters I have hanging from my purse strings. Even so, I do know a place or two. Popular with business types where real hookers don't fit in. Escorts maybe, from time to time. High end gals well-connected. Same goes for rooms once you're connected. If it don't look respectable, it's not. Do not go in."

"That's what I want, respectable. Thank you."

"I suppose I'm doin' some good." He chuckled. "Won't be easy though, goin' home to the wife." He pulled to the curb shortly after, twisting in his seat. "No. You go ahead and keep the money, miss. The meter's been off since we started talkin'. My contribution. One last thing though. Inside, order a real drink. A tall one and take things slow. Don't make yourself a target, take control. Those other girls, they drink sodas. Set yourself apart. There ain't a guy inside who, once seein' you, won't start dreamin' of a much improved evenin'."

"Thank you." Her smile was genuine and warm. "Sorry about the wife."

He pursed his lips, nodding. "I'm truly sorry I ain't ten years younger. Good luck, miss."

She slid out, stepping onto the curb, waving at him through the window. Striding into the lounge as confidently as she could manage, most heads turned on cue. A reaction she expected, was accustomed to.

The ambiance was subdued with low lighting and soft music, a refuge from blaring jazz and Bourbon Street's pre-teen entrepreneurs. Ties and jackets preferred.

She stood deciding between a bistro table and the male-dominated bar where every second stool was empty. Which wasn't good, neither an invitation nor a snare. They simply wanted their personal space and she would come off as a hooker. They were all dressed in suits, hunched over on folded arms or slouched against their seatbacks with their thumbs tucked into their belts. A table was positively the better choice. Getting to Mister Right, let alone choosing him, was an impossible feat. She couldn't, no way. And the chance of any guy invading that personal space to test his luck with her was worse than slim. Better that one of them should choose her.

Most tables were occupied by trendy couples holding hands, or staid couples not holding hands who should have opted for the borrowed spontaneity of others on Bourbon Street. A couple more were commandeered by lone businessmen needing more solitude than the bar would provide.

Seated, she would have died for a double Silent Sam with a splash of soda. Instead she ordered a single measure diluted with sparkling water, in the meantime feeling conspicuous sitting with her hands empty. She was being stared at by everyone around her, assessed by single men, talked about by couples: A beautiful woman dressed to kill sitting alone. Of course they were leering and talking about her. Someone, she hoped, wondering for how long.

Twenty minutes later, her tasteless cocktail down by half, the waiter stopped at her table.

"Miss, the gentleman to your left in the dark grey suit very much wishes to meet you, unless you're expecting company this evening."

She glanced sideways, doing her own assessment: Twenty-something touching thirty. Clean-shaven, very good-looking and stylishly attired. Thick blond hair, no tan and no ring. He wasn't a local. God, yes!

She smiled at him, turning to the waiter. "Please tell the gentleman I would be delighted to share his company."

The waiter returned moments later carrying the man's old-fashioned.

"Thank you. I was holding my breath, hoping you wouldn't think of me as some sort of predator. I find sitting alone excruciatingly monotonous. An all too frequent event, I'm afraid, and not much better than a hotel room. My name's Anthony."

She extended a hand. "I'm Adrianna, Anthony. Good evening, and thank you for coming to *my* rescue. It's difficult for a girl not to feel a little conspicuous sitting alone." She waved a hand across the table. "Tell me, do I detect a Northern flair?"

"You do. Boston. And you, Adrianna?"

He sat and for half an hour they spoke seamlessly. She

arrived in South Carolina from France when she was seventeen with her parents who later died in a tragic car accident. When he commented on her flawless English she explained Charleston and her four years at the university there, and how from an early age her parents would speak to her in English and often vacation in the English countryside.

She recently arrived in town from Charleston, transferred by her ad agency where she worked as the firm's regional copy editor. Although with female envy and deflated male egos interfering with making friends, she decided strangers might be better company than no company at all.

"Thank you for making my evening incredibly enjoyable, Anthony."

"The truth is I'm incredibly pleased with myself, that I didn't give way to cowardice in the face of such stunning beauty." He signalled the waiter. "May I order you another, Adrianna? And then, may I invite you to a late dinner?"

Her eyes sparkled. "Yes, you may. A Silent Sam with a splash of soda would be wonderful."

Thirty more minutes were consumed in conversation. He was often in New Orleans on business from Boston. He had a wife who was punishing him for being successful by suing for divorce; he didn't have kids, didn't want any, and was in no particular hurry to return home to a house that would very soon be his in mortgage payments alone. Nor was he in a hurry to date, not until his current scars were no longer visible.

He helped her from her seat and went to the bar, settling the tab before joining her at the entrance. Stepping onto the sidewalk, she didn't hesitate. She couldn't. She had no time and too much to lose.

"Anthony, I am looking forward to dinner with you.

Though first I must know. Do you want or expect to sleep with me later this evening, sleep being a euphemism, in exchange for your very charming company? Is that why you invited me? Is this all a quaint ruse to get me in bed? Please tell me the truth."

"Naturally the thought crossed my mind, is crossing my mind. What normal guy would not want you? You are seriously drop-dead gorgeous, Adrianna. And more, a lot more. I do want you in bed. Of course I do, unless that fervent wish cancels out our dinner."

"It does not, I simply needed to know. In fact, I promise you will never get a better lay again in your entire life." She took his arm. "Being new in town, the job, that is all true. But for good reasons I will not explain, getting me into your bed, as much as I want to because I do feel a real attraction, will cost you an even 300 dollars in advance. Not negotiable, Anthony." She was resolute. "Let's just say it's a matter of personal well-being. That said, if you're rethinking taking me to dinner, if we are not passing by an ATM, tell me and we'll part company with no hard feelings."

"So…what? You were inside waiting for me, for someone with three bills in their pockets?"

"For someone, yes. Though not just anyone. I am not a hooker, Anthony. I am not a whore, or an escort, if that's what you're thinking. Understand that. I'm an honours graduate with a good job. It's a situation, a bad one. It's why I left Charleston, pure and simple."

"I believe you, Adrianna. I do. We all have stories to tell, some worse than others. "He chortled, throwing back his head, pressing a hand over hers. "We'll do dinner first, then an ATM. Three hundred's a really good deal compared to what my wife's getting for screwing me over. Especially if I'm helping you out of a personal crisis serious enough to bring us together this way. Besides, she's probably getting laid tonight in my bed anyway. Which pretty much gives me a green light. Fair is fair, right?"

"Spite doesn't pay dividends, Anthony." She smirked. "Most times."

He held her at arm's length, admiring her. "I beg to differ. Believe me or not, this is a first for me, which I am seriously regretting did not happen many months ago. That's the truth."

"I could say the same, Anthony. Really I could, however you probably wouldn't believe me and I wouldn't blame you. The truth is, we both have something the other one needs...or wants. Or I suppose both at the moment. I'm just glad you're the other one. If I had met you months ago, or someone like you in Charleston, I wouldn't be in this situation. I wouldn't be doing this with you, certainly not for the money. I think we might have become good friends."

"Who says we won't, particularly if that means you're staying with me for breakfast?"

She needed to say no, her imploring eyes telling Anthony otherwise. "I can't. For one thing, I don't have a change of clothes. I wasn't expecting to stay the night with you because I'm not particularly clear on the protocol for this sort of thing."

"Neither am I, though I do know good friends do not abandon each other in times of need." His smile was warm. "An in-room breakfast then."

"Can we walk, Anthony? I'm starving." They did, arm in arm, the length of an entire block, giving each other space, neither one pressing. "Okay, maybe an in-room breakfast. I'm good with that. Then I'm gone, and gone early. Please understand."

"Adrianna, I'm thinking more like, I don't know,

changing my flight to Saturday and dinner again tomorrow. You know, thinking out loud."

Yes! She drew in a deep breath. "That is impossible. Not unless you've got enough in the bank for two nights with me, Anthony. As good as I'm feeling with you, and I am, I'm in serious damage control mode. It's not the money per se, more like really bad timing. I'm out of options."

"This situation, which I'm assuming is a Charleston boyfriend thing, is what? An abortion? A legal one, I hope."

"Yes, a legal one, with not many days left."

"We're talking what, exactly?"

"Less than a week and six hundred, with what I already have."

"Is that all?" his grin and the glint in his eyes asking what was her problem.

She jerked free of his arm, her liquid eyes crystalizing into a frozen glare. "Excuse me?"

He grimaced, reaching for her hands. "I didn't mean to sound glib. What I meant was, I'm good with six, including breakfast on Saturday. The hotel has a laundry service and I'll even throw in some new undies. I want to spend time with you. I want to know you." He regained his smile. "Thinking of you with some other guy tomorrow doesn't work for me. I think we can do better."

"Anthony, really? You're serious?"

"I am very serious…if I can keep a pair of those undies to throw at my wife."

"Deal!" She kissed his cheek, hugging him, breaking a hooker's time-honoured code. "Keep them all. Smother the cheating bitch…and I *will* need that money this evening. Sorry, again."

True to his word they stopped in to a boutique where he bought her panties and a teddy for each evening. Not much else would be needed by her or wanted by him. Dinner was light and fast at a courtyard café-terrasse corner table, Anthony desperately wanting Adrianna in his hotel suite more than Murielle wanted her money. Whatever else they needed or wanted to learn about each other would come on Friday.

Very soon after, the monetary portion of their evening concluded, Murielle could not believe her good fortune. She not only completed her funding, the Bourbon Orleans was pure luxury.

14

In his bedroom she laid out her lingerie in the armoire, wondering whether the cabbie was thinking of her. She kicked off her shoes, pushing her skirt to the floor, methodically unbuttoning her blouse and shrugging the silk from her shoulders.

She posed in front of the mirror from all angles. She was flawless, disarming even to herself in her green camisole, matching flounced panties, matching garters and nylons. She was ready. In for a dollar, or six hundred, in for a pound. Except for Stonewall she had never before played the demure seductress. She didn't care anymore. What she did care about was her deepening hate for him, about keeping alive her promise to him. That she had wasted an entire year of her life being a whore for someone her father's age made her nauseous.

She sauntered through the doorway into the sitting room with scarcely a blush, pirouetting for the man who did appreciate her, who did want her.

"This is a bit more of me, Anthony. No refunds. I hope you like."

His wife in five years of marriage had never worn garters, never a teddy or anything sheer. What wasn't to like. "Whew! Adrianna. Really. I mean, wow." He put aside his Johnnie Walker Black, savouring every inch of her instead.

She beamed. "I thought at least you deserved seeing what you didn't all evening, before I freshen up and change."

"Well you thought right." He stood, twirling her, stopping at full circle, guiding her to the sofa where she snuggled against him in a single fluid movement. "You are exquisite." He passed her a double vodka from the minibar chilled with two crackling cubes, pausing. "I suppose a few cocktails won't matter now. Sorry, no soda."

"Not anymore. Because of you, Anthony. Thank you."

He put a hand on her thigh, teasing the silk ribbons, squeezing gently, bringing his hand to her cheek. "I need to kiss you, Adrianna."

She sipped her vodka. "Then kiss me. It's not like we're pros at this."

He did, amazed by the softness, the texture and taste of her mahogany lips, the silkiness of her palm pressing against his cheek.

Stonewall was right, she mused: Him, the pizza kid, Todd, the jocks and professors; she got off on them all, in the moment, their adoration and their hunger. Now she was getting off on Anthony. She wasn't acting, not simply earning her money. She was completely into him, not the least hint of misguided spitefulness festering in her mind; neither was Stonewall's misconception that she was a whore.

Anthony was not paying for her body. They were each other's true lovers in the moment. Nothing else mattered. That she might be convenient to his requisite spitefulness towards his wife was not for her to worry over. He was helping her; they were helping each other. Win-win. Perhaps the love she truly wanted would come later. Or not. What mattered at the moment was not disappointing him.

They pulled apart.

"That was fantastic. I cannot believe this is happening, that this is not a dream or that I'm really here with you."

"Actually, it's more like I'm here with you." She passed her glass to him. "On that note, sir, I need a few moments. No peeking."

She pushed against him, prancing her way into the bedroom. She didn't have to glance over her shoulder see that he was taking her in. Of course he was.

Alone in the bathroom she undressed and showered, luxuriating in a cloud of steam, half expecting or hoping he would come in at any moment. That he didn't was his loss.

In the bedroom she put her lingerie, her skirt and blouse into the laundry bag, selecting the deep yellow décolleté and very backless teddy Anthony refused to leave in the boutique. The thing was made for her, he insisted. And he was right, the woman blowing her a gleeful kiss from inside the mirror was spectacular.

In the sitting room she twirled her way toward the sofa, toward Anthony who was already standing.

"That is seriously dangerous."

"I know. I couldn't help admiring myself in the mirror. You really shouldn't have, Anthony. But yeah, wow."

"Where were you five years ago, Adrianna?" He took her hands, truly captivated. "I am really feeling cheated."

"I was in high school." She giggled. "Where were you five months ago," she patted her stomach, "before this? That's a better question."

"I was in Hell with a demon, dreaming of you."

Her smile evaporated. "I thought he was a nice guy, Anthony, a good man. Until this happened, when I discovered the bastard's married with enough influence to ruin my career. That's why I was doing this...*was* doing this. Now being here with you doesn't feel wrong at all. Thank you for helping me."

He snorted, smirking. "Then I should thank the bastard and the demon. I could have flown out this afternoon. I had no particular reason to stay through tomorrow. Not until meeting you."

"I do not want to think about that." She kissed him. "What I am thinking about is us, in bed, after your shower. Or, you know, we could stand here talking all night."

He kissed her. He loved her voice, the sparkle in her brown eyes whenever she laughed. That anyone would even think to hurt such an adorable woman was inconceivable. Then to desert her was even more hideous.

When he was gone Murielle topped off their drinks. When she heard the water running she went into the bedroom. She put the drinks on their tables, threw back the duvet, stripped away her teddy and lay on the bed thinking she could actually like the guy, that he definitely liked her. She was certain he did.

When the water stopped she propped herself onto her elbows, waiting serenely. When he came through the doorway wrapped in a towel she could not have been more thrilled by her choice. He was everything she expected, had hoped for. He wouldn't be bending her over a desk, pushing up her skirt to do her through his zipper; he wouldn't be ripping and tearing at his clothes like a frenzied pizza boy tripping over his boxers; and he would not run out on her in the morning. He would not. He wanted her, as a lover. No way was she purely a return on his investment. The man was in dire need of her.

She believed he was actually nervous, that he had never cheated on his demon wife. That he was truly in need of the love she could give him through to Saturday morning in a bed far more comfortable than her own.

"Is that demon living in your house blind, Anthony? Or possibly a lesbian?"

"No. Pretty much your basic spoiled bitch who married a guy not as rich as her daddy."

"Her loss is my gain." She pushed herself onto her knees. "This is the rest of me." She pointed to the towel. "And you? Didn't you say something earlier about fair is fair?"

The towel opened and fell away, Anthony closing the space between them, Murielle crawling to the edge of the bed. A moment later they were laying together in a tender embrace as though they had been lovers for those many past months. She was in another world, a distant and glorious world. An hour later they were slick with each other's sweat. His heart was pounding, his pulse racing; Murielle's face plastered with her long matted hair, her breasts and belly heaving. She collapsed over him, framing his legs with hers.

"Anthony I know what this is, this thing we're doing. Still, no way was that all business." She breathed deeply. "Not for me anyway. Am I wrong?"

"Nope. That was sensational. You're sensational. I've had hundreds of meetings, never one like this. Forget the money. It's not about the money. It's about needing and wanting." He pressed his palms against her damp flesh from her shoulders to her buttocks, kneading the firm mounds. "But if this is your way of thanking me for the little I did, is there something more I can do for you?"

She squirmed slightly backward, straddling his knees. "I believe that is a yes. So let's work on that, shall we?"

They did, until he had done all that he could and she had exhausted her gratitude, waking late and ordering in room service. When he left her in the hallway in her panties and hotel robe he went first with her ensemble to the concierge who assured him the items would be delivered to his room early that afternoon. When he returned later in the day, pretty certain she would be there, she was dressed, his JW Black was waiting for him, and she was ready for dinner.

He took her for the finest filet mignon in Louisiana, then to Royal Street through art galleries, strolling hand in hand, and to a voodoo shop she wasn't much impressed with. They discovered a romantic hideaway, talking endlessly through to a late-evening cocktail. Not once was either one lost or searching for words.

Later in his suite privacy was a non-issue. She stripped for him, first losing her blouse, which she neatly folded. She unhooked her belt, dropping it to the floor; she unzipped her skirt, walking in place, shimmying it past her knees to her ankles and stepping free; she inched her camisole to her breasts, past them, pausing teasingly, her eyes piercing his, seeing in them what was very obvious to her through dinner, throughout their entire evening.

The flimsy silk sailed into the air, Murielle bending deliberately from her waist to retrieve and fold both pieces by her blouse. She was completely absorbed, Anthony utterly spellbound.

She went to him, planting a patent leather stiletto on his knee, tapping the silk-covered clasp on her garter and waiting. He caressed her calf and her thigh, lingering over the bare flesh, mesmerized, inching his hand between her legs, pressing gently into her moist heat, evoking an exotic and guttural groan that was real. He was lost in a dream as though he had died and gone to Heaven, lamenting that his wife hadn't died and gone to Hell.

He knew what Adrianna wanted, what he should do. Instead he guided her foot to the floor, running his hands lightly from her knees to the panties he bought her that were by no means practical, sliding his hands behind her and under the silk, pulling her closer, pressing his cheek and his hands into her bare flesh. Murielle's hands clasped his head.

She was moaning, the throaty sound at once sensual and sad. Almost, he thought, as though she was crying deep inside, realizing he was inflicting his own needless torture as well. He needed her naked, sliding his hands between her hips and her panties, hooking his thumbs under the band, in one fluid motion guiding them to her ankles.

He pressed his forehead into her belly, fixated, inhaling deeply. "Adrianna, stay the way you are. Really, if I die in this bed, not a big issue."

"Not for you maybe." She raised his head, kicking aside her panties, once again planting a foot on his knee. "But the shoes and stockings have to go. Unless you want to wear them."

She didn't think so.

They devoured each other repeatedly until early Saturday morning, each one depleted. Each one as battered and bruised as the other. Murielle was first surrendering to unwanted sleep. Anthony needed more time with her, propped against the headboard sipping a JW Black well past his usual hour, pondering what Adrianna would do, where she would go once he left for the airport. Who was she really, the Adrianna he hadn't yet come to know in such a short time? He needed to understand her, he needed to understand himself.

He loved her smile and her eyes, her throaty voice and soft lips, her glistening straight hair, her smooth and flawless body. She was sexy and sensual, smart and funny. He loved the way she laughed, her accent. That she even could laugh or wanted to when faced with such a terrible few days alone amazed him. She was amazing, resilient, what with her parents dead and gone and the SOB who got her pregnant deserting her.

He swallowed what was left in his glass, flicking the light switch and sliding in beside her. He kissed her cheek,

spooning her body and cupping her perfect breasts, not many seconds later drifting into his own dreams.
*

Murielle woke first. She eased from his arm and the bed, padding to the bathroom to shower and assess her damage. She reeked, her reddened and swollen labia screaming out for attention. They would have to wait. She showered and towelled herself quickly, not wanting to wake him. She needed alone time. She dressed in the sitting room, into the second silk pair he'd bought her, her camisole and skirt, leaving her legs bare.

What she was contemplating was not insanely ridiculous, not borne of a fanciful epiphany, the possibility becoming more real with each palpable heartbeat since dinner.

She made a neat pile of the underwear she had worn, her yellow teddy and the green one that would have detracted from the previous evening, fitting everything into her handbag. She had no intention of walking through the frigging lobby carrying a five-cent plastic laundry bag.

Life was shit. Her life was shit. Totally. He was a nice guy married to a total bitch. He didn't care that she was pregnant, that she was aborting, almost as though…Shit. With her troubles gone, in part due to him, working at Gilmore would not allow much time for romance, let alone finding someone to share romance with, and dating in-house was absolute bullshit. Like putting out for college jocks when professors absolutely served a higher purpose. Really, what was the point?

So what if he lived in Boston? What they shared was real. He was divorcing, not interested in dating, and together they were special.

"You're muttering, Adrianna. What's up?" He was wrapped in a towel and smiling, his shoulder pressed against the doorway. "Going somewhere?"

"No I'm not going somewhere. You're buying me breakfast, just not here. I don't want to stand here watching you leave and I don't want you to watch me leaving. We should leave together, not me feeling like a …"

He cut her off. "A phenomenal lover, an incredible companion?"

"Yeah, that. Like an incredible girlfriend, like I'm going home to Boston and not an empty condo where I'm going to die of total boredom after all this."

"My flight isn't till noon. We own the entire morning."

She scrunched her face. "Four hours. Then how do we say goodbye? When do we say goodbye? Do we shake hands or what? I wasn't expecting to feel this way."

"Four wonderful hours. I'm thinking breakfast at the airport, perhaps an early cocktail. Like you're seeing me off, like I'm coming back in very early December. In fact I'll fly in on the first, with enough time until then to discover whether we were simply licking our wounds the last two days, or that this is some sort of surreal destiny. You'll have the procedure and fully recover. I'll finally be rid of the demon and if the creep who did this to you comes crawling back that's fine too. At worst, we'll be good friends with something pretty unique to remember. If that's what you want. Sound good?"

"Seriously?" He nodded. "Yes, I do like that."

When Anthony was showered he dressed in casual slacks, a crisp shirt, a blazer and loafers. At the workstation he wrote his personal number on his business card.

"You call me whenever, Adrianna. Let me know when all this will happen. This has to be on you. You have too much going on for me to take the lead. Your timeframe. No rush. No worry."

"I will call, Anthony. I will. And December does sound

good. Really good." A glimmer of a smile brightened her eyes. "Then Christmas in Boston maybe."

His seamless "I'll book a chalet this week," surprised her. "Ever eat snow?"

"No. Why would I?"

He didn't really know. "Okay. Ever build a snowman?"

She shook her head, taking the card. Charles Anthony Vincent. She knew what was coming, the one thing she purposely kept from him. She hadn't anticipated staying with him the first night. Or with anyone. She figured three-hundred, giving whoever, giving herself the best possible bang for his buck and getting out. Or the second night. Or the incredibly heated passion they shared. What whore ever stayed over for breakfast? What guy ever cared about a whore's name or bought them sexy lingerie? What was the big deal about a name? That part of her she would keep to herself.

"Adrianna, after all our time and excitement together, I still don't know your last name."

"Dupree," the told him easily. "I'm Murielle Adrianna Dupree. No one calls me Adrianna."

He didn't laugh or smile or furrow his brow with disbelief at hearing the deception. "A beautiful name for a beautiful lady. And very French sounding."

"I am French, Anthony. I told you I was born in France. I wasn't going to tell you my real name, not at first. Not until I was sure, which I was last night. Then we got busy."

He went to her and kissed her. "No explanation is needed or wanted, Murielle. Your real name, given the circumstances, might well have led to future complications. Smart thinking on your part. Nevertheless, like I said, you take the lead on this."

"So...December?"

"Yes, December. Nine days. Then Christmas," he

pinched her cheek, "Mademoiselle Dupree."
*

Sex would have been a tease, hurried, somehow seeming lewdly desperate after countless tender caresses and soft whispers. At the airport Murielle and Anthony relaxed over a breakfast, before meandering through the concourse until 11:00 when a glass of wine didn't seem at all decadent.

She would call the clinic that afternoon for an appointment on Monday, she promised, reluctantly accepting money for cab fare that would get her home safely. He insisted, and she would call him Monday evening. Tuesday at the very latest. Yes, she would.

At 11:56 they kissed ardently at the gate. Last-minute boarding wasn't a big issue in First-Class.

He didn't wish her good luck, explaining that New Orleanais were superstitious, spooked by ghosts and voodoo. Conversely, patting his cheek, Murielle did wish him luck with the demon.

15

Jackson and Melinda Belmont returned to the lawyer's Mississippi office on February 07th with the remaining five K in cash. Week-old Jackson Junior was ready for pick-up at the foster home along with his birth certificate and a heartrending letter from Keller, handwritten by the lawyer's secretary an hour earlier and stained appropriately with teardrops from the water fountain. He wrote how he and little Jackson's mother, now an angel in Heaven, would always love and want the best for their boy.

Within the hour the chic couple were parents, returning home along the I-10 in Jackson's Mercedes C-Class; Melinda's Vantage roadster simply would not do. The other thing that would not do was bullshit. As genteel and stylish as Jackson Belmont was, he was also a man down-to-earth. Lowering the sedan's window he deposited the letter into the air.

"Jackson, what…?"

"Pure fabrication, sweet thing. A critical difference that separates us from hillbillies is the ability that allows us to detect bullshit before we step into it, moments ago avoiding a substantial mound of the stuff. Junior has no sisters and if there is a mother in someone's heaven she is entirely unrelated. Whatever his origin, the brilliance in his eyes speaks of his bright future. I truly believe we have spared Junior from a pointless life, a continuum of meaningless days."

The home was a stately carriage house sitting on a half-acre of manicured lawn in a gated and guarded New Orleans community. Little Jackson Junior would have a nanny and eventually private schooling. He would have an in-ground pool where his Latina nanny in her string bikini would teach him to swim while father observed closely and proudly, and a tennis court where father would ensure Junior was passably good at tennis. He would learn etiquette by osmosis at home, Spanish for his future Latino clientele and ballroom dancing with qualified instructors for his proper melding into New Orleans society far removed from the stench of livestock, coveralls and pitchforks.

He would learn to ride his own horse and at sixteen would drive his very own Mercedes. He would attend Tulane like father, learn good business practices and one day take over the family-chain that was expanding yearly.

He would as well learn the importance of rank, of forming lasting friendships that would benefit him through life. He would also learn that, once graduating into a more common world, tainting that tightly knit circle with a lesser pedigree would endanger those relationships most fundamentally important to him.

By the twelfth grade he was fully bilingual, better than father at tennis and was driving a BMW convertible. Four years later, at age twenty-one, he graduated Tulane with a degree in Commerce, had long forgotten his Mexican nanny who had contributed in no small way to his fluency, and was brought in the next day without fanfare as Belmont Tailors' newest junior sales associate.

He knew profit and loss, fine dining, fine wines and fashion. He did not know he was a week older than he believed, or that his real parents who never thought of him were a renowned marine biologist and a high-priced attorney on the East Coast. Nor would he ever know or care that the Kellers were found dead and mangled in a Mississippi swamp several days after their shack blew apart years earlier during a hurricane old Wilbur did not believe was coming.

Jackson Junior existed in an idyllic world. He lived a gilded life, was an independent member at the golf and men's clubs, no longer tied to father, striving on his own to create and nurture those friendships he deemed worthwhile and worthy of the future he envisioned for himself. He was on track, yet a year later his world and his life imploded with the sudden death of Belmont Senior.

One day after the funeral Jackson Junior became CEO of Belmont Tailors, a grief-stricken Melinda assuming the dual role of comforting mother and adept business consultant. By twenty-five he owned a downtown penthouse. His friendships were solidified, many of them tested, and he was learning the hard way that besides healing all wounds time quickly erases memories, most of his father's friends gradually distancing themselves from his mother. Apparently a widow unwilling to remarry or find a suitable companion was a burden, difficult explain, more difficult to seat at functions better suited to couples.

Two years later Melinda was no longer involved and the business was flourishing as Jackson Senior would have hoped, albeit for a very different reason: Women. His son broke with a long-standing tradition. Belmont Tailors was hiring young and pretty female sales associates with a flair for men's fashion. The innovation was an immediate sensation with clientele and male associates alike. Business soared, bringing in an ever-increasing younger clientele.

Despite which he had no girlfriends to complicate his life, preferring instead to vacation each quarter, availing himself of cheating or rebounding girlfriends and wives.

Good times had by all, never once tainted by out-of-the-blue moody tantrums or sudden poutiness brought on by the unstable female condition. Life was good.

Close friendships were one thing, a business thing, which he would not extend to dating or marrying their sisters or daughters. Nor did loving his father imply that he wanted to become one simply to prove he didn't shoot blanks or to give her, any her, a valid purpose in life.

He did not want or need a supercilious stay-at-home débutante-cum-mom for a wife he had probably known since the first grade, both of them forever trapped on a mundane merry-go-round existence of dinner parties and backyard barbeques by the pool. He wanted spectacular and independent. He wanted an outsider.

Finding women was not the issue, getting to them even easier. He was infused with Southern charm. He was genteel, easy to approach and be with. He was educated and eloquent, successful and wealthy. Yet he was never pretentious, never full of himself, often working the floor at his Belmont flagship location to stay level and current.

Weekends were invariably consumed with work, most Sundays enjoying dinner with Melinda who had moved away from the gated compound to a friendlier milieu. Most Saturday evenings he would spend perusing travel brochures for his next ten-day break from demanding twelve-hour days, seldom dining out, never good with sitting alone in restaurants. Business travel was different, anonymous. However that Saturday he had worked later than usual. The evening was agreeably warm, inviting after being confined to his office the entire day. He was tired and not particularly hungry, which made the thought of cooking seem very much like an unnecessary and avoidable chore.

He had been to Angelo's lounge countless times over the years, invited by suppliers for a couple of hits before dinner in the dining room and occasionally joining his sales associates for Happy Hour hors d'oeuvres, customarily and good-naturedly stuck with the tab before leaving them to innocent flirtations. He was well-known and recognizable to the staff, though never seen on a weekend.

Inside the lounge was quiet, not New Orleans boisterous, a safe haven from the impossible-to-appreciate clamour of jazz.

Studying those around him was instinctive, as inherent to him as breathing, essential to his trade. Most men defined other men as they themselves were defined: They didn't bother, they didn't care, if they could even find the words. Whereas gentlemen, particularly Southern gentlemen, were held to a higher accountability, taught from their privileged births to preserve their elite caste from extinction amidst the undiscerning and dishevelled hordes. Two divergent worlds: The Envied and the Envious.

Not that he was aristocratic in his judgement of others, he was not. He merely abhorred men and women who saw no need to respect themselves within their means, to define themselves in the best possible light. Such as the men lining the bar when several tables were not yet taken. Simply because they could not. Tables were not their domain. They understood their place, their limitation. They were ordinary. They were lacklustre clones in appallingly lazy denim and khakis worn straight from the dryer or suitcase. Divorced or outsiders stuck in town for the weekend. Or both, with nothing worthwhile to say to each other, sitting inches from a stranger's personal device on a Saturday night nursing expensive beer because the expensive beer was cheaper than the expensive booze. Each one predestined to leave the bar alone without the remotest possibility of something equally desperate and biologically suitable joining them. Someone they could maybe drink pretty by closing, a species that would never see the inside of Angelo's.

Conversely, men sitting in the ambiance of linen-covered tables and the flickering glow of candles were attired in button-down shirts and jackets accented with silk pocket hankies, neatly pressed slacks and polished shoes. Others he observed were dressed in suits and ties, defining themselves for others, discreetly declaring pride in who they were and respect for the ladies seated with them.

The ladies, each one delightful, each one lightyears beyond the paygrades of the Khaki Fraternity, each one dressed in trendy silk dresses or short skirts and billowy silk blouses, were deservedly and demurely commanding due respect and certainly more appreciative glances from their peers seated at surrounding tables. Couples holding hands, leaning in to each other, exchanging furtive whispers for their ears alone, relishing the culmination of a perfect evening; Jackson fully aware that he, too, was being critically judged.

The guy working the bar waved to him with a broad smile. Charlee, a cute twenty-something bargirl greeted him by name as she pranced by balancing a full tray in low-heeled pumps, flared dress shorts and a cashmere sweater. The surprise in her voice was real. She was happy to see him, beaming, telling him to sit at whichever table.

She wouldn't for a second expect Junior Belmont to mingle with the rabble. He didn't belong at the bar, not dressed in a Belmont suit for which his clients like her father would willingly part with two or three grand. Not to mention the indispensable accoutrements and the man's blue-gold Rolex. They wouldn't want him there. Not even his staff sat at the bar; so why would he, particularly since the arrival of the female contingent that she had once been invited to join?

Of course he would take a table, one that for the time

being would intrude as little as possible on her other patrons, for his solitude as much as theirs. Tables were private spaces, others welcome by invitation only, from which one was not expected to snap one's fingers while holding a depleted tumbler or goblet in the air as an expression of need. That was Junior Belmont: Considerate, kind, and sort of very hot.

He nodded, following her, thinking someone somewhere was very and truly blessed. She was bouncy and petite, completely adorable. Not imagining was impossible, not thinking 'what if' would be unnatural to any male of the species. So he did both: She was a divinely naked cherub in someone else's Heaven, who would likely break his heart. Perhaps his vacations weren't such brilliantly planned escapes into freedom after all. Perhaps what he wanted, what he was missing, was right before his very eyes. Or not.

Once he was seated he felt conspicuous, fairly certain the periphery of lovers encircling him were expecting him at any moment to sit gazing into the glare of a phone or some other device destructive to their dreamy moods. Until he forgot them when Charlee set down his Johnnie Walker Blue enriched with a strict splash of soda on a coaster within easy reach.

He asked about her second year in med school, a little-known fact he had discovered when offering her the position at Belmont weeks earlier. Discovering as well that his esteemed client, Doctor Bernard Boyette, was her father. She wasn't a spoiled brat living off a wealthy daddy who happened to be a surgeon. She was level, working hard for what she wanted most.

She asked whether he was expecting a guest, or decompressing solo. He was decompressing, he told her, winking. All the pretty girls were either taken or busy serving drinks to the lonely and unwanted like him. She commiserated as best she could, frowning. She understood his very deep sorrow. She did, patting his shoulder, consoling him; the sparkle in her eyes somehow not terribly convincing. He shooed her away. How could he possibly attract a woman, he grumbled, swirling his drink, with her hovering over him? "Go!" he told her, raising an open palm, thinking to smack her tush, rethinking maybe not.

With that threat she left to fill her tray, promising not to leave him feeling stranded.

His limit was two, in public alone. Anymore would transmute him in their eyes and Charlee's from privileged to pitiable.

His watch read: 9:05, his thoughts leisurely drifting from business to vacations to his mother, often returning to Charlee who did stop at his table from time to time, checking on him without being intrusive, bringing him a refill thirty minutes past the hour. Not being envious of other men in the lounge, or Charlee's special someone was impossible when remembering what his parents once shared.

Still, he did realize he wasn't ready for a relationship that would detract from Belmont. Whenever he might be, with whomever she might be, she would commit to marrying the name as well as the man. He could imagine himself married to a cute doctor, since college boyfriends seldom lasted. The timing was simply wrong.

He had no reason to check his watch. The empty snifter was telling him to leave, to make room for more deserving couples or more desperate singles. He would pour another at home, very possibly a double. Anyway she was coming toward him, Charlee understanding his pleasant shrug and scrunched expression. She brought him the chit moments later when he gave her a crisp hundred and stood, not expecting change.

He wished her good-luck with her upcoming mid-year. She hoped to see him again soon, he was good people. Then he stopped listening, completely distracted. The woman came through the doors alone, slowing her pace to a full stop. She wasn't glancing over her shoulder at someone, or scanning the lounge searching for someone. Certainly no one among the bar clones who were staring her down, stripping her naked. She was looking for space, her private space. She was poised and confident, to-die-for beautiful and impeccably dressed, openly comfortable with the collective approval rating coming from the tables.

For the slightest instant the woman's eyes crossed his line of vision, though he might have been invisible.

Charlee squeezed his arm. "Sure you want to leave right now, Junior? Personally? I don't think I would."

"Do you know her, Charlee?"

"Nope. First time. And yeah, sort of gorgeous. You know, in a really gorgeous sort of way." She put the chit and the hundred in her apron. "You sure, Junior? I can bring you a soda on the house. You know, if you want to sit a while longer. Because you're sort of not blinking." She reached for the empty snifter. "Would be nice to see you in here with a girl sometime." She patted his chest. "I promise I won't be jealous."

"Gee, I think I'm hurt. I was hoping you would be, Charlee." He put an arm around her, hugging her. "But yes, she is gorgeous in a really gorgeous kind of way."

"Yeah, she is. She can also see us talking about her. So what's the plan here, another lonely and blue Saturday...or another expensive Blue and whatever?"

"I think another Blue fits the occasion, strictly as part of a covert mission to assess and strategize. And while we're discussing my evening, this 'whatever' thing is fully on you, Charlee. I mean it. If this thing doesn't go well, if I get beat up. I am definitely dating you. I'm starting to believe my life actually does suck. So wish me luck."

She didn't. She didn't have to. Guys like Junior didn't need luck. He was every girl's dream.

16

Saturday afternoon in her flat Murielle called the clinic. They had an opening Monday that would allow her a full week to recover before her first day at Gilmore and the entire month of November to make herself ready for Anthony.

Yes, she told the doctor. She was committed with not the least sense of guilt or remorse. She was doing what was right, what she must for her and them. She was surviving on her own. She would not ruin her life, or her career, or condemn them to certain unfortunate futures. She was doing the right thing. She was adamant.

Pressing END she sat on her bed studying the colourless walls, the drab and worn furniture, loathing the place more than she believed possible after her nights of luxury with Anthony.

Without the abortion that would be her miserable future, which would not happen. No way. She was resolute. Three more weeks and she would get out with her first paycheque. She would go back to where she belonged, to the Garden District, to a better class of people, her people far away from the Jakes of the world.

She stared at her closet, at her beautiful wardrobe: a kaleidoscope of silks and satins crammed into the tiny space. No way could she spend the weekend alone, not after Anthony, not facing a gruesome Monday alone without anyone to comfort and support her. She could not be alone. She had to get out, and she would.

She stood and went to her mirror, stripping matter-of-factly, turning sideways to critique her body through a man's eyes. Her breasts were a little fuller and rounder. Cupping them she smiled contentedly. That was a good thing. Any man would adore them. Her belly, not as flat as it very soon would be, was slightly rounder, her skin soft and smooth. Her buttocks were flawless and firm, perfectly formed. He would see her as exquisite, perfection, the natural beauty of her ancestral complexion somehow more radiant.

She was exhausted after her marathon evenings with Anthony, not trusting herself to wake before dark. Instead she tugged her way into microfibre short shorts and a sports bra, appraising herself, palming her contours. She tugged a sweater coat from the closet and went to the gym for an hour with her trainer who always gave her his utmost attention, who always ensured each muscle group was properly stretched-out and warm prior making her curse him with each grunt.

Returning home she showered and styled her hair. She slipped into a silk robe, reheated leftover red beans and rice and painted her nails while she ate.

Shortly after eight o'clock she poured a Silent Sam and did her makeup. She took her time dressing by the mirror, planning her evening in the Quarter, beginning with a deep violet three-quarter bra and panty set, each trimmed with delicate lace. She was thinking sophisticated sultry: a fine balance of dazzling good-looks and subtle Southern allure that would work best with sheer charcoal thigh-highs, a short leather skirt in rich purple and a sheer silk blouse in a paler lavender that would certainly accentuate her allure and his need.

When she was finished, her outfit almost complete, she poured another vodka. Stilettos would not do, turning sultry into slutty. No way. Neither would a clutch or coat that would spoil the total look. What she needed were leather knee boots, a leather handbag and a fleece-trimmed bomber…all in black.

Then she was done, her admiring smile growing wider in the mirror. She couldn't imagine anyone not wanting her, not filling their minds with lewd and natural fantasies.

She spent the next fifteen minutes standing, staying pristine for him, switching between the flat screen and her reflection until 9:30 when she called the cab company asking for driver 185. She wanted to thank the man, to tell him about Anthony.

As much as she did like Anthony, as much as she missed him and was eager for December and Christmas, she walked out at 9:45 thankful Jake wasn't lurking in the hall.

*

His name was Mack, he told her, opening her door while nodding his approval.

"So how's the wife, Mack?"

"Doin' her best to be human, I suppose." He chuckled. "Got a long ways to go, though." He peered into his rear-view. "Got to thank you, miss. No one's ever called for me before. Makes a man feel special."

"Had to, Mack, for what you did, for all your help. I met a guy, a really nice guy because of you. He took me to dinner last night and this evening I'm meeting him at Angelo's. He's single and I believe he really likes me. I know I like him."

"I'm assumin' he knows all the particulars, miss? Pardon me for askin'. You got to be up front with a man you're likin' more than just a bit. Angelo's ain't a place for strangers, or nasty wives for that matter. The gentleman invitin' you there means somethin' good for you."

"He knows, Mack. He does. He gave me the money I need. He's even coming with me on Monday. He understands." She leaned closer to the partition. "Because of you, Mack. Thank you."

"Nothin' to thank me for. Like I told you, if I was ten years younger." He inhaled an exaggerated breath. "Kinda wish I'd done some listenin' of my own back in the day, when ol' dad told me to run fast and run far. Didn't listen, though." He pulled to the curb. "Glad you did. Glad I was the one, miss."

"Adrianna. My name is Adrianna."

"Well, Miss Adrianna, you take care. I won't be prayin' for you." He chuckled. "Bein' that I'm livin' in Hell, can't admit to knowin' much about God. I'll be thinkin' of you though, wishin' you the very best." He opened his door and stepped out. At her door he took her hand, shaking his head. "You got better need of that, Miss Adrianna." He helped her onto the sidewalk. "I sure would like to hear news come Monday if the mood suits you."

She hugged him. "The mood does suit me, Mack. Very much." Midway between his cab and Angelo's entrance she stopped and turned. "Mack...don't think I would have cared about you not being ten years younger." She blew him a kiss. "Bye for now."
*

Inside the double doors the hatcheck girl expected Murielle's jacket, she got a polite refusal instead. To the right was the popular dining room, more brightly lit than the lounge, filled to capacity with upscale friends and lovers, the brass plate at the maître d's lectern discreetly forewarning: Reservations Required. Dress Code in Effect. The sign might also have warned: You Cannot Afford This, Murielle. Which was true.

She pushed through the darker glass doors on the left, stepping for the first time into the dimly lit lounge for a drink that she could afford.

She ignored the string of losers sitting at the bar. They had no idea, not in their best fantasies. The couples seated at intimate tables were less obvious. They were appreciative, their rapt smiles welcoming her, their muted exchanges complimenting her. Of course they were.

The guy standing with an arm around the bargirl was hard to miss. They both were. The girl was absolutely cute. More importantly, he saw her. He was fascinated with her, talking about her, which wasn't indicative of anything. What was, was that he had paid his tab. He was ready to leave and now he was sitting watching the girl sway her way to the bar with his glass on her tray. She wasn't a girlfriend, but they certainly had something going on.

Murielle ignored him, not surprised the best seating was taken. She chose a low armchair that would face her away from them, toward the doors and inhibit intrusive banalities. She wasn't interested, not unless anyone joining her that evening was single and fit her criterion. Otherwise she would nurse a glass of wine and leave early.

Shrugging the bomber from her shoulders and draping it over the arm, she was comfortable with being the main attraction, sitting as Charlee waved and came closer.

She passed Murielle the beverage list, explaining that everything was by the glass, that most ladies preferred the fifteen-dollar six-ounce, agreeing the Beau-Séjour was an excellent choice. Returning, she went first with her tray to Jackson, placing the JW Blue, telling him the girl was hot, very hot, that she didn't have a ring and that he should sort of get over there.

Then she carried the red Bordeaux to Murielle, commenting on how lovely she looked in her outfit.

"Thank you."

"Are you expecting a companion this evening?"

"Not this evening, no."

"No problem. This is a great place to sit quietly. No jerks."

"Thank you. Seems the jerks always try their luck first, while the good ones stand back and watch the public executions."

Charlee glanced past her, toward the loner in the dark blue suit sipping his cocktail. "Yeah, I know a few like that. One anyway. What a terrible waste." She tucked her tray under her arm. "Anyway, you sit and relax. I'll be around."

Murielle turned her head. "Him?"

"Yeah, him."

"He's not yours?"

"Nope. Just a likeable guy, a real sweetheart." She scanned the lounge. "My name's Charlee. Enjoy the Bordeaux."

When Charlee was gone Murielle sipped her wine and sank deeper into the leather armchair thinking about Anthony, about what he might be doing and with whom, about the demon and December. She was so eager to get what was inside her out, thoughts of Monday's invasive procedure were practically eclipsed. Of one thing she was certain: She would never again devalue her body to anything less than what she was worth. She was through making mistakes, through screwing up.

But she would never, never forgive Stonewall for what he did to her, for how he mocked her and shamed her. He was beyond sick, a vile predator enticing innocent girls who didn't know better into his sick world with luxurious living, lavish gifts and travel. No. She would think about him every day of her life.

She jerked in her seat, startled.

The guy was standing by her table, his lips pursed together in a curious grin. He was 5'10, maybe a bit more, and older, late twenties and impeccably attired. A sky blue silk hanky accented the tailored dark blue suit, the Mediterranean blue shirt a backdrop to the bright silver-blue silk tie perfectly knotted. His hazel green eyes betrayed the slightest surprise; he was a man in control, his mousy blond hair neatly tousled. He was positively gorgeous. Excellent.

"What?"

Jackson took a step backward. "Forgive me, miss. I didn't realize you were drifting into a far off world. I don't intentionally alarm young ladies. My name is Jackson Belmont. From all accounts I'm a nice guy and was hoping I might join you. Charlee over there thought you might appreciate some company."

"You must excuse me, I did not mean to sound rude."

"You didn't. However, as you can see, I stand before you with empty hands given the real possibility that Charlee is wrong. In which case she is fully cognisant of the severe penalty awaiting her for leading me into a terribly embarrassing situation."

"The severe penalty being what, exactly?"

"Dating me."

"Well that's a heavy burden I wasn't expecting this evening. How could I ever let that happen to the poor thing?" She waved an open palm toward the seat facing her. "Please do join me, and thank you. I would enjoy a gentleman's company, especially one who's been pre-approved."

He nonchalantly turned to Charlee, tilting his head. A moment later she was at their table with his drink.

"Now you see, Junior. Not that difficult," she told him, pinching his cheek, visibly pleased with herself. "You did very well for a beginner. You are such a good boy."

He accepted the gleeful condescension in good humour, thinking he really should smack her tush. When she left them Jackson leaned forward for his JW as Murielle reached for her crystal goblet.

"She likes you."

"I am positively not tipping her this evening. It's like I've adopted a bratty kid sister."

"What exactly did she mean by beginner, and why Junior? If I may pry a little."

"Almost everyone calls me Junior, including some cheeky bargirls. My father was also Jackson. The beginner thing because I don't date when I'm working. Pretty much a bad habit, I suppose. Something I have to work on. Particularly since Charlee seems to have become my self-appointed advocate."

"It's pretty obvious that she likes you. I think a lot."

"The feeling's very mutual. Sadly though, she has more refined tastes. I'm more of a mission for her."

"How terrible for you." She tested her wine, humming her approval. "What is it you do, Jackson?"

"I work in men's clothing. Administration mostly, although occasionally they do relent and let me near the clients."

Christ! "You're that Belmont, the men's clothes Belmont?"

He sipped his JW. "That would be me, yes."

Shit! No way! She knew Belmont. She knew of him. She knew the feel and the rich texture of the imported woolen fabrics and the finely crafted Italian leather footwear. She remembered the superbly tailored made-to-measure shirts and the sheen of Stonewall's silk ties and pocket hankies. She was also abundantly aware that Belmont would never pay to experience the rich textures and silky smoothness of her finely crafted body.

141

"My name is Murielle, by the way. Murielle de la Sorbonne."

"Well, Murielle, thank you for unknowingly colluding with Charlee. I will definitely compliment her on her excellent taste in women. You are beyond lovely and I would be unforgivably remiss as a gentleman were I not to also compliment your ensemble. Divine."

"Thank you, Jackson. These days we girls don't hear that as often as we would like." She sipped her wine. "I suppose since you are *the* New Orleans Belmont, returning such a gracious compliment would sound a little trite to say the least. Let me say instead that I'm very happy Charlee waited until this evening to remedy your social dilemma." Her short laugh was soft and exotically sweet. "I don't believe she was very worried at all about being severely punished by such a good boy."

They spoke for an hour, Charlee keeping her distance. He liked her. She was beautiful and bright; and she liked him. He was soft-spoken, more interested in her than talking about himself, never interrupting her. He was educated and successful, obviously well-to-do and single. He was a keeper, the kind of man she deserved and he would absolutely ask to see her again.

From a distance she might even mistake him for Anthony. He was the same height, though slimmer and not as muscular. His hair was the same colour, though purposely dishevelled, and his clothes were clearly more exclusive. They might have been brothers, Murielle musing as he spoke that she might easily love them both once home from her upcoming vacation.

Then she noticed Charlee practically gliding across the carpeted floor toward them, balancing her empties.

"Don't have to ask how you guys are doing. You look sort of fabulous together."

"Murielle and I have already mutually agreed to your advantage that you do deserve a tip commensurate with your superior female instincts, Charlee. No need to self-promote." Jackson put an arm around her waist. "But thank you."

She reached for their glasses. "Another JW Blue and a Beau-Séjour. Gee, now I can afford a tie on sale at Belmont for my dad at Christmas."

He did smack her tush, one side anyway, evoking a high-pitched girlish yelp.

Watching her prance away, "That felt so good. She has had that coming for such a long time. In addition to which we do not have sales and her father, a top surgeon, is one of our regulars."

"Really, a surgeon? And Charlee's working…?"

"Yes, her way through med school."

"I'm not surprised. However I am impressed. A gentleman who's a connoisseur of exquisite scotch, an excellent dresser and interesting. How rare is that? Are you always this tasteful in your choices?"

He coughed a quiet laugh. "The scotch is a once in a while recompense for my continued self-neglect, the suits are advertisements I get at cost. In my defence however, I also drive a ten-year-old Beemer that I do wash and wax myself in shorts and sneakers about as old. They're pretty disgusting."

Charlee placed their drinks without a word, Murielle and Jackson exchanging quizzical glances. She was clearly pleased with herself, smug in fact, patting his head as she left them.

Murielle discreetly turned her wrist, palming her skirt. Last call was 2:30, which was impossible. Her cut-off time would be midnight, latest. She wanted to see him again and he would not do that if she stayed longer, transmuting the

143

evening's dynamic into suspicion or a one-night stand that would end badly. If she appeared too easy, too eager to go home with him, he would do her and forget her, effectively barring her from Angelo's and raising a red flag with Charlee.

She liked him, truly enjoying her evening despite the resultant negative cash flow. The ride home would deplete her wallet by a good thirty bucks plus the tip she was expecting to well-afford because she was not expecting him, or anyone like him, or his cute little guardian. In fact the lounge was a terrible choice unless she was wrong about him, that she might be the evening's diversion, that he wouldn't invite her on a date, intrusively vivid thoughts of Anthony and Todd, Stonewall most of all, enjoying their evenings without her impossible to ignore.

He leaned slightly forward, reaching for the scotch, whispering, "Am I losing you to that faraway place?"

She blinked, returning to him. "No, you are not. I'm sorry, Jackson. I was simply wondering where the last hour has gone."

"Into a vault of fond memories with ample room for more. The evening isn't over." He swirled the Blue in a warm palm, savouring the aroma. He raised the glass. "Here's to stopping time, if only for us, if only for this evening."

She took her glass by its stem, confused, conflicted. She didn't know what to say or do. Too much was happening at once: The abortion, Stonewall, the four guys she'd fucked like a whore since he threw her onto the street like a whore, three of them absolute creeps. Because of him. Zachary was the worst, all the while laughing at her, Murielle thinking she would order another pizza to smash it into his smug face. Yes, she would.

She touched the rim of her glass to his, thinking she

really didn't need that table separating them. She wanted him closer. She wanted to hear that she wasn't wrong, for him to read her mind and sit closer. "My fault. I should have come in earlier." She moistened her lips with the Bordeaux. "Okay, this time you're drifting."

"I wasn't. I was questioning why I came here this particular evening, and why you did, each of us for the first time. In my case subconsciously coming to terms with my flawed work ethic, I suppose. Or possibly my seriously impaired social life."

"It is weird. I haven't dated for so long I can't remember. I was all about school, about getting on that all-important honours role. I don't know. Even when I left the restaurant earlier I hesitated, not certain I should do this. I was pretty nervous walking in here alone."

"Yet you seemed completely at ease, confident. I wish I had known. I would have loved taking you to dinner, Murielle. You're enchanting. In fact I am really not liking this dance-floor of a table between us."

Precisely what she needed to hear. He would absolutely ask her out. He hadn't permitted himself a single glimpse of her legs across which she had discreetly allowed her skirt to ride, hadn't once dared to gaze past the sheen of her blouse to the swell of her breasts which was very much contrary to plan. Difficult to even believe and very disquieting until then.

Throughout their second hour she was indeed confident, measuring each sip, at last placing her glass on the table and glancing at her watch: The telling moment.

"Jackson, what a very lovely evening. Thank you. I enjoyed your company immensely."

"And regrettably, we are too quickly at an end. Murielle, please come to dinner with me tomorrow."

Her surprise was real. "Jackson, I've been hoping for the

last hour that you would ask me out. I would love to, I really would. The thing is, I can't. I have a noon flight to Paris to visit my grandparents, their graduation gift to me that completely slipped my mind with everything else we were talking about. They're very old, Jackson, and grandmama is not well. Grandpapa is very nervous about what might happen to her. I want to spend as much time with them as I possibly can."

Disappointment erased his pleasant smile as though she had ruined their entire evening, causing her heart to skip a beat.

"With your folks, I suppose."

She gulped air, emitting a barely audible plaintive gasp. "No, Jackson, which is why I must go to them. My maman and papa were killed almost two years ago in a horrible car crash, while I was here at school. In a way I'm glad I was here, that I did not have to see them in such a horrible way."

He lurched forward. "Murielle, I'm so sorry for you. Are you alright? I mean, financially. Can I do something to help?"

"I'm fine, thank you. They were loving parents who continue taking care of me. And, of course, soon I'll be working."

"I wish I could go with you. How long will you be gone?"

"Three weeks today, the eleventh. I'm really sorry, Jackson."

"Don't be. Your grandparents need you. We'll do dinner on the twelfth, when you can tell me all about your trip." He put down his glass. "At least allow me to escort you home." He crossed his heart. "I promise, once you're safely inside I'll be gone. I will not run out of gas and I will not whimper or whine for a nightcap."

"That's very sweet of you, Jackson, and dinner does

sound wonderful. Still, driving me home would make me feel incredibly awkward. And you."

"On the twelfth then. Promise?"

She wouldn't allow her momentary melancholy to dampen her evening. "What I promise is that if we remain intrigued with each other after our dinner, we'll come here for a nightcap with Charlee because my condo is being renovated and I've got weeks of dust to clean and furniture I haven't seen or sat on since moving in. When they are finished, finally, I will take *you* to dinner and invite you in for a nightcap. I promise, if we remain intrigued, and because you are such a good boy."

"Thank you. You know, I really should have smacked her little tush a little harder." He sighed, reaching into his suit jacket for his business cards, passing her one with a pen. "Then call the good boy the moment you land... unless you fall in love with some undeserving Frenchman."

"Not to worry. Grandpapa is very protective of me. He is very old-school. Besides, I really do want to see you again and wouldn't do anything that would get in the way of our dinner plans." She reached into her shoulder bag for her notebook, printing her number and name. "Better yet, you call me Saturday evening unless you change your mind."

"Not a chance. Charlee would seriously hurt me." He stood, reaching for Murielle's hand, holding her at arm's length, at last fully appreciating her. "I like intrigued." He helped her into her bomber, signalling to Charlee.

She hugged them both tightly. "Am I good, or what? I mean, really?"

"You are more than good," Murielle said. "Thank you, for sending him over, Charlee."

"Yeah, for such a cool guy he's sort of slow at times."

"I believe, though, he will get better with some intensive

long-term care. He's showing positive signs. He invited me to dinner."

"He did? Wow, a second date. Impressive."

"No, a first date. And he's standing right here, ladies." Jackson added, tucking three fifties into Charlee's apron.

They both looked at him, shrugging, hugging each other again the way women do when on a mission or plotting, as though some sort of female bond was being formed. He imagined they could evolve into very close friends in time, with or without him. Or co-conspirators, better said.

He tapped his watch, reminding Murielle of her flight that morning. Then he thanked Charlee in a whisper with his arm around her shoulders for her limited involvement in his overdue reformation, turning her toward the bar and ever so tempted.

Once on the sidewalk he hailed a cab, raising a forefinger to the driver. "The twelfth. I'm thinking relaxed dining. Dress code: Casual elegance. The way you are right now, the way I'll be thinking of you for three unbearable weeks."

"I'll remember that when I'm shopping in Paris." She leaned in to him, squeezing his arms, lightly kissing his cheek close to his lips. She would never call him Junior, confident that very soon he would become a Darling or a Sweetheart. No way could he ever be anyone's Dear or Honey. Whatever she might one day call him, for the moment a simple "Adieu, Jackson," would suffice. He opened her door wanting to ask her, deciding not to. She would tell him when she was ready. Leaning in to the front passenger window he passed Diego de la Vega, driver 89, a fifty that would get Murielle anywhere south of Lake Pontchartrain and Diego a six-pack or a bottle at the end of his shift. "Por favor, compadre. Cuída de esta chica bonita. Ella es mi novia. ¿Comprendes?"

"¡Claro!" He connected a loose fist with Jackson's. "Con mi vida, amigo."

Driving away she asked the young driver what Jackson said.

"He told me, señorita, to take good care of the beautiful girl who is his girlfriend. I promised that I would."

17

Sunday Murielle woke feeling elated. In twenty-four hours she would climb out and slam the lid on the dumpster Stonewall had maliciously and cavalierly tossed her into. She would have her career. She would have the life she wanted and deserved.

She would have the procedure the next afternoon and call Anthony Tuesday morning. She would tell him how she missed him, because in a very real way she did, intent on spending as much time as possible through November at the gym with her trainer prepping her body for the rigours of December 01st.

In the meantime she would spend her Sunday and her free days until Gilmore pampering herself, recovering and preparing for her first day of work. She had a lot to think about, not the least of which was a credit card, a short-term bank loan and finding a newly renovated condo in the Garden District. Not just for them, for Anthony and Jackson, because it's what they expected. For herself as well. No way would she ever again not live the way she deserved.

*

Monday, October 23rd, she woke late, not certain what she should think or feel. She wasn't worried, she knew what to expect. Nor was she as cheerful as the day before. She was doing what was proper, what was right for her. Neither Anthony nor Jackson would ever want her with a baby, let alone two. At least Anthony was good with her aborting. Although Jackson, she believed, would view her in a different light that would cause him to wonder, to pollute his mind with suspicious thoughts.

Two exceptional men in three nights, one already a lover. Or he would soon become a lover unless December was a cruel and tactless lie, his money not meant to help her but to pay her what she was worth. The other was very likely already falling in love with her in his thoughts and his dreams, eager for the moment when he, too, would actually become her lover.

She showered and towelled, clamping a barrette at the top of a damp ponytail, dressing in sensible underwear bought for the occasion that she would soon after discard, a flared cotton dress and flat suede boots. She forced herself through a breakfast of juice, dry toast and coffee, pacing the floor throughout the entire morning, dreaming of her next time with Anthony and her first time with Jackson that she would make certain he would never forget. Keeping her options open was key.

At 12:30 she left for the bus stop. An hour later she was at the clinic filling out forms with four other girls, next to last taken into the small theatre where she was asked to undress and cover herself in a paper gown as the nurse reiterated the doctor's previously detailed explanation of the procedure.

"Murielle, in your case we will perform an aspiration." The woman held out a miniature paper cup containing two gel caps. "One is a sedative, given your age. The other will lessen your discomfort. Before the doctor comes in we'll lie you on your back for a little while to help you relax, to help the medication take effect. When he does come in we'll get your feet in the stirrups and make very certain you're comfortable before he inserts a speculum to open and clean the vagina. Then he'll give you a local to numb the cervix before using a tenaculum, a kind of clamp with handles, to hold the cervix in place while it dilates. When you're wide enough he'll insert a cannula, a tube connected to a suction instrument, into the uterus which pretty much takes care of business. You shouldn't feel much discomfort. He's very good."

"Then I go home. Right?"

"It'll be over in ten, fifteen minutes. Then we'll put you in a private room until we're certain you're good to go. Like I said, he's very good."

Within minutes Murielle was on her back, drifting into la-la land, not caring about her vagina, her two men, or anything else with her head held in place on a leather pillow with padded clamps.

"Good afternoon, Miss de la Sorbonne. I'm pleased to see you made us your preferred choice. We'll get this done and get you out of here as soon as possible. All I need from you is to relax and let me do what I do. Agreed?"

Whatever, and twenty minutes later she was staring at the ceiling in her private room, her innocence successfully rejuvenated. They sent her home near six o'clock, once the doctor had completed his post-op exam, assuring her the procedure would not in any way preclude her from producing healthy babies whenever she might wish in the future. She was good to go, responding by asking where and when she could permanently take care of business with a tubal ligation.
*

Monday evening she went to bed early, waking to her dawn of a new era. Kicking away the covers she pressed a palm against her belly, cupping the other between her thighs, thinking she felt no worse than she would or did after a sleepless free-for-all night with Anthony. She didn't feel nauseous at all, or guilty. What she felt was freedom.

At noon she called the number the surgeon had noted on her prescription for the pain and nausea suppressants she wouldn't be needing or paying for. They booked her for a consult and pre-op exam the coming Friday morning. She was done with the patch, cursing Stonewall for never telling her he shot blanks. What was the big deal, other than he didn't trust her?

Her lunch was a bland soup with crackers and water while she scribbled an agenda for the coming week. Then, when she was dressed in her prettiest panties and bra, jeans and cashmere sweater, at once brightening her mood, she called Anthony.

"Anthony Vincent speaking."

"Mon dieu, how formal is that?" A pause. "Murielle Adrianna speaking, the stunning girl in New Orleans. Remember me? I hope."

"I do. Of course, I do. I've thought about you each minute since leaving you, especially yesterday. You're okay, Murielle? Everything went well?"

"Yes, thanks to you."

"Good. Then I assume we're still on for December and Christmas and lots of phone calls in-between."

"We are."

"Which means I've got some shopping to do for Christmas."

"I suppose we do. That said, let's keep things simple, Anthony. Let's not embarrass each other. Size six, if you're wondering. No jewellery and absolutely no cotton."

He chortled. "Duly noted, Miss Dupree."

"So how's the demon? Still breathing fire?"

"Don't think a good acid rinse would be a bad idea. More importantly, she's gone. Or I am. Her rich daddy cut me a cheque for half the house and changed the locks. I'm bunking with a good buddy until I relocate."

"A boyfriend?"

"No, not a boyfriend. A male friend, a bachelor buddy from Boston U. He knows about you. We tossed a few back over the weekend, catching up. Guy stuff."

"I'm happy for you."

"I'm happy for me. I'm finally able to sleep with both eyes closed. Feels good. You feel good."

"Still weird though, you and me." She sighed into her phone. "Thank you, Anthony. Really. You saved me, big time."

"Good things happen to good people…eventually. Listen, got to go. I'll call you. If I had your address I would send flowers, yellow roses for missing you. They represent love at first sight."

"How romantic is that! However they would wilt in the sawdust and paint fumes, pretty much like I am. But thank you, Anthony. I'm missing you too."

They disconnected, each one promising to call the other. Murielle, flopping onto her bed, thinking of Charlee, wondering how she would feel to have a buddy, someone to do girly things with. When she woke the parking lot outside her window was pitch black.

*

Wednesday, feeling good, her discomfort practically nil, she dressed in a navy blue suit, silk blouse, low-heeled pumps and went with proof of her employment to the Credit & Loan.

She needed a credit card, suggesting a five K limit, and a short-term loan of ten-thousand required to secure a rental condo in the Garden District that would be safe for a woman alone and to furnish the place. She got both and went shopping immediately after for six more outfits that would ensure she was the best dressed junior researcher at Gilmore, a tablet, several bottles of wine and a Silent Sam.

That evening she ordered a medium all-dressed and a more manageable small pizza without toppings and extra tomato sauce. When the kid knocked on her door she answered in jeans, leather boots and a tee-shirt with the bill of her ball cap pulled down. She asked him to wait while she went for her wallet, returning with the small pizza instead, smashing it into his face, the shock more than the impact propelling him backward onto the floor.

"No tip tonight, Zach. No money either. This is on you. Thanks a bunch. And to be very clear about what happened here, the asshole across the hall, if I let him do me, and I will if I have to, he will substantiate that you just raped me." Murielle tossed her cap behind her. "Maybe use the money Stonewall's shithead lackey gave you."

She slammed the door shut and forgot him. The rest of the evening she spent circling ads for suitable condos and eating her complimentary pizza with a glass or two of exceptional Bordeaux. She wasn't going anywhere except forward, deciding she would begin her search with the one she believed was the best, the one she was drooling over while studying the details and photos on her tablet in bed with Silent Sam.

*

She began Thursday on the phone, making notes. She primped herself for an hour, sweeping her curtain of straight lustrous hair into a sophisticated updo. She dressed in a blood red and fashionably short yoked skirt, a paler red silk blouse and a matching jacket accented with oversized black buttons that would perfectly complement her three-inch stilettos and shoulder bag.

155

She took a taxi to the Marriott for lunch where she ordered a green salad and Chardonnay, prepping herself with silent answers to unspoken questions she had no idea about. Nevertheless pleased with how far she had come since Stonewall and her father's heartless rebuke.

She sat savouring her wine as most other patrons left her for parts unknown. She didn't want to arrive early or appear eager, letting the doorman help her into the cab minutes from her 2:00 PM appointment.

The second-floor apartment was one of four in the two-storey building, recently renovated, painted, and newly equipped. The place was pristine and unlived-in since the upgrade. The kitchen was modern and spacious, the cozy living room overlooking the quaint and colourful Prytania Avenue not far from the edge of the park she remembered all too well, its front balcony connecting as well with the bedroom's garden doors.

Walking through practically breathless she fell in love, picturing her new bed, her personal touches, the wall art she would buy on Royal Street and Anthony waiting for her to come home. The bonus room would work as her private gym once her membership expired, since she fully expected Gilmore would seriously cut into her personal time.

The en suite bathroom and powder room were modern, not masculine or feminine, all the amenities top end. She adored the place. She couldn't imagine not living there, not blinking when the building's off-site owner at last mentioned the rent. Not a problem. She would be an ideal tenant. She was single with a good job; she didn't smoke and she didn't have very many friends. Two grand monthly was in her budget, a bargain to live in luxury a mere four blocks from Stonewall's private whorehouse.

She wrote the man a cheque for six-thousand against the first three months. She signed a provisional lease and took a taxi to her flat where she waited anxiously for her phone to chime.

*

Friday she woke more tired than when she went to bed, a plethora of design concepts invading her mind throughout the night, each one vanishing as the next one crept in, robbing her of sleep. She was excited, thrilled that the condo was hers whenever she wished to move in. Murielle answering the man, "Not whenever. Saturday."

The doctor was first, then her trainer before shopping for a bed. The rest could wait. Most importantly, no one at Gilmore would gossip about the girl who lived under a freeway in Chinatown.

Squirming into her microfibre tell-all gym shorts and top, she supposed that most doctors probably cared more about their Beemers and being called Doctor than fashion, since most seemed to prefer uninspired white lab coats and pretentious stethoscopes dangling from their necks.

Slipping on her sweater coat and suede boots, she dangled her sneakers opposite her shoulder bag. She didn't need a sports bag, she never showered at the gym. She would never feel comfortable being naked amongst those who clearly resented her during her sessions, the less attractive and less shapely of them gawking at her, envying her, inwardly wishing for digital clones of her to emulate and admire.

The pre-op was a formality, her abortion lending a good deal of credence to her argument. In spite of which, why did she not want children?

Duh!

What if her future husband, her ideal man did want children? What then?

No man anywhere was that ideal or worth the pain and suffering she would endure. They had a different mindset:

They were all about bravado, about themselves, about proving their tiny guns were fully loaded, beyond which they didn't give a good shit. She did. She cared about her body and her life, about what could go terribly wrong with either.

Thoughts of creating something special, something unique, someone to remember her long after she was gone didn't appeal to her?

No. Nor the very real possibility of bringing another mental or physical deficiency into the world that would forever alter her life, ruin her dreams and likely cause Mister Ideal to not come home. No. Her body was her body. Period. End of conversation.

The procedure was booked for Saturday, November 11th, and Murielle went to the gym.

After her workout she lunched at the centre's health food bar, passing by her flat to shower and change before heading downtown to shop for a bed the store would deliver the next morning. She went to a movie and an early dinner, unwilling to endure a moment longer than needed in a slum across the hall from Jake.

When she did return to the flat she busied herself freeing one wardrobe from the closet, protecting each outfit with a clear garbage bag and stacking them on the bed. She stacked the other one in the original bags and boxes by the door. When she was done, she poured two-fingers of Silent Sam neat, sat on the bed flipping channels and fell asleep in her clothes.
*

Saturday morning she couldn't care less about the black deluge battering her window, breakfast, or how she looked. She put on bright yellow rain boots, a bright yellow rain cape and a matching Sou'wester that she strapped under her chin. And she was gone, pressing in to the driving rain, hurrying to the corner liquor store for a dozen or more empty boxes.

Again in her flat she first she thought to call Mack, instead requesting a van for the brief trip, telling the guy to forget the metre unless he didn't want an even hundred for thirty minutes work, tops. He did, following her inside, and together they moved her out in half the time.

Satisfied the hole was empty, he went to the van; Murielle went to Jake's door, not surprised he was in a singlet and camouflage fatigues, work boots and a ragged ball cap.

"Kinda early for the next rent, sweetie."

"Yeah, right. Just came to say good riddance. Can't say it's been fun. I did leave my bedding though. I thought you might like to sniff the sheets or put them on your bed as a keepsake. Whatever."

He snorted. "Wouldn't mind us gettin' them soiled together, Murielle. I got the cash. Been savin' up, thinkin' we might need some mutual assistance, you and me."

"Spend it on tissues or floor cleaner, Jake. Ciao."

He stepped into the hall, his eyes glued to the exotic bare skin between her boots and flared cape. Damn.

"I'll go two-fifty, Murielle. Like I said, I got the cash." All he heard was laughter. "Hey, where exactly you goin'? C'mon, now. There ain't nowhere in these parts better priced than where you're at."

She didn't answer. She had no reason. He didn't exist.

Hearing his fare's address, the driver was impressed. She seemed like a nice kid, like she deserved a lot better than her Chinatown shithole.

On the half-hour they were done, the transaction complete. He wished her well in getting settled and drove off. An hour later, with all she possessed in the world organized in boxes, put away or tumbling in her very own washer and dryer, her bed, her satin sheets and duvet were delivered.

When she was alone she peeked out from her bedroom doors. The sky had darkened, the rain much heavier than minutes earlier. The street was deserted, the balcony next to hers made private by the building's pillars, the balconies across the avenue concealed behind mammoth oak trees.

She stepped out, her tap pants and camisole instantly drenched, her hair plastered to her face and neck. She closed her eyes, tilting her head backward, letting the rain splash and dance on her face.

She stood lost in time, feeling cleansed. She was free of them, fully independent. She had done that, no one else. They could all go to hell, totally, her father and Kenneth Stonewall most of all. The only men she could imagine wanting or needing in her life at the moment were Charles Anthony Vincent and Jackson Belmont, Jr. Both young and successful handsome men.

Let the best one win her over.

Her body convulsed with a sudden and violent chill shooting through her, her feet skating uselessly on the heavily beaded tiles, her squeal hardly one of delight as her feet flashed past her into the air and her bum absorbed the brunt of her crash. She sat for a moment, dazed, massaging the offended soft flesh, exploding into a fit of laughter.

She loved that she was completely alone in the middle of an avenue, and that she would be throughout the summer. She pulled the slick camisole over her head, dropping it between her legs, wriggling from cheek to cheek, pushing her high-cut panties to her feet. She wrung both pieces, sliding on her bum to the open doors, carefully laying them inside the bedroom where she could later step on them.

Crawling onto her hands and knees, she slipped and slid her way to the wrought iron balusters spaced with heavily smoked Plexiglas, pulling herself to the top rail. Standing, she palmed rain from her hair, feeling the rivulets trickle down her back. She palmed her face, her chilled breasts, her belly, her bum and her legs, sweeping away a coating of glistening beads, dripping with more before she was finished, hating that she had to go in.

Inching her way around the balcony to the doors, she stood inside for long minutes completely exhilarated, taking in the view, the balcony and her body, thinking she would always stand or sit or lie outside in the rain…with a towel on the floor. Her tan that coming summer would be flawless.

Closing the doors, she added the clammy lingerie to her washer. She poured a deep and steaming bath no one else had ever bathed in, pondering her evening, her Sunday and Gilmore, suddenly realizing she was starving. She hadn't eaten breakfast or lunch, no food at all other than her wine and vodka and no way was she about to risk being seen in the Quarter or any restaurant where Jackson might see her.

Instead she towelled herself dry, styled her hair, finished her laundry with another glass of red wine, squirmed into a teddy and her rain gear and went out for groceries.

When she got home the cabbie helped her to the front door, grateful for the tip. In her condo she filled her pantry and fridge, made up a bowl of wieners and beans and put together her flat screen.

She spent the rest of her evening in her bed flipping through channels, making do with her cardboard night table.
*

Sunday she knew exactly where to go. She knew what she wanted and by the time the store closed she had completed her condo and gym.

She prepared a dinner of roasted chicken, baked potato and steamed veggies that she ate with a glass of milk while sitting on her kitchen counter deciding what she would wear to Gilmore the next morning.

18

Monday morning came quickly, her alarm screaming her awake at a rarely seen 6:00 AM. She showered, conditioned and combed her hair into a straight auburn curtain; she creamed her body, painted her nails and glossed her lips in a rich shade of prune, piercing her ears with sapphire studs and draping a simple sapphire pendant at her neck.

After her coffee and toast, not trusting herself, she continued the morning ritual with sheer thigh-highs, a cream-coloured satin thong and bra. She had decided the previous evening on navy blue pumps and cream-coloured tailored slacks, a cream-coloured blouse she would emphasize with a dark blue open front bolero jacket and a navy blue hobo bag that would complete the chic fashion statement.

She twirled in front of the bathroom mirror, pleased with the results. She was good to go.

The Gilmore building was a glass and steel high-rise on Canal Street, yet far enough from the Quarter, far from Belmont Tailors. She stepped from the cab, striding through the main entrance at 7:55, greeted by the head of HR who introduced her to security and handed her a pass before escorting her to his office.

The paperwork and a more detailed history of The Group and its mission lasted the better part of an hour before she met her supervisor who she remembered from her initial inquisition. She was given a full tour of the building, lastly putting names to the several faces in her department. She was given a desk with her name on a brass plate, a stack of files to proofread by day's end, and was left to climb or fall from the very bottom rung of her career.

At noon the department took her to lunch, a first-day protocol. After which, they explained, she would seldom have time for more than a sandwich or power drink at her desk. She could expect many twelve-hour days, more late suppers at home than extravagant corporate dinners, and not much help if she fell behind. Gilmore hired the best, expecting no less from each team member. All of them agreeing she would fit in nicely, though the prying nature of women being engrained through the ages, too inherent to ever be eradicated, her female co-workers weren't satisfied with her honours B.A. or where she interned, inviting her for after-hours drinks on Friday.

Back at her desk she called the furniture store early in the afternoon, asking for the latest delivery possible. At seven o'clock she put her day's work on her supervisor's desk and went home exhausted.

The truck arrived at nine. By 10:00 the condo was complete save the bare walls and Murielle sat sipping a mild vodka and soda stretched out on her brand new sofa, peering into the flickering fake flames of the electric fireplace that would stay propped against a wall until the weekend.

She hadn't spoken to Anthony since Tuesday, wondering if he might be in bed, or in someone's bed, or what. He did say to call whenever and she was eager to tell him the good news. Screw the time. She opened FAVOURITES on her phone, pressing a fingertip to the second name.

"How are you feeling?" he asked right away. "How's

the condo coming?"

"I'm fine, Anthony. And the place is finally liveable except for all my wall art crammed into boxes. And you?"

"I'm good. Missing you and sleeping on a blow-up till Wednesday. I found a place forty miles south, practically on the ocean, which pretty well obviates the need for that December chalet. We're talking brick fireplace, wood stove, Jacuzzi, a loft. Kind of small and very romantic. Ever gone snowshoeing?"

"No. I do like romantic, though…with an extra two weeks to vacation with you if we work out. I quit my job at the agency today. The Gilmore Group heard about me somehow. The offer was too good to refuse. Assistant to the VP of Research and Corporate Relations, with a lot more money. I start next week. I couldn't tell you until I was absolutely certain. Sorry."

"That is very exciting stuff. I'm glad you called. Congratulations."

"Thanks. It's a pretty big deal, and I want you to stay here in December. They did a really super job. I also have an empty closet and a driveway. But Anthony, this job is a big challenge and comes at a pretty steep price. Very long days and some weekends. Can you schedule your next trip from Sunday to Sunday? I'll make it up to you at Christmas. I promise."

"No problem, and yes you will."

She giggled. "I don't have a winter wardrobe. Not yet."

"You won't need one. Fireplace, remember?"

"I do. And a tree, Anthony? Please. I've never had a Christmas tree. We don't do that in France."

They disconnected, Murielle telling him she was eager for more than hello and goodbye, more than Anthony and Murielle if they were meant to be; Anthony answering that he was in love with her already, that he must be because he

165

couldn't stop thinking of her. But yeah, the cutesy names would come later.

The long day left her feeling languid with barely enough energy to lay out her clothes for the next day. She opted for a skirt. She abhorred pantyhose and never wore them. There was nothing remotely sexy or sensual about them. With slacks she wore thigh-highs, without a doubt preferring skirts and dresses which would usually demand garters with nylons guaranteed to heighten her sense of self, her femininity and appeal.

Tuesday through Friday were repeats of Monday. When she wasn't reading, adding words, more effective words, condensing, questioning what message or thought was intended and rephrasing, she was studying personal and corporate profiles. She was learning, she was being noticed.

Friday at 6:00 files were stored away, managers and executives decamped from their respective offices and floors with their secretaries to convene in the top-floor conference room for several shots of expensive booze while the lesser minions poured from the elevators through the lobby onto the street.

The younger ones hurried to the most popular pick-up joints to test their skills or assets or both. The older women preferred more sedate hotel lounges while their eager male counterparts headed toward time-honoured gentlemen's clubs for some beers and ephemeral infatuation before going home to their wives from working late.

Murielle's contingent were four other women her age, all Gilmore aspirants dressed for success, parading their way to a piano and wine bar popular with trendy twenty-somethings who didn't have to worry about hooking-up.

They all lived at home, saving for weddings or cars or vacations or whatever. That she lived alone, free from curfews and intrusive parents, and on Prytania by the park, made her an instant celebrity.

At least they did have parents, she corrected them, telling them how that tragic loss in her life had compounded the unbearable torment of her shattered romance with Anthony, about how he moved to Boston within days of crushing her heart with the news of their breakup after all the dreams and hopes for the future they once shared. He devastated her, leaving her feeling lost and alone, until a few weeks earlier when she met who she believed must be the most wonderful man in the world.

And for the next hour they interrogated her about the suave and sophisticated owner of Belmont Tailors.

Saturday she went shopping on Royal Street for affordable wall art, confidant she would not run into him. She spent Sunday decorating her walls.

*

Friday, the 10th, the gaggle of four went without her for wine and free Happy Hour hors-d'oeuvres, Murielle promising to join them the following week. She was meeting Jackson who was taking her to a couples' spa in Biloxi for the weekend and she would absolutely give them all the romantic details.

In lieu of which she spent the evening bored to tears. She hadn't spoken to Anthony since Monday when he called to ask about her first day at Gilmore and she wanted to hear his voice, to be completely honest with him.

"Hey, twice in one week. Things are looking good."

"Yes, they are. Listen, Anthony, I need to tell you something pretty serious. I'm having a tubal tomorrow. My choice. I am not having children. I do not want them or need them to feel whole. I know who I am, and that is not me. I want a career, not a totally messed-up life and body. Just too many negative variables. I thought you should know. I guess what I'm saying is: No more sharing you with prophylactics, or no more us. Sorry for swearing."

"You should have told me before. I should be with you."

She inhaled a loud breath. "You are, Anthony. That's all I needed to hear." She paused. "You really don't care?"

"Of course I don't. I care about you. You've been through a lot these past weeks. I never did understand the blind compulsion. Most of us humans simply and stupidly do not consider the real consequences. It's a basic social equation that contradicts the product of negative numbers equalling a plus, which works fine on a blackboard in grade eight. Not in life. In life it's the complete frigging opposite, when two minuses are a very big negative. Especially these days. A family on one income is downright insane. Thanks a bunch, but my career and a good life, not to mention a whack of disposable income, over strollers and dirty diapers and working till I'm dead to feed a college fund is a no-brainer."

"I didn't mean to set you off. So…that was a no? I guess. I hope."

"Yeah, that was a definite no."

"Good. Because there's something else I should tell you about my week."

"Listening."

"I think I'm missing you too much not to be falling in love you. It's weird, Anthony, I know. Anyway, it's how I'm feeling."

"That's a good thing. Listen, you call me tomorrow. Keep me current, sweetcheeks." He chuckled. "Very sweet cheeks as I vividly recall."

She would, she promised. Disconnecting she was lost for words and went to bed early, falling asleep late.
*

Saturday she arrived at the private clinic at 9:00 AM, signing forms and assigning the 1800-dollar fee to her credit card. The procedure was over by 11:00, Murielle coming around from the general anesthesia near noon, lying in bed pondering how she had, in such a short timeframe, altered her life for the better.

She was allowed to return home by the dinner hour, deciding against remaining overnight, assuring the doctor that her girlfriends were waiting to fuss over her. She understood the precautions and the side-effects. The reason she needed a cab was that no one she knew owned a car.

They believed her, a male orderly wheeling her through the lobby and main doors as a courtesy, piercing the air with a shrill whistle.

At home she threw her clothes into the washer. She poured a deep bath and soaked for an hour before slipping into a silk robe and ballerina slippers on a Saturday evening when other girls her age were at dance clubs or bars having a good time, enjoying themselves. She was at home alone really wanting a vodka, settling for a small bowl of her homemade shrimp bisque and a glass of Chardonnay at her dining table, listening to Francis Cabrel serenading her softly from the living room.

She called Anthony when the bowl was empty and the wineglass was half-full, happier than she was disappointed when he didn't pick-up. She left a brief message. She was fine. Really she was, just tired. She was going straight to bed, to dream of him, to dream of them.

She disconnected. She wasn't in the mood for conversation, a tad pissed-off with herself without knowing why. She had no reason, she simply was. All the bullshit of the past several weeks and Chinatown were totally behind her. They never existed, her long-awaited and deserved renaissance happening right then and there.

Her phone chimed, Murielle muttering a muted "shit." Not that she had forgotten him.

"Hello."

"Murielle, hi. It's Jackson. Welcome home. How was Paris?"

"Absolutely wonderful, Jackson. Thank you. Yet I feel as though I never left."

"Strange. I feel as though you were gone forever."

"Meaning we're still intrigued with each other? Meaning you with me, I hope."

"Very intrigued. We're reserved at Angelo's for dinner tomorrow at seven-thirty. A corner table."

"Jackson, isn't that a little fancy for a first date?"

"I want to make a good first impression with after-dinner drinks with Charlee per your instructions. We're expected. She's very excited about seeing you again. You were a big hit with her."

"I like her a lot. She's really sweet."

"Thing is, I'm not good with meeting any lovely lady on a street corner, particularly the one I'm trying very hard to impress. Unfortunately I don't have the lady's address. Do you see my dilemma, Murielle?"

"How thoughtless of her, Jackson, especially since the lady in question heard from a very reliable source that she is your, hmmm, your novia. Did she get that right? Something about her being your…your girlfriend, a chica bonita?" She giggled. "Gosh, why didn't you tell her?"

"I was waiting to surprise her, to tell her tomorrow at dinner while holding her hand and telling her how incredibly lovely she is. Because you're exactly right, the lady does deserve to hear me say the words, particularly since she did kiss me. I'm certain she remembers."

"Yes, I'm sure she does. And by the purest coincidence I believe I can help you with your address dilemma. I don't think she'll mind. She lives on Prytania, Jackson, close to the park. Do you have a pencil handy?" He did. "More importantly, she'll be wearing green and wants to avoid looking like twins. Please do not wear anything green."

"Some little thing from Paris?"

"Yes, from Paris, and little, which won't help her very much if she doesn't get some beauty rest. It's three in the morning for me, Jackson, with more than a little jetlag."

"You're right, of course. I'll see you at seven. Now go to bed, and sweet dreams."

19

Sunday Murielle spent the entire day pampering herself, laying out her evening outfit and lingerie, neither of which she would be taking off for him. Her condo would be a shambles of sawdust and shavings for another week, by which time the blue and yellow tinges on her bruised belly would have disappeared along with the less than romantic smell of fresh paint.

By 6:30 her hair was braided à la Française, her skin sparkled with silver body dust, her lips and nails were glossed and lacquered with her favourite shade of prune and she stood admiring her full-length reflection for the umpteenth time since her deliveries. Which was, until then, an unaffordable luxury since Stonewall.

The emerald tear-drop earrings and pendant were his Christmas gift to her in the Bahamas. An eternal reminder that, unlike her, they were too delicate and unique to simply discard like yesterday's scraps.

All that and the effect of her three-inch closed-toe stilettos in concert with an emerald green thong with detachable garters attached to sheer stockings was exquisite to the eye. She was exquisite standing there posing, wishing he was there to see her, cupping her bare breasts, pushing them slightly higher the way he would see them in his tortured mind throughout the evening from under the bodice of her cocktail dress: The pièce de résistance in a shimmering deep green that was silky and strapless and short, the flighty hem falling to a hand-width above her knees. Something else his masculine mind would secretly explore.

A coat would ruin her creation. Instead she cloaked her bare shoulders with a simple black shawl. She was ready, standing by her bedroom door as he drove up, standing by her intercom when he pressed 2B. She would be right down.

Jackson Belmont, Jr. stood in wide-eyed awe. "You are ravishing, Murielle. Stunning beyond simple words."

"Merci, Jackson. I wanted to look my very best for you."

He reached for her hand. "This is incredible." He kissed her cheek lightly. "Now we're even."

"Perhaps, yes, if I were your sister." She put a warm palm to his cheek, pressing her lips to his not as lightly. "Now we are no longer even, monsieur."

The evening was perfect for being in love, pretending or hoping; Murielle musing as he opened the passenger door of the Infiniti Q60 that the man was positively head over heels in love with her.

"Thank you, Jackson."

"For what?"

"For not finding a girlfriend while I was in Paris." She twisted in the plush leather seat. "You didn't, did you?"

"You're my girlfriend, remember? What about those single-minded Frenchmen? Any broken hearts cluttering the streets of Paris?"

"Not that I know. Perhaps the ones I chose to ignore. This is possible, I suppose."

At Angelo's the valet took the keys, disappearing in Jackson's two-door luxury around the corner. Inside the hostess watched them come closer, openly admiring Murielle's ensemble, greeting the couple with a wide smile.

"Mademoiselle, your outfit is divine." She leaned over the lectern, whispering. "You will be the centre of everyone's attention this evening. And the gentleman is no less elegant."

"You're very kind. Thank you."

"A special evening for a special couple?"

Jackson said, "Belmont. Corner table for two. And yes, very special."

She led them to their table, pulling out the gentleman's seat as Jackson seated his date. A moment later their server arrived on cue. The lady would have a Jean-Marc XO, splashed with soda. No citrus. The gentleman, very impressed with her polished manner, ordered a JW Blue neat. She was no ordinary date; she was familiar with the good things in life.

"Jackson, I want to give you something before the table gets cluttered with plates and glasses. I suppose I want you to know I was thinking of you while I was away." She clicked open her clutch. "I hope you like them. I couldn't exactly get Mister Belmont Tailors a tie or pocket hanky, could I? Anyway, the thought is more important. N'est-ce pas?"

She paused a moment, letting their server place their drinks. When he was gone she slid a slim velvet box across the table.

"Murielle, thank you. No one's ever given me a box before. I love it. How did you know?"

"No, monsieur, not a box." She smirked. "Perhaps you should open it."

He did slowly, teasing her, his surprise real. "Murielle, you cannot afford this. You just started working."

"They're titanium. They will go better than plastic with your Rolex and thousand-dollar suits, I believe."

He beamed, sliding the pen and pencil from the case.

The smooth black metal was cool to his touch, minute sparks dancing in the candlelight. "They are spectacular, Murielle, and very over the top extravagant. I love them. Thank you." He stood, putting a hand gently against her braid, and kissed her, garnering curious stares and envious smiles. "Three magnificent gifts in as many weeks. I am the envy of every man in this room."

"Three, really? The other two being?"

"The first came from Charlee, when she brought us together; the second was from you a few moments ago, hearing that you were thinking of me in Paris."

"What a charming thing to say."

Murielle ordered turtle soup garnished with baby spinach, grated egg, and splashed with sherry; Jackson selected roasted oysters in a Manchego crust soaked in smoked chili butter, complementing the appetizers with a half-bottle of Louis Michel "Montmains" Chabis 1er Cru.

Her entrée was lacquered roasted duck served with ginger, chickpea panisse and watercress. He opted for the filet of beef Stanley served with parmesan herb roasted bananas, porcini mushrooms, horseradish yogurt, a perigourdine sauce, and a red Elvio Cogno "Bricco dei Merli" Barbera d'Alba.

His desert was a Tahitian vanilla crème brûlée. Her choice a wiser and lighter in-house sorbet with coffee. Charlee was waiting across the entrance to serve their nightcaps.

She took Murielle by the shoulders, twirling her. "You are to die for." She glared at Junior. "If he didn't say something nice to you this evening I'm giving up on him. We already know he's a little slow with the girls."

"He did, Charlee. I really do believe that together we can save him."

Charlee took the RESERVED card from the leather

loveseat. She put Junior's hand over Murielle's and went to get their drinks. When she returned with her tray, placing the drinks, Jackson slipped his free hand into his suit. He held out his gift to Charlee who was suitably impressed, reminding him that "Christmas is only six weeks away, Junior." Then she left them.

"She's actually worse than a kid sister."

Murielle squeezed his hand. "Jackson, thank you for another wonderful evening."

"You have that a little backward, Murielle. You got a meal. I have a beautiful date in a stunning ensemble and an incredible gift."

"And we're even again." She sipped her Jean-Marc. "On that note, Jackson, this novia thing, this girlfriend thing…care to elaborate before I go buying anymore gifts?" Nothing. "Monsieur, the lady is waiting."

"It's complicated. Girlfriend is a very poor translation, much too adolescent for an incredibly lovely lady. Novia also means sweetheart, which is old-school, something my grandfather would say. A prometida kind of novia is a fiancée, and the casada kind is a bride. You do see my dilemma, Murielle, don't you?"

"You poor man. I've caused you another dilemma. How terrible for you."

He nodded. "In fact a very serious dilemma, given my current mental state. Simply put, you are not a sweetheart, not that way. We aren't engaged and I can't properly marry you until we are engaged." He sipped his scotch, she waited. "Clearly, a very important element is missing from this conundrum, Murielle."

"I'm a conundrum. Thank you."

"Yes, you are. A very breathtaking and intriguing conundrum, which does nothing at all to obviate my problem."

"Doesn't sound like much of a problem to me. Sounds pretty nice. So what exactly is this mysterious element that you believe is missing?"

"I'm not an expert. Still, I would think that somewhere between second-date and prometida there should be something like, I don't know, curling up on a sofa with hot cocoa and talking. You know, you and me talking."

"Talking, you and me on a sofa talking?"

"Yes. Without suits and ties, beautiful dresses, waiters and…" he glanced over to Charlee, "cute bargirls. You and me."

Murielle leaned in to him, not letting go of his hand, swinging her feet onto her cushion "Then what, Jackson?"

He knew she was teasing him, making him sweat; the sensual curl of her pursed lips, the twinkle in her liquid brown eyes mere inches from his, the delicate scent of her perfume making him crazy.

"Excuse me?"

"After the cocoa. What happens after the cocoa?"

"Okay. We forget the cocoa. We pour some wine and search for the missing element. That might be a better plan."

"Plan?" She swirled her vodka. "Just to be clear, I'm a dilemma, a conundrum, a problem and a plan. I am not your girlfriend or sweetheart, which I understand. Yet you want us together on a sofa drinking wine and searching together for an elusive element." She shrugged, putting down her glass. "Okay, I'm good with that. I really don't like cocoa. Silly me, though, particularly since we're snuggled together here on a sofa. For a moment I thought you were hinting at making love with me, that you were having an epiphany, actually discovering the lost element while sitting here holding my hand." She kissed his cheek, whispering into his ear. "Isn't that the missing element between girlfriend and prometida, Jackson? Lover. Making love with me when we eventually become more than each other's date? Which we are this evening, to be very clear."

"Murielle, may I loosen my tie? I believe I'm experiencing a mild stroke."

"Yes, of course. You do seem a little distressed, Jackson. Are you alright?"

"Thank you. Yes, I'm fine." He tugged at the 100-dollar Belmont accessory. "Whew! I might be wrong, but I think you enjoyed that."

"Maybe a little." She was relishing the moment. "I'm sorry, Jackson. However that is what you wanted to tell me."

"Yes. That is what I wanted to say. I don't want to lose you. Thinking of you with anyone other than me is unbearable. I can't tell you how much I've missed you since leaving you that first night. I've lived the last three weeks in a daze."

"Well that's certainly much better than cocoa, Jackson. Charlee would be very proud of you."

"She's in huge trouble with me, that girl. Because of her everyone at Belmont is gossiping about my to-die-for gir...about you."

"How cruel of them, given your current mental state, causing another dilemma, another conundrum and problem for you."

"My actual problem is leaving you at your door this evening and going home without you, which I will never openly admit to. They can think what they want. If I'm left alone in my misery to dream, let them imagine whatever they want."

Murielle followed his gaze, commiserating. The man was displaying incredible restraint. The time had come to reward him, guiding his hand to a bare knee.

"Does this ease your misery even a little, you poor man?"

"You are killing me."

"Well try to stay alive a while longer. I'm inviting you to dinner next Saturday, at my home. No fancy clothes. No phones. No movies and popcorn. Just you and me, talking and dancing. I'll prepare a simple dinner with candles, we'll dance to soft music, and we'll enjoy a digestif on my sofa. That means no bedroom, Jackson. Not then. I have not had a boyfriend since high school. I'm about as pure as a teenage nun and I will stay that way until we are certain about each other. Are you good with that, monsieur, or do we remain good friends without our glistening bodies ever joining urgently together, never hearing each other's tender words, never feeling our hearts frantically beating together?"

He put his glass to his brow. "Yes, I am good with that. Just be aware that if I appear a little cold toward you next week it's because I'm wearing an icepack."

Charlee stopped by to check on them, grinning. "Murielle, what have you done to him? He looks positively frazzled. Should I call 9-1-1? Should we give him CPR?"

"I believe that would make him worse, Charlee, the two of us pressing our warm lips to his. He's already a little flushed." She put a palm to his forehead. "Possibly the beginning of a bad cold." She slid a hand under his jacket, concerned, pressing into the warmth. "Yes. Something is definitely distressing him. His heart is really beating quickly, pounding frantically. We should go, Jackson. I would hate for your condition to worsen before our dinner next weekend with candlelight and soft music. I would miss you very much, sitting quietly alone on my sofa without music, so miserable with worry, thinking of you, your body glistening with fever, your poor heart threatening to explode with no one by your side to care for you." She smiled up at Charlee. "Can you possibly imagine such a terrible dilemma for me, Charlee? How wretched I would feel?"

"Okay. Alright. I'm missing something good here. Something's going on. But, hello. Gifts and dinner at home. How cool is that?"

"Very cool, Charlee. Unless he's too sick with his cold."

"Charlee," Jackson broke in, "no doctor, no cold. I'm perfectly fine. The one medicine I want is another JW, and personally I think our pretty French amiga here has had enough."

"I would love another, Charlee, to end a truly enchanting evening with our charming amigo here. I believe he's feeling much better, well enough to drive me home and kiss me at my door."

Which he did an hour later, strolling hand in hand to her entrance where even a single word would destroy the mood, Murielle taking the lead to once again alter the score in her favour. Her first kiss was passionate, her second stole his breath.

20

Monday morning the four girls crowded Murielle's space for the basic data. They would hear the full details on Friday, satisfied that Jackson Belmont, Jr. was an ardent and attentive lover, gallant, and an exceptional dance partner.

Throughout the week she planned a Saturday she would begin in her kitchen. She created her menu and her outfit, ensuring the evening's mood with a precise selection of fifties' crooners, romantic ballads he wouldn't understand and Latin tunes that he would understand.

She spoke with Anthony once on Thursday, telling him everything about her blossoming career and spending her days preparing for Gilmore's annual weekend conference. She was editing her boss' presentation and finalizing details with the hotel. She was totally exhausted, totally elated, and she missed him terribly.

She spoke with Jackson twice, refusing to put herself on Skype. Though Wednesday morning she did surprise him with a selfie attached to his personal email. She was curled into her sofa, dressed in dark thigh-highs that he would think are tights and a raglan sweater with her fake flames flickering in the background. Jackson responded quickly with one of his own, depicting him signing a document with a black titanium pen.

Thursday morning they were framed on each other's

desk, the women at Belmont each with a different reason to drop by his office, the men simply going in as one to see what all the fuss was about. All of them agreeing the boss had superb taste in pens.

The Gilmore Research Sisterhood, seeing Jackson's photo on her desk, could not believe that everything Murielle had told them was true. What girl didn't exaggerate about a newfound beau with superlatives? But this guy, her guy, he *was* every girl's dream. Murielle smugly refusing to say another word about him until the next day.

That evening she got home late. She had gone to the liquor store for wine to complement her four courses and a bottle of Johnnie Walker Blue, then to a music store where she asked for the best in Latin love songs, and a hardware store for a can of paint.

Friday she woke early, eager for the week to end.

She closed her desk at 6:15, joining the girls and the tagalongs they felt sorry for. The guys had nowhere else to go. Gilmore departments were cliquish, each one more critical to the Group's success than the others. Outsiders, particularly interns, were never invited to share in a competing department's heightened sense of self.

No sooner were their cocktails served, than: God! Jackson was so totally handsome. How old was he? Did he have a brother? Was he coming to the Christmas Party?

"What!"

"The Christmas Party, Mur. At the Marriott in two weeks. Like, what, no one told you?"

"No. No one told me."

"Well, you're going. It's a company must-do. Everyone will be there. You included."

"She's right, Mur. It's totally awesome. Live music and dancing, Santa Claus and presents and an open bar. All the managers and bigshots, they all leave early."

"No one told me."

"We're telling you now," Cerise corrected her, "and it's a couple's thing. We all have dates. So you have to bring Jackson. Really, we have to see this incredible guy of yours up-close."

Shit! "When is this thing?"

"December 02nd, and it's formal." Cerise leered across to the guys already on their second beers, who had no particular opinion on Murielle's rich and wonderful stud. "Formal. Understand you two? That means standing when a lady asks you to dance, if you're too slow to ask her, and escorting her back to her seat. It does not mean gawking at our chests while you're chewing gum with beer leaking from your mouths."

Vicky added, "Mur, these losers are going as a couple. No surprise there. I mean, really, check them out. They belong in the Bayou with each other."

Shelly, the girl framing them on the left, scolded, "You will also press your pants, you will iron your shirts and you will ask your daddies to properly knot your ties. God! You are so sad."

Valerie on their right added her jibe. "And you will both wear jackets that fit. Or sit with someone else. We ladies deserve gentlemen at our table, not riffraff out for a free meal."

They understood, mutely nodding their heads in concert. They were sitting with like the five hottest females on the entire Research floor. What was a little abuse? Bring it on! Yeah, like totally.

The girls actually did like Everett Dumb and Quintin Dumber, occasionally inviting them to tag along. They were easy targets, typical twenty-something millennials in wrinkled cotton shirts straight from the doorknob, loosely knotted ties, tan Dockers with no crease, and either thick-soled shoes or shoes four inches longer than their toes, whose mothers continued doing their laundry and packing their lunches.

Then the girls noticed Murielle's brown eyes, as though a system of complex gears was kicking into emergency mode behind them.

"Mur, you are going to that party," Cerise chided her. "Do not even think to make up stupid excuses. You are going."

"I'm not. It's just that…"

"There is no 'just that'."

"You're going," the four insisted.

"Okay. I'm going." They leaned in to her, glaring. "What?"

A gleeful chorus of "Jackson!" assailed her.

"Of course I'm bringing Jackson. The poor man's like a puppy missing his master. I'll tell him tomorrow. He's coming over for a romantic candlelight dinner." Her smile was coquettish. "It's not as though he'll have trouble finding something to wear."

They all breathed sighs of relief. They liked her, and they hated her thoroughly. Valerie, the girl seated beside Dumb, commenting that the most she ever got from her boyfriend was a dinner special at Appleby's on Valentine's. Five sets of glossed lips wide-open and speechless when Dumb told her confidently out of the blue that "Maybe then you should go with me to the Christmas Party, Valerie. I would never treat you that way."

Murielle and the four girls left with Dumb and Dumber after a second cocktail, making sure the guys got on the right bus before going their separate ways. She went to the market, scratching each item from her extensive list, wishing when she was done that she owned a car and thanking the cabbie with an extra five for helping her to her door.

Once inside, her groceries stored, she poured a Silent Sam and sank depleted onto her sofa. She was exhausted after her week. All she wanted was to think of him, to dream of what would come next in the days and weeks ahead.
*

She woke ten hours later completely dishevelled and excited, squealing and hopping around her living room like a giddy teenager mere hours from her first date. She was on her first date. She was, with Jackson Belmont in her very own home.

She brewed a richly aromatic coffee, stripping from Friday's outfit, tossing her nylons and delicates into her washer along with five other days of silks and satins. She put the opened paint can in a corner where she wouldn't kick it. She made toast, poured a coffee, and padded into her bedroom to scrutinize her body. The bruising was virtually gone, not that it mattered. By the time she deemed Jackson ready to caress her, to kiss her from her lips to her toes for the first time, she would be perfect for him. She would be his.

She dressed in panties and a tee-shirt, doing an hour on her elliptical and Bowflex, getting a serious sweat on. She dusted and vacuumed, watered her flowers and set her table. At noon she taped four sheets of paper to her cupboards; she hadn't cooked for anyone since Stonewall and, even then, not very often. Her evening, their evening, would be extra special.

Inhaling a deep breath, filling her lungs to the point of rupture, she began the second course first. Her chicken creole gumbo required more time and attention, which she began by browning the chicken to perfection.

The first course came next, a simple Romaine salad sprinkled generously with Roquefort cheese and bacon chips. She would add the vinaigrette and whipped egg yolk before serving him.

Until then she placed both in the fridge alongside the Sauterne that stood chilling.

Her entrée would be a petit filet mignon seared to perfection with braised raisons, coarse black pepper and brandy that she was marinating, fully expecting to complete the succulent dish with freshly steamed legumes and her very own and lightly spiced puréed pommes de terre au four while he hung over her shoulders being a nuisance and drooling.

The requisite red wine was a Château Capet-Guillier Saint-Émilion Grand Cru that was worth every exorbitant penny.

Still working on the gumbo, the dessert was last on her list near two o'clock: Perfectly formed balls of vanilla ice cream topped with finely sliced strawberries soaked in brandy that she put quickly into her freezer. The wine sauce she would let simmer for another thirty minutes with orange slivers, limes and cinnamon before draining and chilling the delicacy to later serve at the table with her favourite Armagnac.

Pleased with her work she sealed and concealed the paint can under a cushioned wicker chair on her front balcony.

At 3:00 she poured a bath, luxuriating in the warmth and quiet until her skin began tingling. She massaged herself by the mirror with a rich penetrating cream before scrunching her hair with mousse. She lacquered her nails and glossed her lips in a dusty rose, enhancing her eyes with a shimmering pearl champagne.

She cleaned her tub, organized her vanity and put out a

fresh towel before dressing in bronze-coloured thigh-highs, a satiny gold thong and matching three-quarter bra, a short cinnamon tweed skirt and deep V-neck cardigan in bright yellow. If he wasn't all of a sudden blind or gay, he would be completely spellbound.

All that remained was the waiting. She set her fireplace to a slowly flickering flame and low heat, slipped a CD into her stereo and poured herself two-fingers of Silent Sam with a splash to quell her excitement fifteen minutes before she expected her intercom to buzz.

Which happened precisely at 6:00. She greeted him at her door, studying him, searching his eyes. Realizing her instant success!

"Hi, Jackson."

He stopped midway on the staircase. He was expecting "Good evening, or "Nice to see you again." But the "Hi," her voice a sensually throaty purr, her glistening eyes that could melt his heart, told him the evening would become as wonderfully agonizing as their last.

"Murielle, how can you possibly be more desirable each time I see you, more glowing. Last week an enchanting sophisticate, this evening an adorable angel sent from the stars to torment me. You are radiant."

"Thank you, Jackson. And you are very handsome this evening."

He kissed her, holding out a dozen red carnations. "You deserve more than quotidian roses. Red dianthus, for love and devotion as deep as the colour. Dios Anthos, divine flower, named for the Greek god Zeus yet surely created for you, Murielle. You are truly a radiant goddess."

"They're gorgeous, Jackson. Thank you." She kissed him. "You do know how to make a girl feel special." She took his hand, leading him inside, closing the door with a stockinged foot. "The place still smells a bit of paint,

Jackson. Sorry about that. Otherwise we would have waited another week or more and I didn't want that."

He put a bottle of Beringer Cabernet Sauvignon into her other hand, doing a three-sixty. "Wow. Very nice. Do I get the grand tour?"

"Yes, of course you do."

She acknowledged his wine selection with effusive appreciation as a recent graduate of Stonewall's Advanced Wine Studies, scolding him that a Special Reserve '84 was a little much for a home cooked meal. Yet somehow he didn't think so. In her kitchen she put the carnations into a vase, adding them to the dining room table. She poured a JW Blue neat, slipped her arm through his, and guided him through her private life.

When the tour was over he was visibly impressed. "Am I missing something here, Murielle? A beautiful home, my favourite scotch, my beautiful gift, not to mention your sensational outfits."

"My papa always told me to dress and act for what I want to eventually achieve in my life, for how I want people to perceive me. He would be happy for me, Jackson, to know I have achieved the career I wanted so badly. At least the beginning of one." She palmed her sweater and skirt. "I also do this for me, to feel good about who I am, and for the man I will eventually deserve. My papa would also be happy with that man, I believe, Jackson." She guided him to a familiar sofa, patting the space beside her.

"Solis. You didn't tell me you like Latino."

"They told me he is the best, the most popular everywhere." She laced an arm through his, pressing in to him. "Did I choose well?"

"Absolutely an excellent choice." He sipped his scotch. "By the way, my mother's excited about meeting you. Until she sees you she won't believe you're real."

188

They spoke for half an hour before sitting for dinner, Murielle asking him to open and serve the Sauterne while she seasoned and served the Romaine salad, throughout which the conversation was as light as the appetizer.

She loved dancing; he loved old movies. She enjoyed working out and staying fit. No kidding. He enjoyed working and hadn't used his ten-speed in months. She once adored cycling through the parks of Paris, becoming too absorbed in her studies since arriving in America to make the time.

When they were finished he was strictly refused entry into her kitchen, ordered to sit and relax.

Jackson was a New Orleanais born and bred. He understood the people, the quirky customs and the unique cuisine. Her creole gumbo was the finest he had ever tasted, Murielle delighted when he asked for more. She was even more delighted when he took her by the hand into the living room where they danced to Solis' impassioned Sin Ti.

When the woeful ballad ended she wrapped her arms around his neck, feeling incredibly sad, telling him that despite not understanding the words she had never heard a more wretched plea for love.

He refused to be left alone, helping her prepare the table for her entrée and following her into the kitchen where he noticed the Saint-Émilion standing by the Cabernet Sauvignon.

"Where did you study wine, Murielle? Capet-Guillier is a little rich for most college grads."

She was busy at her oven and stovetop, tying her apron. "With papa, of course. This one I brought from Paris for us. At least I was hoping for us, and less expensive than you think. We French drink wine with our dinners at home to savour each drop, Jackson, to relish each morsel with our families and our friends. Here you Americans prefer guzzling tap water while you gorge on factory-made food at tables surrounded by strangers as though you are afraid someone will steal it." The oven door thudded shut. "In France it is also customary to begin with our guest's wine, Jackson." She turned, facing him, furrowing her brow. "What is it? Would you prefer French this evening?"

"Actually yes. I would very much prefer something French this evening." He reached for the Beringer and corkscrew. "More to the point, madam. We are in New Orleans. We do not guzzle or gorge. We devour our delicacies with enthusiasm, which is what I am fervently hoping to demonstrate in the very near future." The cork popped. "À la Française, s'il vous plaît very much."

She patted his cheek. "The red wineglasses are in that cupboard, my sweet darling. Please do not pout."

The filet mignon was tender and succulent; her baked pommes de terre sprinkled with spices and buttered legumes, at first too picture-perfect to disturb, was a fanciful epicurean journey. The wine was full-bodied, smooth and delicious, she commented. He agreed, no less a joy to the palate than she was to his eyes and his heart. Without question far superior to tap water.

"Murielle, absolutely heavenly. You and you're dinner, two heavenly gifts."

"Thank you, Jackson."

She went to stand, Jackson leaping from his seat to help her. She ordered him into the living room with their wineglasses while she cleared the table humming to Cabrel's latest pop rock. She took the ice cream from the freezer, sprinkling each frozen globe with brandy-laced berries before adding a drizzle of thick exotic sauce. She placed the mouth-watering indulgences on the table to set, pleased with herself, pouring Armagnac into snifters for balance before she joined him on the sofa, pressing against him.

"Jackson, I want to dance. First though, I have a very big favour to ask."

"However I can help you, Murielle, is not a favour. The correct words are my heart's desire."

"In two weeks Gilmore is having a Christmas Party. I didn't know until yesterday. Would you be my date if you're not busy? It's formal."

He creased his brow, swirling. "That's a really big problem for me, Murielle. I'm sorry."

Her disappointment was visible. "I understand. You work often on the weekends. I'll be fine on my own."

"No. It's not work. It's me." He sipped his wine. "I wouldn't want to embarrass you. You know, what with my guzzling and gorging. How I wish my manners were, you know, French."

Her mouth opened wide, her eyes wider. "You will go with me!"

"Yes, I will go with you. Of course I will." He chortled. "If I can find something to wear on such short notice."

She grabbed his head, smothering his mouth. "I will be the prettiest girl for you, darling. I promise."

"Okay, that's two darlings. Things are looking up."

She squirmed away. "Three. Dance with me, darling. This time I will tell you the words. This evening is even more special than I could have wished for."

They danced through five songs, scarcely moving, not for a moment releasing their tight embrace until Murielle's electric squeal jolted them apart "Misère! Mon dessert!"

Jackson didn't quite see the problem, wiping away her tears. Chilled vanilla wine and strawberry soup was his favourite. How did she know? All he needed was a spoon, or maybe a straw.

She wasn't consoled, padding to the sofa with slumped

shoulders, plopping backward with her arms crossed, waiting for Jackson and a restorative digestif.

"Sorry about that. I'm annoyed with myself," she muttered. "I wanted our evening to be absolutely perfect."

"Our evening is unbelievably perfect. Besides, I must assume full responsibility for your little dessert disaster." He sat with her, passing her an Armagnac and resting a hand on her thigh, kneading the soft silkiness with his fingertips. "We weren't here. We were transported to a distant galaxy, dancing in a world of surreal dreams. The one where we are deeply and ardently in love."

"I have fallen in love with you, Jackson. I wanted to tell you after dessert, while we were dancing, that I do really love you, that after the Christmas Party I want you to stay the night with me. I don't want a world of dreams, I want a life of memories...passionate memories."

"You're certain, Murielle? You're sure that's what you want?"

"Yes Jackson, darling. That is very much what I want. I want you. I want us."

They danced until midnight when they kissed at her door, suspended in a curious limbo, each teetering at a precarious precipice and urgently wanting to leap, each one uncertain of the other.

"I hate that you're going to South Carolina and Florida. That I will not see you for two entire weeks." She wrapped her arms around his neck, pressing her cheek to his, whispering. "That I cannot love you tonight."

"My employees deserve the recognition, Murielle. They are Belmont, not me. Through to Christmas will be my busiest time. And yours."

She inhaled a deep breath, squeezing him. She *was* certain; she needed him to be certain. "Jackson..."

"What?"

She turned in his arms, taking his hands, drawing them under her sweater, cupping them to her breasts. "I love you. That is what."

Their sudden gasps might have been one.

"Then please stop trying to kill me."

"I'm sorry, darling. I could not wait to feel your hands closer to my heart."

He pressed his lips into her hair, his hands gently caressing. "I can feel your heart, Murielle. I can feel your heart beating."

"Beating wildly, darling, for you to stay longer. I will think of you every minute."

He inhaled her fragrance, sliding his hands reluctantly to her bare waist, turning her. "If I must go, which is not at all what I want, at least I have more of you to remember."

She kissed him, pressing a palm to his cheek and opening her door.

When he was midway on the stairway she called his name. He twisted from the hip, praying she had changed her mind, his impossibly loud and guttural groan bringing a wide smirk to Murielle's face. Jackson Belmont, Jr. was hers. She owned him.

Murielle de la Sorbonne was standing enticingly backlit in her doorway; her skirt was gone. Her legs were crossed at her ankles, slender hands hugging her sides, bunching her sweater into mesmerizing folds under her breasts.

"I never wear tights, Jackson. Or very much else. I thought you should know. Goodnight, darling."

She blew a kiss scented with her sweet breath, letting the sweater freefall to her waist. With a mischievous twirl she strutted into her condo.

Inside she leaned against the door, smiling contentedly. She was pleased with her evening, the ice cream an unintended mishap, not believing for a moment that he was actually dying on the stairs.

21

Sunday Murielle slept in, Jackson and Anthony blindly crossing each other's path behind her closed eyes, each one adoring her. One treasuring each heated breath and spasm until he would see her and love her again; the other cherishing his final glimpse of her, committing to memory the warm swell of her breasts, the flawless symmetry of her near-naked body.

She spoke with Anthony several times prior to his Sunday flight to the Swamp, telling him on the Saturday of her Christmas Party and how she was excited about modelling her Northern Christmas wardrobe for him. She missed him. She was fully recovered from her surgeries and the work on her condo was finally complete.

That he decided to stay at the Sheraton on Canal Street rather than in the Quarter made sense to both of them since she worked long hours and he often entertained after-hours. The hotel was a short walk from Gilmore, meaning she could spend most evenings with him without staying over. She rose weekdays at 5:30 doing an hour in her gym, perusing files with her morning coffee and toast before dressing and getting to the office by 7:30.The mornings would simply be too hectic without any time for each other, although their evenings would be wonderful. That said, he was very definitely invited to dinner on the ninth and he would stay over. No excuses.

However she spoke with Jackson almost every evening except the next Saturday when she worked all day and late into the night, going straight home to bed, waking to a day of housework and gym time. Sundays were always for her, she told him, for pampering and personal maintenance, whether in the New Year he would spend them with her or not.

Speaking with him on the Friday before the party Jackson asked what time he was expected. Dinner was at eight, cocktails from seven o'clock, Murielle suggesting cocktails at her place first at six. She wanted time alone with him before sharing him with her Friday Research Sisterhood, while she finished dressing, while he put away the clothes he would wear on Sunday and helped her with her zipper.

Then she asked him to wait, someone was at her door.

He said, "I hope you like the colour. You did say green was your favourite."

She scurried first to the window. She wasn't expecting anyone, certainly not a Belmont Tailors van. At the intercom, buzzing the door open, she asked what was being delivered. The voice replied, "A green ten-speed for Miss de la Sorbonne from Jackson Belmont, Jr., ma'am."

By the time she remembered the phone Jackson was boarding his return flight feeling good.

*

Saturday she woke when the morning's bright sun gave her little choice. She had lots to do before Jackson.

She missed her rigorous workouts at the gym, her trainer's personal attention and being seen. She missed their envy, especially with her body fully restored to its previous flawless state.

The weatherman promised a calm sixty-three-degree day, ideal for a run. Which she didn't do. She never ran.

She saw no point in running, bouncing up-and-down at intersections, stop 'n go, going nowhere and seeing nothing day after day. What was the point of any drop-dead gorgeous woman evoking envy and arousal if she herself wasn't completely aroused?

Instead she pulled on her yellow Lycra halter, matching short shorts, white leg warmers and sneakers that would complement her metallic green ten-speed along the trails of Audubon Park, thinking she would ride by Stonewall's whorehouse on her way home, somehow suspecting that Jackson would not approve of his future fiancée wearing such a scanty outfit while biking with him anytime soon.

That she did understand, for the time being, until he would fully understand her. Nevertheless she would have her private balcony throughout the summer. As for European beaches, the French and Latin Caribbean during their exotic vacations together, he would simply have to adapt to his girl's phenomenally tight bare ass and her spectacularly perky tits turning the heads of women resenting her while men of every description would openly desire what was his.

She skipped down her stairway and along the driveway to where the bike was locked. He would learn to deal with it starting near midnight. As much as she was looking forward to the Gilmore Party, she owed poor Jackson an even more special evening.

She hadn't biked since her childhood, cycling more on sidewalks than reserved lanes until reaching Audubon Park where she dismounted, adjusting her shorts to achieve the desired balance of comfort and tasteful sexual appeal.

She passed serious runners and clumsy joggers, often standing on the pedals to cruise short distances beyond them, certain they weren't puking. Her fellow cyclists passing her were smiling approvingly and waving, all of them fit, many of them giving her a thumbs-up that she acknowledged with her own bright smile. She was in her element. She was hooked, committed to adding Saturday mornings and yellow Lycra to her workout regimen. That morning however she added a yellow cap with a long curved bill to her outfit after twisting her hair into something nameless and playful.

She rode for an hour before leaving the park, returning partway home along safer sidewalks until stopping a block from his condo, locking her bike to a lamppost.

He would always stay over Friday and Saturday, frequently on week nights with little or no notice. He would take her to fine dinners twice weekly when he would dine with personalized cutlery, though he never once allowed her to choose the restaurant or cuisine.

He never expected or wanted her to do his laundry, never once asking her. Always leaving her late Sunday afternoon, taking with him a suitcase of clothing he would later have laundered and delivered to his downtown office or wherever else he might live. What he did insist upon was a clean pillowcase and sheets each night and that his condo be maintained spotlessly clean, which meant she was never to invite her college friends into his home.

He showered in the mornings and at night, never once sliding into her body without a thin sleeve of latex between them. The first time she stood naked before him, her arms outstretched, twirling, he tore the birth control patch from her hip: something the college jocks who made it that far never cared about, something her professors never saw or thought to ask about. Not when all any of them wanted or needed was spontaneous relief, her tight pussy instead of a limp dick in a soft hand.

But Kenneth was different. He was attentive, taking his time exploring her and probing her. He taught her what no university ever could. Until he threw her away, believing he could possibly replace her for another twelve months with some other girl he would mould into a privileged and personal whore. He taught her refinement and elegance, spoiling her with trendy designer fashions, jewellery and alluring lingerie, exotic trips at Christmas, Spring Break and too many spa days to remember. He introduced her to a lifestyle she could never and would never give up.

She walked the full length of the block in both directions while she imagined he was inside getting laid. She squirmed onto her saddle, propping her weight against the lamppost where she was protected by trees and shadows, more curious about the girl than Stonewall.

Several random thoughts later a faint shudder jolted her when unexpectedly the girl she was hoping to see stepped onto the walkway from the building's entrance with Stonewall behind her, walking with him to the midnight blue Bentley.

Suddenly she felt completely consumed by hatred. Stonewall hadn't changed; she hadn't expected him to, ever the consummate gentleman and dressed for a pleasant fall day of golf.

The girl with him was her age, plus or minus a year, as tall albeit slimmer, and pale as a ghost. All white women were pale in the Swamp, blaming the blistering heat of summer as an excuse to sequester themselves from the sun.

He put a hand to her shoulder shooing her away as though he were her father and not the whore's master. Stonewall never displayed affection in public, never called her anything other than Murielle in private or 'my dear'. His sole idea of romance necessitated her being on him, under him, or in front of him. Everything else was about appearance. He had taught her that much, that outward appearance is the cosmetic of internal flaws, and she was an

A student.

Before the car started moving Murielle was on her feet, coating her arms and her legs with water, hurrying to dribble what was left across her back and into her already show-all shorts. Cause and effect. Cause: Getting herself practically naked in public, for him. Effect: Him drooling as he passed by, craving her, his sick mind reviving someone lost to him, someone practically her twin. And good for anyone else who might see her and crave her. Right place, right time. Even better if they might see her again.

Though whether Stonewall might ever see his most beautiful and vibrant whore again was irrelevant. She would definitely see him many more times. She would never forget or forgive, a de la Sorbonne trait instantly instilled in her with blunt force trauma seventeen months earlier when her mother stood by and did nothing.

As he came closer she faced away. She bent deliberately forward with hands planted on her hips, raising and lowering her torso in slow motion, stretching, letting her dampened shorts freely accentuate the curves of her cheeks and taut legs. When he was gone, after slowing to an expected near stop, she stood straight and snickered. The man was a predator, a sexual marauder continuously on the prowl for his next unwary victim.

Climbing onto her bike she pedalled toward the girl, needing to satisfy her curiosity, needing to see for herself what Stonewall believed was more beautiful and unique than her.

She had to be kidding. She was wearing grey three-quarter tights over full briefs that she might as well have worn on the outside, a loose off-the-shoulder grey tee-shirt concealing a breast-compressing sports bra, florescent runners and a black fanny pack. Her black hair was in a tail, swishing from side to side. She was speed walking, something Murielle believed was the primary sport of blue-haired seniors in malls doing what little they could to delay the inevitable.

Murielle pedalled farther on, stopping, planting her feet on the ground, abruptly glancing over her shoulder and smiling. The girl's eyes were glued to her wet shorts, visibly appalled. Stonewall's whore was a prissy bitch, a skinny prissy bitch. She reached for the bottle. Empty.

"Hi there. I'm Brenda. Any idea where I can get a refill around here? I got such a sweat on I had to douse myself. Now I'm dying of thirst. Go figure."

No shit! She was speed walking on the spot. Hips gone wild, her elbows moving like pistons, possibly in the hope of pumping up her flat tits.

"Well you really should have sipped first, and poured a little on your wrists. That's the smart way. There is a corner store several blocks down. But dressed like that, I don't know. Good luck with that."

"Yeah, I know. Kind of wet. Tell you what, though. I'll get a shitload better service by showing my bare wet ass than you will in that outfit. Including from your slavering father. When he saw me I was surprised he didn't crash through his window to do me on the spot. He certainly wanted to. Big time. And I can't say I would blame him. You look ridiculous. Any chance you come from Nebraska?"

She stopped. "Fuck you. That was my boyfriend."

Murielle's laugh was hysterical and guttural. "Get real. He is no one's boyfriend. He's Kenneth Stonewall. He's forty-two, not whatever he told you, and you're his current whore. It's what he does. You've got seven months left on your knees to earn whatever you negotiated with him. You're going to the Bahamas in a few weeks for Christmas and somewhere south in the spring because he has a sick penchant for nubile T and A." She glanced at the girl's chest. "This year in particular, I suppose. Then you'll be gone and he won't give a good shit. He's probably cheating on you as we speak, interviewing much prettier mid-term replacements. Because really, you are not his type. You are definitely gone. So get real. If I were you I would lose the old-lady briefs pronto and start wetting my pants instead of my wrists."

"Who are you anyway, apart from a complete bitch?"

"I'm you, just infinitely better." She raised a foot onto a pedal, smirking. "One word of good advice, do not go fucking any pizza boys or anyone else before he's finished with you. The entire condo is wired 24/7. He likes to watch and he's got you for a lifetime. So yeah, good luck with that."

Murielle pedalled away, humming. At home she stored her bike, did an hour in her gym, laid out her ensemble for the evening and fixed a quick lunch thinking she might visit the prissy bitch again on June 30th to compare notes.

She did her laundry while she bathed and pampered herself. She put fresh linen on her bed and made space in her walk-in for Jackson.

22

Jackson arrived at 6:00 sharp, Murielle opening her door to an impressive Southern gentleman dressed in a black Belmont single-breasted accented with a silver pocket hanky and white boutonnière. He complemented his silvery-grey shirt with a darker silvery tie, emphasizing the French cuffs with discreet black pearl studs.

His green eyes sparkled. "This feels very strange standing here without a bellhop assisting me to my suite, Murielle." He passed her a clear plastic box wrapped in white ribbons, dropping his over-nighter. "A corsage for the lady."

"Thank you, darling. You can help me with it later. I must say, you are very debonair this evening. Très élégant, monsieur."

"And you are *the* most delightful vision, Murielle. I love your gown. Asian-inspired, I believe."

"That is not funny, monsieur." She closed the door. "I won't sit in my dress until we're in the car. The thing cost me a fortune." She kissed him. "Thank you for my bike, Jackson. I rode to the park this morning. I felt wonderful. Thank you."

"I dusted the cobwebs from mine also, hoping you might need a security detail at some point."

She sighed. "Believe me, Jackson. No one was paying attention."

He examined her with a critical eye from head to toe, his cheeks pinched into a grin. Fearing a severe backlash, he chose not to call her a liar. "No. Obviously not. I can see why."

"What!" She punched him, pointing to her bedroom. "Go, before I really hurt you. I made a place for you in my closet. I'll prepare our cocktails."

When he came in she was sitting on his favourite sofa in her silk robe, her ear lobes and neck glittering with ruby studs and a delicate ruby pendant. She was patting the space beside her, her crossed legs alluringly bare to her mid-thighs shimmering in nude stockings, a three-inch evening pump dangling from a small foot keeping time to her mood. He draped his suitcoat over an accent seat, joining her.

"So, I'm thinking those aren't tights."

"You know they are not, darling. Something much nicer." She put a hand on his thigh. "I missed you, Jackson. Very much."

"I had a pretty rough couple of weeks myself because of you. Something to do with you not wearing tights."

"That's right, I don't. I'm a stocking and garter girl. When did you ever fantasize over removing a woman's pantyhose? Or her tights for that matter? Not once in your life. Am I correct, monsieur?"

"Pretty much."

She paused, pensively.

"What?"

"Please tell me you do not wear cotton boxers."

"I do not." He sipped his Blue. "No boxers, no cargos or briefs. I'm a square cut guy, in Italian."

"And pyjamas?"

"Not even from the Belmont collection. Three-quarter silk robes. One of which is hanging in your closet."

"Thank you."

She blew a long breath, showing relief, pressing a palm to her chest. Then without warning his Rolex read 6:30. Murielle put down her glass, moving to stand, Jackson at once springing to his feet, taking her hand.

"I should touch up my makeup and put on my dress, Jackson. Or we'll be late. You stay here and finish your cocktail. I won't be long."

"Won't you need help with your zipper? I can do that."

She patted his cheek. "Not after almost killing you on my stairs, darling. Seeing me in stockings and very little panties is far too dangerous for you. Besides, how would I explain walking into the party unescorted after all I've told them?"

"I'm stronger now. Truly, I am. You made me stronger."

She thought for a moment. "Well if that's true, I will call you when I need you. At your own risk."

She sauntered away, loosening her robe, letting the silk ties dangle at her sides. Fifteen minutes later she called his name, not surprised that he came quickly into her bedroom, not surprised that he stumbled to a stop as she was bending slightly forward ready to pull her ruby-red and sequin party dress with a bustier top and mid-thigh flared skirt from her knees to her waist.

"Jackson, I didn't mean that you should run." She glanced over her shoulder, demurely, pulling the dress inches higher and waiting. Her garter and the narrow ribbons clasped to her stockings were red satin, the matching red panties framing the most incredible ass he had ever seen in his entire life were high-rise and sheer. "Please close your mouth, darling, and say something appropriate. I'm feeling a little undressed and awkward standing here."

"If I were an artist, I would recreate you on canvas; were I a sculptor, I would immortalize each magnificent detail for my eyes alone until my cruel death would steal you from me."

"You die quite often, darling, for such a handsome man." She faced away, pulling her skirt to her waist. "I didn't want you seeing this much of me until after the party, Jackson. But since you have, come help me."

She wrapped her torso into the bodice, cupping her breasts while Jackson aligned the back, zipping her in when he was certain the chain was properly aligned and the slider would work without the least chance of pinching her or sticking.

"All done."

"Are you certain? You don't want another five minutes?" She twirled, facing him, framing his cheeks with her palms. "I'm nervous about after the party, Jackson. Yet I am also so anxious to share my body and my heart with you. Because of that, because I want to love you completely, perhaps I will undress myself."

She twirled, letting him follow her into the living room, shaking her head and lustrous scrunched curls at his assurances that he would work much more quickly and skillfully at undressing the most stunning lady at the party. She let him adorn her wrist with the corsage, letting him drape her deep-red wrap across her bared shoulders. He hooked a thumb into the inner collar tab of his suitcoat, swinging it over his shoulder and they left.

At the hotel the doorman went to the lady's door as the valet went to the gentleman's side, catching the keys mid-air, Jackson properly attired by the time Murielle took his arm. Inside the hatcheck girl took her wrap, drooling over her gown and her man.

A moment later Jackson faced the Friday afternoon stampeding herd.

"Here they come, Jackson. Just a little FYI. I kind of told them you're head-over-heels in love with me. You're also an awesome lover, which wasn't really a lie."

"Good to know, mi amor. Because I am head-over-heals in love with you...actually."

"Yeah, and we also had a spa weekend in Biloxi. Sorry."

"Then we did. And we will for Valentine's unless you discover I am not an awesome lover."

They circled him, walking around him, assessing him. They patted his suit, examined the knot in his tie and his shoes. They examined his hands, taking turns at squeezing his biceps. His wavy blond hair was gorgeous, his lightly tanned skin smooth and flawless, his to-die-for eyes telling them at once how he adored Murielle.

Cerise dared to lift his upper lip from his good-natured smile, not surprised to find perfect white teeth, asking Murielle, "Okay, so what is wrong with him? Does he come with a motor, or what? Six toes?"

"Girls, leave him alone. You're scaring him."

Cerise countering, "Okay. But I get the first dance after you, Mur. I've got seniority."

Vicky added, "And I'm next. But does he talk at all, or just grin a lot?"

Shelly burst in, "Talking? Who cares about talking?" She looked straight into his eyes. "God, he must be so totally..."

"He is, Shelly. Very totally."

Valerie asked, "Does he have a brother, Mur?" She heaved a melodramatic sigh, hunching her shoulders. "I'm solo tonight. I finally dumped the village idiot. The jerk came to my door in a rental and sneakers. Daddy threw him out."

"Very commendable of your father, Miss Valerie. In which case I'm certain Murielle will allow me the honour of dividing my devoted attentions between the two of you this evening," Jackson told her. "Unless of course some worthy gentleman intends otherwise. I cannot for a moment imagine you not capturing some man's heart. You and Miss Shelly, Miss Vicky and Miss Cerise are breathtakingly stunning this evening, a veritable palette of Southern beauty and charm."

Murielle gaped. What the hell! He knew each girl's name.

"Murielle has told me…well, almost everything about you ladies. I'm delighted to finally meet each of you in person." He took Murielle's and Valerie's arms. "However perhaps now we should join your dates at our table."

Once there, assisting Murielle and Cerise into their seats, he introduced himself first to Cerise's date and the other two gentlemen, excusing himself for a brief moment.

The junior researchers were seated together with an anticipated ten guests, Dumb and Dumber assigned seating at a singles table with the other less fortunate. In fact, by 7:30 they still hadn't arrived. When they did appear fifteen minutes later, the five girls were visibly dumbstruck watching them come closer. Dumb strode directly toward Valerie, Dumber pausing to acknowledge the girls before moving on.

Murielle immediately jabbed Jackson with a disbelieving "No!" She was familiar enough with Belmont to recognize the brand.

"The blends and styling do seem familiar, mi amor. I must ask them."

"Good evening, Valerie. You're very lovely this evening. I hope that later we can maybe dance. You know, if you want."

She didn't answer, shamelessly studying him, dissecting him in equal parts. Then, "Whoever you are, what have you done with Everett?"

Murielle jabbed Jackson in the ribs again, this time with

a curt nod. He got the message.

Everett's unkempt hair was gone, replaced by a stylish comb-back. His shoes were Italian leather, his suit a dark blue Belmont with a Belmont shirt, French cuffs, links, silk tie, silk pocket hanky and belt. The works.

Jackson stood. "Good evening, Everett. I'm Jackson Belmont. Apparently Miss Valerie's date received some unwelcome news recently that precludes his joining us this evening. That being the case, and with Miss Valerie's permission of course, perhaps you would consider changing your seating assignment to complete and complement our table. I'm sure Quintin will find his own way this evening."

"Valerie?" Everett ventured.

She looked to her protector. "Jackson, you won't mind?"

"A gentleman must first and foremost consider the wishes of a lady, Miss Valerie. I will, however, maintain a close eye on the fellow."

"Thank you, Jackson." She turned to Everett. "Yes, you may join us."

Cerise adding, "I'm watching you too, Everett."

Dinner was an epicurean delight, the wine selection superb, and Everett didn't once spill food or wine from his mouth. After dancing through several songs with Valerie he even dared to invite Cerise to dance, returning her to her date when the song ended.

Jackson danced with each girl according to their earlier ranking, the first dance of the evening belonging to Murielle who was the star attraction, everyone from every floor soon realizing her stylish escort was the Belmont of Belmont Tailors.

"Darling, I believe you are keeping things from me, important things. Lovers should never do that."

"I don't understand, mi amor."

"Mi amor, hmmm. I think I like mi amor, darling. Murielle was beginning to sound like Miss despite your charming Southern drawl." She put her cheek to his. "Now what did you do?"

"Regarding what exactly?"

"Regarding two millennials living at home, both wearing exclusive Belmont suits."

"Oh, that. Quite the coincidence really. Everett and Quintin happened into Belmont one Saturday interested in a current style for an upcoming Christmas party. Quintin mentioned something about Everett needing to impress a girl, a Valerie. I simply connected the dots. I remembered you mentioning an Everett and a Valerie at work. Et voilà."

"No, no. There is no et voilà here. No. Together they couldn't afford a pair of your Belmont socks. You phoned them, didn't you? You called them at the office, didn't you? After our dinner at home, you called them. That's why they were acting weird with me all week. That's where you were last Saturday, doing your charity work."

"Not charity by any means. An equitable arrangement between gentlemen."

"That's why they didn't join the girls yesterday. They went to Belmont for the other stuff and a final fitting."

"Not stuff, mi amor. Accessories, please. And you must believe me, your suspicions are entirely unfounded."

"Suspicions? Really, darling? That's why you left us. That's why Everett marched right over to her empty seat." She twirled away and into his arms. "Good evening, Everett," she mimicked, managing a passable imitation. "I'm Jackson Belmont." She put her arms around his neck. "You are too much, my darling. No wonder I love you."

The oldsters in their forties and fifties left as early as good manners permitted once the music became unbearable to more refined ears. Then as the evening began winding down on the morning side of midnight the younger guests began slowly filtering out. Jackson and Murielle were amongst the first, both Everett with Valerie and Quintin with his ad hoc date calling out to them.

The three men shook hands. Murielle and Valerie hugged and kissed.

Then Valerie went to Jackson, hugging him, whispering close to his ear. "I'm not making any promises here, Jackson. We'll see where this goes, and thank you. I couldn't help peeking inside his jacket. You did this for me."

"Purely a happy coincidence, Miss Valerie. I give you my solemn word as a gentleman. You must realize that when we as gentlemen covet a rare jewel, as I believe our mutual acquaintance does, we do what we must to put all in our favour." He kissed her hand. "More importantly, your glow is radiant."

Throughout the ride home nothing more was mentioned of what might or might not have transpired behind the intimidating brass doors of Belmont Tailors, Jackson refusing to look at her. Murielle, curled into her seat, was determined to stare silently at him until he crumpled under pressure and confessed.

Once at home Murielle dropped her wrap onto a seat, guiding Jackson's suitcoat from his shoulders. She tugged the 100-dollar strip of silk from his neck and unbuttoned his collar, staring into his eyes, persisting.

"The subject is closed, mi amor." He put a finger to her lips. "Gentlemen do not accept charity. We agree on reasonable terms and shake hands. Enough said."

She sighed, defeated. "Then pour us a nightcap, darling. I want to sit quietly with you before going to bed. I want to savour every precious moment with you. I've waited a very long time for this evening, for you. Before Gilmore called I was ready to join a frigging convent."

She ignited the fake flames, kicking off her shoes and easing onto the sofa, enjoying the muted hum of the fireplace.

"Everything's possible, I suppose. Dressing for morning devotions in garters and stockings certainly works for me in a big way." He passed her a snifter. "You know, Mardi Gras isn't far off. Could be a theme for another Gilmore party."

"The virgin and Brother Belmont. You're making jokes and I'm sitting here worried about you seeing me naked in the morning."

"While I can't wait for the sun to rise, illuminating you." He sat with her, resting a reassuring hand on her knee. "On that note, mi amor, I am in perfect health. No bed bugs one might say, if that's a concern. Though I did think to bring…"

"All that worries me is becoming a good lover for you." She sipped her Armagnac, gazing into her lap. "Whatever you brought, Jackson, please don't bother. I don't want anything between us."

"You went to your doctor, Murielle. Good."

She inhaled a deep breath, resting a delicate hand over his. "I did, last week. Just not for that, and maybe not so good for us. The truth is, Jackson, I can never have children. I can never give you a baby. I went through a female procedure when I was a teenager in France and something went terribly wrong. An unfortunate complication that was no one's fault. The thing is, surgery was required to save me. The decision was my parents'." She shrugged. "Long story short: No kids. Not ever. I suppose sometimes things happen without much reason." She cupped a hand against his cheek, searching his eyes for the slightest disappointment or sadness. "I had no reason to tell you until this evening, Jackson, because having kids was never a thing for me. I always knew I wanted a career." She put down her glass. "Is making another Belmont a big thing for you, Jackson?"

He didn't hesitate, hugging her closer. "No, mi amor. Not with my lifestyle. My big thing is Belmont while I'm alive and having someone to share my life with. When I'm gone I'm sure Belmont will go with me. I wasn't raised to think family. The truth is I never wanted children, particularly now when I see twenties and thirties still living at home. I wasn't raised that way. The day I graduated I was gone. Not quite here, but I was gone. On my own. Nor would Belmont ever engage such a person. Our clients deserve the highest integrity. Of course, mi amor, I would have modified my thinking for you, though really the world is already sufficiently populated and the much greater blessing is having you to myself."

"You're certain?"

"I am very certain."

She shifted, straddling his legs. "In that case I am AMA approved for heart-pounding sex, which by the way came with an excruciating lecture on the demerits of informal acquaintances. I believe that's how he put it." She put her forehead to his. "Are you informal, darling?"

"Well I suggest we find out, Miss de la Sorbonne."

He put aside his glass, heaving their weight from the cushions, carrying her to the bedroom where Murielle did not turn on the lights. Instead she stayed straddling his waist and clinging to his neck until she opened her blinds to accommodate the early morning sun.

Jackson gently eased her to the floor by her bed, kissing her, facing her away, trailing his fingers from her shoulders to her elbows to her hands that he brought to her breasts, making certain they were firmly affixed before sweeping away her hair and kissing her neck. He freed the slender slider at her zipper from the edges of her dress, sliding it effortlessly and wordlessly to below her waist, sliding his hands between the warm silk lining and her soft, smooth flesh, pushing down gently.

Kneeling, he guided the dress to her knees, planting his hands at her waist so that she might step one foot then the other from the satin heap. He palmed her bare back as though committing each inch to memory, caressing the length of her legs to her ankles with tender pressure, his fingertips inching their way between her legs with deliberate and titillating care to the bare flesh between her stockings and the irresistible heat emanating from the narrow and moist swath of satin.

He pressed his cheek into the soft mounds, believing her ass more spectacular than any he had ever come across in his frequent travels, pressing a kiss into one and then the other. He freed the back of one stocking from its clasp, then the other, working blindly to free the front clasps. He unhooked the satin belt, inhaling its scent, dropping it to the floor.

Standing, he went in front of her, holding out her arms, his eyes devouring her. He cupped one breast, pressing his lips into the unique softness. Her reaction was immediate, her guttural squeal heightening the pleasure of the pale caramel nipple growing taut between his lips. He kissed her mouth, her chin and her neck, trailing more kisses to her other breast cupped in a warm palm, that pale crown at once erect, Murielle wrapping her arms around his neck not wanting the wonderfully unfamiliar sensation to stop.

They kissed eagerly in a feverish embrace, their lips and their faces smeared with crimson gloss, lost in separate deliriums.

Her moans were sensual and arousing, her breathing hard and sweet, shrieking when without warning he swept her feet from the floor, his hands firmly grasping the soft mounds still fresh in his mind.

He laid her effortlessly onto the duvet, standing back to absorb all of her in the dim light. Kneeling, he encircled a stockinged leg in his hands, pushing forward, squeezing lightly until once more he felt the warmth of bare flesh, pressing the edge of his hand again into moist satin.

He tucked his fingers under her stocking's lace, pulling the silk away and onto the floor, placing her bare leg over his shoulder. Her other stocking came away no less attentively, that leg raised and lowered onto his other shoulder.

Her legs were smooth, scented with cream. He caressed them to her knees, leaning forward. He braced his arms against the bed, raising her weight from the downy cover, trailing kisses from one inner thigh to the other and across her panties, inhaling the pungent fragrance.

She was in a place far away, her lips pursed. She was purring, her delicate and attentive hands temporarily barring access to her breasts.

He pressed his cheek into her heaving belly, content to retrace his kisses past her perfumery of corporeal and cosmetic fragrances, not content to wait. Planting his knees under her, he tucked his fingers under her panties, tugging them to her knees, raising her legs into the air, pulling them past her feet and onto the floor. Lowering her legs, framing his body with them, he sat there mesmerized.

Her eyes were shut tight. "What?" Nothing. "What, Jackson? Don't be cruel. I'm kind of really vulnerable here, in case you haven't noticed." She squirmed. "I'm not opening my eyes until you say something, Jackson."

"Good. You stay exactly as you are because I am noticing. Really noticing. I'll never see you like this for the first time again. So don't do a thing to spoil my moment.

Just lay there and be noticed."

She obeyed, her closed eyes intensifying every sensation. She felt her body lower, the coolness of the duvet, his slacks and the strength of his legs moving away, his palms gliding from her belly to her thighs to her feet.

All that moved were her breasts, heaved by a pounding heart.

She heard the rustling of his shirt torn from his slacks and his arms, the swoosh as he whipped it into the air. She heard the tip of his belt yanked from its buckle, his slacks guided to his knees, each leg freed in turn, the flutter of them as he straightened them and laid them on her chair. She heard his muted groan as he pulled first one then his other executive sock from his feet.

She pictured him standing at her feet, in Italian silk, consuming her delicious body, titillating and teasing her.

She was nervous, too exhilarated to speak, her throaty voice trembling. "I am so happy, darling, that no one has ever been where you are now." She gulped air. "Say something. Please tell me you like what you see."

"Shhh, mi amor. No words. Words are for the morning."

She didn't want to speak, her body eager for his; her mind crowded with men and boys past and present vying for attention. She was enumerating, trying to remember them all.

The pimple-faced kid often on her bed from Easter through to the close of grade ten did everything to bruise her, nothing at all to arouse her, leaving more on her than in, and he never came back. The one who followed her into grade eleven wasn't much better when a toilet or Kleenex would have served the same purpose.

The guy from Christmas to her graduation that year was the best. He wanted her naked to see and grope all of her. Six months of sex for fun. Something to do. If not her body, someone else's. None of them once telling her how beautiful her body was.

Her first, second and third in college, each one an all-star braindead jock, brought her more status than desire: matter-of-fact social sex with the hottest girl on campus when not putting herself out there would have singled out even her as peculiar. Not one of them enduring through the first week of those summers when she did whatever she could while interning to ensure a promising future. Not one of them paid off, their promises all lies; working for nothing while letting them strip her, fondle and do her like adolescents in closet-size offices Fridays before going home to their wives.

The other four professors throughout those years were different, each of them an excellent investment. She had no interest in Macroeconomics, Ethics or Sports in Communications, least of all her time wasted in Children and Youth Culture. The four were easy and they were married, too burdened with wives and kids to afford hotel rooms when keys to their offices and lecture halls worked just as well.

Of course they each wanted to see her naked, which she did for them occasionally when time allowed between classes, something to remember and arouse them when making the best of their tired women at home. That she understood, beyond which sex with them was as lacklustre as their lectures, most times bent over a desk with her skirt up over her back and her panties off or missing.

Then came Stonewall as she commenced her fourth year with two other professors readily disposed to ensure her impressive grades in Grass Roots and Myths. Men in their middle and late fifties no better or worse than her younger professors, though eager to see her naked more often while bending her over a table or desk for expediency, which she agreed was quite fine.

Stonewall treated her well, nearly convincing her that sex could be good, until the day he truly screwed her over. Then Zach the all-star tripping his way onto her bed because he had never seen anything as exotic and spectacular; then the janitor and the Todd guy, until by some long-deserved miracle Anthony came to teach her the meaning of volatile, insatiable sex that had left her practically debilitated and needing more.

Now Jackson was savouring her, exploring her, crawling naked between her legs. He was easing his hands under her bum, raising her hips, bringing the most secret part of her to his mouth as she brought her hands from her breasts, locking her fingers into his wavy blond hair, expelling a sweet gasp at his first daring and wonderfully intimate touch.

His warm lips kissed her soft folds with tender pecks, brushing them into her pungent wetness, tasting her, inhaling her, the tip of his tongue penetrating her, exploring and probing her seconds before her eyes flashed open. Her shriek was loud and piercing, the violent spasm racking and twisting her body from his comforting hands as though he had sent a million electrifying volts surging through her.

He put a fingertip to her lips, kissing her mouth, her cheeks and her nose, intoxicating her with her own bittersweet nectar.

He braced his taut arms again on the bed, staring into her dark eyes. He wasn't smiling or smirking; he was searching. He was asking if she was ready, if she was certain. She was. God she was, nodding her head deeper into her pillow, sliding her hands tentatively from his bare hips to his buttocks, impudently pulling him closer.

He went into her easily, deliberately, not wanting to hurt her, kissing the wetness from her imploring eyes. His rhythm was unhurried, the tempo gradually reaching a crescendo in sync with the pressure of slender fingers digging into his buttocks and back, her happy tears and sensual whimpers, the reek of their combined sweat puddling between them. Until, as though instructed by some invisible director, they shuddered and convulsed together, their mouths too numb to kiss.

He rolled onto his side, onto his back, smiling at her quiet tears and heaving breasts. "What, señorita? Not good enough?" he asked, fairly certain he had surpassed all previous and restricted records.

She struggled to prop herself onto an elbow, squirming and groaning, breathless and soaked with sweat. She couldn't imagine any twenty-second being any more outstanding or even necessary. Not with Anthony and Jackson so skilfully attentive and passionately in love with her.

"No, darling. I mean yes, very yes." She was breathless, panting, thick strands of auburn hair plastering her face. "I guess. I mean, I don't know. How would I? I've only ever had doctors in there," she answered. "It's just that…"

"Just what, mi amor?"

"Well, it's just that I love you. I do, but is that all. Somehow I thought we'd be making love until morning. I am definitely tingling inside and my heart's threatening to explode, but if you really need rest I suppose that's alright. Honestly though, how can you turn me into such a complete mess, get me all excited, and not expect me to keep going on my own? I was kind of hoping those sad days were over." She filled her lungs, expelling a long and sorrowful sigh. "It's no big deal. I really don't mind. Particularly since I'm naked and, you know, hot." She patted his cheek. "Goodnight, darling."

He chortled, reaching for her. "I was being a gentleman,

giving the lady repose."

"Then please stop being a gentleman. This lady has reposed long enough."

23

As the sun rose Murielle padded to her en suite. She showered away their sweat, towelled her body dry and stood relishing the lure and symmetry of her reflection: her curtain of dark hair, her flawless face and disarming eyes, her perfectly shaped breasts and sculpted belly, her slim waist and hips, her delicate folds too rosy and tender to deny recent and persistent use, her toned legs and her delectably smooth ass he hadn't stopped kissing and caressing until collapsing into a comatose sleep.

She wrapped her head in a fleecy turban, her body in a silk kimono, and went to make coffee, smiling at Jackson wandering alone in a world of dreams far away from the sun illuminating her radiant body.

On her balcony she stretched out on a cushioned chaise-longue reliving their night, absorbing the warmth of a balmy sixty-five degrees, dreamily musing that her favourite numbers going forward into a welcoming future were twenty and twenty-one. What would her dear papa think about that? Not that she cared.

Anthony was slightly more muscular and conditioned, an incredible lover. He was educated and travelled, an industrial consultant and essentially a bachelor 1400 miles away. If not for that he was Jackson in a less expensive suit. Jackson was Anthony in a slimmer body; he was CEO of a successful company and wealthy. He was genteel and gentle, as good in bed as he was good-looking, and he adored her. He could drive to her home in twenty minutes, and probably less now that he fully understood what was waiting there for him.

She swung her feet onto the tiles, loosening her robe, pushing herself to her feet, squirting lotion into her hand. She raised one foot to the chaise-longue, coating that side of her bum and her leg to her foot, then the other with more lotion. She moisturised her hips, her waist and her belly, quietly moaning, enjoying the soothing warmth of her hands pressing lightly into her reddened lips. She massaged her breasts and her shoulders, unravelling the turban, dropping it onto the lounger, combing her hair into straight filaments catching the light…and gasping.

"You must be an angel, mi amor. I have never seen anyone or anything as heavenly."

He was leaning against the doorframe, dressed in dark blue straightbacks, beaming.

"Thank you, darling." She threw the towel at him. "How long have you been standing there spying and smirking?"

"In minutes, don't know. In body parts, pretty well everything. Is this a morning ritual, mi amor? Because if that's the case, I am definitely moving in."

"My weekend and summer ritual, darling, and very private as you can see. I told you, I don't wear very much at home and I hate tan lines."

She reached for her robe. Not for modesty; she simply wasn't risking the unlikely possibility that he might become immune to any part of her, taking her for granted.

"Are you okay this morning? No damage, no regrets?"

"Yes damage, lots of damage which is completely your fault, monsieur. Though no regrets and you're officially invited anytime."

"Good. What's for dinner?"

"Pizza with a bottle of Château Capet-Guillier Saint-Émilion Grand Cru. Then I'm sending you home." She patted his cheek. "Don't pout, darling. I have an early day tomorrow."

"Capet-Guillier with pizza?"

"No. With my lover. We're celebrating my long overdue enlightenment. Then you're going home and we'll miss each other until next Sunday. Saturday is a workday for me. Year-end stuff. Sorry."

They made love once in the afternoon, lasting most of the afternoon with long tender strokes, quiet murmurs and kisses. He sat watching her shower while he ordered an all-dressed from a parlour she hadn't yet tried. The last one she ordered was absolutely the worst, she told him.

He towelled her with utmost care, making certain she was completely dry, and sat watching as she pampered her body once more and dressed in a lacy satin baby doll and G-string. In the living room they toasted her remarkable transition from disgruntled virgin to insatiable vixen and lover, talking and listening to Solis while they waited for dinner, Murielle sending him home as flight 1802 from Boston was landing at Louis Armstrong International.

When he was gone she replaced her winter wardrobe from under her bed to the front closet. An hour later her phone chimed.

"You didn't forget me."

"I did not forget you. Are we on for a late dinner?"

"Not this evening, Anthony."

"I'm up to my eyes in campaign notes. Tomorrow, yes. And I'm staying late. For free this time."
*

Monday she went to work early, not surprised to see Everett sitting side-saddle on Valerie's desk. His recently bought slacks were not Belmont but were fitted and pressed, his shirt was ironed and his tie was properly knotted at his collar.

When they noticed her, Valerie sent him to his desk and came over.

"That man of yours is something really special, Mur." She glanced over her shoulder. "Dumb took me to the park yesterday, then to dinner. He and Dumber are getting an apartment together and I'm getting him an iron for Christmas. He's really a nice guy."

"We all kind of knew that, didn't we? Maybe just a little stuck on slow?"

"He's picking up speed. Anyway, they are officially barred from our Friday afternoons because we can't very well talk about them if they're sitting with us. I just informed him. He's okay with it."

"Like he has a choice."

"He's learning that too."

Cerise joined them with Shelly and Vicky. Jackson was absolutely to-die-for. Those eyes! God! Did he stay over? They wanted every detail. Then they noticed Valerie smiling at Everett. All five marched to his desk, Cerise pulling him to his feet by an ear, inspecting him, poking his chest with a rigid finger and threatening to shoot him with her derringer if he ever thought to hurt Valerie or revert to his android state. She would definitely be watching him.

He understood.

Near 6:30 Murielle left with them, explaining she had some shopping to do before going home, leaving them at the bus stop. When she was out of sight, certain they were gone, she crossed Canal and strode into the increasingly familiar Marriott.

They kissed at his door: Rabid and illicit lovers to anyone at Reception monitoring the floor. Not that anyone cared. She certainly wasn't a hooker. Hookers didn't dress in winter white linen slacks, blue tailored blazers or low-heeled pumps. Nor would even the highest-priced escort deem to put her reserved and private mouth on a client's.

Once inside he poured a JW Black and Silent Sam, the way he remembered. "Two-fingers deep with a splash of soda for the lady." He stepped back, taking her in. "Nice outfit, very nice. Very chic, very executive looking."

"Thank you, Anthony. Not the same girl you helped with 600 dollars." She reached into her handbag, putting an envelope on his suitcase. "Six-hundred in crisp fifties. Repaid in full."

"No. That is not necessary, sweetcheeks."

"Yeah, it kind of really is."

He acquiesced, dropping the envelope into his attaché. The lady had pride.

"You are not at all the same girl, Miss Dupree. You look wonderful."

"I feel wonderful."

"Good, because we're eating out." He never ate hotel food in the South unless faced with driving rain or wind. "I've reserved a romantic table at Angelo's. It's top end. Know it?"

Shit! "Yes I know it," she snarled, Anthony taking another step back.

"Oookay. So now I'm thinking, hmmm, not such a good idea. That I might want to cancel. Is that about right?"

"The woman who runs the place is a complete bitch. I went there a few days before I met you, asking for part-time work as a waitress. Guess why, and guess what? So yes, please do cancel."

He did, reserving a table in the hotel dining room, learning during dessert that 'sweetcheeks' was cute when they were alone, when they were all sweaty and hot, which was moments away. However when they were out

225

'sweetheart' would convey the same sentiment.

She left him close to midnight, freshly showered for the morning. If she wasn't a whore she had no desire to smell like one. And thus went her week, speaking with Jackson each evening before leaving her desk, telling the girls not to wait, her supervisor duly noting her commitment to Gilmore.

Tuesday they ordered to the room, Wednesday they went into the Quarter since Jackson had gone to Biloxi for the day and was staying over. Thursday she wanted to try a bistro in Midtown, each night increasingly difficult for them to part.

Friday he understood the Research Group's end-of-the-week review, that she would come to him as quickly as possible after the meeting. The girls wanted to try Angelo's, Murielle not expecting for a moment that she would walk into Jackson and a dozen or more of his staff decompressing after a demanding week.

The men at his cluster of tables all stood, while the Belmont women stared at their boss with gaping mouths. His girlfriend was utterly gorgeous.

Charlee came over with a Silent Sam, a tight hug and kisses, the men helping her make room for their unexpected guests, the seating arrangement becoming a more equitable division of the sexes.

Two hours later she crossed over to the restaurant for dinner with Jackson. Waiting until they ordered, she excused herself to visit the ladies' room. The meeting was running late, she told Anthony, they were ordering in. She felt horrible and would take a taxi to the Marriott the minute the meeting was over. In fact he should check-out and not wait until morning. Why wouldn't he spend Friday and Saturday at her place?

Jackson stood as she came nearer, grinning.

"What?"

"I know a secret."

"Which is?"

"I know how exotic you are naked and glistening. I've added the Cote d'Azur to my bucket list. There must be thousands of you over there."

"What would you possibly do with thousands of me, darling? If I recall, and I do, I believe one of me might be too many."

"Good point."

"A very good point. Especially now that I see the girls at Belmont are exceptionally pretty, darling."

"They have boyfriends, mi amor. Big guys, Navy SEAL-types. Definitely no need to worry."

She put a hand over his. "I missed you this week, and really looking forward to Sunday with you and something tastier than pizza. I'll stop by the store on my way home tomorrow, I've been pretty busy this week."

"Don't bother. We'll do dinner at my place with a view of the Mississippi and the city, tomorrow and Sunday. I'm pretty good in the kitchen and you're way tastier than pizza."

"No, darling. I'll see your place at New Year's when I stay over. Tomorrow I'm doing my laundry, cleaning my home and steaming my dresses. Sunday I'm doing girlie things and cooking for you. You're expected at four and you're staying over."

"Girlie things on the balcony?"

"Yes, girlie things on the balcony."

"Naked and glistening?"

He inhaled a deep breath at her blasé reaction, expelling a mournful sigh. "Perhaps tomorrow I should buy a drone. I think I will."

"Yes, darling, I think you should. And I'll buy cotton

pyjamas and thick socks to wear with my flannel dressing gown and hair curlers."

"Another good point. I'll be over at four with the wine."

The first course was served with a golden Crozes-Hermitage Blanc as they made plans for Christmas. Both Belmont and Gilmore would close on the 22nd and reopen January 02nd. Nobody was interested in expensive menswear or campaigns between Christmas and New Year's.

They were spending the holidays in Vail, somewhere she had never seen. She would learn to ski, drink hot toddies and make love with him by a real fireplace. Most of all she was eager to meet Melinda on the 20th for a pre-holiday dinner, Jackson's mother no less curious about the incredibly wonderful and warm French girl he could not stop talking about.

The entrée was filet mignon drizzled with peppercorn and wine sauce, Jackson selecting a bold red from the Rhône to complete the succulent dish, Murielle entirely rapt throughout the meal listening to his memories of New Year's Eve in Time Square. She could scarcely imagine the fervour and excitement. She had never been to New York. What a wonderful idea for Easter, she thought aloud, declining the waiter's suggestion of dessert. No way, not with Christmas and New Year's coming when she would look her absolute best on the ski slopes and après.

He would be so absolutely proud of her.

He was proud of her, fully expecting that Monday she would be the primary cause of female chatter in the Belmont lunchroom. More importantly, he insisted, he would drive her home. New Orleans cabbies, the ones who weren't off-duty cops, were as bad as the cops. He was taking her home, end of conversation.

At her door he didn't ask, beg, or pout. He kissed her,

waited until she was safely inside, and drove home to a lonely penthouse and a nightcap.

Once in her home Murielle called the Marriott. The VP had insisted on sending her and the other ladies home in taxis, she told him. She couldn't very well tell her boss she was stopping by the hotel to get seriously laid. Could she?

He chuckled. He supposed not.

She gave Anthony her address and precise directions, telling him where he should park. Disconnecting, she steam-cleaned the long day and stressful evening from every sumptuous curve and crevice in a scalding shower, stepping in front of her mirror with a fleecy towel before hurrying to change her satin sheets and dress for him.

Satisfied, she went onto her balcony to help her tousled hair air-dry. When Anthony arrived, stepping from his rental, she called his name, blowing a heated kiss through the pleasantly cool air.

When her intercom buzzed she pressed a fingertip to ENTER. When the heavy footfalls stopped, she opened her door.

"Hi."

"Whoa! Wow! What is this?"

"My winter outfit," she twirled, "for our Christmas together in Boston. And the weather had better be frigging cold and snowy up there, Anthony. My credit card is still recovering from severe shock."

Her fur-trimmed bucket hat was a rich forest-green suede; her matching coat, the collar and cuffs fur-lined in black, fell to below her knees. Her scarf was a thick wool and deep green. Her kid leather gloves were black, sensual to the touch, passing her wrists; her black Cossack low-heeled boots buckled with stainless-steel faux-spurs protecting her to the fur-trimmed bottom of her coat.

"Phenomenal, sweetheart. How can you possibly be

lovelier each time I see you. How do you do that?"

"That's for you to wonder about, darling."

"Darling, I think I like that." He stepped through the doorway, putting down his suitcase and attaché. "I do like that." He kissed her as though her lips were a rare delicacy, as though he hadn't once touched anything as soft and warm. "A better question might be, what happens when we come in from the snow and the cold, sweetcheeks? Where is that wintery ensemble?"

She closed her door, stepping into her living room. She bared her hands, dropping the gloves, unbuttoning the coat matter-of-factly and shrugging the cozy warmth from her shoulders to the floor.

The sight of her in boots, lacy white silk panties and satin bra meant to incite more than cover, draped in her scarf and smiling wickedly as she strutted in a tight circle with her arms outstretched, was too much.

He closed the gap quickly, going in low, one hand reaching out for a delicate wrist, his other wrapping tightly around creamy smooth thighs, shifting her easily onto his shoulder.

"Where's the bedroom?"

24

Saturday they woke late.

They showered together, dressed together, and made breakfast together.

Murielle showed him the bike she bought with her Christmas bonus and took him to the park where they walked and talked until finding an out-of-the-way spot to spread their blanket and set the basket for an intimate lunch of wine, cheese and pâté. The day was ideal for a romantic picnic.

Back in her condo they watched movies and talked about Christmas. Gilmore was closing from the 22nd at noon to the 27th. She would arrive in Boston in time for dinner and fly out late on the 26th. Four glorious days together. She was excited.

That evening they prepared a light dinner and went to bed early, falling asleep hours later covered in sweat between damp sheets. Sunday morning they woke with barely enough time for Anthony to shower and repack, Murielle's nicely battered vagina serving unwavering notice that visiting hours were over.

He showered and dressed alone while she brewed coffee and heated Danishes. They ate standing and kissed at the door moments before noon. Neither had much else to say that wouldn't make their parting more difficult, not after Murielle's "I love you, Anthony."

She waved to him from her balcony. When he was gone she went inside. She stripped and remade the bed. She washed her dishes and cleaned the apartment while her laundry was spinning and drying, bagging and hiding her winter outfit under her bed with what remained of the JW Black. She showered and shampooed her hair, sanitizing her body. She did her makeup and nails, dressing in dark thigh-highs, a short tweed skirt and loose-fitting sweater before calling a cab that would take her to the market and liquor store.

At moments to 4:00 she pressed ENTER, swinging open her door to Jackson dressed in cords and a cable knit sweater holding a grand cru with the leather over-nighter hanging from his shoulder.

Dinner began after cocktails with a simple chicken gumbo, followed by grilled Gulf shrimp over a pilaf of golden rice sautéed in oil, lightly seasoned and mixed with peas, corn, and dried fruits. Dessert was a vanilla sorbet layered with a thin coating of melted chocolate.

She didn't feel like cooking.

With the dishes done they sat for a while holding hands and listening to music, their desire for each other too fresh and exciting to waste the evening watching stale actors struggling to reinvent themselves. They were in love.

She snuggled close to him. "I never imagined my very first love could be this incredibly wonderful. It's like I'm living in a fantasy world I don't deserve, that I never believed existed."

"Our fantasy world, mi amor. One we both deserve."

"Last weekend was totally amazing. After you left me my heart needed most of the week to begin beating normally again. Funny though, thinking back, not a single college girlfriend ever talked like it was anything more than…you know, something to do. Nothing special."

"Compliments humbly accepted, mi amor. Then when I saw you on Friday…Did you glisten this morning?"

"Darling, I've glistened nicely every evening since Sunday, since our first time…our fourth and our fifth, reliving you in my bed, which I cannot believe I'm telling you. Friday after our dinner most of all, dreaming of this evening. And this morning I really could not help myself, waiting for you, remembering how you kissed me and caressed me, how you watched me on the balcony. I had to do something to pass the time. I mean, hello." She twisted, wrapping an arm around his neck, pressing her mouth urgently to his. "A primary survival technique for lonely and desperate college girls. Still, I wasn't alone, darling. You were with me every moment, watching me. You know, panting and glistening."

"I imagine this primary technique requires regular practice, mi amor, to ensure the continued survival of girls everywhere."

"Yes. In the most critical cases very regular. Until we lose all hope and we lapse. Like me, before you. I lapsed."

"Though happily for me your skills are finely tuned once again."

"Yes, darling. I believe better than ever. Because of you I'm a survivor."

"The very reason I implore you to demonstrate this requisite technique for me, mi amor. You must, and very soon. I should have every possible treatment at my fingertips in the event you experience a serious relapse. Don't you think?"

She did not think. Particularly since who else but he would be the unwelcomed cause of her relapse? And how would that work in his testosterone-impregnated mind?

He nodded, understanding the contradiction. Despite which they went to bed, Murielle relenting only after she had fully depleted him. Jackson then selflessly suggesting a possible beneficial side-effect to her survival technique, merely suggesting a plausible solution to her distress.

She quietly considered the pros and cons while he waited with calm dispassion, her eyes brightening with a mischievous glint. He was right, of course. Depriving the poor man meant depriving herself, which was many times worse.

Yes. She did understand the benefit, gleefully pushing herself back against the headboard so that he might more closely observe and learn. Which he did completely in awe, fully trained in her Relapse Therapy by midnight and passing the hands-on examine with remarkable ease; Murielle succumbing to sleep first, nestled in his arms and purring contentedly.

When she woke oblivious to the aroma of freshly brewed coffee, he was propped against her headboard gazing at her.

"What time is it?" she yawned, stretching, her body mildly shuddering.

He put aside his cup, reaching for his Rolex. "Seven-ten."

"What!" She jerked, struggling from the twisted sheets. "Shit, Jackson! Shit!"

"What's wrong?"

"Aaaghh!"

She bolted to the bathroom, running a shower to heat the water while she peed, muttering, shocked at first when he nonchalantly ambled in.

"I made coffee while you were sleeping. The very least I could do after your amazing tutorial last night."

Standing, patting, feeling a tad awkward, she flushed. Pulling her hair into a ponytail tail she took the cup, sipped, gave it back and scampered into the steaming downpour.

"Can I join you?"

"No! You cannot join me. Shit!"

"I made breakfast too."

"Jackson, I'm going to be really late. Shit!"

"Can't say I'm particularly familiar with the feeling. I own the place. Being late isn't a real issue for me." He leaned into the shower, studying the soapy nude, sipping his coffee. "Is that a bad thing, being late?"

"Yes it's a bad thing, a really bad thing. I have a frigging seven-thirty breakfast meeting. Jesus, Jackson! You knew that!" She stopped the torrent, thrashing beads of water and frothy suds from her body. "I am really not liking this side of you."

"Would you rather a towel, Murielle? You seem a little harried. You know you could save time by skipping the underwear. Two, maybe three minutes."

She snapped the towel from his hand, stepping out, bending and stretching. "Would you please get my phone, Jackson?" He nodded, walking out. "God, Jackson can you possibly move any slower?"

He ambled back in, tapping his Swiss timepiece. "Well that's entirely weird."

"What?"

She was whipping a thong, the matching bra and thigh-highs from different drawers onto her dresser.

"Well apparently I misread the time. It's actually six-fifteen." He beamed. "How could that happen, do you think?"

"What!" Her shoulders slumped, her body plunking onto her vanity stool. "You bastard. I mean, really. You bastard. That was decidedly not funny."

He didn't believe her, she was laughing. "I wanted to show you the humorous me, my lighter side."

"Then please learn some anecdotes. Shit!"

235

"I'm driving you. I'm working at home, the one you haven't seen yet. It's Christmas bonus time which means I won't be seeing you until the party on Saturday."

She threw her bra at him. "Good. And I hope you enjoy dancing alone."

*

By which time she had decided she might possible forgive him, not that he shouldn't dangle a while

Jackson spent his week speaking with his employees across the Southeast, acknowledging each one personally for their part in Belmont's continuing success, working with his accountant to ensure their bonus cheques would be received before their respective Christmas parties.

Saturday he was a guest at his own soirée, giving his secretary, and his father's before him, carte blanche to organize the event. Cocktails were from seven o'clock, leading to a sumptuous dinner at eight, gifts and an open bar until closing. Everyone would arrive by taxi, leave by taxi, and submit their receipts: House rule.

He arrived at Murielle's promptly at 7:00. She greeted him in a small blue satin tube top mini-dress detailed with a scrunched-ribbon, standing at the door in three-inch open-toed blue sandals that put her two inches taller than him. Her ears were pierced with glittering cobalt blue and stainless steel artisan open-drop earrings, highlighting a Cleopatra-straight curtain of dark hair, a matching long-chain pendant drawing attention to her shoulders shimmering with silver dust. Her bare toes and fingers were tipped with clear lacquer, her lips shimmering with clear gloss; she didn't want to detract from her jewellery or gown.

"You are divine, Murielle," he told her, following her in. "Truly a celestial creation."

She put a palm to his chest, enjoying her revenge. "My

gloss is too fresh, Jackson. I might kiss you later. Maybe."

In the kitchen he poured a JW Blue and Silent Sam with a splash. "I don't see why, mi amor. You're flawless as you are and we really shouldn't be late. Remember that being late is a bad thing. Inexcusable, I would say."

She ignored him and went to the bathroom with her drink for a final critique and touch-up of her eyes and lashes. She knew very well he preferred giving his staff the hour to mix and mingle, that he never sat at the head of the table or remained past midnight. Neither had Jackson, Sr. or Melinda.

"I left my overnighter in the Q60," he explained, following her in. "I wasn't sure I was being invited to stay over. You know, not having spoken since Monday morning."

"Just as well. Because I'm not sure either, Jackson," she answered, casually brushing a light blush onto her cheeks. "I really haven't thought about it. Let's see how the evening goes."

He leaned into the doorway. "I'm excited about showing you off to the rest of my staff, mi amor. I want everyone to see how lucky I am to have you."

She shifted on the cushion. "Have me, Jackson? You mean like your fancy Q60. You want to show me off like a car? Does that include test drives, Jackson?" she wanted to know, her voice flat.

He let that one go. "You're sitting on your stunning gown. I came early hoping to see…Don't you always make yourself beautiful before you dress?"

"I'm not sitting on my dress. I'm not sitting on anything except a cushion," she answered, focused on her mirror. "And make myself beautiful? Excuse me?"

He chuckled. "Even more than you are at six in the morning with suds gliding across your exotic curves and various other exquisite features, mi amor."

"Then I hope you have a very good memory, Jackson." She sipped her vodka, not impressed.

"Or, you know, sitting on the toilet peeing. That was pretty special, an historic Kodak moment. How could any gentleman ever forget something like that?"

Vodka sprayed from her mouth and nose across her mirror. She lurched forward saving her gown, gaping at him with disbelieving dark eyes and soft pink lips encircling an incredulous and toothy 'O', the stool crashing to the floor behind her as Jackson's hands pressed securely into her sides.

She grabbed for a tissue to pat her face and mouth, catching her breath.

"What an absolutely horrible thing to say to a lady."

He countered from behind. "Or from the gentleman's perspective, what an absolutely wonderful sight for him to witness and cherish forever: A dark-haired and exotic angel sitting vulnerable and naked and, you know, speechless. His dark-haired and exotic angel. My angel."

She regained her composure and dignity. "Okay, alright. Timeout. But officially and until I say otherwise you are a bastard." She shrugged him away. "And the least you can do to redeem yourself, Jackson, is get your stay-over bag to spare your exotic angel from feeling like she's dragging home some pathetic homeless person…darling."

The New Orleans Christmas Party was being held at Angelo's, his staff voted. They liked the place and they liked Charlee who was their bargirl exclusively throughout the evening in the restaurant's private salon, who wasn't wearing her usual flared shorts and sweater. Not that evening. This was a Belmont party. Even the women who sat at sewing machines all day would show up wearing something close to designer. If not their own original designs created during lunch and coffee breaks.

Charlee was wearing a fashionably short, sleeveless wrap-around woolen coatdress, teasingly décolleté and snug, with sheer nylons and patent leather pumps. Not a chance she would wear an apron or money belt. Not that night.

The moment Murielle and Jackson strolled through the doors at a quarter to the hour, all heads turned. The men remained as they were, if not their eyes, drinks in hand, the store's senior associate with a JW Blue at the ready; the women went at once, weaving between chairs and tables, to take possession of the flesh and bones version of the girl framed on their boss' desk, dragging Murielle away.

Charlee came soon with her cocktail, both girls admiring each other, kissing and hugging each other, promising they would talk later.

Near eight-fifteen Junior's secretary asked for attention, prodding thirty festive souls into the dining room across the hall with their drinks.

The wine was plentiful and delicious, the four-course meal superbly created for Belmont by one of New Orleans' premier chefs. When the table was cleared Junior remained seated. The evening was not for speeches, ergo the previous personal visits. The evening was for them, their wives, husbands and significant others. And gift-giving. Each one personal, each one shopped for by Junior's right-hand. She was a forty-year Belmont asset, his asset, and the evening's Miss Santa.

Her gift for four decades of dedication, she was fully aware and flustered about, was a ten-day Caribbean cruise with her sister. But what, she asked standing with her Black Russian in-hand, does one possibly offer a man who has everything, especially a lovely young thing whose name is Miss Murielle? Certainly not a tie, or socks, or a gentleman's underthings. Not even a gold Rolex.

"I trust you do appreciate our quandary, Junior."

"I do, Miss Clara." He shrugged, grinning. "Though certainly not the first time I've stood in the proverbial corner for causing you undue distress over the years."

"Yes, well your entire staff has agreed with my suggestion, Junior, agreeing that something should be done. The ladies in particular since the gentlemen of Belmont seem to consider gallivanting and womanizing as somewhat of a curative for male loneliness. An opinion on which we ladies place no value." She sipped her cocktail, ignoring the drumming hands and male chorus of "Hear! Hear!" She raised an open palm, inducing silence. "The time has come for you to get a life, Junior, to get out of the office. Wandering who knows where like a lost puppy, whimpering, hoping desperately for some young and pretty owner to adopt you, to rub your tummy and scratch you behind the ears. Which was not at all acceptable until, according to reliable and anonymous voices," she glared at the men, "of a less raucous quality, others of us became aware of credible evidence suggesting that finally your tummy and your ears are being quite well attended to."

The ladies were covering their mouths, the men once again thumping the table in unison. Murielle causing abrupt laughter when she rubbed said tummy and scratched said ears, bringing Junior's light dry tan to a moist shade of crimson.

"Mister Belmont, your entire staff has come together to send you and Miss Murielle to a luxurious three-day, all-inclusive spa weekend in Québec City during that city's winter Carnaval.

Murielle gasped, clapping a hand to her mouth.

The gift was beyond the pale, exceptionally extravagant. What was worse, he could not refuse. He pushed his chair from the table, his mind racing to do the arithmetic, to compose a meaningful script. Making his way to Miss Clara's side, he embraced her warmly as a close and dear friend.

"Miss Clara, ladies and gentlemen, I stand here truly speechless. Which I suppose is a good thing since we have kept Miss Charlee agreeably busy this evening. Your gift is way over the top, particularly when I feel sufficiently gifted to have all of you here, and your colleagues to the east of us, to rely upon. We thank you, Murielle and me. We are as deeply grateful as we are shocked and truly humbled." He raised his glass. "To all of you, and to our very sensational Charlee who now joins us."

Thump, thump! Hear! Hear!

Junior first cleared the invitation with Angelo, inviting Charlee to join the party for a relaxed and well-earned refreshment. She'd been on her feet for six hours, not missing a beat.

He discreetly passed her an envelope that would take care of the wine service. A second envelope would come Monday once the bar bill was tallied. Then he gave her a fifty for a cab after closing, Charlee not hesitating when Murielle invited her to dinner on Sunday for girl talk without *him*. They were close in age and neither one had a real girlfriend. The girls in med school were haughty and Murielle, as much as she did like the Gilmore girls, wanted her home as a sanctuary from work.

They left at midnight, running a gauntlet of men's hands and women's hugs before escaping into the cool early morning air and waiting for his car.

"Darling, those people absolutely adore you. Québec City! Wow!"

"Have you ever been to Québec?"

"I've seen pictures. I suppose now I will have to teach

you some French."

He supposed so, opening her door, passing the valet a fifty.

At her condo he poured nightcaps, Murielle slid a CD into her stereo. Thirty minutes later he was fully forgiven for the previous week's poor judgement, Jackson recounting several of Miss Clara's admonishments from the time he began working summers as a delivery boy.

Sunday they slept in talking about Christmas and New Year's in Vail, Murielle eager to discover everything she could about the spa, about Québec and the historic Château Frontenac overlooking the majestic St. Lawrence River.

25

She kicked a love-weary Jackson out at noon. She had things to do before Charlee arrived and each evening before their dinner at Melinda's on the 20th. She had shopping to finish, outfits to buy for Christmas, New Year's to plan and gifts to wrap for under the tree in their chalet.

Charlee arrived at three and got the full tour. She was envious of Murielle living independently. Living in her parents' guest house separated from the mansion by a pool and tennis court, despite the 100-dollar rent she insisted upon and buying her own food, wasn't the same.

Her father each school year wanted to buy her an appropriate car as part of her school loan that she would repay once holding a scalpel, though she didn't need the extra burden. Buses were fine. Besides she would probably become a taxi for dykes on a dare or medical dickheads more interested in curing a lesbian than plush leather seats.

"Lesbian? You're lesbian, Charlee?"

She nodded, pursing her lips. "Lesbian, not a steel-studded dyke, and currently unattached. Is that a problem, Murielle?"

"No that is not a problem. Not ever. You are the cutest thing, you're adorable, and absolutely everyone loves you including me. What do you mean, a problem?"

"I suppose now you can tell Junior. I'm okay with that."

"No. You tell him, whenever, if ever. Anyway, he won't

care. He adores you." She chortled. "Hey, at least now I know why."

"Okay, what why?"

"Why you gave him to me so quickly."

More importantly, did she play tennis? No. That didn't matter either. Did she own a bikini? She did, a very tiny one. She was French after all. Good. Then she was definitely invited to stay over for a weekend, Charlee promising not to hit on her out of desperation; Murielle replying with glistening brown eyes and a warm hand squeezing her friend's.

They spoke non-stop for hours through drinks, dinner and Cabrel, often times giggling at Jackson's or Junior's expense. When Charlee was leaving, not wanting to, they hugged as though they had been friends for years, each one certain they would be friends for years.

When she was gone, Murielle called Anthony. She wanted to tell him about Cerise and the girls inviting her to Québec in February for the famous Carnaval.

Chuckling, he wished her luck. He'd done the must-do carnival thing once while in university and was still in recovery mode. All he remembered was the hotel staff waking him and his buddies on the third day sometime after check-out and, by some miracle, getting home.

Monday she told the girls, and her supervisor who was fine with Murielle taking an extra day for such a special occasion. When her workday was over she spent what was left of the evening at the mall deciding on a silk scarf and leather gloves for Melinda.

Tuesday evening she went home to a light meal and to wrap her gifts, thinking Miss Clara was right. No way was Jackson easy to shop for. She put the gifts into a Christmassy shopping bag, showering before clambering onto her bed where she sat propped up with a glass of wine pondering the previous five months and her future.

Wednesday she rushed home in a taxi to cry mournful tears and phone Jackson who would understand. Melinda, being a woman, would certainly understand.

She had put the requisite ingredients on her counter that morning. She prepared a coffee and ran into her bedroom to strip and fill a suitcase with laundry. Dinner with his mother was at eight, Jackson expected at quarter to the hour. Standing naked on her balcony she threw a handful of finely ground pepper into the air, walking into the cloud with wide-open eyes. The burning and tearing came instantly. Again in the kitchen she added warm cream and lemon juice to the coffee before padding single-minded to her bathroom to chug the ten-ounce concoction as quickly as possible.

What followed erupted quickly: the sweating and trembling, the cramps and the retching until the expected tempest of sour vomit roared from her mouth into the toilet.

She washed her mouth and face, dressing in panties and a robe, calling Jackson half an hour before he was set to leave.

"Darling," she wept. "I'm so sorry."

"Murielle, what the hell's wrong? What's happened?"

"My grandmama passed away this evening. Je ne sais quoi dire."

"I'll call my mother to cancel. I'll be with you in fifteen. I'm staying with you this evening. You cannot be alone through this."

"Jackson, I'm leaving for the airport. Grandpapa has bought me a ticket. I must go to him, my darling. I'm his only family. I fly first to Boston then to Paris to be with him by the afternoon." Her voice was weak and raspy. "I've been crying for an hour knowing I will miss our first Christmas and ruin your mother's dinner."

He was with her in twenty minutes when, he had to admit, she looked as though she'd walked into a serious shitstorm. A fleeting thought he would keep to himself.

She let him take her luggage and gave him a bag of presents. At least a very little part of her would be with them in Vail, she told him. He and Melinda were to have a good time and he would teach her to ski in Québec in February. N'est-ce pas?

They were at Louis Armstrong International when they should have been walking into Melinda's home. She was not to worry about her tickets to Denver: An insignificant detail. She was to call him whenever she learned her return details, whenever she needed or wanted to talk. Things would work out.

She left him at Departures, insisting that he go to Melinda's. She didn't want to think of him alone in his condo worrying over her. She was feeling much better, because of him. She loved him so much. She would call him from the gate before boarding and please tell Melinda how embarrassed she was.

She ordered a tall vodka in the lounge, nursing it, nursing herself. She felt terrible. When the flight to Boston was announced she called him, thanking him for being concerned, weeping when Melinda took the phone to express her deep sorrow and wish her well. When she disconnected she went home, emptying her suitcase into her bin. She showered, managed a bowl of bland soup and crawled into bed feeling like shit.

She struggled through Thursday, spending her evening in the kitchen and bedroom, keeping her living room dark on the off chance Jackson might do a drive-by. Waking early she pampered herself, ensuring that when arriving in Boston she would be Anthony-approved.

She took a taxi to Gilmore in her new winter dress

boots, jeans and a cashmere sweater. The one day of the year casual dress was permitted.

Casual Friday was verboten, a guaranteed prelude to a career change. This time her suitcase was filled with outfits appropriate for the ten days she had planned, her winter coat, scarf and hat stuffed into a Belmont suit bag. She was ready for Vail, she told the girls over late-morning spiked eggnogs. Jackson was meeting her at the airport, where she arrived while he was still at home packing with the most beautiful girl in the world on his mind.

26

Flight 902 arrived in Boston at 4:30 in the midst of a white-knuckle blizzard, frightening for most passengers whose idea of snow came from uninspired postcard scenes of gingerbread cabins, prancing cartoon reindeers and sleigh rides along unreal pristine white trails. Not their plane under assault by battering crosswinds at 200 miles an hour over a runway no one could see.

Though all that was forgotten once on the tarmac as all save one passenger applauded their individual survivals, everyone waiting unbelted and tense for the ping to signal a frantic race to the Jetway and their respective destinies.

Anthony was waiting outside Baggage Claim, beaming as she sauntered toward him dressed for winter's assault. The Belmont bag was gone. What she needed was Jackson, not an explanation about him.

She looked great in her outfit. He loved her, Anthony explaining the next four days as they drove ninety minutes through heavy traffic, icy white-out and white-knuckle conditions to his newly acquired safe haven forty miles south of the demon.

The evening was theirs to enjoy each other and talk. The next day they would decorate her first Christmas tree, maybe find creative ways to enjoy the Jacuzzi, and dinner was Italian at eight. The weather was expected to clear by Sunday when they were going on a sleigh ride by the ocean, warm their cockles with hot toddies and do some tobogganing.

Maybe not. No way was she sitting wrapped in a DNA-infested blanket behind a horse. "I have no clothes for a sleigh or toboggan, darling. I packed for us. And, whatever this cockle is, I would prefer that you warm mine."

"Well actually you do, in florescent green and yellow in case you get lost. You're favourite colours and you'll be easier to find in the snow."

"That's very thoughtful, Anthony. Nevertheless I would prefer that you do not lose me."

He agreed that was the better strategy, adding another surprise to her weekend. "I've invited some friends for drinks and munchies Christmas Eve. Strictly casual. I've told them about you, sweetcheeks. And I cannot wait to show you off. I know they'll absolutely love you."

Another one, really? More stupid man-speak for "Hey guys, get the hell over here and check out what I'm fucking."

"They're good people. We're also celebrating my divorce. The final papers came today. The wicked witch is dead in time for my first real Christmas in years."

She was happy for him. He deserved better, she told him.

Christmas morning they would sip hot toddies under the tree and open their presents. He would put together a phenomenal Christmas dinner, with her help, and go snowshoeing.

That was all very nice, she hoped, convinced that flight 902 had delivered her into a frozen Hell. She did not like what she was seeing, not when a year earlier she was strolling a Bahamian beach in a thong and nothing else. Snow and cold she could tolerate, but this was the frigging ice-age.

"But Tuesday, darling, I want the entire day inside by the fire with you." Or get me the hell out of here.

Turning onto the street where he lived lined with the amber halos of lampposts, she had to admit the scene was postcard-perfect: Christmas trees flickering in blues, greens and reds, windows and doors glowing in silvers and golds, rooftops the precarious homes of reindeers, gift-laden sleds and unflappable snowmen jerking and snapping in a whirlwind of swirling snow.

Just not perfect for a girl who hadn't once in her life seen, touched or eaten snow.

Turning into his long driveway at the end of the cul-de-sac, she was impressed. The place wasn't as small as she imagined, with large bay windows and cedar cladding. More importantly, he was driving directly into the double garage.

Inside she was even more impressed. The living room was decorated with modern furniture, a huge brick fireplace, and the vaulted ceiling was dotted with halogen beams. The loft spanning the entire width was his leisure space with lounge seats, a day bed, a library, a sixty-inch flat screen and the Jacuzzi. The kitchen was small and au courant, the bedroom fitted with a king-size boasting a bay-window view of a forest she wouldn't see until morning, a walk-in and bathroom fitted with a soaker comfortable for two and His and Hers fleecy towels. Anthony stressing how the 'Hers' had never been used.

There was no guestroom, he didn't need one. That was his office fully equipped with an oversized map on the wall and a framed blow-up of her clutching a towel she had weeks earlier reached for not a second too late.

She liked the place. She could see herself living with him, being a couple. What she saw even more was her tired body sinking into his soaker filled with steaming and perfumed water. Dinner could wait. He could wait. The flight was a total bitch, the perilous drive home not much better if not worse. She needed decompression time.

She filled the tub while Anthony brought real flames to a roar in the living room and went for her luggage. When he came in with a Silent Sam mildly splashed with soda, she was up to her breasts in a cloud of suds, her face beaded with sweat. Then he left, which surprised her. Murielle thinking or hoping he would have stayed to see more of her.

Stepping out, her skin lightly coated with oil, she went into the walk-in not bothering to wrap herself in a damp towel. She emptied her suitcase, hanging her outfits on the unused side of the closet, storing her delicates and her presents for him in unused drawers. Then suddenly she was starving, squirming into silk tap pants and a camisole.

Passing through his bedroom her lips curled into a smile, seeing that he had made their bed ready for sleeping.

Anthony was sitting with a JW Black by the fire listening to carols, watching her come toward him, absorbing every delicious part of her. Dinner was homemade pea soup, French bread and pâté on the floor by the warmth of real flames; Murielle surprised by the size of the tree and the cluster of decorations scattered on the floor and in boxes.

While Anthony did the dishes she pressed her nose and palms against the frosted glass of the patio doors, recalling how she was naked and warm on her balcony a mere forty-eight hours earlier. She didn't much like the sensation, her body retaliating with a sudden and violent shudder.

She wanted to make love right there by the fire and fall asleep in his arms. That's what she wanted. That's what they both wanted and when he returned moments later with pillows, a blanket, and puffy duvet Murielle was laying naked on her front by neatly folded silk, her body's natural hue all the more exotic with shadows dancing across her undeniably alluring contours.

This would be her best Christmas ever, she told him, drawing their lips into a heated kiss.

The next morning she discovered that waking to a huge hole in the wall lined with dirty brick and filled with grey ashes, then scurrying to the bathroom to hover her pretty butt over a cold toilet seat while trying to pee and rub heat into her arms, was not her idea of romantic. Despite the very impassioned romance of the previous evening.

Then came Christmas music and the thick aroma of rich coffee wafting through his home as she dressed in her jeans, thick woolen socks and cable sweater, ready to trim her first tree. She was excited and she glowed.

The tree trimming was done by one o'clock, lunch completely forgotten. Murielle was fully into the joyful season studying their glittering work from the heated and swirling Jacuzzi and musing. Counting her three Spring Break vacations with her jock dickheads and Stonewall's love of the Bahamas, she hadn't once experimented in the ocean, a pool, or even a bathtub. What her body and mind were experiencing then and there, her legs straddling his, her breasts pressed against his chest, was delirium. Her face was dripping with sweat; her lips were numb, smeared with gloss. Brassy eye shadow stained her cheeks, made worse by Anthony thumbing away her happy tears, her hair sculpted into a slick headdress from sweat melding with steam and the pressure of her hands and his. Heated water swirled between them, around them and under them, splashing against her back, her soft and tingling flesh undulating under the erotic power of invisible jets probing impudently where Anthony had not yet thought to reach.

When the swirling died they crawled over the edge, depleted, Murielle questioning why he was reactivating the jets. He didn't answer, Murielle not understanding when he took her by the hand, hurrying her down the staircase to the patio doors while she was still heated and giggling. Until she shrieked as he swept her over his shoulder and opened the doors.

She got the idea much too late, pounding his back, begging him to be a gentleman.

Her pleas were wasted, falling on deaf ears, her toned legs thrashing the cold air until contact, until her piercing screech, her body kicking and squirming its way deeper into the pristine snow.

"You bastard! I hate you!"

He collapsed beside her, waving his arms and legs, the sparkle in his eyes warm and loving.

Then he wasn't a bastard. She didn't hate him…much. She was laughing and screeching, creating her very first snow angel. She hadn't once in her life felt as naked or as cleansed, the cold snow burning her skin, snowflakes melting on her legs and her belly, arousing her nipples, minute frozen crystals falling onto her tongue and into her wide-open mouth. She was eating snow, reaching for his hands and pulled to her feet, dashing through the house to the stairs, to the Jacuzzi, clambering breathless into the agitated and steaming water.

When Anthony went for a bottle of wine wrapped in a fleecy robe, needing a few minutes to set up, Murielle kept briskly towelling herself.

She stood peering over the railing, taking in the room below, her lover and her disappearing snow angel, conceding mutely that she was having a good time, wondering how she could possibly survive her time in Vail, wondering what Anthony was doing. When he looked up she blew a kiss through the air. The angel thing was fun, once. Not the same as a ski slope, not the same as teetering on strips of polished wood and plummeting into a wheelchair with broken legs when Stonewall's skinny whore was getting tanned and topless in the Bahamas. Shit!

"What?"

"Come on down, exactly the way you are."

Which meant naked, which she did.

"What is all that?"

"A massage table, never used. Demons don't like oil. She probably suspected I'd put a match to her. Anyway, get on." He patted the thin cushion. "I'm pretty good."

"Darling, I've never had a massage. Wow!"

"Backside first. Male prerogative. And no talking. Moans and groans are permitted, Miss Dupree, squirming is verboten."

She clambered on, lying flat, resting her head on crossed arms. The darkening sky, the heat from the fireplace and flickering tree lights quickly luring Murielle into another place and time, a fantasy world.

He trickled oil from the nape of her neck to the small of her back and into his palms, beginning with long and light strokes to warm the tissue under her heated skin.

Starting at her right shoulder he kneaded and pinched meticulously before digging an elbow into her entire upper right quadrant. Then he placed one hand over his other, pressing the heel of his palm into her flesh from the curve of her buttocks to her shoulders, his pressure constant, her seductive purrs mixed with throaty moans. Changing sides, taking a moment to savour his wine, to savour her, he repeated the process.

He dribbled oil across her bum, into the compelling divide, down one leg and up the other where he continued kneading, digging his thumbs into one cheek then the other, sliding a hand between them, kneading and probing, reminding her not to squirm, continuing down her leg to her foot, thumbing her arch with both hands and pulling at her toes before once again pausing for wine. Changing sides he began once more at her bum, evoking longer and throatier moans, working one cheek then the other, sliding the edge of his hand again into the heat between them, continuing down her leg to her other foot and delicate toes.

He trailed kisses from her feet to her shoulders, pausing midway, ensuring each side equal attention. Her purring and the oil's heavy fragrance were intoxicating, threatening the completion of his good work.

Determined not to let that happen, for her own good, he selflessly drummed rapid and noisy smacks across what he told her was a very spectacular ass, telling her to flip over. She did, petulantly, earning her another smack; Murielle serenely yielding to the gentle pressure parting her legs from her thighs to her knees to her ankles.

He dribbled oil over her breasts and between them to her belly, first smoothing her skin with long gentle strokes to warm her, beginning with a deeper pressure at her shoulders until reaching her breasts, attentively working each one in turn with both hands, squeezing tenderly as though reshaping them, pinching and plucking her nipples. Leaning over her face he worked her abs with the heels of his palms from between her breasts outward, applying more pressure at her waist and her hips as though clutching her.

He rubbed more oil into his palms, reaching for one arm, coating and pulling the slender limb from her shoulder to her wrist, squeezing her palm between his thumb and his fingers, pulling at each of her fingers and thumb, laying that arm by her side before quietly reaching for her other.

When he was done with her torso he paused for a swallow of wine; his hands were beginning to ache, skimming one lightly across her breasts and belly to ensure the oil was evenly applied.

He trickled more from one foot to the smooth folds of her vulva and down her other leg where he began anew, kneading her calf and her thigh, noticing her shallow breathing, her breasts and her belly barely rising and falling. He went to her other foot, working toward her calf and her thigh, parting her legs slightly farther apart.

At first he pressed a thumb lightly and deliberately over each fold, opening and closing her lips, inhaling her body's exotic perfume, his pressure gradually increasing, her body twitching once, twice. He drew her lips apart, the tiny pink nodule peeking out, glistening on its own. A single fingertip took over his work, strumming the delicate jewel, each minute stroke enhancing the hot breath against her moisture, her breasts and her belly increasing their rhythm until at last her legs flailed wildly and she lay panting.

He wasn't done. With his palms freshly oiled he cupped his hands under her head, pressing his fingertips into her hair, massaging the back of her head and her neck. He pressed his thumbs across her forehead from her hairline to her eyebrows, his palms lightly across her cheeks and under her chin, once more cupping her breasts, pinching her nipples and kissing her forehead.

He braced his arms against the corners of the table, studying her, adoring her, watching her drift into some past or future dimension where she had dwelled for most of the sixty minutes.

He covered her with a sheet, leaving her flat on the table, and went for more wine to sit by the fire and watch her. When she finally stirred the only light came from the fire and the tree, the only murmur from Dean Martin's Christmas.

He didn't see her eyes flutter open, her furrowed brow or the worry. He heard the gasp, waiting several moments as she journeyed from her private world into the one they shared.

"Darling, how long have I been lying here?"

"Two hours. I let you sleep, though not much longer. We have to leave in an hour."

"That was fabulous, darling. Absolutely fabulous. The demon must really not have liked you very much."

"She doesn't like herself."

"We absolutely have to do that again."

"We will. Just not tonight. My hands are dead." He eased from his leather couch to help her. He gathered the sheet into a jumbled mess, dropping the bundle onto the table. "I poured you a bath. You're a little slick, sweetcheeks." He swept her into his arms, kissing her. "Your wine and your shampoo await, Miss Dupree."

When she next saw him he was dressed in casual slacks, a turtleneck and blazer. He was leaning against the doorway watching her blow-dry and scrunch her hair with mousse. He followed her into the walk-in as she sank into the armchair to pull on one dark thigh-high, then the other, standing to pirouette and pose for him. She selected a thong with flounced edges that she stepped into and shimmied to her waist, fluffing the ruffles. She selected and stepped into a short green suede skirt that would complement her boots and her coat, she told him, asking him to do her zipper.

From another drawer she chose a yellow heavy-knit cowl-neck sweater that she pulled over her head and bare breasts, pausing, her expression questioning. Unless he wanted her to wear a bra. Do you, darling? Does the restaurant impose a dress code?

They did not, and neither did he; Anthony quietly regretting they weren't staying home for a plate of homemade spaghetti, a bottle of Chianti and her.

Instead the candlelight dinner was everything Italian from the zuppa Toscana, to the fettucine Alfredo and crisp

Pinot Grigio to balance the heavy sauce, to a succulent mascarpone cheesecake and chilled dessert wine.

As they drove home he gave her a tour of the town, snow falling into the silver-white beams of his headlights like microscopic stars. Main Street was cute and enchanting with strings of coloured lights, lined with boutiques and restaurants. Side streets were lined with mid-range homes and American-made cars both guarded by pudgy and armless snowmen.

Couples were actually walking on sidewalks cleared of snow, holding hands and smiling as though they weren't living in the frigid North. Fathers were dragging their kids on sleds, mothers walking alongside with cellphones freezing their frozen faces in the moment. Good for them. Trapped in monotony. Most of them were as white as the snow and, from what she had observed at the snooty restaurant, just as warm.

At home they went to bed, made love and fell asleep, neither one fully recovered from the massage.

Sunday morning they arrived at the farm early. Anthony was dressed in jeans and winter boots, a parka and thick gloves. Murielle was warmly tucked into a shiny green snowsuit trimmed with shiny yellow stripes down the arms and legs, yellow fleece-lined boots and green reflective mitts, scolding him first for spending the money, secondly for tampering with a lady's private closet.

She had never trudged through snow or felt a horse's tail whip her face. She had never seen a horse's backside up-close and personal, absolutely refusing the woolen blanket, thoughtfully suggesting another older couple might prefer the front row. Though she did accept the famer's tin cup and steaming hot toddy.

The sleigh ride along the snow covered ocean-side trail lasted an hour, the ancient beasts lazily pulling the sleigh over hills and into valleys, along craggy cliffs and the edge of a pine tree forest. No one was talking. The scenery was too picturesque, cellphones capturing the moment, Anthony's Nikon capturing Murielle.

The farmer reined in the horses at the bottom of a slope that Murielle quickly estimated at 400 feet. At the top were benches and a food truck spewing out steam, Murielle asking the man what the smaller shacks were. He answered "For your comfort, miss."

She turned to Anthony and said "Not going to happen." Which he believed.

She had never been on a snowmobile or sat behind a farmer's pubescent son, clinging to his chequered jacket for dear life in a swirling maelstrom of powdered snow at thirty miles an hour. Nor had she ever eaten a hotdog with steam escaping her nose and her mouth.

While Anthony went for a toboggan she watched others hurtling their way to the bottom, those who weren't bouncing into the air creating all manner of crash landings and sprawled bodies.

"Comment ils sont fou! No way am I sitting in the front. Misère."

"Whatever else you said I don't think you have much choice, sweetheart." He was behind her, grinning, standing with a six-foot cushioned toboggan. "Not unless you want to push me and this thing to a running start. You know, for momentum."

He lowered it to the snow, demonstrating how she should sit before helping her onto the cushion and attaching her hands to the safety line that he told her was pretty well useless. If she was meant to fly, she would, and seconds after she nodded she was gripping the thin line tightly enough to stop blood flowing to her fingers.

She was bouncing and jerking, on snow, not on snow,

crashing into him, lurching forward. Now he was he yelling in her ear to hold on, pointing past her face to a veritable launch pad mere seconds ahead.

Wrapping his arms around her, he yelled "Here we go, sweetcheeks! Hold on tight!"

Then he wasn't holding her. He was gone, which, during that split second, wasn't her primary concern. Her disarming brown eyes wide-open behind yellow-tinted goggles had no time to blink, her mouth too wide open to scream. She was flying freestyle, crashing, rolling and tumbling, laying sprawled on her front, her face buried in icy snow, her feet wide-apart, her arms outstretched.

Anthony scrambled to her on his hands and knees. "You okay, Murielle?"

She didn't answer, raising her head, licking her lips, her eyes dark holes in a white crystal mask: A Nikon's Kodak moment. Click. Click. He checked her legs and arms, her eyes and her mouth, cupping her face in his hands. She was fine.

"Now that is eating snow."

She burst into a fit of laughter. "That was so totally wild, darling."

He helped her to her feet, checking his watch. The bus wasn't leaving for an hour, Murielle leaving him to drag the thing up the slope into an onslaught of screaming snow lovers. She went to the farmer's kid, pressing a warm hand to his cheek, bewitching him with her finest accent and broken English, getting to the summit several minutes before greeting a breathless Anthony with a hot toddy.

She challenged the slope twice more, safely, videoing Anthony's fourth and solo flight through her phone.

The bus ride to his car was short, the half-hour drive to his home pleasant. Just not pleasant enough, Murielle refusing to hold his hand. Road conditions had improved somewhat since the horrors of Friday, however avoiding death on the slopes did not mean she wanted the Jaws of Life prying her mangled body from his crashed car. Both hands, please.

At home they showered and dressed for the evening, Murielle asking what 'casual' meant in Boston. He said Dockers for men, slacks and sweaters for women.

He had to be kidding. She said, "I don't think so." Woolen mid-thigh leg warmers, a short woolen skirt and biased cashmere sweater were much more appropriate. Any problem with that, monsieur?

Apparently not a single one.

Near 6:30 five couples flooded in with Tupperware filled with Christmas goodies and booze.

She was an instant hit with the men. Each one slapped his back, congratulating him as though he had created her in his workshop. The women, late-twenties, early-thirties, loved her outfit, her warmers and painted toes. NOT! Bitches. She read their eyes like a frigging tablet with flashing fonts. Her skirt was too short, her thighs too bare; her sweater was too revealing, the cowl neck practically putting the swell of her dusted breasts on a platter for their husbands to drool over, the biased cut flaunting her to-die-for abs. What was their problem?

She didn't know or care, deciding she wouldn't compliment their perma-press slacks and cardigans over cotton blouses. She couldn't help pondering as she sat pressed into Anthony, while the other women were sitting beside their husbands with their legs crossed as though in a waiting room dreading a pap smear, whether they were wearing six-to-a-box full cotton briefs.

When they left near midnight the men's hugs were tight, Murielle lightly brushing their cheeks à la Française. The women didn't hug her. They didn't know how. They leaned in to her, smelling of drugstore perfume, their cheeks not touching, making faint puckering noises as though they were kissing the cold night air.

Closing the door Anthony couldn't wait to say "The guys really liked you, sweetheart." He followed her into the living room. "I kind of got the impression the ladies were a little envious of you."

"Naturally they liked me. They spent the entire evening wondering."

"Wondering what?"

She snorted. "Seriously? You're asking me what? Well I think the word is fucking, darling. Your friends were wondering what it's like to fuck me."

"What! No."

"Yes. And the women, they are absolute bitches. Believe it. Each one of those guys is taking shit right now. If you'll pardon my French."

"For what?"

"For me. They're living with prissy bitches who dress like nuns with panty lines and use hairspray and makeup like preservatives. I mean, hairspray, really? Who does that anymore?" She patted his cheek. "For looking up my skirt all night, darling. That's for what."

"Can't say I blame them. I mean, hello. Gorgeous. Sexy. Hot. Isn't that a compliment, admiring a woman?"

"Gentlemen admire, pigs slaver. Your friends are pigs, darling. Pigs and bitches."

Which about said everything, setting the tone for a restful night's sleep. He checked his watch, retreating into the kitchen, preparing a snack he wouldn't eat while she looked on with a quizzical expression,

They went to bed without a nightcap, Murielle lecturing him with each item she dropped to the cushy armchair on the advantages of sexy and short, silk and satin, or nothing at all as she flung her sweater into the air. Anthony, very much enjoying the rant and seeing the wisdom in keeping his mouth shut, dutifully nodded on cue.

In the morning Murielle woke to Christmas carols and him softly calling her name a dozen times from the living room. She went to pee and comb her hair, dressing in a teddy and leg warmers before joining him by the fire and a glittering tree.

He had crept from under the sheets once she was asleep, leaving behind the warmth of her body to put Santa's presents under the tree, standing in the dark chuckling. He loved her. Seems Santa had already come by; seems Santa noticed the cookies and milk little Tony had put out.

"Merry Christmas, sweetcheeks."

She took her hot toddy, sipping. "Joyeux Noël, darling."

They sat gazing at the tree, at their gifts wrapped in silver and gold, red and green glittering foil. Far too recent with each other to suffer through the inspiration required for stocking stuffers.

Anthony went to the tree, Murielle telling him which he should open first. He loved the collection of silk pocket hankies, Murielle scolding him that well-dressed gentlemen must always be complete. He should know that from all his time spent in the South. And she loved her silk scarves, draping them over her shoulders. Then another toddy was in order, not rushing away the morning. This was Murielle's first real Christmas since the death of her parents, and his since his wife's horns and tail first became apparent.

Then came blue and gold, Anthony's eyes opening wide. The Johnnie Walker Blue was an extravagance he was not expecting, Murielle even more delighted with the silky cinnamon baby dolls she would wear for him that evening.

This time she hurried across the room to gather the

remaining gifts. They had agreed to open the finer gifts last, Anthony suggesting ladies first.

She nestled herself into the soft leather beside him. She was excited, carefully tugging at the blue ribbon and silver wrapping, honestly surprised. She absolutely adored the Nikon point-and-shoot. Her very first camera. Wow, darling. Anthony no less taken aback with the black titanium pen and pencil set that every successful businessman must own.

They finished the morning with a third toddy, Murielle thinking to give him something to remember, wanting to give herself something to remember. She went into the bedroom to freshen her makeup from the evening before, going nonchalantly to the Jacuzzi and flipping the switch, telling Anthony to set their cameras for outside. Standing by the doors she tugged her snow boots over her warmers, pulling the teddy over her head, wrapping her woolen scarf around her neck and leaving him to follow. Which he did in a hurry.

They hurried in after clicking a hundred or more shots of Murielle bending and twisting this way and that, stretching and squatting, throwing snowballs at him and creating a more superior snow angel. She was shivering, exhilarated, kicking her feet free and scurrying to the swirling hot water, making the most of the heated moment with a chilled Chardonnay and each other.

When they were dry, their bodies and their minds tingling, he changed into casuals and began creating their intimate Christmas dinner made easier with a thawed man-made ball of turkey. She changed into her cinnamon baby dolls, poured another Chardonnay, and watched him while she transferred the images to His and Her flash drives for viewing on his flat screen after dinner. Not imagining for a moment what was coming.

From his homemade soup to the French sorbet and Biscotti biscuits the meal was delicious, the second bottle of Chardonnay finding its way to the loft where the lovers were stretched out on the daybed watching a tantalizingly chilly Murielle fade from one unabashed position into another.

Except for standing in front of a mirror, or the doors to her balcony, or the hurried selfies of her with the pizza kid, she had never seen herself naked in a photograph. Stonewall wasn't into youthful spontaneity or exceptional memories, just spying, and she hadn't gotten there yet with Jackson.

Now here she was in high resolution being shamelessly hedonistic on a sixty-inch screen. She was completely absorbed, her fascination occluding their difficult dinner conversation, a less concerned Anthony suggesting with a chuckle that her moaning was a tad self-indulgent.

So what, she countered silently, smiling at him coquettishly? When did the demon or any of the five Artic bitches have as good a reason to moan? She didn't have to ask. She was stunning. Her body was fabulous with not a single flaw, the exotic hue of her skin even darker against the pure white snow. Though she did concede that laying with him, a man she had met a mere two months earlier, a man she had slept with as often as Jackson, both of them watching her romp and jump and roll naked in the snow, was totally weird.

What followed was a natural and ardent conclusion lasting into the third or fourth slideshow, Anthony driven to perform at his best as one Murielle became increasingly infatuated with the other.

They collapsed into a deep sleep where they lay, Murielle waking first the next morning to her snow-splashed double waving and smiling at her. A gleeful and rosy smile she didn't return. She couldn't. He would be driving her to Logan International in eight fleeting hours, her mindset far removed from the dynamic energy of the night before that somehow seemed more urgent and appropriate to the moment than the sensual massage he had promised.

Not so much their conversation over Christmas dinner which, she had at once determined would not spoil the rest of their time together.

Padding to the bathroom to shower and dress into her jeans and sweater she was despondent, not at all certain what to do. And not because her vagina was once again in lockdown mode, this time happily. Despite absolutely wanting him, any sex before leaving him would be a disaster: a mechanical and disappointing carnal function she would easily replicate once at home.

The day was beginning as an absolute bitch and the man wasn't even awake. Sex would really make things so much worse, so much more confusing. Christmas was different. They were euphoric with presents and pretty lights and her acting like a carefree cherubic nymph in the woods. Until he thoughtlessly chanced to steal all that at dinner.

That he wanted her forever in his life was a no-brainer. What man would not want her forever? She poured a coffee and sat by a bay window waiting, trying to figure things out in the quiet. Though by her third cup she was entirely miffed, wondering whether he might have died in his sleep. Then:

"Morning, sweetcheeks."

"You're alive." She didn't have to check her watch. "It's nine-thirty. You do remember this is my last day?"

"Sorry. I was lying in bed thinking, giving you time to think. I guess we have things to talk about."

"Yes, we do."

He sat beside her. "You don't believe someone will snap

you up? An attractive young woman who's also vivacious and a bilingual honours graduate? That is pretty impressive stuff."

"Moving here is not an option, Anthony. That will not happen because somebody has snapped me up, a Gilmore VP. You don't walk away from something like that. I would take a major career hit. You know that."

He nodded, pursing his lips. "I also know we should be together. This is very special. Not everyone has this, this you and me."

"Then come to New Orleans. Your HO is in Chicago, Anthony. What's the difference to anyone whether you travel north to south or the inverse? Move to New Orleans."

"That is not possible. I could never live there, especially in the summer. They have one season, the heat and the rains are miserable, and let's not forget the hurricanes. In fact you're the one compelling thing about the entire place and how you're managing to survive after living in Charleston is a complete mystery."

"As much as I would never be happy here, despite being together. I despise winter and I hate snow. Yes, all this was fun for Christmas. But after four months of it I would go insane. Also, Anthony, I have friends in New Orleans. You would have friends, real gentlemen I would never think to call pigs, or their snooty bitches."

"Friends are transient by nature. And didn't you live through snowy winters in France?"

"Of course, one or two inches when I was younger. Not ten feet, not blizzards that kill people."

She shifted, bringing up her legs and crossing her arms, tucking her hands into her sides.

He inhaled a deep breath. "So what do we do?"

"I suppose we tell each other the truth whenever the time comes. You don't want to marry again, which I understand. The same way I chose never to become a mother. Both situations equally repugnant for different reasons. The real difference, Anthony, being that I can never change my mind. You can."

"Until which time, which is unlikely…?"

"We remain good friends and lovers. After all you've done for me, after all we've shared I would not like to lose you as either. I would not like that at all."

Charles Anthony Vincent and Murielle Adrianna Dupree shook hands as friends and kissed as lovers: Status quo until something might or would change. The difficult part was over. What remained was a simple test of their resolve.

He prepared a light brunch, mostly to kill time while Murielle packed. Neither was hungry. Then either as victims of melancholy seeking comfort in each other's arms, or zealous lovers desperately clinging to their final seconds entwined, they found themselves naked and dripping with sweat in his dishevelled bed, the afternoon too quickly behind them with scarcely enough time to shower and dress when for the last time she shuddered and collapsed onto his chest.

No way was she leaving her snowsuit and boots, especially since she was going to Québec in February with the girls, which he reminded her with a smirk was white and snowy and cold.

The drive lasted under an hour on dry roads, Anthony walking with her into the main concourse. They kissed at the gate, Murielle's eyes tearing. She hated leaving him, promising to call him, Anthony promising to see her soon in the Swamp.

Flight 901 departed Logan on time at 8:00, landing in New Orleans at 10:00 local time after a monotonous three-hour flight.

She walked into her home near eleven, leaving her

luggage, her coat and her boots by the door. She poured a two-finger Silent Sam, neat. She was exhausted, plunking onto her sofa, pressing a fingertip to *CAV* in her contacts. They spoke for ten minutes. She got home safely. They loved each other. They missed each other. They disconnected.

The next morning she did her laundry. After lunch she dressed in runners and warmers, snug microfibre shorts and a halter, and went for a bike ride in the park under a bright sky and a comfortable sixty-seven degrees remembering her weekend, Christmas and her ad hoc photo shoot.

In the evening she did a workout to the point of fatigue. She soaked in a bath and rummaged through the fridge for something fast and easy. She stayed up late, watching herself prancing in the snow, and went to bed setting her alarm to wake her every hour on the hour.

When she finally did clamber from her bed she looked terrible. She ate a light breakfast, pushing herself in her gym for an hour, and went biking.

In the afternoon she went shopping for something special to wear for Jackson, for their first New Year's together, though not for skiing or frolicking in the snow. Then she went to the French Market to browse for the perfect trinkets from a bygone era. Returning home she was pleased with the memorabilia she would treasure forever, spending what remained of the day selecting other outfits for her flight and her time in Vail, ensembles she had also worn in France and her stopover in Boston.

For dinner she heated leftovers in her microwave, spooning the chunky mélange distractedly into her mouth while meandering through her condo. She missed him. She was eager to see him, eager to smother him with kisses and wrap her body tightly around his. She danced to Solis as though swaying in his caring arms, as though Jackson was twirling her, embracing her, caressing her arms. She did another hour in her gym and went to bed with her alarm's setting unchanged.

At seven the next morning she shrieked at the shrill sound, her chilled and exhausted body violently jerked into the air as though by cruel and invisible hands.

Dragging herself from her bed she went to the kitchen for a strong coffee. In her bathroom, squinting into the mirror, she managed a thin smile. She not only looked terrible, he would positively believe she had lived through the worst week of her life.

She ate a full breakfast before showering and shampooing, lingering under the hot water. She massaged rich cream into her body and did her makeup, dressing in tailored slacks and a loose-fitting sweater.

She called for a cab and left, departing Louis Armstrong for Denver at noon.

27

Murielle arrived in Denver on the 29th at 1:30 local time. In the Arrivals concourse she found a quiet area and called Jackson. He answered on the first buzz.

"Murielle, finally. Where are you? How are you?"

"I'm in Denver, darling. I'm at the airport. I wanted to surprise you. I needed to surprise you. They are both gone, Jackson. My family is gone. Grandpapa could not live another day without her. I believe he lived to wait for me, to say goodbye and kiss me. He passed in his sleep to be with her hours after we buried her. I have so much to tell you, Jackson." She sniffled, wiping her eyes. "How are you?"

"That's not really important, mi amor. I'll be with you in a couple of hours."

He told her where to go, a quieter more soothing place than a hectic airport. Disconnecting, he explained things to Melinda who told her son to get real. She was going with him. She would not wait a moment longer to meet that poor girl.

In Denver Murielle took a shuttle to the Fairfield where she sat nursing a double Silent Sam for an hour before sitting disconsolately in the lobby to wait for the man she loved.

*

Melinda recognized Murielle immediately, striding ahead of Jackson like a woman in control to embrace the distraught girl.

Murielle stood, smiling weakly, the full extent of her weariness imprinted on her face. She had seen wallet-size photos of his mother, which did her no justice whatsoever. Melinda Belmont was smaller in stature, Murielle judging 5'6" give or take. She was petite, her face lightly tanned from the glare of snow-covered slopes, her golden-blonde pixie hairstyle wispy and youthful, long bangs swept diagonally across her forehead. She looked more like his older sister than his sixty-year-old mother, her clear ice-blue eyes telling Murielle everything would be fine.

"I'm Melinda."

"I am Murielle."

The tight embrace was momentary and meaningful.

"Come. Let's get you out of here." She took Murielle's arm, turning to her son. "Junior, please attend to your lady's luggage."

He did, not intruding into Melinda's domain of being a mother. Murielle had unquestionably been through hell, deserving of a mother's comfort and understanding. In the rental Land Rover the women sat in the back holding hands, Jackson listening intently to her nightmare.

Her grandmama gave up her life on the Thursday, the evening of Melinda's dinner. Upon arriving in Paris she went directly to the old couple's cottage several kilometres outside Paris. Together they spent the entire Friday sitting with her grandmama, saying goodbye, each of them weeping, reliving her childhood with them in the country, remembering her own loving maman and papa who were taken from them so tragically.

On Saturday she was cremated. Murielle and her grandfather, the old man so weak and frail, took her home one last time to spend one last night together in their home. And in the morning "we buried grandmama in their little forest behind the cottage where she would often sit to hear the birds and watch the little animals. The forest was her favourite place, Melinda, where I left grandpapa to his sorrow. He remained the entire day talking with her."

"Who was caring for you, Murielle? They must have friends and neighbours."

"Their friends are all dead and the neighbours, they're too young to care. I was fine. Taking care of grandpapa brought joy to my heart. I made his favourite meal and gave him a small glass of wine." Murielle wiped her eyes, smiling. "He told me stories, naughty secrets about their first love that made us laugh and cry until I sent him to bed. He was very tired. He kissed me and hugged me, anxious to open the little gifts I sent them in the mail." Tears trickled down her cheeks. "In the morning I was calling and calling him for breakfast until at last I went to scold him for sleeping in on Christmas. I found him lying fully dressed on their bed, clasping a picture of grandmama to his chest. He looked happy, Melinda. His sadness was gone."

"What!" Jackson pulled off highway, twisting in his seat. "Jesus, Murielle. You found him Christmas morning?"

She reached forward, touching his face. "I could not call you, Jackson. Not on Christmas morning. Besides, what could you do? Nothing. I was happy to know you were with Melinda."

Melinda squeezed her hand. "Murielle we tried calling you often. Your phone was out of service the whole time and we couldn't locate your grandfather. You poor dear."

"That is my fault, Melinda. They are my mother's parents. Their name was Dupree. I did not tell Jackson this. I'm so sorry, Jackson."

Melinda politely ordered Jackson onto the highway. She needed to get Murielle into a warm bath and clean clothes.

"I should have been with you," is all he said, twisting.

"No, Jackson." She gazed into her lap, to her hand clutching Melinda's. "The police came and took him from me. He was cremated the next day and I brought him home to bury him in the forest beside the woman he loved all his life."

"Jesus H Christ!" Jackson blurted, his mother telling him sharply to keep his eyes on the road.

"Then I think I drank too much vodka," Murielle confessed shyly, "and the next day I went to a lawyer who will be the executor for me."

"I wouldn't worry about the drinking part, dear," Melinda assured her, patting her thigh. "I think we'll all be doing a bit of that very soon."

"And the home?" Jackson asked.

"They were simple people, Jackson. Perhaps after the expenses and the legal fees, a few thousand euros. I kept all that is very personal to me. What was personal to them I burned in their fireplace or took to the lawyer. The rest is going to charities. It's what they wanted. Then yesterday I flew to Boston and this morning to you and Melinda." She inhaled a deep breath, laying her head against the headrest. "Now I must also scold Jackson, I believe. He speaks often about his mother, though he never once told me how very lovely you are."

She closed her eyes, letting her head fall gently against Melinda's shoulder, moments later humming a soft purr.

Arriving at the chalet in Vail near six o'clock in the dark they woke her with quiet whispers. Once inside Melinda helped Murielle from her coat and hat. They followed Jackson into her bedroom where he put her suitcase onto the bed. His mother, essentially dismissing him, asking him to prepare cocktails, went into the en suite bathroom to run the water. When she came out Murielle was sitting on the bed staring at a square of crumpled tissue paper framing her grandfather's silver pocket watch that was her grandmama's wedding gift to her beloved husband. In her other hand were their simple gold wedding bands.

Melinda sat with her for a few moments. She understood how special grandparents could be.

As sad as she was for Murielle, wishing she could assuage the girl's terrible grief, she was happy for her son being with such a lovely and caring young woman. She felt certain in her heart that something good would happen between them.

When she was alone, promising she would take her time, Murielle eased into the scented and foamy water. She was glad the day was over and that she liked the older woman. Melinda was down-to-earth, not the least haughty or full of herself, Murielle very confident they would become close. She blow-dried and scrunched her straight hair into whimsical curls, feeling if not looking much better.

Dressing in jeans, thick socks and a cable sweater, her clothes put away, she went to join them. She was at once taken aback, her surprise vivid at seeing the Christmas tree alive with flickering lights and that none of the gifts had been opened.

"Thank you for coming to get me." She eyed the colourful packages. "I'm sorry I ruined your holidays."

"You ruined nothing, dear," Melinda told her. "Come, sit by the fire. We'll do Christmas tomorrow, now that we're together. Nothing under that tree is more important than you." She turned to her son, arching an eyebrow. "Junior, are your good manners for some reason temporarily in a state of suspension?"

"Excuse me, mother. I am simply spellbound by the beauty of two incomparably bewitching women." He went to Murielle, passing her a Jean-Marc XO enhanced with a discreet few drops of soda. "The stunning women I'm taking to dinner this evening. If you're up to dining out, Murielle."

She scrunched her face, turning to Melinda. "He always calls me mi amor. I think he's embarrassed."

"He's trapped in his formative years, dear." Melinda sipped her fifteen-year Glengoyne single malt. "Perhaps with your long overdue help the little that Clara and I have managed to accomplish will not have been wasted."

"I'll do my absolute best. And thank you for my bath, I'm feeling much better." She reached out, taking Jackson's hand. "Dinner sounds wonderful."

The evening was the very medicine she needed to cure her emotional ills. Dinner was ski-resort casual, the ambiance bright and vibrant, Murielle enjoying herself for the first time since flying to France. At times she smiled at hearing a mother's anecdotes and insider information, other times managing to chuckle.

Back at the chalet Melinda joined them for a nightcap and retired early, leaving them to enjoy their belated Christmas Eve. First telling her son that Murielle needed sleep more than anything he could as easily tell her in the morning, a raised eyebrow requesting verbal confirmation that he fully understood.

When Murielle was ready for bed she went to her room, changed into a teddy and fell into a deep sleep without him. Her one proviso for Christmas in Vail once hearing of the arrangements was separate rooms. She could not and would not share his bed while his mother was sleeping in the next room. Wasn't going to happen, darling.

In the morning she woke to music, the aroma of rich coffee, and voices. She came out in her silk robe and bare feet into a picture-perfect Christmas and bright smiles greeting her. The fireplace was blazing, casting shadows and throwing out heat; the tree was sparkling, the stereo playing age-old carols from a CD. Melinda was in the kitchen setting up for a later brunch of sausages, fruit-filled crêpes and French toast, Jackson explaining that he was testing his first hot toddy so that his second and the ladies' would be beyond reproach.

He went to her, kissing and hugging her, Melinda blowing her loving warmth across the room from busy hands, suggesting that Murielle could add more wood to the fire. Then no sooner were the logs crackling than Melinda was hugging her and Jackson was setting their toddies by fireside sofa.

They each had two gifts to open, Jackson freezing the event for posterity with his Nikon. Mother and son were wealthy, though Christmas was not at all about exchanging expensive or eccentric gifts that neither one needed or wanted. The day was about remembering a devoted husband and father and, this year, being a family to Murielle.

Melinda asked for Murielle's gift first, promptly delivered by her son. She methodically played with the ribbons, neatly folding back the paper, expecting she didn't know what, evoking a squeal of delight and surprise at the limited hardcover edition published in Spanish on the Mayan culture.

"Gracias, querida," she said, pressing one palm to her chest, pressing the other to Murielle's cheek. "Jackson, how precious a gift is this?"

Her gift from Junior was equally extravagant and unexpected: balcony seats for a sold-out Broadway show that he had bought months earlier for his mother's Easter getaway with a girlfriend.

The requisite tears of Christmas had begun flowing.

Murielle opened Melinda's gift first, gaping at the delicate crystal bracelet. She hugged the older woman tightly, real tears welling in her eyes, remembering when she once had a mother. Jackson's gift to her was a Lady Rolex, Murielle looking first at his mother who smiled and shrugged. What could she say? Her son was in love. A time when certain rules must never apply, dear.

Jackson's gift from his mother was a heavy cable sweater she had spent the last year knitting, which he put on and modelled to applause before giving mom lots of kisses and a tight embrace. When he went to open Murielle's gift she put a hand over his.

"You said to keep all this simple. That's what you said, Jackson. Which you did not do. No way are my beautiful bracelet and watch simple. Yours on the other hand cannot be simpler. That is on you. So next time don't say things you don't mean. Misère."

Mother and son shrugged. Whatever. Tearing at the gold foil he opened the velvet box teasingly, his expression changing from mischievous to curious. Inside was a stainless steel keychain inscribed with jBj, the small ring was attached to a key inscribed with 2A.

"A beautiful gift, mi amor. The key to your heart?" he guessed.

Murielle and Melinda exchanged telling glances. Junior was an idiot.

"No. Not the key to my heart, Jackson. It's the key to my home because I kind of love you."

He knew that. He chortled, facing his mother. "She always calls me darling. Go figure."

Melinda spent her Christmas Day peacefully reading her gift in the chalet while Jackson took Murielle on a tour of Vail, surprised when she began clicking dozens of photos of him with the camera she bought at the Paris Duty Free. She didn't show him before because she had no idea what her gifts would be, she told him. And yes, she also wanted his photos of her happiest Christmas in such a very long time.

That evening mother and lover worked at creating dinner while Junior transferred his and Murielle's photos to a flash drive she hadn't thought to buy in France, adding more to the mix as he attended to the wine. Recognizing them as women of distinction and worthy of the very best, he assured them, he would first test for texture, flavour and aroma. Then with his women served he lay by the fire to observe them, harbouring no doubt whatsoever that "you lovely ladies will perform passably well without the slightest interference from me."

They ignored him.

*

The next morning at breakfast Murielle was absolutely feeling better because of the memorable Christmas they had given her, one she would never forget.

She wanted them to enjoy their final days on the slopes together, not spoiling their time with a newbie. Besides, she had no intention of celebrating New Year's Eve in a cast or in traction. That wasn't going to happen. She would learn to ski in Québec, maybe. Instead she would photograph them on the slopes from inside the warm lodge while drinking hot cocoa. Which they did after a lazy morning, Murielle sitting crossed-legged on a sofa with Melinda listening intently to stories about Jackson's father.

Throughout the afternoon Melinda skied gleeful circles around her son, doing that female thing with her hips, snuggly fitted into a glittering silver suit and candy-red goggles. The woman was decidedly youthful and desirable, Murielle mused. That she was alone in life was impossible to believe.

Tucking her camera into her coat she left the lodge, strolling over crisp and blinding snow to the chalet. Inside she poured a glass of wine, scrolling to *CAV* on her phone and pressing SEND.

279

"Anthony Vincent."

"God, that's formal, Monsieur Vincent"

"I'm expecting a business call."

"Sorry."

He chuckled. "Some things are more important than money, like pretty French girls."

"I wanted to wish you a happy New Year. Some single girls from the office are coming over for dinner and whatever. We're having a New Year's lingerie night and sleepover."

"Fun stuff. And the 'whatever' part meaning...?"

"Meaning I'll be wearing my Christmas baby dolls. The rest I'll leave to your hyperactive male imagination, darling, although I do suppose we'll have to kiss each other at midnight."

"Thanks for the imagery."

"You're very welcome. And you?"

"Nada mucho. No one to kiss. No friends this time. Me and a swirl or two of my JW Blue and probably a slideshow. Actually, very definitely a slideshow."

They spoke for twenty minutes, making plans for a week together in mid-February after her weekend away with the girls. A short seven weeks away.

From the outside terrace at the lodge she photographed mother and son slipping smoothly from the chairlift, coming toward her arm in arm with skis balanced against their shoulders. They were understandably turning heads, oblivious to the attention. That they might actually be an item was easy to imagine, easier still to envy them having each other.

Lingering over Spanish coffees they talked about the approaching evening and dinner at the Grotto renowned for its squash soup, Peruvian octopus served with charred sweet potato and its ash crusted wagyu sirloin served with smashed marble potato and black truffle chimichurri.

When Jackson asked innocently what each of the ladies would be wearing, he understood at once not to pursue the matter.

At the chalet Melinda delved into Mayan culture by the fireside while her poor babies were taking separate naps because they were exhausted.

When Jackson reappeared the lovely ladies were sitting with cocktails waiting for him. He was so taken aback, despite their conspiratorial smirks, which he suspected wasn't particularly a good thing, he rushed into his room for the Nikon.

Mom was sitting in stocking feet, a shoeless foot lazily kicking the air. Her silk dress was fashionably short and décolleté, her jewellery understated, her blush, lip gloss and eye shadow expertly applied by one Mademoiselle Murielle.

Murielle would dance with him later that evening in clear thigh-highs and a simple yet sophisticated sheath dress with spaghetti straps, her hair swept into a cute updo by one of New Orleans' most sought-after hair stylists. Her one piece of jewellery was Melinda's crystal gift.

Worse, they were holding hands, leaning in to each other and whispering when he hurried in to capture the mood he suddenly wasn't sure about.

"Ladies, words fail me. You are delightful angels beyond any mortal's greatest expectation, without question too much for one man's heart to endure."

"Thank you, Junior. You're as gallant as your father and very handsome this evening. You and Murielle will be everyone's envy this evening."

"Those who care to envy me, mother, which they should, will believe I happily gave up my life for the single purpose of stealing incredibly beautiful seraphs from

Heaven."

Murielle kissed Melinda's cheek, Jackson freezing the moment.

"We were talking about you, Jackson. Girl talk while we were doing our hair and makeup."

"Anything I'm privy to, perchance?"

"No, something I'm privy to, darling. We have to talk about these frequent vacations you have been taking." The women exchanged telling glances. "In fact, I would love to see your vacation pictures. Your mom made them sound so," she paused sipping her XO, "erotic. Yes, erotic."

Melinda brought up a delicate hand between them, correcting Murielle with a furtive whisper, their eyes piercing his with that 'care to explain' female thirst for the truth.

"Oh, darling, I'm very sorry. I meant to say exotic."

He put down his SLR, reaching for his cocktail. "I believe, ladies, I was seriously mistaken. My angels are apparently metamorphosing before my very eyes into delightful little she-devils. As for my previous vacations, those days were spent in peaceful solitude for the purpose of meditation and meaningful introspection, the cleansing of body and soul, returning home each time revitalized and enriched."

They believed what he said in part, the part about purpose and body, letting the rest go as they went for dinner.

The restaurant setting was elegant with fashionable ladies and refined gentlemen, candlelight tables and a concert of muted whispers. A must-do for the well-heeled.

After dinner they went for cognacs and dancing, Jackson not really into arm swaying and bouncing off hips, leaving that to the ladies. He was more into slow and Latino. Dancing with Melinda they were the envy of every couple on the floor, Murielle seeing more than a graceful lady and charming young man. He was a devoted son, she a loving mother. When he danced with Murielle, Melinda saw in their eyes they were deeply in love.

At midnight they brought the New Year in with champagne, neither woman caring to divulge her resolution, both stopping Jackson with palms in the air since they already knew he had a cleansed body and enriched soul. Whereas Kenneth Stonewall had no need of pointless resolves, the domain of the weak-willed, returning to his Bahamian beach resort villa with his twelve-month whore midway through her term as Charles Anthony Vincent lay awake in his bed pondering what he should do.

He was twenty-seven and divorced, pretty certain he could not go through life waiting for her in hotel rooms six weeks a year, or sleeping in her bed like some sort of privileged guest, or waiting all year for a few days at Christmas and a two-week vacation. Still, he was infatuated with her. He loved everything about her.

The next day mother and lover went window shopping in Vail, enjoying the quiet streets, each other, and the relative warmth of January 01st. Jackson hit the slopes, returning early afternoon to suitcases by the door.

28

The last Friday of the month Murielle received closure from the French executor of her grandparents' small estate. In accordance with her wishes the cottage was auctioned-off for a quick sale. After all debts and fees were honoured the remaining inheritance amounted to several thousand euros which she wisely added to her 401K, she told Jackson during dinner at his condo the next evening, effectively putting an end to the old couple's convenient existence.

His 'unpretentious' condo, she couldn't help noticing, was a top floor penthouse with a private terrace boasting a Jacuzzi and wet bar, the interior decorated with European designer furniture. The place was spotless, prompting Murielle to ask which room the maid slept in.

"She comes and goes Fridays," he replied. "She keeps the place looking respectable, does my groceries, and she's a fabulous cook."

"Is she old and very ugly?"

"Not in the strictest sense, mi amor. I would describe her more as a twenty-something Costa Rican beauty. She's a student at Tulane and I pay her more than a coffee shop would. She's a nice kid."

"And does this Latina beauty qualify for any employee benefits, darling?"

"A Belmont year-end bonus, of course. Also a key to the

pool and fitness centre downstairs." He grinned. "When you look that good, mi amor, you have to maintain. It's expected. Practically a moral obligation."

"A Latina maid with a gym bag and a cookbook. How nice for you, darling."

He had to agree. "I have to say, with a to-die-for Latina housekeeper and an incredibly lovely French lover, my life could be a lot worse."

She patted his cheek. "Not your life, darling. But certainly the rest of your evening."

She left him, muttering sweet-sounding gibberish, marching into the kitchen with the dishes, Jackson thinking with a mischievous smirk that learning a little French wouldn't be a bad idea.

Twelve days later they were flying First-Class to Québec without his skis for romance and purification during the final three days of the Carnaval, Jackson reluctantly agreeing they would scarcely have time for the slopes, commenting with a frown upon arriving that he had never in his life seen so much snow.

He hired a limousine for the circuitous ride to the spa where they were greeted warmly by an all-female staff dressed in red togas at La Réception. They were given their schedules, a carte du jour of treatments, a dinner menu, and escorted to their suite by exceptionally lovely ladies in blue togas. Jackson insisting that he would manage the luggage, commented to Murielle that, yes, bringing his skis would certainly have intruded on their weekend. Though seeing the trendy snowsuit and snow boots she bought in Boston during her stopover he forewarned her that she had no excuse not to romp in the snow.

"It's fabulous, mi amor. Why didn't you wear it in Vail? Think of the hearts you would have stopped."

"I was thinking of your heart, darling. I didn't bring it

with me because I bought it for here. The boutique couriered the outfit to my home. Then I couldn't wait to wear it for you."

They had two hours before dinner, relaxing in fleecy robes and flipping through channels. Walking into the dining room casually dressed for dinner the lighting was subdued, the tables spaced for intimacy.

He was impressed. Of course he was, Murielle suggesting the reason might be the bevy of nubile waitresses dressed in short togas and ballerina slippers. All of them pretty Aphrodites, goddesses of love, beauty, pleasure and procreation. In case he wasn't sure. Duh!

Dinner was light vegetarian or non-crustacean seafood, meat entirely absent from the menu. Wine was available, white only, albeit discouraged. Jackson telling their petite Aphrodite that he would become grievously sad without wine with his dinner. Dessert was a selection of fruits, Jackson fully convinced that by Sunday he would be too weak to walk.

After dinner they donned their snowsuits and boots, strolling the property under a full moon, not diluting the tranquility with words. In their room she changed into the cinnamon baby dolls she bought especially for him the week before, setting the mood that lasted until midnight.

Day one began with a breakfast of fruit juice, a fruit plate, dry toast, skim milk or green tea.

The first treatment was tropical, a gentle exfoliation of their entire bodies before stepping together into a warm shower to cleanse their bodies and revive their spirits, completing the treatment with a relaxation massage combining the heavenly essences of lime and coconut butter.

Jackson doing his best to disregard the fact he was naked in a room with three women, one of whom was also naked three feet away and apparently completely at ease, wondering why they even bothered with the tiny towel over his parts. The dining room had bigger napkins and it's not like his toga girl closed her eyes when he clambered onto the table or flipped over.

The second treatment before lunch was another full body affair, a mud mask of winter green, camphor and red pepper massaged onto their skin after a second massage with hot basalt stones to tighten their already tight skin. Then they were somehow cocooned in thermal linens, drifting into separate and peaceful spaces during face, scalp and foot massages, the muted lighting and soft music discouraging speaking.

Lunch was an extravagance of fruit juice, spring water, crudités, more skim milk or more fruit juice.

The first afternoon treatment was a Swedish Couple's Massage, plant and flower extracts blended with oils to ease pain and relax specific tension. His toga girl asked where; he answered his shoulders. He couldn't possibly say what he was thinking, wondering how Murielle's breasts could possibly feel tense.

Left alone in the dark for fifteen minutes, he had to ask.

"My breasts are perfectly fine, darling. Very fine. I simply wanted to experience a young woman's smooth hands on them. You know, the sensation of warm oils and gentle squeezing. I've never been massaged. I wanted to know, and now I do. It was very, I don't know, relaxing."

"Relaxing."

"Yes, darling." She inhaled a deep breath, expelling a long and sensual sigh. "And she seemed very pleased that I asked. I could tell. She made the treatment extra special. I would say tender. Her touch was a lover's gentle touch, darling. She enjoyed cupping them, feeling the soft warmth, fondling them and pressing into them as much as I did. I can't imagine if we had been alone in the room. She might still be here."

He shouldn't have asked, thankful the girls had gone. Things were getting a little tight under the wrap.

Dressed in robes and slippers, two more girls guided them to the Eucalyptus Room for a deep steam wrapped in hot eucalyptus-soaked linens to soothe tired muscles and rid their bodies of toxins, one in particular that Jackson would pour two-fingers deep once in their suite.

Which he did before falling asleep for an hour.

Dinner was a green salad without dressing, baked tuna or trout, a half-bottle of Pouilly-Fuissé and frozen yogurt sprinkled with fruits.

Once again in their snow gear he introduced Murielle to snowmobiling. She had never been on one, wrapping her arms tightly around his chest as they followed the trail well marked with reflective poles and flags.

Back in their suite Murielle lay on her front in her baby dolls watching him flip through channels, stopping at Bleu Nuit. He didn't know those words. He didn't have to; he understood 'adulte' despite the extra 'e' and lay beside her. Not many minutes later they were performing as well as the actors.

The second day began with juice, a hardboiled egg, dry toast and skim milk or green tea.

The first treatment was another exfoliation, this one more invigorating with a brush made of coarse hair. After which came a deep steam wrapped in towels, a rejuvenating hydrating application on self-draining tables, their therapists washing streams of warm water across their bodies with ultra-soft sea sponges which, in Jackson's case, made his miniscule modesty patch virtually useless if not completely silly.

The second treatment was the Milk and Sesame Stone Wrap, their bodies again massaged with basalt stones before a deep rub with butter milk and sesame seeds. Then another wrap in thermal linens for the duration of face, scalp and foot massages.

Lunch in robes and slippers after another fifteen minutes in la-la land was spring water, juice, a crunchy veg bowl, more juice or skim milk. Jackson certain that Miss Clara wanted him dead.

The first afternoon treatment was Reiki, the toga-clad girls explaining universal life energy creating balance, harmony and wellbeing by way of their light hands transferring a flow of energy to Murielle's and Jackson's bodies. This when the flow of energy in his body was precisely what Jackson was concerned about.

The last treatment of the day was a back cleansing. More heated basalt stones laid across his back over more herbal formulas where he lay motionless on his front for an hour in a heated room with his head on a pillow facing Murielle with his eyes closed until the girls returned to de-stone him. Jackson feeling confident that he could pretty well go anywhere from then on completely naked, wondering aloud why they never bothered covering Murielle's private parts.

"Because, darling," she answered, "what is there to cover? And besides, we are all girls."

Dinner was a potage aux carottes et gingembre, pommes de terre au four served with a mélange de légumes, a rôti de bœuf par excellence accompanied with a fine Bourgogne, and a gâteau au fromage et chocolat. That's what he wanted. What he got was juice, broiled salmon, more crudités, another half-bottle of the Pouilly-Fuissé, low-fat biscuits and frozen yogurt or a rhubarb purée.

Escaping to the solace of the one JW Blue Murielle allowed him, they suited-up and went snowshoeing. Trudging through the woods, following a glow-in-the-dark rope between tall dark trees and shadows in the moonlight, Murielle put more images of her lover into her camera's memory card. She was having fun, invigorated by the cold night air, by yet another novel experience. Stopping him she kissed him, telling him how she loved him, how she hoped they would always discover novelties to share.

Despite his life possibly being much worse, for which she finally forgave him, hers could never be better.

Feigning several moments of deep reflection he promised he would give her concerns due consideration, suggesting that in the meantime Bleu Nuit was pretty novel, not to mention instructive. She decided not to punch him. Instead she raced him back to the lodge.

Their last day began with a dozen other couples wandering in for a breakfast looking younger and refreshed in robes and slippers, a concept that for Jackson was beginning to lose all meaning. The juice Murielle was trying looked like green mud, he went with unsweetened apple; she wanted a poached egg with spring vegetables, he selected French yogurt; she had unsweetened homemade blueberry jam, he tried for butter with his toast only to discover that le beurre n'est pas disponible, Monsieur Belmont. Which he understood was a 'no'.

He ordered bland field berry instead.

Friday for Murielle was an earth stone facial, a treatment designed to nourish, relax and soothe her tired skin, the formulas specifically chosen for her skin delicately applied with hot basalt stones. Jackson had to admit his facial was soothing, the treatment less complex than Murielle's, getting him into the steam room sooner.

When she did join him, the vapour trapped behind glass doors hung in the air like a dense grey cloud. She left her robe hanging by his, walking into the thick air barely pinching together the corners of a fresh towel at her waist. Seeing that he was alone and smiling, she let one corner fall away.

"I'll stay like this until someone comes, darling."

"That towel doesn't do much."

She shrugged. "I believe that's kind of the idea, darling. Remember? Love, beauty, pleasure. Or we would have bigger towels." She looked down. "And who are you to speak, monsieur, should some other young and beautiful woman see you?"

"How did you know I was alone?"

"I did not." She tossed him her towel, cupping her breasts. "They're breasts, darling. Not magical or unique, not in a place like this. Besides, no one here will ever remember me."

"Your breasts are spectacular and everyone here will always remember you. I should have gone to our suite for your camera."

She leaned in to him, kissing him. "I will pose for you before we leave. I promise."

He leaned to one side, peering past the door, pulling her closer. "We should make love, right here, right now."

She wrapped her arms around his neck, straddling his legs, grinding into him. "No, darling. I couldn't possibly. The girls might come in and see us like this."

"So what? They've seen us naked for two days?"

"Because darling, that would be fucking and I'm not ready for that." She patted his cheek, wriggling backward onto the tiled floor. Tugging him to his feet with one hand, she yanked away his towel with the other. "Not yet, anyway. But I will shower with you."

Then she turned and walked out dragging both towels, dripping with sweat and laughing.

*

Back in their suite his Nikon SLR came out quickly, Murielle timidly agreeing to pose in her boots and scarf in the snow between six-foot privacy fences framing their patio. However soon she was beaming, elated by being naked in the open air.

He loved her! Of course he wanted to see her naked in the snow. That he would ask her was a no-brainer. What surprised her was that he waited until their final day. What she particularly enjoyed, what induced her bright smile, was her reflection in the darkly tinted doors.

What surprised Jackson was Murielle without warning laying in the snow, waving her arms and legs, telling him how as a little girl she would make angels in the snow. He was all the more astonished when she abruptly turned, putting her rosy and chilled bum in the air, suggesting that essentially they were in the privacy of their suite.

She didn't have to ask twice, Jackson responding as any gentleman would to eagerly assuage his lady's distress. Lost in the moment, neither one certain whether they shuddered together with completion or suddenly shivered from bone-chilling cold, they scrambled to their feet prancing into the suite and a hot shower.

"Just an FYI, mi amor. To be clear. That was definitely fucking, you mischievous nymph."

The apparent revelation seemed for a moment to mystify her. "Really? We were fucking?"

"Oh, yeah. Big time."

"Wow! Then darling, I am absolutely ready for more...very soon...and very often."

They skipped lunch, departing the spa once Jackson had appropriately acknowledged each of their therapists. He was in dire need of food. Whatever energies the treatments had not massaged, pressed or twisted from him, Murielle had gladly depleted throughout their three days.

Friday's limo driver brought them to la Grande Allée, an avenue lined with lively bistros and elegant restaurants that was notably the nation's premier dining experience.

Murielle was accustomed to entering the finest restaurants without first checking the carte du jour at the entrance, given her easy transition from Stonewall to Anthony and Jackson. Whereas for Jackson fine dining was the norm. Walking into a burger joint or peering through the sneeze-shield of a food trough simply never occurred to him.

Relying on the chauffeur's recommendation they were not disappointed. Leaving the restaurant they were driven along the avenue into le Vieux-Québec, through La Basse-Ville to the Château Frontenac where they strolled in and out of boutiques, Jackson wishing he had taken several more days, out of the blue asking Murielle if being in Québec provoked memories and images of her mother France.

"Of course," she replied. "How can I not remember my beloved France, darling, my Paris. If anything at all in la Nouvelle-Orleans is truly French, it is me. Go to the French Quarter and speak French. You will see. However the France that I loved, to me now, is a land without friends or family, a land of strangers. In New Orleans I have friends. I have you and Melinda who I adore very much."

"As much as she adores you, mi amor."

They had three hours before the domestic flight to Montreal, enough time to give her a little more French flair, Jackson guiding her to an outside bistro table. Apart from the gaiety and rowdiness of the Carnaval's final afternoon, lovers were strolling hand in hand or sitting at café-terrasses cupping glasses of wine or mugs of hot chocolate between thick mittens. All of them smiling, or laughing; men walking with men, women kissing women. The joie de vivre permeating the air was palpable, Jackson pondering how she would enjoy her summer vacation in the continent's French enclave. He was thinking June or July which, without question, would be his fiancée's prerogative.

Her palm felt warm against his cool cheek returning him gently to real-time. "Where did you go, darling? I lost you for a little while."

"I can't tell, mi amor. Suffice it to say you went with me. I think happily."

Relishing the ambiance, the final few drops of heated cider and brandy Sangrias, neither wanted to leave. The flights home suddenly seeming arduous, incongruous after three days of exotic romance.

29

Monday Cerise and the girls wanted details which excluded Everett and Quintin from the lunchtime female inquisition. At Belmont the women were no less curious. They had all perused the spa's brochure on Miss Clara's desk, Miss Clara giving them full rein to tease and interrogate their blushing boss.

Wednesday Jackson drove home earlier than his usual late night at the office. He was preparing a special dinner for Murielle who hurried to finish her day's workload near 6:00, leaving a bouquet of red roses on her desk. She had a dinner date with Jackson and the limo would be coming for her at 7:30.

At home she stripped away her day, stepping into the shower, wondering what he would give her for Valentine's. Since exhorting promises to keep things simple seemed pointless, she didn't waste her breath with the lecture.

Towelling herself dry she combed her hair into a perfectly straight curtain, laying out her outfits for the evening and the next day. She was staying over, calling Anthony before leaving to thank him for the flowers. She loved him, eager to be with him in five days.

With most of his meal organized, Jackson showered and dressed for the occasion in a navy blue Belmont, a dark blue shirt and crimson tie. Murielle's stockings were sheer, her gartered panties backless and satiny. Her leather skirt was short, zippered from her waist to the hem. Her three-quarter bra, several shades darker than her sheer blouse, was meant to be appreciated.

In front of her mirror she was breathtaking. Anyone seeing her would absolutely adore and want her. And he would, her low-heeled boots and bomber taking him back to their first evening at Angelo's. She was ready.

The chauffeur arrived promptly, helping with her overnight bag. At the downtown condo he assisted her from the limo, accompanying her into the lobby. Belmont was a preferred client who expected the best. Inserting her key into the unmarked slot far from the public elevators, she stepped into Jackson's elevator, stepping out to see him waiting in the exclusive foyer.

"You are ravishing, mi amor." He reached for her bag. She unzipped her bomber, shrugging it from her shoulders. He didn't need reminding. "Hmm, hmm. Déjà vu. I will never forget that first evening. Did you believe I would?"

"No." She kissed him. "Happy Valentine's, darling. You're very dashing this evening. Are we going somewhere extra special for our first Valentine's?"

"We are. We're eating in. Not my fanciest creation, admittedly, though passably appetizing. I'm still recovering from being healthy."

"And pretty girls in togas, I suppose. Has your week been difficult without them?"

"Very difficult…because of them."

She sauntered past him into his dimly lit living room, recognizing Francis Cabrel's voice. The air was filled with a medley of aromas, the glow of candles illuminating an intimate dinner setting. In his bedroom she organized her clothes for the morning, neither one quite ready to do each other's laundry despite their toiletries being a fixture in each other's bathrooms since New Year's.

They talked and danced for an hour, mostly about Québec, about trading Vail for French for their next Christmas and New Year's, Jackson coughing a mouthful of expensive JW Blue when she suggested with a straight face that Melinda would probably enjoy a few days at the spa with them.

Dinner began with his curried carrot soup splashed with brandy and topped with a swirl of sour cream. His second course was filet mignon seared to perfection, served with lightly crusted puréed potatoes, steamed broccoli, and a robust '97 Pauillac.

While he cleared the dishes, preparing the table for his mixed berry trifle and dessert wine, Murielle went into the bedroom coming out with a small package wrapped in gold foil and silver ribbon. He joined her in the living room after refreshing her wine, appearing not the least bit nervous.

"Didn't we agree Valentine's is a girl's day, mi amor?"

"I didn't comment at all on that silly suggestion, darling…if you recall."

She patted the cushion beside her. "I hope you like them. They're exchangeable if you don't."

He teased her with acute slowness, earning a punch.

"Aviators! Alright! Thank you." He put on the gold Ray-Bans, Murielle smiling into the mirrored lenses. "They're incredible, mi amor."

"All you talked about flying to Québec and at the spa was getting an airplane. Pilots need pilots' glasses. Happy Valentine's."

He kissed her. Point of no return. He stood and left her, disappearing inside his office. A moment later he sat beside her, Murielle wondering what he had bought her that could possibly be that heavy. Carefully tugging at the ribbon, she neatly folded back the silk wrapping paper Miss Clara had found for him. She placed the linen box on the coffee table, carefully removing the lid, clamping a hand to her mouth as the four sides fell away, at seeing the delicate life-size crystal hand and wrist mounted on white onyx.

"Darling, what an incredibly beautiful sculpture. Thank you." Reaching to take the art in her hands, she squealed. "Jackson! What is that?" She punched him again. "What is that?"

He chuckled. "It looks pretty much like a diamond engagement ring, mi amor. Unless you don't want to marry me."

"Seriously! I mean, shit! Seriously? You want to marry me?"

"More to the point, Murielle, do you want to marry me?"

"Shit! Yes I want to marry you!"

Jackson slid the diamond and platinum bauble from the slender crystal finger onto the one that was as slender and trembling, asking if she was certain, Murielle's head bobbing like a dashboard puppet.

She straddled him, plastering his face with wet kisses and tears, her skirt bunching at her hips, pushing herself to her feet, adjusting her skirt. She had to tell someone, scurrying to the phone in his office. She didn't care that Melinda already knew. She was going to have a mother-in-law. She was going to have a mother.

Half an hour later, his delicious pièce de résistance forgotten in the name of love, she emerged with reddened eyes. Crying softly, she dropped onto the sofa beside him.

"You two have a good talk, mi amor?"

She nodded. "She told me she was thrilled having me as her daughter." She gulped, taking his hand. "I will have a mother, Jackson. She said she loved me very much."

He wrapped an arm around her. They talked and danced until midnight. Or rather Murielle talked until midnight and

Jackson listened. First and foremost, she was not religious. The entire notion of adults willingly coming together en masse to gaze up at some holier than thou guy, probably dressed in jeans and a tee-shirt under his fancy robes, condescendingly chastising them like some omniscient guardian, was ridiculous. The notion of a traditional wedding no less outdated and creepy.

She wanted a simple civil ceremony before a Justice of the Peace and a reception for their closest friends on October 21st, a year from the day they met. Melinda would be her witness, in a sense giving her away since both fathers were gone. She also wanted Charlee included in the private ceremony as she was the one who brought them together.

Jackson agreed with 'simple' to a point, intimating that some would construe overly simple as snubbing which would have a negative effect on the Belmont name. Although he cared nothing about religion as a philosophical concept, he did believe in himself and in being a good person. He saw no correlation between the two, no reason why he should spend his precious Sunday mornings demonstrating to strangers that he was in fact a good person. His one suggestion when he did manage to get a word in, was that the ceremony and reception could be held on a riverboat reserved exclusively for them. No clerics, no prayers, no blessings. Nothing creepy. A JP in a private setting to preside over the formality and a reception on the Mississippi for friends and associates.

She loved the idea.

At midnight Jackson carried her to the bedroom, not that Murielle had run out of things to say. She could barely keep her eyes open. Still, no way was she sleeping on the most special night of her entire life without making love to her fiancé; Jackson finding her dead to the world and purring when he came in from the bathroom.

Dessert became a delectable breakfast Thursday morning with coffee instead of wine.

Once in his Belmont office Jackson called his mother who apparently was already aware of the twenty-first and the riverboat. She was happy for him, happy for them. They were a lovely couple, meant for each other, and Murielle would be an adorable bride.

He then told Miss Clara who told the other Belmont ladies who were almost as excited about the upcoming wedding as Murielle, barging into his office for first-hand information which soon spread across the Southeast.

Of course they took full credit for the engagement that came suspiciously on the heels of his three starry-eyed days of romance and heated passion. At which point he stood, corralling them in wide-open arms, guiding the gleeful pack into the main office.

The men slapped his back and shook hands as they saw him throughout the day, his most senior associate, a long-standing employee and good friend of the late Jackson Senior, thrilled to discreet tears when Jackson asked if he would consider standing together with Melinda as his best man and witness. Who better than his mother and his father's close friend?

Things were no different at Gilmore. Seeing the ring waving its way toward Murielle's desk the girls went crazy jumping up and down, hugging and kissing the bride-to-be. Only Cerise noticed Quintin and Valerie's slowly metamorphosing Everett sitting nonplussed at their desks, pulling them into the commotion by their ears, telling them exactly what they should do and say. The poor guys just as quickly jostled out of the way by a flood tide of excited females swarming in from other departments.

They were taking her after work for Happy Hour drinks. When they asked her where, she replied "Where else?

Angelo's, where I first fell in love."

Charlee wasn't surprised, she was ecstatic. She was certain from that first night that Junior would become completely addicted to her. What did surprise her was being invited to the private ceremony, as special a moment as Murielle inviting her to spend Sunday afternoon together. She wanted to hear everything about the French spa weekend.

Thursday night alone was anti-climactic. Jackson was working late, preparing for the coming week in Georgia and Melinda was out with her friend. She had no one to continue sharing her excitement with. After a light supper she poured a Silent Sam with a splash and called Anthony.

Friday she came home with her roses. She changed into short and provocative and took a taxi to the mall to shop for a hostess gift. Jackson was working the floor, staying level, giving his clients Belmont Tailors' most personal attention.

Saturday she did an hour in her gym, cleaning her condo before pampering herself and putting her flowers on the balcony moments before she buzzed him in. Jackson was taking her to dinner at Melinda's for the first time, Murielle excited to talk about her wedding with her future mother-in-law and friend, Jackson not quite as eager for his mother's looming lecture about him becoming a pilot. She didn't like the idea one bit.

What Murielle didn't like was that he wasn't staying over, which meant not making love, which he suggested driving her home was a clear benefit of a personal aircraft. He would never again be restricted by someone else's schedule.

Sunday he packed and left home for an early flight to Atlanta. Murielle went for an early morning bike ride, enjoying the attention, calling Jackson once at home simply to say she loved him. She did a strenuous workout, showering and dressing for an afternoon with Charlee who drove her daddy's late model Jaguar into the driveway at precisely at 1:00.

She was a cute little thing, Murielle mused, waving from her balcony before hurrying in to press ENTER on the intercom.

In suede boots, a short knitted dress cinched with an oversized belt under a suede topper jacket and a Carolina Herrera handbag, Charlee Boyette was a heart stopper looking very much as though she belonged in a Jaguar, not winding her way between bistro tables with a money belt.

They did the indispensable hugging and kissing, the twirling and complimenting, Charlee commenting that she really needed to start operating on people. As much as she loved the guest house and pool, she could do without the constant reminder that she was alone. Her social life sucked, telling Murielle that the first possible pool-day of the year they were definitely getting a burn on.

If she imagined her life was already dismal, seeing the roses and listening to Murielle's recount of the weekend superimposed an even bleaker picture. Worse yet: She had no date for the wedding.

"That's why virgin is still a dictionary word, Murielle. It's because of me. Webster's wants everyone to know I'm a desperate lesbian."

"That's a good thing, Charlee. You never had to worry about college jocks who just want to get it wet and don't stay long."

"Med dickheads are worse. They think we're like bedpans to be cleaned out and used again. Put a stethoscope on a guy's neck, he becomes a real asshole really quickly. Smile at them, they get hard and scurry around searching for a room with an empty gurney."

Murielle commiserated. "I got through college with my

panties fully intact. Now I've got Jackson because of you."
She sipped her wine. "Proof positive that waiting pays huge
dividends, Charlee. And while we're on the subject, do you
remember Cerise from the other day?"

"With the beautiful long crimson hair and deep green
piercing eyes? Not really."

"Yeah, right. Anyway, she remembers you and she's
coming to the wedding solo. So I wouldn't worry too much
about not having a date. I kind of think your biggest
problem might be who drives who home. You know,
thinking out loud."

Murielle easily convinced her friend to stay for dinner
and a coffee to dilute their bloodstreams. When Charlee was
gone she put Jackson's toiletries with his photograph in her
dresser, putting Anthony's photograph in her living room
and his note by her roses on the coffee table. Tired, though
not ready for sleep, she went to bed with her tablet and flash
drive.

Monday, she didn't want to meet him on a street corner.
She hadn't seen him in eight weeks and wanted to do things
right. After work she went directly to his suite at the
Marriott with her diamond ring tucked safely into her purse,
relaxing with a minibar vodka while he showered and
changed into Boston casual. The rock and a hard place was
that she had a large and beautiful home, and her own bed;
he needed a workstation, proximity to his clients and a hotel
room to expense.

Truthfully she did not see the issue. His days always
finished early. He could easily wrap up loose ends by the
time her day was done. They would drive to her home and
they would spend their evenings and nights together. In the
morning they would drive to the Marriott to begin their
separate days and meet later. A no-brainer. She wouldn't
feel like a whore walking through lobbies and he wouldn't

feel like finding someone nowhere as good in bed or as alluring as her. Given that he would understand.

At her home he saw the roses and note, visibly pleased. He followed her to her bedroom, sitting on her bed, watching her leisurely undress while wondering why him. Why had fate brought her to him, or the inverse? Trailing her eagerly to the bathroom he watched from her vanity stool as she stretched, bent, and twisted in the shower. When she stepped dripping from the tiled stall, pointing to a freshly folded towel, he leaped to his feet with an impossibly wide grin.

When he finished meticulously drying her, she handed him a bottle of body cream telling him "everything except my face, darling."

He worked attentively and tenderly, as though creating her with his hands and not simply arousing her. When he finished she stepped away, casually sitting at her vanity, treating her face and combing her hair while he leaned against the doorway entirely captivated. When she was finished, satisfied with her body, certain he was primed and ready, she pushed herself to her feet.

Squeezing past him, she took his hand. Pulling him into the bedroom she told him she needed a good one. She wanted his best unless he was tired and would prefer watching, shrieking as her feet left the floor.

An hour later they were panting together in the shower, Murielle thinking her body would not survive the week. Then no sooner would he be gone than Jackson would naturally want her, with scarcely a day between them.

She slipped into her Christmas baby dolls, choosing a wine while he called for an all-dressed.

In the living room, the fake flames flickering on low and throwing out heat, she curled onto the sofa beside him.

"I love you. You know that, don't you?"

"Of course, I do. And ditto that big time." He clinked his glass to hers. "I have to admit, this is a lot better than a hotel suite."

"And soon I'll make space for you to work. You'll be able to stay longer the weeks you're in town, the weeks I'm alone. Or the evenings I could be working late."

"I don't think that came out right, sweetcheeks. How can you be alone when I'm with you?"

"Okay, I need you to listen and understand. I have a friend. Her name is Charlee. She has a brother who wants to see me. Wants to see me, Anthony. I have not slept with him. I promise you. What I'm saying is that you call the place I live a swamp and, as much as I had a good time playing with you in the snow…once, I absolutely despise the cold. Not to mention your warm and cuddly friends, your current fear of marriage or our blossoming careers." She squeezed his arm, leaning closer, searching his eyes. "We have something special, something fantastic that will not survive in the long-term unless we get real about each other."

His expression derailed her. He had none. He had learned years earlier the advantage of maintaining a neutral façade when hit with bad news. Despite which he was stunned, his mind flashing back to the day he came home early to discover the demon bitch frantically pounding some unfortunate bastard as though she'd won the national lottery.

He glanced at the fingers digging into his arm. "How does that work, Murielle, exactly? You, me, and some guy you will eventually sleep with."

"Anthony, in France we have a custom we call cinq à sept. Five to seven in the evening, a time when gentlemen visit with their lovers before going home to their wives. A time for men to cheat, a time for their wives to react. It's all very acceptable, keeping marriages alive and stimulating. My father had a lover, my mother also on occasion. Otherwise how boring would life become? Divorce in France is very unusual, darling. That is what I am saying."

"You're saying that we see other people, and each other when I'm in town. That's what you're saying?"

"Yes. Seeing other people will keep us together as lovers. Otherwise one of us will eventually cheat. People cheat and tell lies, Anthony. It's normal, something neither of us should want. This way, at least we will be honest with each other."

"And when does all this happen?"

"I won't tell you. And you should never tell me."

"And if this guy somehow gets promoted to husband, what then? Does he move in, do you move out? What?"

"Of course I will marry one day, and you will be my secret. As I will be yours because, whoever I choose to marry, he will cheat."

"I have to ask, Murielle. Was this guy the girls in Québec, the girls at New Year's? Was that all a lie?"

"He was not. Charlee and those girls are my friends. They were not a lie."

He nodded, sipping his wine. "I can't picture you sleeping with someone else. The guy in Charleston, I get that. But what you're suggesting is weird, expecting me to share your bed with this guy."

"Not my bed, Anthony. I would never do that to you. I promise. This place is for us, darling, for you and for me. Married or not, I am keeping my home as my private place...for us. "

The pizza delivery was timely.

"I wish you hadn't dropped this shit bomb on me while you're wearing practically nothing, Murielle. Tactically very smart, though not really fair."

"All is fair, darling, in love and in war. I am in love, *with you,* fighting to keep *you.*"

He went to the door, buzzing the kid in, taking his time. He needed breathing room. Topping off their wine he sat facing her on the coffee table. "Christmas seemed like four hours, not days. New Year's Eve I was alone and for Valentine's I sent flowers I didn't hand pick. Now, sitting with me practically naked, you're suggesting I should find someone else and cheat on her with you."

"Not cheating, sharing. Once you find the right girl, someone to share special times with, until you can truthfully say you no longer love me. That is not cheating. That is sharing, like most of the world. Your demon wife was cheating. If she were honest you would still have your house and me because you loved me the first moment you saw me. That is why divorce in France is almost taboo. How often, here, did you want some pretty girl in your bed before me?"

He snorted. "I'm strong-willed."

"Until you met me, darling." She patted her cushion. "There is always a 'someone' because the ennui of living the same day every day of your life eventually becomes unliveable."

He sat beside her. "Did this epiphany come to you before Christmas?"

"It came to me because of Christmas, as I flew home, counting the days I would miss you, counting how many times I would miss you. When I arrived here, Anthony, I felt...je ne sais quoi." She shrugged. "I felt incredible loneliness, such emptiness."

"Is this an ultimatum, Murielle? If not me, do you find someone else to balance your time or your life with this girlfriend's brother? Would this have happened if I moved here?"

"Not an ultimatum. I have my lover, darling. The real questions is, will you keep yours?"

PART FOUR
30

He didn't have much choice in the matter, if not sharing her with a stranger meant losing her.

Saturday morning he left Murielle depleted and purring contentedly in her bed after ardently damaging her, mutually agreeing they should speak once each week. At the airport, as he had done all week, he pondered her logic. She did have a valid point. Pretty well every man he was acquainted with cheated, cheating with women who cheated, like the guy he caught bagging the demon.

That Murielle would marry one day was a given. She was too sexually charged and driven to live her life waiting for his next business trip and statistically her husband would cheat, in essence allowing her equal opportunities.

Men and women entertained divergent views on marriage, until shit hit the fan, until those differing views collided in court. Most women viewed the concept as an assurance of stability and security, which was complete bullshit. Most men saw the overrated institution as pragmatic, an unpredictable means to an end.

In all probability the woman he would inevitably meet would sooner or later want his name, which was problematic because when travelling he would always wonder.

He couldn't blame Murielle or the other guy. She was

young, deserving more than a drop-in lover. Her body was magnificent and the girlfriend's brother would soon discover that sex with her was tantamount to getting laid by a short-circuited delirious android. She was insatiable.

Flight 902 was called, which he ignored, letting the masses board first. The flight was full, evenly balanced with experienced business types and all others who weren't.

The plastic female attendant gave him a one-second peripheral once-over he wasn't supposed to recognize, smiling as though she was greeting a dear friend. She wasn't. She was rating him. She was estimating his age, his height, his strength, whether he was intoxicated or a smart-ass who would cause trouble, whether he would be of any use in an emergency that didn't first kill everyone onboard. Apparently he passed. She returned his stub, telling him 7C at the bulkhead as though he couldn't read.

"Excuse me, miss. I believe you're in my seat."

The woman looked up, Charles Anthony Vincent instinctively giving her the same peripheral once-over she wasn't supposed to recognize. However being a female, a very pretty one, one he assumed was accustomed to being ogled, she did. He was rating her, estimating her age, her height, whether she was a bitch or worth talking with, whether her skirt would ride any higher as she wiggled into the centre seat.

As she gave him a passing grade her weak smile scarcely masked her disappointment, which was unfortunate because aisle seats would forever trump gentility.

When he was seated, she turned to him. She wasn't smiling, her eyes and her voice were. "You're a last-minute gate crasher, 7C. I hate last-minute gate crashers."

"I feel badly, Miss 7B. I do. Honestly, I can't think of any worse creature. Tell me, is there any way I can possibly nullify the ill feelings I've created between our neighbouring seats?"

"No. Thank you, 7C. I'm beginning to feel better."

The conversation stalled with the customary tedious announcement spoken for the benefit of grandmothers and first-timers. No one else paid attention. At altitude, with in-flight service beginning, Anthony's mind was a whirlwind of doubt and frustration, eagerness and expectation. Thing is, he didn't lie. Never did, not really. So what would he tell her when she asked the obvious and inescapable question?

She was good-looking, very good-looking, twenty-six or seven. She had great and long legs, most of which were nicely on display, and she wasn't wearing any significant ring. He had no doubt she would look fantastic naked. Her skin was smooth, her long black hair shimmering over her shoulders, her green eyes sparkling with sandy brown speckles.

He was rebounding, seriously aching from the demon, numbed by vivid images of someone else in bed with Murielle. What he was considering was irrational and pointless. She would politely and demurely refuse him, her species' tactful way of telling him to get lost.

He inhaled an invisible deep breath, fortified against probable failure. "Excuse me, Miss 7B. I've been pondering how best to ease the obvious tension between us. Would you please allow me to offer you a beverage?"

"I'm sorry. I don't drink with strangers."

"A minor impediment very easily remedied. I'm Charles Anthony Vincent seated in 7C. We spoke previously. I have no criminal record and I am not a predator. I'm unattached at twenty-seven through no fault of my own and I live alone near the ocean. I have a degree, a good job, I dance fairly well, I drink Johnnie Walker Black in moderation and I'm a fairly good cook. I can also offer references on demand."

He was grinning, waiting.

She wasn't blinking, staring directly into his eyes as though probing his brain. Or searching for one.

"I'm Karine Fenway. No relation. My brother's a Boston detective and I hold a third dan in the unfortunate event you do become a predator. I'm single because most of you are complete jerks. I have a master's degree in sociology and a very good job. I'm a terrible dancer and a fantastic cook. I'm old enough to drink, and I prefer wine with a real cork to hard stuff. A red wine would be wonderful. Thank you, Charles Anthony Vincent."

Karine's wine came with a twist cap. Not his fault, he immediately made clear. No worse than his JW coming with a red label, he added.

Too soon, as the attendant took away their glasses nearing their final approach into Logan, he said, "I really want to say something that doesn't sound trite, Karine. You know, like I'm really happy I met you."

"Then don't. Say what you mean, Anthony. You want to ask me out. So ask me out. It's not as though I'm not going to Google you. I am definitely going to Google you."

"I would like to invite you to dinner, Karine. Not tonight, whenever you're free."

"Next Saturday works for me. March third." She ignored him for a moment, reaching for the attaché at her feet, fully aware he was admiring her legs. She passed him a business card. "If I don't answer, leave a message, Anthony. If I don't return the call it's because you're a sociopath or a reformed criminal. Giving you the benefit of doubt the mandatory requisites are bright lights and meeting at the restaurant. Can you live with that, Charles Anthony Vincent?"

"I can very nicely live with that."

From his in-flight success to the baggage carrousel they spoke about restaurants, when they should meet, and when he should call to confirm. She was first off the shuttle with a simple "Call me." And then she was gone. A curious instance when shaking hands would be ridiculous, given that Saturday she would be saying "yes" to a second date. He hoped.

Driving south to his home he revisited the entire week. He hadn't once cheated on his wife or Murielle. Yet because of her he had a dinner date with a remarkably good-looking sociologist, which wasn't cheating according to her French rationale. The only one cheating would in fact be Murielle on the other guy. How bizarre was that? Though one thing she did say was true, that by not knowing the specifics of time and place he likely would never dwell on the insane duplicity she actually made sense of. The foremost rule of their socially venerable cinq à sept: Be discreet.

Throughout the three hours onboard, strolling through the airport and onboard the shuttle, he hadn't given her a moment's thought. Which wasn't the case while driving in the dark along the I-95, wondering who was taking her to dinner, who would later sit on her sofa, wondering what she would wear, wondering how many more dinners she would deem requisite to sleeping with him.

He shook his head free of her, rekindling his brief time with Karine. The single proof of her existence, that she was not some cruel fabrication of an injured consciousness in desperate need of repair, was the card in his shirt pocket.
*

Tuesday he called Karine, pleased to hear that Google and her cop-brother had approved him for dinner. He wasn't a sociopath, a stalker or predator.

She did like Italian and she knew the restaurant that was not overly posh or romantic or a playroom for bratty kids. And well-lit, he made clear. She asked what he would wear.

Casual: Slacks, a blazer and open-collar white shirt. She was looking forward to the evening. As was he; she was his first sociologist dinner date. And a professor to boot. Something she hadn't told him. Was she going to analyze him, he asked? She would not, she promised. That was a fait accompli.

*

Anthony was right about Saturday, about Professor Fenway wanting to see him again.

She met him at 7:00, greeting him as she stepped from her Lexus, handing her keys to the valet.

Inside he took her coat and scarf, passing them to the hatcheck girl, watching as she transitioned from her boots to her stocking feet to her patent leather pumps. Standing, palming her snug woolen dress, she was a vision.

Throughout dinner they talked about work and travel, his home by the ocean and her martial arts, Karine assuaging his worry. She would not beat him up without good reason. She hadn't dated in over a year. Her several previous attempts at something resembling a relationship were instant and dismal failures. They were either intimidated by her being a professor, or her black belts, or believing that sex with her the first night was a reasonable return on their dinner investment. They were wrong.

He was recently divorced as a result of discovering his ex's comparative studies of the male nude and its ability to please. The scars were healing; still, he was glad he asked the fascinating and lovely lady in 7B to move over, amazed he had somehow found the courage to invite her to dinner. Despite his trust quotient plummeting into the single digits, he would have regretted not knowing her.

After dessert, after non-stop conversation without trespassing into unsafe territory, he took the leap.

"I have to say, Professor Fenway, I don't find you intimidating at all. Nor would I ever think to fight a girl, which makes your ninja thing a non-issue. That said, I do want to see you again. I'm good with more bright lights in a public place."

She had a way of smiling with her eyes. "Then I'm good with seeing you again. I literally cannot remember the last time I wasn't at home grading papers on a Saturday night. Or when I last enjoyed a man's company, particularly with one I've known," she glanced at her watch, "a total of six hours."

"Dinner next Saturday?"

"I do have tickets for an afternoon performance at the Capitol next Sunday, not particularly thrilled about sitting alone between strangers. Given the distinct possibility I'll be told by a charming last-minute gate crasher to move over. Do you like musicals, 7C?"

He did.

Leaving the restaurant Karine Fenway pressed her cheek lightly to his without inferring better things to come, thanking him for a delightful evening without suggesting they call each other in the meantime.

At home later that evening Anthony poured a healthy JW Black, preparing himself for the unpleasant ceremony essential to the life Murielle was imposing on him. He deleted her entirely from his flash drive, closing his framed image of her into a seldom used drawer in his garage since she would never again come to Boston. Not due to Karine who was all too fresh. Because he realized that seeing her two-dimensionally naked, playful and untouchable on his flat screen, or every night by his bed while she was doing some other guy in his bed, was a needless and excruciating torment.

Speaking with her each week would be torment enough.

The following Sunday he met Karine in the lobby of the Capitol. After the performance they went to dinner, talking endlessly, Karine kissing his cheek before stepping into her luxury sedan. The next morning Anthony flew to Chicago, too busy with presentations and meetings during his days and entertaining at night to think about her or Murielle.

When they did speak he invited her for the seventeenth, Karine meeting him outside her Boston condo, ending the evening in her lobby with a sisterly kiss on his cheek and an invitation to a simple home-cooked meal that gave him greater hope.

The following Sunday he arrived at her condo moments before noon in a sweater and cords, Karine greeting him in designer jeans and a crisp white button-down. She opened his Patriarche red first, sitting close to him on her couch, talking about their week, not waiting long to serve her ragout and freshly baked baguette.

After lunch they strolled through a nearby park holding hands, Anthony unexpectedly kissing her lips. Karine apparently harbouring the same urgent need. She kicked him out an hour after dark, after her most passionate kiss, confessing she was afraid. She had to be certain.

On the last day of the month, their fifth date, she drove the forty miles to his home where the snow had practically disappeared. Nevertheless walking into the warmth of a flickering fireplace, soft music and the man she was beginning to, she didn't know, possibly love.

He wasn't a jerk or obnoxious. He was educated, polished and respectful, not once alluding to sleeping with her. He was good-looking with all his hair, was physically fit with no obvious bad habits. She assumed he was anatomically correct, the remaining mysteries prompting her to make the weekend one of discovery.

He was standing waiting as she drove up, leaning

casually against his doorway with his arms crossed, his legs crossed at the ankles. She was impressed. The place was a little wooded Shangri-La. God, she thought, popping the trunk, inhaling a final deep breath…do not let this be a huge mistake.

He was coming closer, beaming. She smiled through the tinted glass, letting him open the door.

"Hi. Welcome to my hideaway."

She took his hand, stepping out, smelling the fresh spring air. She could actually hear birds. "God, I live in a box."

"Something to take in?"

"Please."

He went to the trunk. "That's a suitcase."

"Not a suitcase, Anthony. A decision. I thought all week about this. So you better not have some blonde bimbo planned for tomorrow or I'll really be pissed."

"I don't, Karine. I promise." He reached in for the suitcase, slamming the trunk shut. "She's a redhead." Then he remembered, shaking his head and chuckling, slapping a palm to his forehead. "Silly me. I'm sorry. The redhead was last week. Tomorrow I'm expecting long, black and beautiful, with green hazel eyes and full pouty lips."

She stood staring, not quite appreciating the humour. He didn't seem to care, taking her hand, leading her into his home.

"That was not funny, Charles Anthony Vincent. You wait until I'm ready to sleep with you to show me you're a jerk? Really? After I spent the entire week wondering whether you're a Tony, a Darling, a Dear, a Lover or a whatever? You do realize this is a major leap of faith for me, don't you?" She slid her jacket from her shoulders. "That was a question, 7C."

317

He guided her directly to the bedroom, assuring her he was not rushing things.

"I do realize you're nervous. Don't think I'm not. I thought I was sending you home early. But since I'm unexpectedly the happiest guy in the entire state, please no Dear or Darling and I haven't been a Tony since grade one. Lover? I suppose you'll have to wait until tomorrow, Professor, since you are predisposed to grading. Personally I think 7C works in the short-term."

He left her to pour wine while she unpacked. When she came out he gave her the grand tour, Karine impressed with his housekeeping skills. As he sat in the living room she went to the bedroom telling him to close his eyes. She had a surprise. When he opened them minutes later…

"Happy birthday, 7C. I hope you like it."

His brow furrowed. "What? I never told you my birthday, Karine."

"I knew the day after we met, amongst other things. My brother the detective, remember?"

"This was not necessary."

"Don't spoil my day. Especially now that we're the same age. I won't feel like I'm robbing the cradle."

Tearing away the paper, Karine thanking him for destroying her careful work, he was visibly shocked, the smell of rich leather wafting from the slim briefcase.

He kissed her. "Karine, this is exceptional."

"I can't have my lover walking around with a vinyl and canvas computer bag. This is much more you, more sophisticated." She glanced up to the loft. "I don't suppose you wear anything in that."

"It's usually not an issue."

"I didn't bring a bikini."

"I'll close my eyes. Besides, it's pretty deep and swirly."

"Great. I'm taking off my clothes and you're closing your eyes. Good beginning, 7C."

He pondered the dilemma, running his fingers across the smooth leather. "What if *I* take off your clothes and you close *your* eyes?"

She thought maybe not, patting his knee, thanking him for his genuine concern.

Lunch was more wine and hot clam chowder, calming her churning stomach. They went for a walk through his woods, quietly holding hands, listening to birds chirping over the roar of the nearby Atlantic, returning to the warmth of the fire as the day grew shorter and chillier.

There was no point in waiting. She was well-acquainted with the human condition as a professor of sociology. She knew what he was thinking. He was wondering when, wondering how she would look naked, whether they would be good lovers, or whether sex with her would dampen their feelings. He knew that cupping her breasts too soon might ruin their evening, that saying he loved her in the heat of the passion she craved might scare her away. Thing is, she held the reins.

Staring into the flames, pressed against him, her lustrous black hair soft against his cheek, her legs framed by his, his arms framing her torso, she brought his hands to her breasts, pausing a moment to relish the tender pressure.

"Not merely a lovely professor and a ninja, a psychic as well. Thank you."

"I haven't done this in a very long time, 7C." She pressed against his hands. "They're not the biggest, yet they do seem to go well with the rest of me."

"They seem to go well with me too."

"One rule, Anthony. Please. Do not say you love me because you're all hot and excited. Let's save that for later, if later happens."

"I won't. I promise. I have to say though, sitting here like this tells me that later will happen. I want later to happen."

She wiggled free of his arms and hands, padding to the bedroom, pointing to the loft, telling him to run a bath or whatever he does with the thing. She also wanted him sitting in the swirling water before she joined him. She was already on the verge of a stroke.

Ten minutes later, sitting on his bed in an oversized robe, nervous and wanting to cry, elated and wanting to bounce on the bed with glee, her heart skipped a beat. He was ready with glasses of chilled Chardonnay, sitting naked and cloaked in the swirling and gurgling water, which wasn't by far his first choice. Which she called out wasn't her problem, keeping to herself that she was about to get laid by a man she wouldn't admit she was beginning to love. Seriously laid, she hoped.

At the loft the tension and anxiety drained from her body. His face was beaded with sweat, his lips pursed, his eyes squeezed tightly shut. Despite which, she liked what she was seeing. Imagining the rest of him came easily.

"Okay. I'm really not good at this, though I do believe most girls want to see their lover's very first reaction. If there is a later, we will never have another first time. I need to see your eyes, Anthony."

He complied at once, smiling either contentedly or to lessen her anguish at making herself completely vulnerable, Karine giving him the benefit of doubt.

She faced away, shrugging his robe from her shoulders. Clutching the side of the Jacuzzi she pulled her weight easily from the floor. Her arms and back were flawless and defined, the sensual curves of her buttocks tauntingly suspended over the edge before she lowered her weight onto the slick fibreglass making him want to push his way through the water to pull her in.

Swinging her legs over the edge, planting her feet on the moulded seating, she stood gazing at him with her arms by her side.

"Okay, 7C. I'm not staying like this very long and I am not turning. So have a good look and please be a gentleman."

She was spectacular. She was a couple of inches shorter than Murielle whose body was smooth and shapely by virtue of her youth and daily workouts. Karine's body was tighter and trimmer, her abs sculpted by more intensive training. Even though her skin was much paler than Murielle's olive hue, she was no less flawless. Her voice was sweet, almost delicate; Murielle's was husky and exotic.

She cleared her throat leaning forward, planting her hands on her hips, Anthony fairly certain her pursed lips and glaring hazel eyes meant he should say something.

He shrugged, smirking. "Really? I have to say, not bad."

Her eyes flared open, her mouth gaping. The next instant she was tightly wrapped in his arms. He was kissing her, plunging her lithe body into heated water, and she was certain. She was no longer afraid. She did love Charles Anthony Vincent: Her secret.

31

Her body hadn't once in her life been as expertly or
delicately probed or penetrated, caressed and titillated, her
every sensation heightened by a hundred pulsating jets, the
warmth of fleecy towels and the silkiness of satin sheets
that followed.

The next morning Karine Fenway woke wanting more
of what lulled her into a deep sleep, disappointed to
discover he wasn't beside her. In the bathroom, peering into
the mirror, she cringed. Her hair was a tangled mess; her
face was frightful, marred with mascara. Her lip gloss was
smeared and she smelled worse than a wet dog.

Sitting on the toilet she wondered when he would say
the words, whether he would ever tell her. She certainly
would not. What would loving him matter if he felt
differently? Five weeks was insane, nevertheless she knew
what she felt.

Stepping into the shower she massaged shampoo into
her hair, standing in a euphoric daze, watching the white
foam wash lazily over her breasts and her belly, between
her thighs and down her legs. Stepping out, patting her body
dry and combing her hair into damp tresses, the girl in the
mirror smiled at her more approvingly. Dressed in a thong
and bra since modesty was clearly no longer an issue, she
went to him in the kitchen where he was doing blueberry
crêpes in straight-backs and a compression tee.

They spent the morning walking and talking in the woods, holding hands and laughing. Throughout most of the afternoon, interspersed with time-out in the Jacuzzi, Karine's desire for more was fully acknowledged and amply satiated.

She stayed over Sunday as well, waking early to a pleasant throbbing. She hated leaving him, which spoke silent volumes. Driving to her office Monday morning she didn't care about the heavy traffic, pondering how often and for how long she would make the ninety-minute trip.

Would she always, or would she never again? He couldn't possibly not love her. No one could possibly feign that much affection.

In early April he went on business to New Orleans, using his hotel suite as a work station before going home each evening with Murielle. At the end of April Karine heard the words she hoped for spoken in the heat of passion, in the shower and at dinner. He loved her. She was thrilled. Charles Anthony Vincent was not a huge mistake, from then on missing him more each week until the next short-lived passionate weekend, feeling miserable the weeks he would arrive from business trips late Friday or catch an early flight on Sunday.

At the end of May, and again on the 16th of July, he returned to the Swamp for a week of sweltering heat and miserable sweat. At the end of the month he vacationed with Karine in Miami, soaking up the sun before spending the first week of September with Murielle who was weeks away from becoming Mrs. Murielle Belmont. In Boston for Thanksgiving dinner at Karine's he out of the blue slid a diamond ring onto her finger, lending credence to the proposal on bended knee. He wanted to marry her; he could not bear to think of living without her.

She flung herself into his arms, smudging his face with

gloss, wiping warm tears from her face and his as a prelude to several gleeful yeses, hating that he was flying the next morning to a city he loathed.

*

Murielle over the previous eight months heard not a single word about Karine, how quickly he had met her or of the engagement. Nor did she ask. She was content being with him as often as he could manage being in New Orleans.

She preferred having him in her home, cooking for him, loving him in her bed and missing him each time he would leave her on a Friday morning and not come home to her that evening.

In early May she arrived home from work to see Jackson standing by a gleaming green MX-5 roadster tied with a wide yellow ribbon, wishing her the happy birthday she assumed he had forgotten. He was taking her to dinner, she was driving. Three weeks later Anthony gave her emerald earrings and she drove him to dinner in the car she could finally afford.

By mid-July her wedding plans were complete, adding her supervisor, the four girls and the much improved guys to the almost 200 guests Melinda had invited. She had also given a three-month notice to her landlord, she told Jackson, the man happily agreeing to take her furniture in lieu of continued rent.

In mid-September they went together to the family and Belmont Tailors attorneys to set up a simple prenup comprising a 500 K cash gift the day of the wedding, an insurance policy against his life, and ten percent from the sale of Belmont Tailors to his employees upon his accidental or naturally occurring death with the option of from then on assuming control.

None of which mattered. She was excited about moving into his upscale home as his wife, never again to leave as his girlfriend and lover. Then, too soon, not soon enough, he was kissing her goodbye at her door seven days before her wedding and would not see her until then. He was meeting with suppliers in Georgia, Miss Clara advising him in her inimitable way days early that his presence would be required at the office on the Friday afternoon without fail.

Something was up that he thought wise not to question. Although he would call his lovely fiancée the next evening, a call she missed with her bum in the air kneeling in front of Karine's fiancé. Thursday evening she didn't answer his call either, Jackson correctly assuming she went early to bed.

When Anthony left her Friday morning he kissed the bride-to-be without congratulating her. He had no reason; he had no idea about the wedding. He hadn't once asked her about the man she was seeing. Why would he? More importantly, they would see each other in December if not for Christmas.

Friday afternoon the Belmont girls gave him a catered party at the office that Miss Clara allowed to close early. Each one danced with him, Miss Clara given no exemption from learning basic Latin steps. They adored their boss, hugging and kissing him as things wound down. Miss Clara though limited her emotion to a motherly embrace, blushing at the giggles when he kissed her cheek.

When they were gone, prancing out the door admonishing him with more giggles and scolding fingers before clambering into the waiting taxis he insisted upon, the Belmont men remained behind for another hit. They were taking him to dinner and later to New |Orleans' finest gentlemen's club, Miss Clara making clear to innocent faces before marching out that she did not condone that sort of activity. They should all be very ashamed.

Earlier in the day at Gilmore Murielle's supervisor

325

requested that she stay late with Cerise to finalize a presentation, Murielle keeping to herself that not one of her friends had thought to suggest even a small bachelorette party. When they were done Cerise suggested heading over to the Marriott for cocktails and dinner. Her treat. And Murielle's last chance to legally flirt, she added.

Sashaying through the lobby toward the lounge Cerise took her arm, swinging her toward closed double doors, Murielle at the last second seeing the brass lectern and 'GILMORE' printed in bold script on parchment, Cerise chiding her for believing her friends would ever think to ignore her most special day.

Stepping through the doors she gasped at seeing every female at Gilmore well into the party mood screeching her name, her supervisor included. Seeing Melinda standing closest to the doors was a happy surprise. What shocked her, what stole Cerise's breath, was seeing Melinda wearing a mischievous smirk and the cute dark-haired girl standing beside her.

Cerise clamped a hand to her mouth. "Mur, you are an absolute bitch. You told her!"

"I didn't, I swear." She took Cerise's hand. "I told Melinda. So deal with it."

A moment later, "Charlee, this is the green-eyed redhead. You two work things out. I'm not involved." She turned to Melinda, hugging and kissing her. "Merci, maman, for both of them."

*

Saturday morning a bleary-eyed Jackson woke late, happily confident that those who conspired to leave him with a fairly decent hangover weren't in much better shape, thankful he had a full twenty-four hours to regroup.

He spent what remained of the morning in his Jacuzzi, reading the morning papers, reading in the society column that the next day Mademoiselle Murielle Adrianna de la Sorbonne would become Mrs. Jackson Belmont, Jr.

He spent his afternoon preparing what he would wear for the ceremony and packing for the honeymoon, dedicating his final evening as a bachelor to comparing flight schools and personal aircraft. At 1.35 million the Beechcraft Baron was a good entry model. Notwithstanding his mother or Murielle, each of them firmly against the purchase, the thing was sturdy, had a good history, and at 230 mph he would be anywhere in the Southeast or Mexico on his schedule before he would normally be taking his seat in First-Class.

*

Saturday Murielle's eyes fluttered open uncharacteristically early, jabbing a fingertip punitively against her phone's flashing screen, stopping the piercing shrill. Misère! She'd missed two calls. The first was from Cerise saying that, okay, she wasn't an absolute bitch. She was the best friend ever. She and Charlee were meeting for a lunch, thinking they could be each other's date for the wedding. The second message was from a giddy Charlee. She and Melinda were the absolute best. She was meeting Cerise for a lunch, pretty certain she would have a date for the wedding.

Good for them. Blah, blah. But they were both wrong. There would be no lunch, at least not the way they planned.

Groaning, dragging herself from the soft comfort of her bed, she didn't bother showering. Selecting what she should wear was hardship enough, deciding on jeans, a sweater, and the first thing she pulled from her panty drawer.

Breakfast was coffee and toast, her elation competing against her weariness, her mind skipping freely from one beautiful future into another with them. Though were she to have cared to enquire, were she to suspect for a moment how he was chortling on his balcony several blocks away, his mind festering with cruel ideas, she would have fled that morning as Adrianna Dupree into the cold North.

*

Kenneth Stonewall stood on his Garden District balcony snickering, fixated on the amusing wedding announcement.

He often thought about her, often perusing his Murielle Collection of fond memories, in the dark recesses of his mind never truly forgiving her rude interruption of his evening or her girlish threat. Forgiveness for Stonewall was a fundamental flaw in humankind, a weakness. Now he believed he would always think about her, always remember her. How could he not, given his decades-long relationship with Belmont Tailors?

The little harlot did well for herself in a mere fifteen months, transitioning from bartering her athletic allures without the slightest restriction in exchange for an education to luring Belmont into her frilly panties in exchange for a carefree life after losing her appetite for pizza.

*

JACKSON BELMONT, JR., SON OF MRS. MELINDA BELMONT OF NEW ORLEANS AND THE LATE JACKSON BELMONT OF BELMONT TAILORS, WILL TOMORROW MARRY MADEMOISELLE MURIELLE ADRIANNA DE LA SORBONNE, DAUGHTER OF THE LATE FRANÇOIS-ANISETTE DE LA SORBONNE AND HIS WIFE JACQUELINE MARIE-ANNE (NÉE DUPREE).
THE PRIVATE CEREMONY WILL TAKE PLACE ONBOARD THE STEAMBOAT NATCHEZ FOLLOWED BY A RECEPTION FOR CLOSE FRIENDS AND ASSOCIATES.

*

"Well done indeed, Murielle. Bravo. Very good work indeed," Stonewall spoke aloud, watching desirable and scantily dressed women jog and run along the outskirts of

328

the park.

"What, Kenny?" she asked, his current live-in passing him a fresh expresso as she stepped into the morning air.

"Belmont and his bride," he snorted. "The man's done well for himself. If I could for a moment create in my mind a woman lovelier than you, I would surely imagine his nubile bride. He must surely be proud to marry such a delightful and ostensibly pure young woman." He put a fingertip to Murielle's black and white image, sipping the bitter coffee. "I imagine she's quite pleased with herself, marrying into such an established family. In any event we'll see her in person tomorrow. Won't we, my dear? I am very much looking forward to meeting her, to introducing you. You might well become close friends."

"She'll be a beautiful bride."

"And you, a beautiful guest. In fact I suppose we should expect to see your lovely visage in these very pages in the very near future."

"Oh, Kenny! Do you really think so? I can't imagine how awesomely thrilled I would be."

*

The limousine arrived near 10:00 AM for a special day of makeovers and beauty treatments with Melinda who was already seated in the car with a stunned Cerise and Charlee: Jackson's idea. And he didn't want any of them driving after a night of partying and a full day of pampering.

The second to last stop for them was Melinda's salon for extra special attention from her staff, the last was Murielle's for pizza without Melinda and an early night of whatever girls do on such an occasion.

*

Earlier that morning however as Stonewall was reading his paper, several miles north on the shores of Lake Pontchartrain, François-Anisette de la Sorbonne answered

329

his phone. His neighbour was calling. Her voice was agitated, asking Frank whether he had read the morning paper and, hearing that he hadn't, she disconnected. Moments later his doorbell chimed.

Reading the announcement, seeing in black print what her daughter was telling the city and the world, Jacqueline Marie-Anne searched her husband's eyes through her own that were flooding with tears. Hearing him respond with cold detachment that the girl was as dead as they apparently were, she reeled dizzily and wailed, collapsing inconsolable onto a loveseat.

Frank graciously thanked his neighbour, returning the paper. Closing the door he poured curative cognacs equal in volume to Jacqueline's distress and sat quietly comforting her. He was not a man given to forgiveness or undue emotion. Even so, what could anyone possibly say that would adequately detract from the incredibly repugnant and spiteful malice of a daughter once loved? The girl was incurably and despicably devoid of decency, not in the least way worthy of fond memories or salvation.

As Jacqueline's sobbing and trembling gradually diminished to occasional gasps for air, he squeezed her hands in his. Smiling affectionately, he said in a low and tender voice, "The girl has no soul, mon coeur. She is the dead one, not us. Today is merely the closure so long in coming to us. Now we will live our lives as happily as we once did before her. You and me together."
*

On the outskirts of Lafayette, 150 miles to the west, at the end of a long and winding dirt road was a home that to any trespasser's eye was more ramshackle than humble.

In muted and foreboding daylight chickens ran freely squawking across a front yard littered with all manner of debris, the skeletons of ancient vehicles and Mister

Lebrun's rusted-out tractor, stray cats, his lethargic dog and God knows what else he had forgotten or left to decay. Not a single ray of sun or its warmth penetrated the tall dark trees since Lebrun's grandfather put the place together plank by plank 100 years earlier. Just bleak dampness from endless grey days of Louisiana rain.

At night, surrounded by those tall trees, shadows never danced in fierce winds; they never crept across the chaotic graveyard when the wind blew elsewhere. No moon could ever be seen, not a single silver glow in those hundred years and the best place for Maurice Beaudoin to hide.

When Lebrun took his missus to the town hall dance that Saturday night, she with her baked goods and he with his jug of cider, the Beaudoin kid stood quietly in the dark until the truck's engine and grinding gears were at last beyond earshot. Then he waited several minutes more before making his way to the porch, to his girlfriend Claudine who days earlier after school promised him that Saturday night she would at last ease his manly discomfort.

Though not in a barn on bales of hay or the back of his father's truck. She wanted him in her bed, to poke her like the proper and good girl that she was.

She was seventeen, an only child and eager to leave her last year of schooling behind in the spring on account of the manager at the food and liquor store promised her a job on account of she was good with numbers and all. She was a tall girl at 5'8" with a bountiful chest always testing the buttons of her shirts, an enviable slim figure and a handsomely rounded backside that was impossible to ignore when she wore her tight jeans to her class.

Maurice was nineteen and taller with his hair cut short. He was lean and hard from labouring with his pa on the farm, eager for spring as well when he would begin work at the lumberyard since the Army had no real use for him.

331

Something to do with his flat feet, he supposed. Though what he did know for true was that with his first paycheque he would buy an automobile and ask old man Lebrun for Claudine's hand in marriage. He could not for the life of him picture himself not married at twenty.

Until that evening he had done what he could to soothe his physical yearnings, each night Claudine invading his mind, each night wanting her more. She had on occasion over the past several months bared her teats for him on the way home from school, once in a while letting him squeeze them and pinch her nipples. And with their shared times at the pond over the previous summer he had a fair imagination regarding her bare backside, not for a moment understanding why she couldn't once show him for real. Stranger still was that she was never once curious to see his cock despite his readiness to show her. Unaware she was assuming the thing was much like a horse's cock, though made much smaller to accommodate a woman's smaller opening.

Stepping into the open darkness and onto the uneven road he made his way to her dimly lit porch. He had seen pictures of all-naked girls, mostly at the drugstore in town where his cousin worked. Still, a live one was better. Had to be based on what he gathered from squeezing her soft teats. Though poking one, his cousin told him that morning…now that there was a real special treat.

She was waiting, standing in bare feet at the screen door in her Sunday dress, hoping that taking off a dress for him would make her appear more like a woman, more so than pulling off her jeans and socks and a tee-shirt he saw every day.

She was teetering between excitement and anxiety. Excitement because no boy had ever poked her, but Maurice was a man. Anxiety because no boy had ever seen her all naked, not even him, and she didn't know how to make herself prettier like those modern girls he once showed her in his cousin's dirty magazines.

She knew all the boys talked about her, thought about her without her clothes, which was different. That was okay. She didn't mind. That's what boys did in their beds, boys she didn't care about. She loved Maurice who was coming to see all of her, coming to poke her because she wanted him badly; she wanted to soothe his yearnings and springtime was too long to wait for her father's permission.

While taking her bath late that afternoon she dreamed of earning enough money at the store, and Maurice at the mill, to one day run away to the big city where she had never been. To the one they called the Big Easy she heard tell of at school, where women dressed in beautiful clothes and men treated them like they were ladies. That's what she wanted; she wanted to be lady like them. She also decided she would not wear underpants. She didn't own any like the pretty ones in proper magazines at the drugstore and she wanted Maurice to remember her body whenever he put his face into those other magazines, not her standing in a limp and shapeless cotton rag.

She took a deep breath, swinging open the rickety door. "Evenin', Maurice. Git yerself in."

"Yer lookin' real pretty this evenin', Claudine. Damn pretty, speakin' the truth. Ain't often I git to see ya'll dickied-up in a dress."

"Figured I should, seein' how yer comin' here to poke me. Seemed fittin' fer the occasion."

Inside they went straight to her bedroom holding hands. They didn't know what else they should do. They had no concept of sophistication, a word neither one knew nor could spell. They were too adolescent to know about romance and intimate dinners, dancing or sitting by a fireplace sipping fine wine.

She did however siphon cider from her father's many jugs in the barn the previous day after school, filling two large mugs that she hid under her bed, figuring that since she would become a woman within hours she'd be old enough to drink like one. She had also pulled back the sheets and fluffed her pillow. She didn't have much else to do, she figured, other than take off her dress and open her legs real wide. She couldn't remember a single time when her ma did more than follow her pa into the room, or the bed squeaking for more than a minute or so.

She pointed to the floor. "Got mugs fer us under the bed, Maurice. Pa's cider."

He nodded, dropping to his knees, passing her one. "Got to admit to bein' a mite uneasy, Claudine. Never poked a girl before. Thought about it enough times though, with you."

"Never bin poked before, Maurice. What I know is, yer the man I want pokin' me first off. Can't think of another I want more breakin' me in."

"Suppose we should gulp a swaller or two." He drained half the mug, wiping his mouth with the back of his hand. "Whew! Good stuff, yer pa brews."

Claudine did the same, coughing, blowing a mist of cider from her mouth and nose. Her pa didn't believe in womenfolk imbibing. The female mind was excessively frail. Drink made them lethargic, disinclined to perform their chores in a timely manner.

She tried again with better results, a deep heat surging to her face. "Ain't nothin' in the school books regardin' pokin', Maurice. All I know is to take off my dress. I'm supposin' the one with the cock should know more. Seems a natural enough thing in the barn."

"Ain't no different in a bed, Claudine. Cousin Arnold,

he told me what to do. He's bin pokin' his girl regular in the storeroom." He gulped more cider, peering into the empty mug. "Says ya'll might squeal a bit, then ya'll be smilin' and moanin' and sayin' bad things in yer elation."

She passed him her mug. "Suppose we should do some kissin' first."

"Ain't required, Claudine. Best way is to git yerself naked and git to the bed on yer knees. When yer ready I do likewise. Says his girl's forever pullin' him into the room. Says most girls once poked suffer a painful hunger fer cocks they can't ever properly satisfy."

Claudine knew she was ready. She felt the warm glow colouring her cheeks, the knot in her stomach loosening, prompted mostly by a foreign sensation invading her. She first plucked free the button at her collar, the next and the next, her eyes fixed on the floor, forcing all thoughts from her mind as the gap between the edges of her dress widened. Releasing the last button, letting the open hem fall to below her knees, she shrugged the dress from her body and made herself vulnerable.

Maurice stopped blinking, lurching forward, staring at the thin patch of brown curls crowning her thighs, mesmerized. He hurried behind her needing to see and grab her bare backside. He moved in closer, clumsily rubbing his hands over the smooth flesh as though deciding which mound he liked more, too inexperienced and unskilled to give her pleasure with tender caresses and kisses along the length of her legs and the curves of her back, too selfish to ease her anxiety with reassuring whispers. Instead he brought up a hand between her thighs pressing into the moisture, ignoring her heaving belly.

Inhaling the pungent glaze coating his hand, he stood. Reaching around her he squeezed her teats, plucking her nipples as though wanting them for souvenirs, not for a moment thinking to kiss the nape of her neck or her thick and lustrous chocolate brown hair.

He guided her to the bed, telling her the best way was to face the wall with her elbows on her mattress with her backside as high in the air as possible.

When she was poised, asking if she was doing it proper like, he nodded. He kicked off his shoes, tugging at his socks. He pulled his shirt over his head, ignoring the buttons, clumsily tugging at his singlet. Tearing at his belt he pushed his jeans to the floor, kicking them into the air, evoking a gasp from the girl waiting naked on her bed. His stained cotton shorts were distorted, not at all like her pa's she was accustomed to seeing each morning in the kitchen, Claudine only then realizing what he was about to jab into her.

Watching him push his shorts to the floor, kicking them away, she thought she had never in her life seen a stranger thing. The bag under his cock might have been a large walnut, the cock itself not at all what she imagined. The thing was pointing at her, bobbing every which way as he came closer.

She closed her eyes as he clambered behind her, holding her breath when the thing rubbed against her leg, suddenly embarrassed that he was seeing every bit of her. She felt him guiding the thing, pressing against her, searching for the right place while his other hand was squeezing her backside. Then she felt the slightest intrusion, the foreign tightness and warmth. A second later her eyes flared open, her distorted mouth sucking in air. He was pounding her, jerking her, gripping her hips, rocking her body to a cacophony of her cries and his horrible grunts.

She shifted her weight, struggling to raise her body, bracing herself against the onslaught with rigid arms and clenched fists digging into her mattress. A moment later his grip tightened. She felt him convulse, twisting her, his final and brutal thrust launching her forward. Then nothing.

Faster than she needed to take off her dress she had forsaken her purity, laying splayed on her front and panting, wanting to cry, wanting to close her legs but he wouldn't let her.

He was breathing heavily, kneeling between them. He leaned forward kneading her backside like mounds of dough, ignoring the slim contours of her back and her legs. Not thinking to turn her over, to lay with her, to see her face and hold her.

"I can't see that yer fine teats alone will ever again be good enough fer us after classes, Claudine. Not after a poke as good as that one. Yer as wet down here as a leaky faucet, the way my cousin told. You should raise up yer backside again while my cock's still stiff as an iron pipe."

She did, thinking maybe the second time would be less awful. However Maurice, puzzled at seeing the pinkish tinge trickling down her thighs, heaved his weight from between her legs to the floor.

"What's wrong?"

"Don't know. I'm guessin' yer insides are cut, Claudine."

"My insides are fine, Maurice. Sore a bit, is all. It's what happens." She sat crossing her legs, watching him lose his strength "I'm thinkin' yer cock's done for the night, Maurice. We should git ourselves dressed." She stood, wincing. "Besides, I have to pass my water and clean myself."

"It'll come back in a little while, Claudine. Let's wait a bit."

She shook her head. "They'll go dancin' other nights, Maurice, till the springtime comes."

She walked out, leaving her dress on the floor, Maurice

following her every footstep. When she came out her insides were as clean as she could make them, her soft curls freshened and damp with well water. Putting away her dress she put on jeans and a tee-shirt, not wanting him to see her drab underwear.

When the Lebruns came home her pa went straight to his bed, her ma opening Claudine's door to see her daughter peacefully sleeping. But Claudine was not sleeping, opening her eyes when the door closed. With a warm palm pressed between her thighs, soothing the numbness and stinging, she was dreaming of springtime, of being married and one day moving to New Orleans with her man.

She had to marry and she would. That's what decent girls did and Maurice was the best of all the boys in her class, though she did think that for his stature his cock might have been a size bigger. Leastways the thing was bigger than a tampon and who was to say the other boys were any better endowed? If that was the best pokin' could be, then he was the man to poke her from then on.

Of course Claudine Lebrun would never in her life see New Orleans; neither would Maurice Beaudoin. They were backwoods Cajun hillbillies. Always would be. Things like that don't ever change.

By Christmas she wasn't yet aware, once in a while managing a poke in the woods with him while straddling a fallen tree or kneeling on a patch of dry leaves. However by New Year's her flat belly was rounded and weeks before Valentine's Lebrun was pounding on Beaudoin's door with the stock of his long gun. Despite the girl being legal he demanded the Beaudoin boy stand up for what he had done, threatening to kill the boy straight out otherwise.

Claudine and Maurice left school on the last Friday in June, their papers attesting to their readiness to survive in the real world, Maurice taking her as his wife before a local judge the next day with God as their only witness. Once married, her disgraced pa wanted nothing more to do with her, Beaudoin's view of his son not much better.

Maurice began work at the mill on the Monday. Claudine began at the store, the owner agreeing to rent her the small apartment upstairs as part of her wages. They were alone to make their way, Claudine giving birth alone three weeks later to a daughter with no possible way of foreseeing that tiny Chloe Beaudoin would in her late teens abandon her unhappy alcoholic parents to disappear behind the blackest doors of New Orleans.

Nor would she ever discover how a young street-wise Chloe Beaudoin would drastically and forever alter the lives of Kenneth Stonewall and Charles Anthony Vincent.

32

Charlee, Cerise and Murielle sat huddled together on her sofa in baby dolls beside the flickering fake flames, gossiping and giggling, eating pizza while being careful with their wine. She had evolved into good friends with them, certain they would evolve into better than friends, certain the three would remain good friends for life. They did not know and would not have cared that pretty Claudine Lebrun was getting her bum and vagina battered by a hillbilly with a small dick. Or that Murielle's and Chloe's lives would one day collide.

In bed, propped against fluffy pillows, the three went on tirelessly until past midnight. Sunday morning, giddy with excitement, they skipped and hopped around the apartment making breakfast and getting ready until Melinda arrived at 10:00 to touch-up the girls' coiffures and help them dress. Dr. Boyette arrived at 1:00 in a limousine with his wife to collect Mrs. Belmont, the bride, his daughter and her new friend who she might finally stop talking about, having steadfastly refused Jackson's financial assistance. To escort five such lovely ladies was a purest delight he could imagine.

They arrived at the Natchez on time an hour later as the crew was preparing to get underway.

They were greeted by the captain, the first and second officers, and thunderous applause from an unbroken row of fashionable guests on the upper deck. The officers gave their arms to the bride, Melinda and Charlee escorting them to the captain's office where the groom and his best man Bradly Connors were waiting, leaving the good doctor to proudly escort his wife and Cerise into the festive throng.

The bride personified elegant simplicity in her knee-length off-the-shoulder deep emerald gown, matching low-heeled satin pumps and delicate emerald earrings she could not resist buying; the groom stood in a hand-tailored black Belmont, an emerald silk tie and white boutonnière.

The ceremony was brief and informal, Charlee passing Murielle a bouquet of flowers after the groom kissed his bride, Mrs. Murielle Belmont. The captain led the small party to the top deck, his many other less privileged passengers looking on in awe, pointing cameras and cell phones, Charlee and the Second Officer trailing behind Bradley Connors who seemed quite taken with Melinda.

Jackson patted his bride's hand. She was nervous about meeting hundreds of people in a receiving line whose names she would never remember, whose faces she would likely never see again: A stationary gauntlet that would endure an hour or more. Although her worry brightened to glee at seeing Cerise with Shelly, Vicky and Quintin with their dates and Valerie with Everett.

Murielle was second in line after Melinda to greet and thank their guests, telling Valerie that she had better be the one catching the bouquet. Though she wouldn't. That lucky girl would be a Tulane student in her final year.

She was doing well, focusing on each guest, not letting her mind or her eyes wander. She was adapting to being a Belmont. Then, almost done, ready to dance and have fun, she froze.

"Murielle, please meet Kenneth Stonewall and his companion Miss Rachelle Sinclair. Kenneth is one of

Belmont's most valued clients and long-standing member of the club."

"I am truly enchanted, Murielle." He held out a steady hand, taking hers. "You are without question the loveliest of brides. And Jackson here the most fortunate of men for capturing your heart before some lesser fellow might. I also understand you're a graduate of Tulane, the ranks of which Rachelle will join this coming spring. As a member of the board of governors I would greatly enjoy hearing of your Tulane experience. Would you do me the pleasure of dancing with the bride on this most beautiful of fall days? Preferably one whose tempo requires the least possible output of energy."

He pressed his other hand over hers, his eyes as cold as she remembered.

"I would be delighted, Mister Stonewall." She pulled her hand away, smiling at his most recent whore. The second since her own kept year ended. "I look forward to speaking with both of you. Especially about my graduating year, Rachelle, which I'm sure is not at all what you expected."

When they were gone, when the line finally ended, a waiter led them to their table. Murielle could not have chosen a more splendid day. The sun was warm, the air perfectly still if not for the gentle breeze coming from the steamboat's slow and steady progress through the brown and meandering Mississippi.

With the bride and groom seated, the first of five courses was served. With tables cleared and wineglasses refilled as the boat eased against the dock three hours after casting off, guests were ushered to the enclosed main deck for cocktails and dancing to a live band when all other passengers had disembarked. The evening sailing was a private and privileged affair.

Jackson danced first with his bride, then his mother, Miss Clara, Charlee and Cerise as most couples left their tables and barstools to join them.

An hour into the evening cruise Stonewall asked the groom whether he might borrow his bride for the duration of a dance. Of course Jackson consented, at once asking Rachelle Sinclair for the pleasure of her company on the floor.

"You are indeed a lovely bride, Murielle. I'm pleased to see you have done this well for yourself. Can you possibly imagine my utter amazement upon receiving my invitation? You and Belmont. You must have worked quickly indeed once cured of your impulsive penchant for pizza."

"Your loss, Stonewall. You threw *me* out. Remember? And don't talk bullshit about pizzas. I met your last whore, the one before Rachelle."

"She was somewhat of a disappointment, though her year went quickly. And Rachelle is very much a welcomed upgrade. Yet nowhere near as exquisite or, shall we say amenable, as the one I continue to miss. The only one who ever thought to threaten me for my undying kindness toward her."

"You paid me for being your whore."

"Very handsomely as I recall, with a tidy bonus which you squandered with your inherent insouciance. A mutually equitable arrangement entered into freely and with full knowledge of the terms and conditions inclusive of the eventual outcome. That you forgot, that you created an improbable illusion is neither my fault nor my concern. That you deliberately chose to fornicate with one of life's failures was fully your decision. What would Belmont think about that, of you fornicating with a pizza boy to save on a tip, of you redecorating my walls with images of your creative fervour?"

"You paid him to fuck me. Then what, Stonewall? Did you jerk off while you watched? Does she know you spy on her? You got me pregnant as much as he did, then you abandoned me and called me a whore. You said I was dirty. Something I will never forget or forgive. I meant what I said. You will pay dearly for that one day."

"I did and said no such thing. I merely put temptation in your way, exposing, if you will, your true nature. We are what we are, Murielle. That you somehow found your way into polite society changes nothing." He acknowledged Jackson and Rachelle with the slightest tilt of his head. "I can almost picture those two together in life. Luck of the draw, I suppose."

"Go to hell."

"Indeed. Which brings us to the brilliant epiphany striking me immediately upon receiving your thoughtful invitation." The music stopped, Stonewall waving an open hand toward the edge of the dance floor. "You see, Murielle, despite my proclivity for freshness and Rachelle possessing an abundance of affection and amenability, I do on many occasions regret our parting."

"You regret not having me in your bed. Pure and simple."

"Precisely. A situation which I believe is wholly remediable."

"You're sick. We are done here."

"I don't believe we are. You see, irrespective of my love of Belmont fashions, there are other exclusive haberdashers. Conversely, which is unfortunate for you, there is not another Belmont for you to marry. Not for you. Imagine his reaction when viewing your début as a porn star, and with what. Or seeing you plaster *my* walls with memories of your very athletic performance. Nor should we dismiss the termination of the sad consequence of that ill-fated evening which you somehow managed to finance."

"What I did, what I was forced to do because of you, doesn't matter. He loves me and I love him. I would never cheat on him."

Stonewall chuckled for the benefit of Jackson and the other guests. "Who would not love the ever-enchanting and quixotic Murielle de la Sorbonne, exotic paramour extraordinaire...until her mask is removed and her true self revealed?"

"I did nothing wrong. He would understand because he loves me. Something you would never understand."

"Love is a malleable intangible, Murielle, constantly redefined, easily squashed or enhanced in accordance with one's circumstances. Or, in your case, revelations. We will talk later, of course. We'll do lunch after your blissfully romantic honeymoon. In the meantime, as food for thought, I propose that you consider becoming my occasional dalliance. A pleasant diversion to enhance my time with Rachelle and her successors."

"You cannot be serious. He's my husband. I love him. What you're thinking is impossible."

"Jackson Belmont and I can live without each other, Murielle. You, however, cannot now live without either one of us. That would be the impossible. You have made that impossible."

"You would do that to Jackson, to me?"

"He and I are business associates. I'm here because I give him eighty thousand a year to assist in my appearance. You're here by way of three unforgiveable deceptions, none of which he nor his mother will forgive. Not the least of which is me, unless we surmise how you likely funded the abortion before somehow making yourself appear more the lady than you are."

He bowed, kissing her hand, returning her to her husband. She was the most endearing bride, he told Jackson. Wishing them a marvelous life together, thanking Murielle for her candid perspective regarding Tulane, he left them to dance with his whore.

With the celebration coming to an end, the steamboat nearing its berth, the younger single women shuffled in stocking feet to form a small and expectant herd, waiting for Murielle to throw out her bouquet. Valerie missed by inches, frowning to the relief of Everett; Rachelle Sinclair jumping up and down, squealing with joy, mistook girlish superstition for a telling omen.

Amongst the last to disembark, Stonewall looked forward to seeing Jackson at the club, while Murielle suggested that she and Rachelle should do lunch sooner than later. Her treat.

Dr. Boyette once again assumed responsibility for getting Melinda, his wife, his daughter and Cerise home safely, Melinda graciously declining. Jackson had earlier assured his best man that if he didn't try he would not know. Take the leap, he encouraged Bradley Connors. His mother was too lovely and too vital not to date. Which, of course, he added good-naturedly, would not in any way affect his career at Belmont.

Though the biggest surprise of Murielle's day came when Jackson carried his bride over the threshold of the Tower Suite at the Marriott, hearing of their 10:00 AM flight to Paris, France.

33

Jackson and Murielle returned to work November 04th, a week later he left New Orleans on business. That week Murielle went shopping for an entirely new wardrobe to furnish her Garden District closet. On the Monday she called Anthony, suggesting that he do the same. On the Thursday she dined out with Kenneth Stonewall who met her later at her condo. He left before midnight with not much more to say than a sincere thank-you for an agreeable evening. After which she showered him from her body and drove home as though nothing had happened.

They agreed on one night each month at her place for an unspecified duration, on an evening convenient to both parties. He would not stay over, nor did he see any particular benefit in feigning romance. He simply wanted her physically and visually. He also encouraged her to appreciate the futility of speaking with Rachelle or any of his future short-term interests, in return for which, and without the slightest inference that she was a whore, he would with each visit leave her a monthly household stipend equal to her rent.

Anthony stayed with her five evenings in early December. They celebrated Christmas early, dressing a tree and opening gifts. Content that he was sleeping on clean sheets he chose not to comment on her diamond rings. Nor did he speak to her of his upcoming June wedding.

He left her Friday morning, feeling a sadness he would never conquer. Hating how their week had so quickly come and gone Murielle hurried to her private retreat that evening to make her bed ready for Stonewall. Saturday she spent pampering herself at home, Jackson arriving late in the day to soft Latin music and a gourmet dinner prepared by an enchanting and loving wife.

On the first of the New Year he began flight school after returning from a week of skiing in Vail with his wife, his mother and Bradley Connors. The morning of February 02nd, a week after Stonewall's first visit of the year, Anthony left for the airport after unexpectedly spending his Friday night alone. His mood was glum, feeling strangely jealous of the other man despite going home to a very beautiful and loving Karine.

At home with Jackson enjoying a rare lazy morning in bed, Murielle decided she would simplify her life. Her lover would no longer stay over with her on a Friday, however Stonewall would those particular weeks. Twelve days later Jackson brought her flowers and took her to dinner; Karine wanted a romantic evening at his home where she was spending more time, where they had decided she would soon be living. In the French Quarter at a quiet table he'd reserved at Angelo's, Bradley Connors proposed. Charlee Boyette was the first to see Melinda's tears and the next morning Junior reassured his mother that Jackson Senior was as happy for her as he was.

In March Jackson ordered his Beechcraft Baron. Early the next month he called Bradley Connors to his office when everyone else had gone home. He was deeply troubled, seeing no other reasonable solution to a difficult situation. He was not comfortable having his stepfather working for him, he told Bradley outright, his tone and candour leaving the older man perplexed. Sliding a document across his desk he asked for a signature that would once and for all put an end to the dilemma.

Confused by the abrupt reversal in their relationship, not understanding why his boss was acting uncharacteristically imperious, Bradley reached for the document. The wording was concise, leaving no room for misinterpretation. He was visibly shocked, staring in disbelief at Jackson who was filling crystal snifters with JW Blue. Signing would make Bradley a partner with a ten percent share in Belmont Tailors.

At Easter Jackson stood as Bradley Connors' best man, giving the couple a Caribbean cruise for their honeymoon as a wedding gift. He left the next day to spend the holiday in New York with Murielle who returned to spend her third week with Anthony and her sixth evening with Stonewall since becoming a Belmont.

In May she turned twenty-four, neither Jacqueline Marie-Anne nor François-Anisette giving a moment's thought to the day. Jackson gave her a spring ensemble, Anthony phoned her and Stonewall left her another envelope before spending the night with Rachelle who was nearing the end of her term.

Anthony arrived in New Orleans again on June 10th while Jackson was in Charleston increasingly eager for his pilot's certificate and plane. He left her Friday morning making room for Stonewall who would come with his usual bottle of wine and envelope. When Anthony arrived at Karine's from the airport she hurried to the door beaming with excitement despite her long day of packing and sorting. Movers were coming in the morning to take her belongings forty miles to the south.

Eight days later she gave up being a Fenway, becoming Professor Karine Vincent in a civil ceremony at the courthouse. Sunday the happy couple departed Logan for a

European honeymoon, slightly hungover from partying with friends.

Friday, the 28th, Jackson took Murielle, Melinda and Bradley to dinner to celebrate his pilot's licence. He was flying them the next weekend to the Mayan Riviera. Melinda thought maybe not, adding that neither did Bradley, and Murielle agreed to meet him there.

On the twenty-ninth Stonewall went to his Garden District condo to spend his farewell evening with the lovely Rachelle Sinclair, arriving late. She was waiting, as he usually preferred, in lingerie she could never afford on her own as a student. Except that she was no longer a student, a week earlier celebrating her graduation in Biloxi with the man she loved. Now she was eager to begin her career and marry her Kenny. Her life was an endless rollercoaster ride of novelty and bliss, joy and wonder, without the slightest clue she was about to crash.

Not in the mood for conversation, seeing no practical purpose, he took her to bed making the best use of her in the fleeting hours remaining. Waking early Sunday morning he showered and dressed and went to stand on the balcony. He had learned a hard lesson two years earlier that he would never again repeat. Rachelle would have until noon to leave without tears or regret. She had nothing whatsoever to cry about. She lived in the lap of luxury for a year. She owned an enviable wardrobe and would leave with a cheque for fifty K, five thousand in cash, and he had booked a room at the Hilton in her name for the coming week at his expense. Sufficient time to locate accommodations more in keeping with her pending income.

What she would not do is fornicate with a pizza kid, or staple lasting memories to his walls, waste his wines or threaten him. She would go and go quickly, driven by his chauffeur while he remained behind to instruct his cleaning service. Her replacement would arrive Monday at noon with a key to begin her twelve-month tenure. She deserved and she would have the finest first impression.

Joining him on the balcony Rachelle learned *her* first significant life lesson. Her mind was too stunned to cry, her body too paralyzed with shock to move. She couldn't believe what he was saying. How could he love her and want her to leave? How could she leave him when she loved him?

He hadn't once in the year used the word, hadn't once in life thought that he might or that he should. To conclude the matter he gave her a choice any clear-thinking woman her age would understand: Leave with her clothes, the cheque and cash bonus by noon or leave one minute later without them. She walked out at 11:00 with a dry face when the chauffeur finished loading her luggage. She wanted to give him the finger and say something hurtful, winning over temptation because he didn't have a heart and she hadn't cashed the cheque.

July 01st Jackson's Beechcraft Baron arrived. His instructor agreed to join him on his maiden flight to Biloxi while two cynical women and an envious Bradley watched and videoed his departure and disappearance into a clear sky from the tarmac. The following Saturday Bradley stood his ground. He kissed Melinda at 9:00 AM, possibly for the last time. He wasn't certain he was coming back to her. He was sorry. He really felt terrible leaving her, he did. Nevertheless he felt obliged to support his stepson and partner.

She wasn't amused, neither was Murielle, watching the Beechcraft taxi to the end of the runway, seeing the men soar past them to disappear over the Gulf of Mexico en route to Havana.

The women of course, affected by the inherent condition of their species, were fraught with worry throughout the entire day. The men insisted they would not call hourly to check-in with their mommies; they would however call from Havana while having a lunch, assuring the worrywarts that lunch would not include anything stronger than Coke.

Near one o'clock when the calls finally came in Melinda and Murielle practically ripped at their purses. The men were in the Cuban capital, safe and sound and drinking Coke. They would depart at 4:00. ETA New Orleans: 6:30. They arrived on schedule executing a perfect landing, giving each other several high-fives as they jogged toward the women.

For Jackson the flight was a dream of a lifetime come true; for Bradley the day was an out-of-character thrill over open water, secretly embracing the adventure as a test of self, believing in part that he was challenging himself as much for Melinda.

Jackson quickly evolved into an accomplished pilot. Although he maintained his travel schedule, he never again left for the airport on Sunday or came home late on Friday or spoiled another weekend. Flying became an integral part of his life. The couple did spend the following weekend on the Mayan Riviera alone and many more weekends in Cuba and Mexico, deciding with Bradley to test Belmont stores in Cozumel and Cancun.

Anthony continued staying at her Garden District private retreat, continuing to reserve his time with her in advance as he would a client or hotel room, Murielle managing to stay with him Monday through Thursday, loving him, missing him each time they parted, adding Stonewall to the mix on the evenings she was ostensibly working late or having a 'girls' night'.

Life was good and getting better nine months into her marriage, going home to her husband in fresh lingerie from working late Friday July 19th, too exhausted to make love with him despite how she adored him. Saturday she woke late to a sumptuous breakfast in bed.
*

Late Saturday afternoon in the backwoods of Lafayette, Claudine Beaudoin asked her boss if she could leave early. She was feeling poorly and made her way upstairs to rest, pouring a glass of cider she hoped would ease her discomfort.

When Maurice arrived home from his day at the mill, his clothes thick with sweat, ready to relieve his dry throat with a few cold beers, he instead found her propped against a kitchen wall crying and sitting in a puddle. Asking why she made such a smelly mess, he hurried hellbent downstairs to tell her boss who called for an ambulance.

Near 2:00 AM Sunday morning a doctor Claudine didn't know successfully pulled Chloe Beaudoin into the world before leaving her and her mother in the care of apathetic nurses.

There were no tears of joy, no jubilation to share with family and friends, and for Maurice no memory of that wondrous day when he first poked a live girl in her bed. He would never take her to New Orleans and never leave the mill. Claudine would become a fixture at the store where they would live upstairs regretting their lives and the girl until living no longer mattered.

Part Five
34

Maurice and Claudine took the girl home Monday and put
her in a drawer. They had nowhere else to put her. They
hadn't given any thought to cribs or diapers, blankets or
feeding the kid and Maurice didn't want anything else
sucking on her teats despite their disfigurement the doctor
assured him was temporary. Instead he went downstairs
with a list the nurses had given them, doing his best to
remember the instructions.

Claudine put herself straightaway on the pill, saving
what she could from her weekly budget over the coming
year to get herself spayed at the clinic when she was barely
nineteen and looked much closer to thirty. She didn't want
another child, not ever again. The one she had was plenty
bad enough, taking up space in their bedroom, taking all the
fun from their lives and causing Maurice to lose interest in
poking her. She needed to make things right for him.

They had no friends. The ones they had known at school
fled quickly to Baton Rouge and New Orleans to find work
in restaurants and hotels. None went to college. Some went
to jail after a while, others stayed behind to work on farms,
or at odd jobs, or at the slaughterhouse believing they
would be better off in jail. Not many were taken on at the
mill and those who were joined Maurice doing menial work
whose sole requisite skillset was staying awake.

354

By the age of three Chloe no longer spent her days strapped in a car seat that had no car and went from a larger bottom drawer to sleep on a mattress in the spare room that had no furniture, blinds or curtains. Nothing on the wall. She had no little friends either, nor toys that were a needless expense. Spending hard-earned money on something lasting a year at best made no sense at all, Maurice declared. Though she did have a rocking horse with no ears or a tail all to herself that he came across one day while walking home from the mill.

She spent her days tethered to the doorknob and forgotten in her room, though to her credit Claudine did continue spending her lunch time and breaks with the girl when she would let Chloe run freely around the apartment. At night she fell asleep early on her mattress without kisses or hugs or a little girl's teddy bear that would keep her safe while she dreamed of little things, rarely tossing and turning, oblivious to her young ma and pa sitting apart in front of the sixty-inch screen sharing a jug of spicy cider.

And so went her life until she began her schooling seven weeks after her sixth birthday that came and went without cake or presents. She didn't know presents or Christmas or Easter. Those times would come soon enough, Maurice told the wife. She knew her room where she preferred being alone since her ma and pa paid her no mind.

The wooden horse was long forgotten, though she did have a comb that was missing teeth and a plastic mirror with a broken handle that someone had discarded near the store. She didn't know school; she didn't know picture or colouring books, eager and unafraid the morning she went with her ma in her coveralls and a tee-shirt to the schoolyard without holding hands. She was curious. Most of all she was curious about the playground with its swings and sandbox and by the time the school bell rang that afternoon she was twice as smart as she was the day before.

Her first day in class was the first real day of Chloe's life. She stayed to herself. She didn't make friends because she didn't know how and her pa had sternly cautioned her not to bring any other kid home. By the following summer she was reading better than any kid in her class, coming to hate her little room, spending her time between supper and her mattress outside at the bottom of the steps with her books, excitedly absorbing each new revelation.

Six years later she was ready for high school with gold stars on each of her papers, receiving her certificate alone. Maurice and Claudine had gone to Lafayette by bus to shop for their first used car.

None of the other parents thought to applaud, nor did her classmates. The girls had never asked her to be their friend, never invited her to a party, not understanding that she stayed to herself because she was afraid they wouldn't like her.

She was used to being alone, to no one wanting her. Which is how she passed the summer she turned thirteen while the other girls were strutting along the shoreline of the pond pretending themselves older and more mature, giggling at the boys wrestling in the shallow water. Though never able to pretend they were prettier than Chloe, and so they decided they would never like her.

Instead Chloe spent her summer at the school library reading and learning. She read about faraway places and the people who lived in those places. She read about fashion and how looks mattered, inwardly disappointed when on her birthday Claudine took her to buy jeans and shirts for the coming school year.

At thirteen she was more striking than her mother who was thirty-one and looked more like her grandmother, the one she didn't know. She no longer wanted to dress like a boy, particularly since over the summer she was losing most of what was girlish about her, entering high school as a young woman if not the sophisticated woman she yearned to become.

She removed the sketches from her wall that she drew in school throughout her first seven years, replacing them with discarded posters from the first teen dance she didn't attend because she had no one to take her. Then one day after school she went to the drugstore a mile farther along the road on a whim. The druggist hired her immediately to work an hour each day and Saturday sweeping and keeping the shelves neat and soon she was buying her very own posters and books, working full days at the drugstore over the summer.

By the end of grade nine turning fifteen she was smarter than her father, her unhappy mother aging several days for every one she endured. Once again working full days through July and August she began buying her own clothes, if not as fine as the outfits in her magazines, Maurice interpreting her independence as his own financial relief.

By the end of tenth grade there was no mistaking that she was becoming a beautiful woman. Her body and her clothes were the envy of every girl at school, and that she was the endless source of wet dreams for every boy made the other girls hate her all the more. They snubbed her and called her names. When other girls were having sweet sixteen parties Chloe read alone at the bottom of her steps.

She was wearing skirts, blouses and low-heeled boots and months earlier had begun changing in the bathroom, locking the door when taking her weekly bath and remaining dressed at night alone in her room until changing for bed. Her pa hadn't once touched her or hit her, though increasingly he was eyeing her in a way that made her uneasy.

Her seventeenth birthday went unnoticed, Maurice increasingly finding the girl difficult to have around. When she wasn't hiding in her room with her books she was acting high and mighty with her fancy clothes. What she needed was a sound thrashing across her backside. That's what she needed, not a gift when he and the wife could scarcely afford their own basic comforts.

Midway through her last year of high school, she asked the druggist a huge favour that she was certain he would grant. He was late-twenties, single and good-looking, and Chloe could see that he liked her. He was constantly watching her when he thought she didn't see. What he felt was obvious in his voice and in his eyes each time they spoke. He wanted her; he wanted to be with her.

She wanted his help buying a computer and needed him to drive her to Lafayette on the Sunday. He agreed. He also agreed to let her keep the laptop in the store and use the storeroom as her study space through to the end of her scholastic year after her work was done. She was thrilled, thanking him without the faintest glimmer of a smile.

Sunday afternoon she left her room wearing jeans and a sweater, telling them without seeing them that she was going to the library. When her pa asked what was in the bag, she said "nothing."

In the drugstore's employee washroom she changed into a skirt, a blouse and suede boots she'd never worn. Happy that she did. She wanted Vance to see her the way she saw herself in her mirror when she was certain they were either in bed or a shared stupor. Vance was always well-dressed under his lab coat, however Sunday he belonged in one of her magazines. He even treated her to lunch, the first time in her life Chloe saw the inside of a restaurant, read a menu or had her seat pulled out by a man.

In February she secretly wrote a letter to Tulane in New

Orleans, receiving an invitation from the committee weeks later. She was excited with no one to tell except Vance who happily drove her to the city for her evaluation the day her ma and pa believed she was working.

She changed at the drugstore into a skirt and blouse bought for the occasion, pantyhose and pumps she had never worn, needing to make the best possible impression at the interview that would define her future. She saw Baton Rouge for the first time along the way and when the road trip was over he took her to a garden patio for lunch in the French Quarter where an elegant waiter called her Mademoiselle and helped her to sit before laying a linen napkin across her lap.

They strolled along Bourbon and Royal, walking into voodoo shops and art galleries, once in a while Vance putting an arm around her shoulders. She was alive in a world she could never have imagined. She was inside her new world. He bought her a beignet and took her to see the steamboats and the mighty Mississippi, disappointment infusing her face as he glanced at his watch.

Weeks from her eighteenth birthday she received the university's letter of acceptance at the drugstore, the first time since the age of three when she was given her wooden horse that Chloe Beaudoin's eyes welled with tears. She was finally leaving the dank and dreary backwoods on the fringes of Lafayette, sobbing quietly in her bed that night for a very different reason when she thought to crunch the numbers.

Tulane was on hold.

In June she didn't attend her graduation or the dance. Instead she went to the school's office on her last day requesting the document and walked out early. She didn't know how to dance. She never had a reason to learn and wasn't interested in socializing with going-nowhere

359

hillbillies who would be married and pregnant within a year.

She was going somewhere and what she did have was a closet full of nice clothes, while the other girls who did know how to dance did so that evening in someone else's dresses rented from a store in town. Dresses they would wear with their legs bare over washed-out underwear, ankle socks and running shoes.

Instead she began her summer schedule at the drugstore, secretly learning to drive with Vance's help, passing her test in town a week before her birthday. On the afternoon of July 21st she borrowed his car to practice, promising she would not go far and that she would stay on the main road. Which she did, stopping at the steps she would later in the evening climb for the last time. She was eighteen and they weren't her ma and pa any longer.

She emptied her closet and drawers, filling the car within an hour. At the drugstore she went to Vance in his small private office.

"What is it, Chloe?"

"I need a place to stay, Vance. I suppose I should have asked first."

He looked up. "What do you mean, need a place to stay? Asked what first?"

"I packed my things. All I've got is in the car. I had no other way, Vance. I did what I thought was the best way."

"You're telling me you left your home, just walked out?"

"The place wasn't a home. Never was. And they can't stop me. I'm eighteen today. I'm legal and free to do as I please in Louisiana. That's true, Vance. I read about it."

"And you're going to stay where, exactly? Did you read about that?"

She nodded. "With you. I want to stay with you at your

place in Lafayette. I won't cause you any trouble. I can cook and I can clean. Besides which I like you and I know you feel the same way about me. I see you looking at me. I remember your arm around me in New Orleans."

"Of course I like you, but what you're suggesting is beyond crazy, Chloe. It's impossible. You're eighteen."

"I know what I'm doing, Vance. I know what I want and I am not going back. I deserve better than them."

"You're eighteen. Get real."

"I am real," she practically snarled. "I'm smarter than other eighteens and getting smarter. I'm also beautiful, older looking than other eighteens. I know you think about me that way. What you don't know is that I'm a virgin, Vance. Never once touched or worse by a hillbilly. I never will be and you don't have a girlfriend. So why can't we help each other? Why can't I be your girlfriend? You're too good and too handsome to settle for whores once in a while, the way I suppose you do because the ones your age around here are either pregnant or stink of manure stuck to their boots. Besides, being ten years apart in our ages is no big deal in Louisiana. Especially in these parts."

"You want to live with me and be my girlfriend. Am I getting that right? You want to sleep with me?"

"That's what I'm saying. I do want to be your girlfriend. Sooner or later I'll be in someone's bed, somewhere. So why not yours?"

He didn't answer because he did want her in his bed.

The conversation went on for an hour until Vance at last nodded his agreement, inviting her to dinner in town. The least he could do given the day was her birthday and that later he would sleep with her, finally see her naked. Not that he hadn't undressed her a thousand times. That alone was worth a good meal. As for her moving in, why not? Putting in twice the hours he should to save on hiring another druggist screwed his social life big time and she was *the* best looking thing in town.

Her elation shone from her eyes, for the first time in her life kissing another person. She liked the feeling, the warmth she hadn't once felt from her parents or the boys at school. She was liberated, feeling free for the first time as she drove his car to the apartment.

Standing by the kitchen door at the top of the stairs she felt years older, infused with confidence that she was doing the right thing.

"Late fer yer supper again." He guzzled a mouthful of 100 proof home brew clear as water. "Where ya bin, girl, all dickied up and lookin' pretty? Treatin' some boy to a good time under yer skirt in the bushes?"

She ignored the slurred rebuke. "I was at work, talking with Vance."

"Well ya can git yer own damn meal." Claudine grunted. "And don't go wastin' the heat. That's what ya git fer always comin' late, fer showin' no respect."

"Don't be stupid," she retorted, expressionless. "I'm not staying. I'm leaving, for good. I emptied my room this afternoon."

Claudine's dulled mind absorbed and processed the revelation seconds after Maurice lurched to his feet. He toppled his chair, stumbling his way to her room, swinging open the door.

"Goddamn if she ain't speakin' the truth. Nothin' left here exceptin' her beddin'."

"And where do ya think yer goin'?" Claudine asked, pushing away her plate, resting her sagging breasts over folded arms. "Ain't nowhere here fer a girl on her own to stay."

Chloe didn't answer. She didn't have to ever again. Instead she sneered, eighteen years of disgust and loathing radiating from her face.

She simply said, "I won't tell you both to go to hell for the horrible life you gave me, because you are both already there."

With that she skipped down the steps feeling reborn. She would have smiled or even laughed, except she didn't know how. Instead she went to dinner with her ad hoc boyfriend cum lover and never once looked back.

*

Chloe was right, of course. Vance did want out badly. He was tired of doing business with pot-bellied and toothless hillbillies in coveralls and unlaced work boots, their women no better in their work boots, tights, chequered jackets and mesh caps. He wanted and deserved a bigger store, a real pharmacy, as much as she wanted a degree from Tulane.

He was born and raised in Baton Rouge. He was accustomed to women in trendy dresses and heels, men in neck ties, clean shirts and suits. He was accustomed to good manners and Southern gentility, though practiced at disregarding tooth picks and cold cigar butts travelling to and fro across sloppy mouths while attempting to explain cautions and restrictions to puzzled minds.

He bought the aging drugstore, the only one he could afford with a loan from his parents after graduating a year before Chloe first approached him to explain compellingly that she would be his best employee. He had nothing to lose then and even less now. She wasn't expensive; she didn't talk a lot, was easy on the eyes and was truly the best part of his days.

After dinner she went with him to his Lafayette apartment with a complimentary patch on her hip, despite which he duplicated the precaution. He was twenty-eight with his whole life ahead of him and he didn't need or want a teenage wife. He didn't need any wife, yet refusing her would have lost him an opportunity of a lifetime. Screwing a teenage virgin was one thing, but doing something as superb as Chloe Beaudoin was no less than a miracle.

She felt no panic or shame sitting on his bed removing her skirt and blouse, that minor problem came with what remained. She hadn't once in her life gone swimming at the pond, let alone anyone seeing her in underwear. Nor had she ever seen a man in his, except her pa in his boxers most mornings. So she inhaled an invisible deep breath and stood, remembering her evenings in front of her mirror when she would pretend that someone who loved her was in the room with her.

Turning from him she tugged her camisole over her head, pushing her briefs to the floor the way she did in her mirror, certain he was pleased. Of course he was; she was looking more every day like those women in her magazines.

She was tall, shapely more than slender, her skin soft and smooth. Her auburn hair was long and straight, her brown eyes piercing yet empty. Her face was sculpted with high cheek bones, a Romanesque nose and sensually full lips. Her shoulders and back were defined and flawless, her arms taut, her unspoiled hands free of calluses and scars from working in dung-filled barns and dried fields under a harsh Louisiana sun. Her bum was pear-shaped and alluring, her legs long and straight. Her breasts were perfectly suited to her body with small nipples the colour of caramel. Her belly was flat by virtue of youth, the downy curls at the apex of her thighs cared for as though she might one day become a glamourous model.

If not for the paler hue of her skin she could well have been another woman's daughter in a far better world, a beautifully exotic woman she would meet in her not too distant future.

She didn't care that Vance didn't love her. She didn't

expect that he would, not at first. And if love never happened, so what? She was fine with that too. He wanted her, which was more than anyone else had ever given her.

Without glancing over her shoulder she crawled onto the bed. Covering herself to her raised knees with a sheet she sat waiting without the slightest indication in her eyes or on her youthful lips or steady hands to betray that she was nervous.

The next morning she woke with a start to his warm hands gently prompting her: an entirely foreign sensation. She was mildly embarrassed at being naked, an uncertainty he quelled with warm kisses, tender words and caresses before once again parting her legs.

When they were finished he threw back the sheet and went to the bathroom, Chloe quickly rummaging through her suitcases for something to wear, her mind still groggy from her first taste of wine the night before. When he came into the room wrapped in a towel with his hair wet, she was dressed. She stood staring, her quizzical expression and wrinkled brow asking the question. Who would ever think to wash themselves every day of the week?

She would, she discovered, while he was making breakfast.

Once at the drugstore Vance posted a FOR SALE sign on the door, surprising his backwoods customers and placing compelling ads in city papers and universities. From that day forward she showered and drove to work with him, soon working the cash, taking on more responsibility and earning more money without the slightest fear of meeting her ma and pa since they regularly obtained their favoured medications from neighbours' illegal stills deeper in the woods.

Most Sundays over the next year they stayed home, sometimes driving to Baton Rouge, sometimes travelling to

New Orleans. Other times he would leave her at home to clean and do the laundry while he supposedly went to the store for the afternoon, driving instead to Baton Rouge.

She understood he was too educated and too particular to be friends with hillbillies, though she was mildly curious why he never once spoke about his parents and never went to see them. Not that she cared. She understood not wanting friends, not needing a family. Perhaps that was the reason he never once told her he loved her. Why would he? Why would anyone?

She understood his longing for a real and proper pharmacy, his quiet disappointment in no one wanting to buy out his business. Because she felt her own disappointments. She needed more than being a clerk in a country drugstore. She wanted an education; she wanted New Orleans, a career, and for once to hear that he wanted her for more than her body.

She was excited about turning nineteen, as though on the 21st she would wiggle from their bed as an adult, secretly excited about her first birthday gift ever. Crazy, she knew, wanting a teddy bear.

Although her real surprise came early after an hour of heated passion and a romantic dinner on Saturday, June 29th, three weeks from her birthday while enjoying a glass of wine with him. Sitting curled into the couch in silky baby dolls she exuded pure sensuality. She patted the cushion, wanting him closer. Vance thinking not such a good idea.

"I finally found a buyer for the store, Chloe, and at a substantial profit. As well as a lender to finance the pharmacy I've always wanted," he said as though he'd bought a pair of shoes. "He starts Monday. He'll be your boss and doesn't believe there'll be a problem. I spoke very highly of you. He's twenty-three, starting out on his own."

What! She was stunned. "You cannot be serious,

Vance." She put aside her wine. "You're telling me this now? Are you kidding me?"

"I wasn't sure how to tell you, or when. I suppose I thought waiting until the last minute would get this over with faster."

"Meaning you and me. You're leaving. You're telling me this when I'm practically naked, after fucking me an hour ago. You bastard!"

"I couldn't leave you without having you one last time, without seeing you like this one last time. I couldn't just walk away from you."

Her wineglass missed his head by inches, smashing against the wall, spraying him with Merlot. A minute later she came out from the bedroom dressed in jeans and a sweater.

"When, Vance? When are you going? Where are you going, and what happens to me? I did not spend a full year in that shitbox of a drugstore for you to leave me stranded in Shitsville with inbreeding hillbillies."

He sipped his wine. "The lease here expires tomorrow. The movers are coming early. I'll be leaving with them for Baton Rouge, staying with mom and dad until I'm settled."

"You never intended to stay with me, never wanted your parents to meet me. You just wanted something nice to fuck. You bastard."

She wasn't crying or yelling, frantic or panicked. For the second time in a year her eyes and voice radiated loathing and disgust, her expression unchanged from when she patted the cushion. The effect was unnerving, Vance gulping his wine to moisten his throat.

"This was all your idea, Chloe. Remember? You got a much nicer place to live and I got you. Like you said, you would have been in someone's bed sooner or later. So why not mine?"

"You should have told me, Vance. You should have given me time, not keep me around to use till the very end. Shit."

"I prepaid a week at the Motor Lodge starting tonight through to Friday."

"Tonight."

"I was thinking of you. I figured you wouldn't stay after what's happening here. I figured a week would give you enough time to find yourself, maybe get yourself to New Orleans to start over."

She closed the short distance between them, crashing a tight fist into his jaw, throwing him backward over a stool, the hard toe of her boot attacking his side with four vicious kicks. She took up a jade statuette scantily cloaked in a flowing Grecian robe, threatening to bash in his head if he moved.

He believed her.

She went to the kitchen for his phone, removing and smashing the sim card, effectively deleting dozens of provocative poses he was no longer entitled to drool over. She went into his office for his flash drives, smashing apart the one containing their short-lived history, telling him she truly regretted she couldn't gouge out his eyes.

Satisfied, she poured a glass of wine. Ignoring his groans she strode to the bedroom to pack her clothes and her collection of books. All she owned in the world, advising him that he owed her 1200 after-tax dollars in severance that she wanted in cash. When he answered that wasn't going to happen, that he arranged for her to keep her job, she left her packing to nonchalantly smash his flat screen and shatter ever piece of framed wall art in the living room.

Paid in full, and then some, she continued packing. When she was done she put her suitcases by the door, walking again into his office. She emptied his wallet without counting, warning that if he did anything stupid like call the cops she would accuse him of rape and abuse. She would post his face on social media, detailing how he abused a teenage girl for an entire year, alerting Baton Rouge and his parents to what was coming their way.

"You fucked me once too often," were her final words.

Then she smashed the Grecian's head from the body, called a cab and walked out leaving him on the floor wincing and looking pathetic. She never saw him, the drugstore or the hillbillies again. In less than an hour her life had completely turned upside down, Chloe believing for the better. How could it possibly be worse?

Monday she checked-out from the two-star Motor lodge with a five-night refund, boarding a bus that would take her to the Big Easy to begin a chapter in her life she could not possibly foresee.

35

Murielle Belmont was Head of Research at The Gilmore Group, deciding years earlier that actual lobbying would adversely impact her life. Cerise climbed the corporate rungs to become Director of Public Relations, maintaining her claim of seniority over her friend, and near the timing of Murielle's rethink Everett and Quintin left as full-fledged lobbyists to represent the company's clients in Washington, taking Valerie and Shelly with them as wives and mothers. Vicky chose another path after meeting Paul Bunyan and moving to the wilds of Alaska as Mrs. Paul Bunyan.

Murielle and Jackson, their lifestyles too hectic to consider the suburbs, moved into a higher and more exclusive penthouse overlooking the Mississippi. Not long after she secretly negotiated a mortgage for the quartet of condos at her Prytania Avenue address as Belmont Tailors was completing their rapid expansion across Latin America despite Jackson losing his mother and Bradley to retirement and Florida on their tenth anniversary.

With his success came a second Beechcraft that went farther and faster, allowing him the freedom to maintain personal connections with each of his stores, flying often on weekends with Murielle to Florida. Their final two flights together were to first bury Bradley before returning several months later to bury Melinda.

Charles Anthony Vincent and Karine adored each other

as much as they did the day they married, early into their marriage mutually agreeing their careers were more important than raising a family.

Karine was committed to her freedom and imparting knowledge. As was Anthony who faithfully maintained his travel schedule to the Southeast and New Orleans, declining several promotions over the years that would tie him to a desk and once explaining to Karine that the key he never used was a keepsake from his youth.

*

The first Friday in May was unpleasantly humid, the air rippling with heat. Even the birds were too oppressed to chirp.

At sixty-four Kenneth Stonewall stood on his condo balcony peering out over the park lost in thought. He was pondering the past forty-four, trying to recall his twelve-month contracts by name or by their faces, discovering he could scarcely remember the last two or three without his visual aids. Not at all surprised that, despite his infrequent visits with her, Murielle remained vividly in his mind.

In spite of his age he was trim and fit, due in part to a surgeon's scalpel which occasionally improved upon his trainer's dedication to keeping him youthful and vital. His eyes were clear and bright, his hair full and dark against lightly tanned skin. To those none the wiser he might have appeared as though lamenting turning fifty, when in fact he was increasingly and morbidly fearing the inevitable finale of his years. Which was why he would never let her go, never release her from her longstanding indenture that she brought upon herself with lies and deceptions.

She was a week from her forty-fourth birthday with not the faintest flaw encroaching on her beauty, as magnificent as the first day he saw her on campus. She was in fact three years past his intended due date of her release and many years older than the one concocting a dinner for him in the kitchen, who would graduate with a master's by the end of her twelve-month term. Yet as that day came ever closer he selfishly faltered.

There would soon come a time when the flow of appealing women eager to open their legs in the hopes of long-term security and luxury would evaporate, when his money and social stature would no longer ensure his youthful appearance, his health, or serve to satisfy his addiction to nubile devotion. A time of regret and transition with Murielle to rely upon when even those in their thirties with history would refuse his beneficence.

Sex with her, of course, would never exceed polite interaction. A degree higher than shaking hands, he conceded. One enduring friend joining with another without ardour or devotion, without tender caresses or whispers, a common bond ensuring her continued marital bliss and ongoing amenability.

He would simply go with her to the bedroom to relish the sight of her undressing after a prelude of wine and congenial conversation. He would slip into her bed with her to once again delight in the textures, the warmth and scent of her body while punishing her for the ancient folly of once thinking to punish him, never once putting his lips to hers. Then he would leave her, each time mystified, each time striving to conceive of any whore giving of herself with any greater dispassion notwithstanding the occasional climatic yelp of delight.

Be that as it may, as it must be, he would never let her go. He could not, never intending to question her regarding the lock on her closet door or the bottle of Johnnie Walker Black in her bar. He didn't have to. He didn't care about Anthony Vincent from Boston who frequently parked his rental car in her driveway, or that the man left her that morning to return home to Karine Vincent, née Fenway.

He stepped inside, snorting, checking his watch. A whore by any other name.

*

Murielle Belmont arrived at her condo after work near 5:30, expecting Stonewall at 7:00. She showered under cool water, not bothering to towel herself. Outside she lay naked on a chaise-longue, enjoying the glistening effect before coating her body with cream, protected from view and the cruel sun by the surrounding tall trees.

She was pleased with herself, with her body. At the precipice of forty-four she was still undeniably stunning. She was seductively shapely. Her breasts were as firm as the day he first put his lips to them, her belly as flat. She was the envy of most women, clearly desired by many of them, and certainly the distraction of any man not debilitated by impaired vision or sexual preference. Her legs were smooth and tight, the firm cheeks crowning them outstanding in her thongs on the dozens of beaches she strolled with and without Jackson who finally accepted that three square inches of clingy wet material did nothing at all to conceal her breasts.

She was also successful in her own right. She earned six figures at Gilmore, managing her own investment portfolio. She owned her condo and three others, and was married to a gallant multi-millionaire who she loved deeply.

They vacationed twice each year, often flying somewhere on weekends as Jackson's way of compensating her for his frequent travels without her. Though not a single day passed when he was gone that he didn't call to say he loved her.

Standing to admire her contours in the garden doors, she recalled her morning with Anthony, the happiness in his eyes as they made love. Then the sadness of yet another goodbye that was painful for her as he waved to her from the car. He never missed coming to her in early May for her birthday, understanding that May 10th was her husband's to celebrate with her.

She knew pretty much everything about Karine, not once feeling the slightest tinge of jealousy. Nor was Anthony envious of Jackson's penthouse, the plane, or the man's obvious millions. He didn't care; he loved her and would forever. They were each other's true love, forced apart by unfortunate circumstance and distance she believed could never be bridged.

During the warm months of spring and the sweltering months of summer she seldom dressed for Stonewall, greeting him in panties and a camisole or loose-fitting halter. Their meetings were perfunctory, not in the least sensual or romantic. He was coming to punish and demean her before driving a few blocks to his twenty-something whore.

In those months they would begin the evening with a glass of wine on her balcony, talking while never discussing. She never prepared meals or played romantic music. When he was ready he would put aside his glass and stand, walking ahead of her to the bedroom where he would sit by her bed to watch as she made herself ready, as she reached into her drawer for a condom that would keep him clean and free from worry and make her feel dirty.

Then he would slip off his Belmont loafers, stripping away his Belmont slacks and shirt to stand in his Belmont boxers deliberately mocking her, fully aware she was enduring the added humiliation solely to save her marriage and her life with Jackson. Each time further igniting her hatred for him.

Despite being perfunctory and unfeeling, his stamina never waned. Nor did his proclivity for variation, Murielle often reaching again into her drawer. And then he was gone, leaving his last remnant on the sheet for her to discard as a clear message.

The intercom buzzed on schedule on the hour. Murielle padded to her door in a thong and cami greeting him by name, taking the chilled Sancerre from him. He never came with a gift for her birthday or any other occasion and three hours later he left her without the slightest pretence of familiarity or kindness or that he might have a heart.

She changed her sheets, removing him from her bed, and stood under steaming water lathered with soap to remove his smell and sweat from her body. Satisfied she was clean she sat wrapped in her towel in the dark on her balcony pondering for the hundredth time in the almost twenty years since her first punishment whether she could actually kill a man.

Whether he was actually right those many years ago no longer mattered. Whether as a naïve college girl she was infatuated with the idea of him, or whether she truly loved him, no longer mattered. She reviled him beyond words, never for a moment forgiving him for the long-ago implication that she was a common whore or for making her cheat on Anthony and Jackson.

But killing him? Sipping a chilled Jean-Marc XO she believed that she absolutely could.

36

Six months later, a month before their Christmas vacation in Vail, Jackson called his wife from his Bogotá hotel suite Thursday evening. He was flying home early the next day. The call ended with an "I love you" he truly felt.

Friday she went home expecting to see him at any moment since he would normally go to the office after each trip. When he hadn't called her by eight she called him, not expecting an eerie silence.

With no connection at nine or ten she called the airport, frantic to hear he hadn't yet landed or made contact with air traffic control. Fifteen minutes later they called back. The plane departed that morning at 9:35 local time, the pilot altering course not long after take-off to an airfield several hundred miles to the south where the plane was refuelled before departing to an undisclosed destination. They would keep her informed.

Distraught, she wandered aimlessly from room to room holding her phone until succumbing to fatigue in the early hours. Waking to the usual morning chimes she called him immediately, not knowing what to think or do when yet another OUT OF SERVICE blinked on her screen.

Struggling not to believe the worst as she dressed, her mind reeling with impossible images, she called Cerise at home wanting someone she loved to be with her.

Cerise came quickly, calling Charlee at the hospital to

keep her current. She wasn't one for false hopes. Jackson would never do such a thing and if he hadn't called in thirty-six hours, if his phone was out of service, all they could hope was that someone else would call.

Near eleven o'clock someone did call, Murielle's entire body chilled to the core when hearing from the doorman that Louisiana State detectives needed to speak with her.

Cerise opened the door to them, telling Murielle to sit and stay calm. A minute later Murielle was sobbing, Cerise sitting by her side to comfort her friend. Jackson Belmont, Jr. was dead, his body found murdered the previous evening on a side road near the private airport. He was shot twice sometime before 9:00 AM, presumably for the multi-million dollar plane that would likely never be found. The body would be flown home Monday. They were sorry for her loss and left.

When they were gone Cerise poured each of them stiff vodkas and called Charlee, telling her to hurry over without telling her why. When Charlee did arrive, seeing their faces glistening with tears, she needed no one to tell her. She'd seen those tears too many times before. But this was Junior and she hurried to sit close and cry with them.
*

Through to the funeral the following Friday morning Charlee and Cerise stayed with her. Monday the coroner agreed with Doctor Charlee Boyette that she should view the body first, preparing Charlee for the worst before pulling back the drape. She slapped a hand to her chest, horrified, grabbing the edge of the gurney to steady herself.

Kissing her fingertips she put a hand to Jackson's shoulder, saying goodbye, telling him she would not allow Murielle into the room. What she told Murielle was to remember him as he was when she last kissed him goodbye. All she would add before taking Murielle home was that

Jackson died instantly without the slightest trace of fear on his face.

Friday all Belmont locations closed for the day, discreet notices posted in storefront windows to assuage worried clients. The ceremony was private; she didn't need or want strangers sharing her grief. She wanted to say goodbye with her closest friends before seeing him laid to rest beside his father, before sending Charlee and Cerise home.

She loved them dearly, but Jackson left her with much to do before returning to Gilmore. She was without warning the sole owner of Belmont Tailors with no idea how to run an international success story she had no interest in. When they were gone she phoned Anthony.

Monday she met with Belmont lawyers and management to appoint a president and CEO according to Jackson's documented wishes. She had no reason to worry. Belmont Tailors would continue to flourish, managed by a newly created board of directors that Jackson wished for her to oversee as sole owner, though she was visibly shocked to discover in a private meeting that her net worth had increased by fifty million.

The rest of the week she stayed home reading through a stack of Belmont legal documents, wondering what to do with a sprawling penthouse and her life. She donated his clothes to the mission, a gesture she believed was completely ridiculous, picturing the city's homeless men at their corners begging for change in Belmont suits and shoes. But what else was she to do? She returned his car to the dealer and shortly after added the insurance cheque for the plane to her millions.

Saturday Cerise and Charlee invited her to dinner, waking Sunday to a clear and pleasant December morning at her Prytania home. She went for a bike ride in the park, scarcely noticing the familiar faces and friendly waves with so much on her mind, suddenly realizing she was more than a widow. She was single.

The next day Murielle went to work, confronting a morning of condolences after a two-week absence. When the day was done she hurried home to Anthony who would stay with her through to Friday without the glitter of tinsel and lights to brighten their premature Christmas. Too soon after, coming in from waving goodbye from her balcony, she changed the dampened sheets as a matter of habit and left.

What she didn't do was put condoms in her bedside drawer because Jackson's death brought her never hoped-for freedom. Stonewall would never again use her body to punish and humiliate her. For the first time in days she was effervescent, free for the first time in two decades. She was ecstatic, for the sake of propriety transmuting into a grieving widow once stepping into Gilmore's bustling lobby. At long last she was rid of him, even though she would see him that evening. She wanted to see him. She needed the satisfaction of seeing him walk away, of losing face. She needed the closure.

That evening, refreshed and excited, she dressed for the long-awaited occasion in a sheer silk blouse, balconette bra and short tweed skirt, lacy stay-ups and pumps. Satisfied, she smirked into the mirror. Her embroidered thong didn't matter because he no longer mattered.

Pouring an XO two-fingers deep without soda or ice she sat waiting, until precisely at 7:00 she went to the intercom feeling practically giddy.

"Good evening, Murielle." She took his hat and coat, dropping them over an armchair. The wine she put by the door. "You're looking exceptionally lovely this evening. A veritable gift for the eyes which this evening you must unwrap for me with the utmost allure."

"When haven't I been the most beautiful of your whores with the utmost allure, Kenneth?"

"Indeed. Though I must say, with Belmont dead these three weeks, you do appear somewhat more jubilant than one might expect. I can't recall when last I saw you this radiant." He made himself comfortable. "Quite the merry widow who sits atop the Belmont Empire."

"In a sense I am a merry widow." She sat across from him. "Jackson did leave me Belmont, he also left me true freedom. He freed me from you, Stonewall. I'm no longer your whore. You no longer have power over me with Jackson gone."

Stonewall didn't flinch, not a single nerve twitched on his face. "How predictable you are, Murielle. Your casual treatment of my hat and coat, the wine by the door. To be truthful I never viewed our relationship as I the superior conqueror and you the vanquished maiden, though most assuredly as an exceedingly pleasant and sadly infrequent diversion lo these many years. Nor shall I in the future. You were, are, simply available to me by reason circumstance and opportunity. Not unlike countless other opportunities presented to me."

"I am not an opportunity and there is no future. You and I are done. We're finished."

He shifted his weight from the sofa making his way to the bar, pouring a substantial Johnnie Walker Black. "Thus I imagine you dressed so enticingly for our final encounter, to tease and titillate an already weakened heart. Look, but do not touch. A lid on the candy jar, in a manner of speaking."

"Something like that."

"For which I thank you. The effect is thoroughly delightful," he sipped the scotch, "and sadly done for naught. You might as well have come to the door fully naked or in a nun's frock." He stood over her. "Your determination is commendable, Murielle. However do allow me for a moment to clear this dense smog of hostility and anger that is blinding you to reality. How do believe a very conservative Gilmore would react to your long-forgotten abortion, to your insatiable frolicking with a pizza kid and documenting the lewd event in remarkable detail for posterity? How would they react to your many years of cheating on Belmont with me, in this your secret love nest? Or to the rapid repayment of your college loan? Or to Anthony Vincent whose scotch I hold in my hand, whose clothes hang in your sealed closet? How would his loving wife Karine view your many memorable years together?" He swirled the amber liquid, inhaling the sharp aroma. "How would Belmont Tailors respond to your illicit and vile treatment of their highly revered Jackson?" He chuckled. "For that matter, how would Vincent view our recurrent tête-à-têtes? Or any future love interest for that matter?"

He swallowed what remained in the glass, returning to the bar.

She was devastated. "You can't be that cruel, Kenneth. You've had me this way for twenty years."

"Imagine what I might do to someone I don't like, Murielle, or at least enjoy upon occasion."

"I have a life to start over."

"That no doubt will include your Mister Vincent."

"I love him."

"You love his never-ending infatuation with you. I dare say you love your various reflections more."

"One million, Kenneth. I'll give you a million to leave me alone."

That desperate remark brought raucous laughter. "Notwithstanding your substantial windfall, Murielle, my zeros far outnumber yours. A distance measured in many prosperous lifetimes."

"Then what, Kenneth? I mean, shit, twenty-years! I wouldn't get that for murder."

"Exclusive of murder, Murielle, I would suggest the one possible escape available to you is the variance in our ages and any eventual diminished faculties that may adversely affect me. I will, however, not seek any modification to our current schedule. Nor will I object to Vincent continuing to occupy my valued space in your bed. Or in you, for what it matters to either of us."

"What?" She wanted to scream.

"I see no merit in further discussion, Murielle, other than my own. Since I am neither a liar nor a fraud and you are decidedly accomplished at both. It's your nature, though you can no longer cheat on Belmont, nor on Vincent more than he sees fit to supplant his wife's most tender affections with yours." He checked his watch, resting his glass. "Come. We should put this unpleasant chapter behind us. Our evening will be better served by rekindling your earlier glow rather than stoking the flames of futile animosity. Moreover I cannot wait a moment longer to see more of you."

"I can't."

"You will."

He left her, walking to the bedroom. Minutes later she followed, her eyes glazed, defeat etched on her face. He was sitting with his feet on her récamier, composed as though in a theatre waiting for the curtain to part.

She sat facing him on her bed, removing her shoes in a daze. Standing, she unbuttoned her blouse without seeing him, freeing the edges from her skirt that she unzipped and pushed to the floor before shrugging the silk from her shoulders. She raised one foot to the bed, rolling the stay-up from her thigh to her ankle to the floor, mechanically baring her other leg before baring her breasts and letting the bra fall to her feet. Then facing away, bending from her hips the way he directed, she inched her satin thong past her knees to her ankles, pausing for long seconds before rising with deliberate and demeaning slowness to step free of them.

She left her clothes in a cluster, walking to her bedside table for the key to her walk-in. Stonewall remained as he was, not the least interested in an average man's wardrobe. When she came out she put the foils on his bedside table, turned down the bed and, doing as she was instructed once more, crawled onto the sheets to wait on her elbows and knees.

For an hour he silently penetrated and probed her, groped and squeezed her without emotion. He didn't once touch her lips or her face, or peer into her eyes while Murielle's mind left her body to visit far off places, to remember Jackson while imagining Anthony behind her, an occasional pinch or misspent thrust evoking an empty grunt that held no meaning.

When he was finished she went quietly to her closet for a long robe, closing and locking the bathroom door. Staring transfixed into the mirror she realized her body was entirely dry, physical proof she had done nothing wrong. Finishing her toilette she went into the living room, hoping he wouldn't stay long. She had nothing to say, nothing she wanted to hear. All she wanted was to change her sheets, go to bed and never wake up.

His coat and hat were gone, the untouched wine standing by the door. She inhaled a deep breath, a torrent of tears washing across her cheeks without warning. Her body and mind might have infused with relief to see he was gone, that she was free of him until he would again degrade and punish her the night of his choosing in January. Instead, for once in her life, she truly did feel like a whore.

37

The next weekend Murielle spent Christmas with Cerise and Charlee at the Boyette mansion.
She had cancelled Jackson's reservation at the resort, giving their skis and his presents to the mission along with his clothes. She never again wanted to see Vail or another ski slope.

They listened to carols and watched old movies the night before, everyone eagerly opening gifts Christmas morning after their second hot toddy. Later, dressed for dinner, everyone seated with their glasses full, Charlee's father gave Jackson a special place at the festive table by sharing memorable anecdotes with Murielle and his family. He ended the last tale with a toast to the man and his memory, Cerise and Charlee both reaching for Murielle's hands.

At New Year's Cerise and Charlee went to the penthouse, all three dressed to kill later in the evening with nowhere to go. What mattered was being together.

They gabbed about their early years as though they were ancient, about Murielle's first day at Gilmore with Cerise and the girls, about Dumb and Dumber who against all odds began to breathe on their own. Charlee told Cerise for the umpteenth time how she brought Jackson and Murielle together that first night at Angelo's, Murielle reminding her friends that if not for her and her wedding they would never have met.

She absolutely envied them, envied them having each other to love, in spite of which she was adamant. She would not spoil their Valentine's with more tears. She was spending the fourteenth in bed, remembering all her Valentine's with Jackson. She would cry, get drunk, and be fine the next morning. That's what she wanted, which didn't mean she didn't love them.

*

February 14th came on a Friday. Stonewall was at his Garden District whorehouse, she knew from experience, playing the quintessential romantic prick. Their January encounter was no better than December's, without the preamble. They understood each other. New rules were in place, hers as well. She met him that bitter evening at the door in a silk robe and nothing else, as she would from then on.

In her bedroom she had simply and quickly shrugged the robe from her shoulders, thrown back the covers and crawled onto the bed to sit facing him with her legs parted. Whores were not girlfriends or mistresses, and she was one whore who would not dress or undress to please her master. Nor would she going forward leave her bed until he was gone.

Anthony came to her the following Monday. They spent four wonderful evenings together and he would stay with her for Valentine's. When she arrived at her second home he opened the door to greet her with flowers and warm kisses, soft music and the smell of fresh baguettes. The evening was hers. Her bath and XO neat were waiting. His delicious cream of broccoli soup and renowned fettuccini Alfredo would follow in due course, accompanied with an ice-cold Sauvignon Blanc. Dessert was a store-bought sorbet.

He shrugged, making her smile. He didn't do fancy stuff.

He left for a short time while she bathed before pampering her body with velvety lotions. He called Karine from the car, telling her he loved her. He asked whether she got the flowers he sent to her office. She did, hating her first Valentine's without him. She missed him. She wanted him home to see her in the beautiful gown and panty set she found hidden in her closet.

He missed her also. He felt terrible not being with her on her special evening. Though he would be home early on Saturday and do his ardent best to make amends.

Murielle also loved the long silk slip and robe in a deep green draping the corner of her bed, pressing a passionate kiss to his lips that his wife could not.

Over the broccoli, fettuccini and wine he didn't ask about Belmont Tailors, her financial comfort zone, or the sprawling condo she lived in alone. He wasn't interested, though evading the obvious question was impossible, Anthony taking the leap, turning a lovers' evening into an unwelcome reality check. With Jackson tragically gone they would still never vacation together. They would never sit openly in candlelight holding hands across linen tablecloths as lovers whispering intimate feelings, not without driving far beyond the city limits. They would never share her friends because of her friends or dream of a future together.

"You're stunningly beautiful," he told her. "You're young and you're vibrant. You are too special to spend so many months of the year alone."

"I have Charlee and Cerise."

"At some point friends won't be enough. You're forty-four, Murielle. At some point I won't be enough. Not this way."

"That won't happen. That will never happen, no matter

what I do. And whatever I do won't happen for some time. What *will* never happen is me moving to the Artic or you moving to the Swamp. I would marry you tomorrow, Anthony. Screw public opinion. You have always known that."

"If not for Northern winters and things here that hiss." He poured more wine. "Why did we never think of meeting halfway, of you returning to Charleston? Charleston I could handle."

"I suppose I was afraid. I left behind some unpleasant history. Or possibly Gilmore." She sighed. "Thinking back, I should have. We would be together and Jackson might possibly be alive. I miss him, Anthony. I did love him. He was a good man, but I have always loved you. You're the one I should have married, not Jackson."

"I never doubted he was a good man. Thing is, you did marry Jackson. And I married Karine, who I love very much. I have since first seeing her. Your rules, remember?"

"But you're here with me on Valentine's, not her."

"Two women I love equally, yet somehow differently. And strangely I have never once felt burdened by guilt."

"I've never seen her picture, though I do know she's very pretty. You would never want anything less."

"She's beautiful inside and out, like you. And, like you, she's very fit. You would like her, Murielle. You would like each other in a less complicated world."

"A woman you will never leave to marry and live with the other woman in Charleston." She sipped her wine. "I would leave Gilmore now that Jackson's gone, Anthony. I would leave New Orleans. I want to leave, but you'll never leave Karine. Why would you when she's beautiful and you love us both equally?"

"I have no reason to devastate her that way." He stood, taking her hand, walking with her into the living room to sit by flickering fake flames. The sorbet could wait. "Cinq à sept, that's what you once called what we do. What you wanted us to do before you married Jackson, before I married Karine. We simply didn't think things through intelligently."

"How do I possibly begin dating after twenty years, let alone marrying someone I don't even know? You were my second, Anthony, then Jackson. How do I do that? How can we sit here talking about me dating other men, sleeping with how many before I find a good fit, some guy who doesn't care about my bank account? What do you think those odds are? It's insane. I mean...shit!"

"It's not insane. It's unfortunate, but something you eventually must do...for you. And who's to say you won't love the guy? You loved Jackson, you love me. And there is something else to consider, Murielle, something that until this evening never crossed my mind."

"Anthony, you are seriously ruining my Valentine's."

He smiled, she didn't.

"I don't have the comfort zone you do, Murielle, nevertheless I am very comfortable. I will have no valid reason to work beyond fifty-five. None. Even working to sixty would require explaining to Karine that I love my job more than her, not to mention that airports thirty weeks a year is the bitch of all bitches. That gives us six years together. Karine's already got the world map pinned to our office wall, which is why you have to find someone to fill this void in your life which is bound to get deeper."

"And you're good with that, other men in my bed?"

"No, I'm not good with it. Thinking about it makes me ill. Nevertheless, such is our reality. Something we do have to deal with."

She put down her glass. "Don't even think of saying such a thing. There is no one I want or could ever love more than you. I would move to Charleston, I would for you. Because I need and want you more than Gilmore, and I would sell Belmont. I would, Anthony. I would for you."

"And do what, Murielle, settle for an occasional afternoon while I have every day and night with Karine? You would come to hate me because I cannot leave her." He drained his glass, wishing he was in bed with his wife. "This place is your home. What you must do is find someone to love the way you loved Jackson, or more. The way you love me, or more. He will come to you, once you put your rings in a box. You are not Jackson's wife anymore, Murielle. He had his time with you. He would want you to do this, and so do I. You must, for you."

"Shit!"

The evening was ruined, a spoiled Valentine's ending with quotidian sex devoid of romantic whispers and sounds, unfulfilled lovers separating, soon drifting into distinctly separate worlds.

*

Murielle saw Anthony five more times by Christmas, Stonewall humiliating her twice as often.

She spent the next Valentine's alone, not once dating over the previous year. Nor did Anthony once think or dare to revisit the subject of Jackson's successor, although she did vacation on four separate occasions at all-inclusive upscale singles resorts where she became an instant hit, filling her life's void to the fullest with heated fervour and indiscriminate variation, forgetting each of her enthusiastic devotees the moment she boarded the plane. She did not want another husband. What she wanted was Stonewall out of her life and Anthony to herself.

On the last Saturday in April, one day after removing traces of love from her bed to yet again service her tormentor ten days before her forty-fifth birthday, she spent the day shopping with Charlee and Cerise who understood her continued devotion to Jackson. If any man did exist who she could possibly love as deeply, he would wait a good while longer. Anyway, she didn't want the day with her best friends to end and she was taking them to dinner.

Walking with them, their arms linked together, she halted the carefree trio abruptly. She was visibly shocked, her flesh chilled and rough, staring at herself in the past, staring at the daughter she might have given life to if not for Anthony's 600 dollars. More unnerving yet was that the girl was gaping at her, at the beautiful and sophisticated woman who in a more caring world might have been a mother who loved her.

*

Chloe Beaudoin arrived in New Orleans midafternoon on July 01st. She spent her first four months far from the Tulane campus she longed to be part of.

She spent those twenty-one days until her birthday clearing tables and washing dishes twelve hours each day of the week to afford a one-room slum and a new bed to sleep in. What saved her from worse poverty was eating three sparse meals at the diner. What saved her sanity was reading books she bought from Tulane's bookstore. She was determined to make her life worth living and whenever that day might come she would be ready.

She quit the diner on the 20th. On the 21st that was her birthday she did something that months later would alter her entire life, something she had no clue about. She strode into the city's best-known gentleman's club asking for the manager who three weeks earlier had turned her away because of her age with no invitation to return. In his office, after showing him proof she was legal, she showed him everything else and was hired on the spot.

The next afternoon she met the girls working the day

shift. They were students in their twenties earning easy money to pay their tuitions or single moms who preferred thongs and teddies to aprons with coffee stains. The ones in their thirties, no longer appealing to the more discerning night crowd, were either addicted to the twenty-dollar attention span of social derelicts or had stripped their way into life's dead-end.

They gave her a locker and a key and told her to dress in her newly bought panties and a bra. They taught her the difference between premium booze and cheap liquor, the difference between good tips and bad and gave her a dozen tables to serve and clean. Which wasn't good enough.

Each afternoon they taught her to strip, to slip off her top during the second song and her thong during a third. They taught her to engage between songs, to ensure a fourth dance and fifty percent of the eighty dollars plus tips for twenty minutes on a stool while her mind was far away.

After several weeks of training and rehearsal, of practicing each day at the cabaret on her own, she was ready to dance for her boss. She began the next night getting that fifty percent. She was the youngest girl, the shapeliest and most appealing. She instantly became the most requested by patrons gladly paying to see all of her up-close and personal, Chloe always achieving the coveted fourth dance and often more. She was the most watched when her turn came to slip and slide on a chrome pole gratis, the most ogled by lowlier regulars who couldn't afford her as she twisted and squeezed her way scantily dressed between her tables.

In a matter of weeks she had successfully graduated from the drudgery of menial work and unpleasant living to pulling in over a grand a week and buying a used Mustang convertible.

She had no friends, which didn't matter. She didn't need

or want friends because she understood that sooner or later they would not want her. She wanted a degree that would be hers to keep forever; she wanted to become someone special.

The girls at the diner added nothing to her life; they had no interest in living, working each day to support miserable existences. The ones at the club either did drugs, hooked after hours, or were single moms, all whose side glances and smirks she ignored. She wasn't interested. She wasn't like them and she didn't care. She didn't do drugs and she didn't do the salons. She was not stripping to feed unwanted kids or doing BJs after-hours to feed a habit. Stripping wasn't a short-lived desperate career or a thrill. She was stripping with a purpose. Her star billing was a means to an end that did not include giving ten-dollar blowjobs to pathetic johns through car windows, which they knew was true, which did nothing to make them like her more.

She worked Tuesdays through Saturdays, the prime nights from seven until closing, never socializing, flopping into bed alone after showering and shampooing away her customers near 5:00 AM and sleeping till noon. Saturday, the last in April, twelve weeks from her twentieth birthday, she went to the gym dressed like an innocent teenager in jeans and a sweater where she trained with a coach and tanned to keep her skin flawless and her body desirable. Then she went to a sex boutique where she bought exotic dance attire, shopping for groceries and wine before going home to a nicely furnished apartment in a middleclass neighbourhood where hookers and dancers didn't belong.

After dinner with another book as her sole companion she dressed more appropriately for her job, adding a fedora and coat that would make her more socially acceptable until she got to her car where she would toss them into the backseat to make herself more commercially viable.

*

At first Cerise and Charlee didn't notice the girl wearing knee-high boots, an indecently short denim skirt and jean jacket unbuttoned midway to enhance the swell of her breasts, wondering why they were suddenly diverting pedestrian traffic onto the street. They didn't see her jolting to a stop as abruptly as they did, clamping a hand to her mouth. Following Murielle's gaze, feeling her shudder, the women inhaled loud and concurrent gasps.

Her bare legs were perfect and smooth, her auburn hair cut straight like a shimmering curtain. Her face was thick with make-up, her eyes and lips painted with garish purple shadow and gloss, though even from thirty feet her brown eyes sparkled in the early evening sunlight.

The resemblance was uncanny, the three women entranced as the girl's expression slowly metamorphosed from shock to dreamy as though confronting herself in the future dressed in fashions she would never afford with a thousand fourth dances. Then she turned and was gone, disappearing behind tall and glossy black doors that *the* Mrs. Belmont, Ms. Quinterre and Doctor Boyette would never for a moment consider passing through.

"What was that?" Cerise blurted.

"My God, Mur that was you," Charlee said, her throat practically dry.

"That was freaking weird. Mur," Cerise added. "I remember you exactly that way, a little better dressed maybe. Though I did think you would make a half-decent stripper whenever things didn't work out for you at Gilmore."

"Just for that you're paying for dinner, sweetheart." Murielle squeezed their hands, mildly shaken. "Why would such a disarming girl possibly strip naked for a few dollars to give a room full of sick creeps a cheap thrill? I can't imagine how she must feel."

Charlee was fixated on the doors, shaking her head. "She doesn't feel. It's strictly about the money for someone like her. The good ones do exceptionally well. Especially the ones doing the private salon thing at two bills an hour. A minute later they wouldn't ID the guy in a lineup. Really, that's almost as good as you two at Gilmore. On the other hand, the ones who strip for loveless adoration are sort of the lower echelon." She broke her saddened trance, facing their quizzical stares. "What? I work with medical dickheads, remember?"

The girl was their primary topic at dinner, Charlee explaining what she would do on her stool for twenty dollars a song or in a salon for an hour at ten times the cost, according to her male counterparts who would on occasion feel an obligation to update their knowledge of the female anatomy in order to stay current.

After dinner Charlee and Cerise drove to the burbs, Murielle to her penthouse home where she lay awake in bed for hours thinking of the girl. She wondered what strange sensations might have whirled through the girl's mind during those several seconds, trying to imagine what wistful hope or expectation lay behind her dreamy gaze.

She gave the girl twenty-two or three, pondering how unattractive she would be at thirty after spending that many nights naked in a smoke-filled cabaret or in a small and dimly lit room being mauled by men desperate for the smooth warmth of nubile flesh. She imagined the girl stripped of her make-up and clothes, rebuilt from head to toe with proper care and attention, wondering what difference that would make in her life. Or did the girl even care? Would she care? If she could spend her nights writhing and wiggling naked on a stool, contorting her exposed and vulnerable body on a pole amidst dozens of faceless men, what else might she do to make her way in life?

Sunday Murielle slept in, eventually making her way with toast and coffee to her terrace with Saturday's unread paper. As though directed by some divine decree, her mind wandering, she absently flipped to the page identifying Friday's dearly departed, reading her mother's epilogue as she would a stranger's, learning without the slightest twinge of emotion that her father had passed on the previous year with no children surviving them. She snorted caustically. She hadn't thought of them in years, nor would she again. Their loss.

Forgetting them, she dressed for a lazy day at home, spending the afternoon on her daybed in the solarium with a grand cru looking out over the river. Her life was far too busy to feel lonely between her weeks with Anthony and her upscale sophisticated vacations without him. She had more money than she could ever spend, loving friends, a remarkable career at Gilmore and she sat at the top of Belmont. What more could she ever want other than Stonewall's sudden and fortunate death? A recurrent dream kept alive by his recurrent cruel punishment. What would she give to see him dead, to flee from him into the idyllic life he kept from her?

How intensely she regretted the day they crossed paths at the end of her third collegiate year, the day he captivated her by saying all the right things. He was older in years, stylishly young in his manner and appearance. Thirty-three, he told her during their first lunch, years younger than the professors whose desks she would often and happily bend over in return for ensuring her best possible future with an honours degree. He was handsome and wealthy, a smooth sophisticate instantly smitten with her. He needed and wanted to know her better. He drove her home in a limousine and kissed her, asking to see her again. And she agreed.

Lunches quickly became dinners, one in particular ending with cognacs in his Garden District home when he had sent his whore away for the weekend, where she was blinded by luxury. One week later she went with him to Biloxi midway through June where, together in bed their second morning, he confessed his deep feelings. She was twenty-one and he believed he could fall in love with her, that she could one day soon love him. He wanted her one weekend at his home, to see each other as they truly were without the glitter of casino lights, exclusive hotel suites and fancy limousines. And she agreed, returning to her parents' home from a weekend at a girlfriend's home.

She stayed with him throughout two weekends, colouring the same lie with different names, one year and one week later making the second worst mistake of her life without which she would not have found Anthony who found Karine, or Charlee who discovered Cerise. She would not have married Jackson who might not have died so terribly. Nevertheless he did die, survived by a young and wealthy tormented widow trapped in a cycle she lived each day for no better reason than an innocent young woman long ago succumbing to Stonewall's incurable addiction to the most beautiful nubile bodies. As appealing as the stripper, she mused, who had most likely forgotten her.

38

Murielle refilled her wine, swirling the deep-ruby liquid. Allowing the girl to again creep into her thoughts, she wondered what if?

Stonewall was sixty-five, admittedly looking late-forties with help from his personal trainer and surgeon. Despite which the last several of his whores were closer to thirty than their lost virginity, studying for their master's and doctorates and eager to repay their staggering bills while living in luxury's comfortable lap.

What would he possibly do or think to see her again as she was at twenty-one, alluring and spirited, eager to please him in any way he wished. What if, before snatching the girl from his tight grip, she would quit Gilmore? What if she would sell Belmont and move to Charleston? What if?
*

Monday at work she waited anxiously for 6:00 to end her day. Before going home she drove to the Quarter, to the glossy black doors where she stepped casually from her Jaguar convertible   to study the girl whose 3-D image and billing dominated the cabaret's window.

Her name was Chloe Beaudoin, the Big Easy's youngest and most irresistible exotic danseuse available to excite and stimulate her every Tuesday through Saturday, though Murielle somehow believed perhaps not. The ever-present 'what if' applied big time. What if she bumped into a

Gilmore man or, worse, a Belmont employee? Absolutely not. Instead she went home to create an appropriate outfit for the next evening.

*

Tuesday she left her Gilmore office early. At home she showered and shampooed, combing her hair into long, dark strands. She dressed in flared, high-waisted tan linen slacks and fitted jacket accented with a green silk scarf, a tan wide-brimmed fedora trimmed with a green silk band, and three-inch green stilettos bringing her to an even and impressive six feet.

She left at 5:30 into an evening that was pleasant, sunny and warm, the tightly conjoined structures and dark narrow alleyways that were the Quarter forbidding the slightest breeze.

The first cop to stop alongside the Jaguar left her after a few minutes of agreeable dialogue. He understood her wanting to help a down and out stripper; he understood her business card and the fifty percent Belmont discount even more, notifying his fellow peace keepers that the green Jag was disabled and waiting for a tow truck.

At 6:30 Chloe Beaudoin came into sight, closing the distance between them at a fast pace, bouncing along insouciantly, her dark hair swaying from shoulder to shoulder, completely oblivious to the stares of envy and disgust from one demographic, lust and desire from the other.

Murielle was standing by the convertible import several feet from the black doors with her arms crossed. She couldn't think of what else to do with them and Chloe Beaudoin had no choice but to notice her.

Not acknowledging the woman wasn't an option. Chloe hadn't stopped thinking about her since Saturday when seeing the woman at once made her shiver, happy and sad.

Who was she and why was she even there? Why would such a chic and sophisticated woman be interested in her when she was nobody? Not knowing why she was standing there waiting, unsmiling, staring at her more intently than Saturday, would haunt her for years.

Chloe slowed her pace to a stop. She glanced over her shoulder for no particular reason, then at the sidewalk. The woman hadn't budged an inch, had not stopped staring, Chloe steeling herself with an invisible deep breath before stepping close enough to prevent intrusions.

"You're the lady from Saturday, the one who stared at me with your friends."

"That's strange. I thought you were staring at me, Chloe." Murielle stood straight, clasping her hands. "More accurately, we were staring at each other for similar reasons. Weren't we?"

"You're here waiting for me, aren't you? Why?"

"Yes, waiting for you."

"Why?"

"Because you and I haven't stopped thinking about each other since Saturday. Because my friends told me what you do behind those doors and I want to know why that is because what I saw Saturday in your eyes does not belong in such a dark place. Among more personal reasons that are not yours to know at the moment."

Chloe studied Murielle from her stilettos to her fedora. She was more striking than Chloe remembered, her softly accented voice sensual and low.

"Who are you? Why do you even care what I do? I'm nothing to anyone, especially someone like you." She stared at the car. "What do you want from me?"

"My name is Murielle Belmont. I do care and I want nothing, not for myself anyway."

"So then why are you here talking to a stripper?" Chloe

wanted to scream, struggling to understand what the hell was happening. "This is too creepy, lady. Leave me alone. I have to go."

Murielle's lips formed a faint smile. "You do not have to go. You do not have to dress that way and what you said about being nothing…that stops right now. That's why I'm here, Chloe. The sparkle I saw in your eyes Saturday and whatever magical dream lay behind your faraway look that came and went in a blink because of me. That is why I am here. Because whatever your dream, nothing good will come to you from behind those black doors."

Chloe hunched her shoulders, not understanding. "What? You're here telling me not to strip, to live a better life? Well, fuck you. I live just fine and I will have a better life. I will. That's why I'm here, for the money. I'm going to university in the fall. I'm getting a degree. So yeah, fuck you and your fancy clothes," she hesitated, "Murielle Belmont."

Murielle stood unperturbed. "Yes, you will have that life and that education, if you're the woman I hope you are. If not, I'm sure your star billing will reopen those doors to you. That said, Chloe, I'm not one for wasting time. This is a one-time offer. So listen very carefully, I will not repeat myself. I will give you a gift of ten thousand in cash to not walk through those doors, to stop this very minute ruining your life. Is that clear enough…Chloe Beaudoin?"

"What!"

"You heard me. Ten grand in cash, and dinner once we wash your face. Don't like what you hear, which I doubt, spend what's left of the evening twirling on your stool. Spend the rest of your life stripping. You'll be ten grand to the good and I won't give you a moment's thought."

"So what do you get for ten K, me for a night, a thrill?"

"That would certainly be an expensive evening.

However, yes. You for the night, without any thrills."
Murielle checked her Lady Rolex." Did I happen to mention
not wasting my time?"

"I don't understand."

"You will."

"You don't even know me."

"I believe I do."

The girl inhaled a deep breath, expelling a groan. She
wanted to stamp her feet and scream, scanning the street in
both directions. She needed space, she needed time. "I can
leave after dinner and still get the money? That's what you
said."

Murielle nodded. "That is what I said. And we forget
each other. Me, because I won't care. You, because any
number of years from now, when that exquisite body goes
to shit, when you're eternally drunk, drugged or dead, you
simply won't remember me. More's the pity."

Murielle watched the girl drift for mere seconds, while
for Chloe her thoughts sped through her past, present and
future. Reaching into her handbag for her cell, she called
her boss. She felt sick and was going home, which was
wasn't entirely a lie. She did feel sick, with no idea where
she was going.

*

Inside the Jaguar Murielle casually dropped an envelope
thick with twenties into Chloe's lap. Driving to Chloe's
apartment she waited as the girl changed into a more
modest skirt and sweater, from a dancer to a teenager, and
washed her face. She was impressed with the collection and
range of academic books and how neatly the one-bedroom
flat was kept.

They went to Angelo's for dinner, a place Chloe had
always wanted to go but she had no one to go with and felt
she wouldn't fit in. They were greeted by Angelo himself

who escorted them to his most private table and left, accepting Murielle's word that her guest was of sufficient age to enjoy his finest Bordeaux. Moments later the head waiter came to the table with a Jean-Marc XO neat and a glass of exquisite red wine.

Through a relaxed dinner Murielle learned of the drawers and the doorknob, the mattress on the floor and Chloe's parents. She listened intently as the girl spoke of her time with Vance and the letter from Tulane accepting her, a letter she could prove. She learned about the diner and the cabaret and the girl's dream of becoming an architect, of one day designing her own luxurious home.

She knew everything she needed to know and wanted to forget about tiny spaces, "anyway, that's my magical dream. That's why I dance. That's what I'm doing with your money. I'm going to Tulane in September."

"Tulane, that's good. It's my alma mater also. Nevertheless it's merely a stepping stone, not your future. That alone won't be enough and this thing you're doing will follow you through life like a dark shadow, always with you, always threatening. I know because I have my own black doors. And please, call me Murielle." She acknowledged the waiter and the crème brûlée with a smile, Chloe didn't. When he was gone, "I don't believe in anything except myself and the ladies you saw me with on Saturday who would do anything for me, and I in return. That said, I must believe we crossed paths for a reason. In that instant I revisited my past, the very way you foresaw your future self in me. Am I right?"

"Yes."

Murielle liked the girl, certain that the weeks and months ahead would cultivate a synergy between them if not a bond. For the next hour over dessert and coffee, a dazzled Chloe learned of her conditional future. Whether

her dream would ever come true was fully dependent on her.

"You will not return to the club, Chloe. You do not need what little they owe you. Tonight you will go home and tomorrow you will sell or give away your car and make peace with your landlord. If he jerks you around, you call me. You will also trash your wardrobe, your entire wardrobe and accessories. This is a complete makeover, no residue. I'll come for you and your books at six and take you to your home in the Garden District that is far from a tiny space. Then you'll spend the night with me in my home."

"The Garden District? Seriously?" Murielle answered with a nod. "But why your place?"

"To show you where I live, how I live, how you can enjoy a similar lifestyle one day if you don't make very many mistakes. Because I'm sure you'll become a frequent visitor and Thursday you're going for a physical by my personal physician and a fast-track passport before we go shopping for a wardrobe and a car. Your choice. The mustang was okay for a stripper, but you would definitely worry my doorman."

Chloe scarcely believed what she was hearing, thinking that at least she had the ten grand if what Murielle was telling her was all bullshit. Though what she heard next made her sweep her napkin to her mouth.

"Friday you're doing a spa day for a full makeover. You've got a few things to learn about make-up and you will never again use a tanning bed. You won't have to when we get back from a week in Martinique. We leave Saturday morning with an extra five hundred in a real leather handbag you don't have yet, after which I will deposit the same amount weekly to your account and pay your full tuition each semester at Tulane. In addition, do well, become that architect, and I will finance your own firm with a cash bonus of one-half million. Or do I drop you off at the club before going home?" She paused, her expression completely indifferent. "Do we have a deal?"

Murielle understood the visible disbelief in the girl's eyes, the hesitation. She also saw hope.

"Okay. We have a deal, if this isn't a dream or a rich lady's sick joke. Yes Murielle, we do have a deal. Thank you. I just can't believe you're doing this for me."

Chloe also agreed to abstain from dating for the first year, which wasn't a big issue for her, and that she would protect herself from the disruptions and complications of motherhood that would be a deal-breaker along with failing to graduate.

Outside the girl's apartment Murielle wished her a pleasant evening and left without so much as a hug. Inside Chloe phoned the club's owner and quit. She was going home to Lafayette, she told him. Disconnecting, she poured a glass of Merlot and sat rocking on her couch. Sleep was entirely impossible. She was afraid that morning would awaken her from a fanciful dream, that the ten grand was an illusion. Instead she went to her closet. She put aside a pair of penny loafers, jeans and sweaters for the next day and Thursday, selecting her best pyjamas for the next evening with Murielle. What was left she stuffed into a bag the mission could sort through.

The next morning she went to her landlord, trading her Mustang for three months' rent, and at 5:00 she sat on the building's stoop waiting with a small suitcase and boxes filled with books. At 6:10 she wanted to scream, five minutes later fighting the temptation to cry. Then she saw the candy green Jaguar coming closer. She saw Murielle's bright smile and she did cry, the deluge unstoppable when Murielle sat beside her on the stoop and held her close.

When she opened the door to her Garden District home with her own key she began believing Murielle had taken her to a heaven that did exist, where people might actually want her, where she could for once in her life be happy.

Murielle poured a shallow XO, giving the girl time to explore. Everything that was, was gone. Anthony from then on would stay at the penthouse and Stonewall would have to kick out his whore one hour a month or pay for a suite. Prytania by the park was Chloe's to restyle as she pleased for as long as she played by the rules.

The condo was one thing, an absolute springboard into luxury. At the penthouse however Chloe stepped from a private elevator into a world of unimagined elegance leaping from the pages of her magazines and her dreams into her reality. Again Murielle gave her time to quietly digest what was happening, to wander and touch in awe, to sit and stand enthralled, to gaze across the glistening black waters of the Mississippi.

Turning her back to the river her eyes were filled with confusion and uncertainty, a thousand questions cramming her mind. Murielle answered the first by taking her hand, leading her to the private guestroom and en suite where a deep bath was steaming. An hour later Chloe padded into the bedroom wrapped in a towel and turban, to the large gift box wrapped in a deep pink foil and ribbons. Opening the box to a silk gown, matching slip and slippers in a deep fuchsia, she skipped quickly into the bathroom to dry and style her hair.

In the living room Murielle was waiting patiently with a refreshed XO and a small Chardonnay.

"Thank you again, Murielle. They're wonderful. I don't know what else to say. I'm sorry I swore at you. I'm really a nice girl."

"I know you are or you wouldn't be here and there is

nothing else say." Murielle beamed, pleased. "You look lovely. And what were you doing in there? I was about to call 9-1-1."

"I was thinking about tomorrow, about the car."

"And?"

"I really like the 2 Series convertible, and I don't need a current model. What I mean is, if they're too expensive."

"They are not, and you do. No hand-me-down ever fits well." She chuckled. "Besides, people would talk. A Beemer it is."

They spoke about fashions and colours and a to-do list that included a passport, a phone with an unlisted number, and a personal trainer because the good life came with certain expectations and obligations. Whatever else she wanted was her call. Women did not buy other women jewellery. Then she was sent to bed; she hadn't slept in thirty-six hours.

Thursday she woke on a cloud, one that was hand-made in France and covered with satin sheets imported from Italy. The doctor gave her a clean bill of health and the passport office promised Murielle by end-of-business the next day. More importantly for Chloe the BMW convertible would be prepped and ready to drive home that same evening.

They went to lunch for salads and sparkling water before spending the entire afternoon with a personal assistant in the city's most exclusive ladies' boutique where cocktails and canapés were served to the well-heeled By Appointment Only. 'Ladies' meaning that Styrofoam coffee cups and beignets escorted by sticky fingers, sneakers and tank tops were diverted at the door to other more appropriate shops.

With a dozen or more bags filled to brimming and Chloe's own clothes discarded with utmost care, Murielle reluctantly agreed to visit one sex boutique for the most daring thongs and bikini tops. They left with a half-dozen each and Chloe drove home after a long day with the Beemer's top down.

First she unpacked her clothes, then she jumped and bounced on her own recently delivered French cloud. Falling flat, kicking the air, warm tears trickled onto the pristine duvet.

Friday she woke to a clear and bright day, the fourth in her life worth living. She arrived at the spa as a beautiful and appealing woman. They pampered and treated her body with steam and oils, they fed her with exotic fruits and herbs, vitamins and green tea; they massaged her and waxed her. She floated weightlessly and naked with no sense of time in the serenity of total darkness, deprived of sight and sound, smell and touch, tasting nothing on her lips; they bathed her and wrapped her in warm towels while they enhanced her fingers and toes; they dressed her in a fleecy robe while styling her hair and sent her home as an elegant young lady.

At 4:45 she was exhausted, officially ready to fly, and by six she had a phone that would keep her safe from her past.

39

Chloe had never flown. She wasn't comfortable with the idea of some stranger driving her into nowhere at 180 miles an hour, squeezing Murielle's hand when her body unexpectedly pressed into her First-Class seatback and the ground disappeared. She didn't like the rattling, the bumping or the deafening roar of the engines. Or that the flight over open water to the French island would last five hours.

What she did like was being with Murielle, more convinced each day she wasn't suspended in a dream. The woman wasn't intrusive or domineering, not once calling to impose herself, and after Tuesday had never repeated herself.

Throughout the entire flight Murielle scarcely spoke a word. Chloe's nose was stuck to the small window, mesmerized by snow-white monolithic clouds and the brownish-green specks that were islands. Although her hand was sacrificed once more at the abrupt drop and unnerving low drone as the jet began its initial descent, through to screeching tires as they touched down and Chloe's body lurched forward as the pilot reversed thrust, Murielle assuring her that was a good thing.

She told Chloe that thanking the pilots was always the polite thing to do, which she did. Minutes later, managing to avoid the gleeful exuberance of the colourful reception committee, the first to pass through Immigration and Security, their Priority luggage was waiting for them.

While confused and sweat-drenched tourists waited ill-humoured in line under a fierce midday sun for buses that would zigzag between several hotels, Murielle hired a limousine. At the resort Chloe was aware in advance to thank the man opening her door, also mindful that she was now a proper lady wearing a skirt.

Inside the grand lobby, as at the airport, she was amazed at Murielle conversing in fluent French. In their suite she hurried from her bedroom onto the top-floor private terrace to stand staring out over thatched rooftops and sparkling pools, blinding sand and gentle waves folding into an endless effervescent white ribbon along the shore.

Turning to Murielle who was stepping out from her adjoining bedroom, she choked on a "Wow", Murielle asking why she was simply taking in the scene instead of being part of it.

Strolling along meandering pathways to the ocean in thongs and tops, sheer sarongs tied at the their hips, they appeared more like sisters than mother and daughter and certainly not as each other's recent acquisition.

While Murielle relished the deserved admiring glances, Chloe was too acclimated to the nuances of testosterone-driven psyches to care. Of greater importance was that she had never put her feet onto hot white sands, or dipped them into warm turquoise waters; she had never swum or felt as free as she did splashing beneath the surface.

Over the next seven days they raced on PWCs and parasailed in tandem. Chloe dragged Murielle into early morning aerobics and noontime aqua-ballet very much against her will, she drove an ATV with Murielle clinging to her from behind and leaped into fresh-water pools from forty-foot crags while Murielle stood her ground to watch and take photos. She was the envy of all other girls during late-day dance classes, one of them asking Chloe where she learned to sway her hips and twirl so effortlessly.

Midway through the vacation Murielle rented a private yacht and crew for the day, Chloe taking her turn at the helm, snorkeling and marvelling at incredible marine life for the very first time, ending that day and others under fluttering canopies and wide-brimmed sunhats sipping wine spritzers.

Evenings were for elegant dresses and sandals, fine dining, Caribbean theatre and the casino. Thursday local vendors came with their wares to the resort, Murielle bargaining agreeably in French while beside her a frustrated Chloe kept adamantly repeating her best price, until…

"Murielle, can you please help me here? He's not understanding me, and why is he laughing at me?"

"He isn't laughing at you, sweetheart. He's saying your price is fair. He simply wants to see my lovely daughter smile, to see your eyes sparkle as a condition of the sale."

"That's crazy."

"Do you want the ring, sweetheart?"

"Yes."

"Then you have quite a dilemma. Don't you?"

Chloe furrowed her brow, pursing her lips, studying the turquoise gemstone mounted on silver. She eyed the vendor, studying his unblinking cue-ball eyes set in an ancient purple-black skull topped with bristly white stubble, his chipped white teeth trimmed with gold a curious backdrop to his thick and smiling pink lips.

She planted her hands on her hips, determined, staring him down. She couldn't remember smiling once in her life. She never had a reason and didn't know how. Imitating the vendor's was impossible. She wasn't a cheerful and carefree eighty-year-old black man with whiskers and she did not understand how Murielle managed to form one side of her mouth into an endearing smile and not the other, like she was the Mona Lisa but more beautiful.

Murielle said something in French to the man that caused his smile to fade. Making a show of straightening shoulders, shaking his arms and hands free of tension, he pointed a commanding finger at Chloe, telling her in French to pay close attention. Waiting until her mother helped her understand he put a skeletal fingertip to one corner of his mouth. Jabbing gently upward he maintained the lip's position as he drew away the finger, indicating with a flourish that Chloe should do likewise.

People were watching and smiling. Murielle was watching and smiling, not being any help at all. She wanted out, feeling a searing heat wash across her face despite her familiarity with leering audiences, determined to have not her ring, but their rings that would mean something to each of them.

She shrugged, giving in. No big deal. She put a polished fingertip to one corner of her glossed lips, pushing gently upward, stopping on command. The old man nodded his approval, moving the other corner of his mouth into position, his pink lips pressed firmly together, again indicating to Chloe to do likewise. She did, feeling silly, her eyes focused on the vendor's.

He brought up his arms, halting her with open palms as though preparing to pull a rabbit from a hat or conduct an orchestra, Chloe dropping her arm to her side, her full cheeks flushed and pinched and quivering, thinking that smiling was too much work.

Again with a flourish the old man spread his arms wide, from his elbows bringing bony hands and fingertips to the tight corners of his lips before gently pulling in opposite directions, nodding to Chloe with his fingertips still attached. He looked comical with his skin stretched and his eyes wide open, the top row of teeth exposed. As for Chloe, she wanted to die deciding she wouldn't. She wanted those rings more and walking away would disappoint Murielle. So she did; she stretched her mouth, baring her teeth.

The old vendor again nodded his approval, slowly lowering his arms to his side, encouraging Chloe whose eyes opened wide with surprise. His distorted mouth was transformed into a beaming smile framing gold and yellow teeth. She lowered her arms, staring at him. Her lips didn't move or feel pulled, her cheeks didn't feel squeezed. She was smiling, into her tutor's plastic mirror.

The applause was muted and friendly. Murielle's arms around her were warm and tender, Chloe all of a sudden remembering the unwanted and unsmiling girl in grade seven whose work book was full of gold stars.

As everyone returned to their own high-level negotiations the old man slipped the ring onto Chloe's finger. She thanked him, pointing to the ring's twin and her mother. Forty USD wasn't ten grand, but a small beginning and meaningful. Leaving, Chloe thanked the man with the one French word she knew. He returned a simple "Je vous en prie, mademoiselle" with a tilt of his head.

Friday after dinner, their last Caribbean evening, Chloe wanted to sit with her mentor in the quiet darkness under the stars by the ocean.

"Murielle, thank you."

"Stop saying that. You made the week special for me, sometimes more special than I really needed."

"I love my home and my car and my clothes. How do I ever repay that?"

"You graduate. That's what you do, you graduate."

"Last Tuesday you said 'Among more personal reasons that are not yours to know at the moment' when I asked why. Will you ever tell me why you did this for me?"

"It's more what you've done for me."

Murielle paused for a moment, not seeing the endless black water glistening with moonlight. "Jackson and I loved each other very much. We wanted a family, until we discovered he could never do that for us. Which we accepted, which in no way diminished the absolutely wonderful life we shared. When he was killed I cried for weeks when I was alone, shutting out the world for months. Not only did I lose the love of my life, I had no part of him, no part of us together to continue loving and adoring. I felt complete emptiness until Charlee and Cerise gave me a timely reality check."

"Will I ever meet them? Do they know about me?"

"They do not know about you. And yes, you will meet them very soon. They will absolutely adore you. They were as shocked by seeing you as I was. You reminded them of me twenty some years ago, when I first met Jackson. Charlee introduced us. In a sense she tied our knot."

"And Cerise?"

"I work with her. I introduced her to Charlee. They're a fabulous couple and we have a lot of shared history. But when I saw you, seeing myself in the past came second. What I saw first was the daughter I might have given Jackson. In a way I still do. It's impossible not to. Nevertheless, I like you most for being Chloe Beaudoin future architect extraordinaire."

"I will be, Murielle. I swear. I just cannot imagine you years ago being like me."

"You mean *my* black doors. No. I suppose not. Though some doors are blacker than others, why I'm so happy we found each other when we did."

"Imagine how I feel. All this, the last ten days, is completely off the chart."

Murielle patted her knee, acknowledging the waiter who came with her cognac and Chloe's mildly diluted with soda.

"After my parents died I was lost. I was in a strange country with no relatives or friends, with scarcely enough insurance money to pay my tuition and survive alone in a small apartment. Until the summer of my final year when the money ran out, when coffee shops and diners weren't enough to pay my bills." She inhaled the pleasant night air. "Then..."

"I know, something really good happened to you. The way you happened to me."

"Not exactly, sweetheart. Though at the time I really did believe that. Instead I stepped through what would quickly become my black doors. Better said, I was lured through. I met a man, an older man, while running in the park one day. I later discovered he was in fact waiting for me, that he had seen me several times. I saw him again the next day by supposed coincidence and we went to lunch together. He was attentive and charming, overpowering for a naïve and inexperienced French girl. We met several times more and went once to Biloxi before I moved in with him a month later. His name is Kenneth Stonewall, the CEO of Southeast Industries. He was much wealthier then than I am today and he's as cruel today as he was then, though during our months together he did treat me well. He took me to fancy restaurants, to the theatre, to New York and the Caribbean. He bought me nice clothes and I believed I was falling in love with him. I was about a year older than you, thinking of marriage and babies. The world was different then, that's what we did. That's what I wanted with Stonewall until he threw me out, literally putting me on the street, making me feel like a whore for what I had done. What I stupidly believed was the heated passion of lovers was actually him using me as his private whore until he tired of me. The one good thing was that he paid my tuition in full. I could graduate and become someone, albeit as a whore, unaware at the time that he would keep me on a leash because of some sick obsession he has for me. Even though he threw me out, sweetheart." She squeezed Chloe's hand. "I have not told a word of this to anyone, not even Cerise or Charlee. They don't know."

"God, Murielle, what a horrible secret to keep from Jackson all those years."

A single tear trickled down Murielle's cheek. "Jackson quite rightly would not have married me, had he known. His family was the focal point of New Orleans society. What I did would have disgraced them, not that what I did with Stonewall was that terrible. I believed we were lovers, which does not exonerate me. Jackson married a lie, which isn't by far the worst part. At his funeral, as my heart was crying for him, I was crying for myself knowing he would never discover the darkest possible truth. He was a good man, a decent man. I believe he would have killed Stonewall had he known. I certainly wanted to, countless times. Stonewall was sick, he is sick. He liked taking pictures of me, taping our romantic moments together, which I believed was fine because I loved him. He made me believe we were creating lasting memories of our love. What I didn't know was that he was watching me when he was gone, recording me in the bathroom and the shower, when I dressed and undressed, when I was in bed. All recorded in high definition for the highest bidder or the most damaging impact. He was creating my black doors, sweetheart. I would say my personal guillotine which hangs over my head to this very day."

"He spied on you and kept the photos, the videos?"

Murielle nodded, forcing a weak smile. "Past and present to this very day. I cannot imagine what I would do

416

should my friends or Belmont and Gilmore ever see those photos and videos, the sole reason I must continuing sleeping with him once each month, some months more often, whenever he tires of his current victims."

"What!"

"I have for twenty years, sweetheart, forced to cheat on Jackson a week after I buried him. I had no choice, I never have, and he is not going away. He not only threatened to tell Jackson throughout our marriage, to show him proof, he now threatens me with telling Belmont and Gilmore. The fallout would devastate the memory of Jackson, his family name and my careers."

Chloe was stunned. "And you can still smile, Murielle? You can still think to help me? How is that even possible?"

"Because what happened to me will not happen to you. You see now why I want desperately to alter your life, why I must. You and I are not from such different worlds, sweetheart. We don't merely share an intriguing physical appearance, we share a life of parallel miseries. Or we did."

"Stonewall's the reason you're not dating? I mean, it's been eighteen months. You're way too young and beautiful to be alone, Murielle. I mean, shit! He's the reason?"

"He is *the* reason, sweetheart." Murielle swirled her cognac, sipping. "I should not be telling you this, ruining our vacation. Nevertheless, six months ago I did meet someone completely by chance, a wonderful gentleman from Boston I met not long after graduating. Anthony Vincent. We didn't date at the time, as much as I liked him. We were strictly platonic, enjoying occasional dinners whenever he was in town on business, our evenings ending with innocent hugs. Nothing more. He was a little older than me and I was getting over my year with Stonewall. And nothing on that level has changed, except that he's miserable at home. He wants out from a marriage that's

417

been a disaster for years, the complete opposite of mine."

Chloe didn't smile. The most she could manage was a mischievous glint in her eyes. "And… what happened? Will I meet him one day soon like Cerise and Charlee? Do you think he'll like me?"

She patted Chloe's cheek. "Nothing happened, sweetheart. We enjoyed a few innocent dinners talking about our early times together, before we were separated by marriage, because I know that's what Jackson wants for me. He wants my life filled with happiness and joy. He wants my life filled with a man like Anthony who's kind and gentle, which will never happen, which is why you will never meet him. Not in this lifetime. Stonewall somehow saw us or found us and, during my subsequent encounter with him, he told me he would courier a complete set of his so-called "Murielle Collection" to Anthony's home along with photos of us walking in the Quarter holding hands if I didn't stop seeing him."

"Which means he found you. The bastard was stalking you, but what I'm not understanding is why you're not completely in tears. What you're telling me is absolutely horrific. Who is this animal?"

"That's exactly what he is, sweetheart, a predator. And he is very sadistic. He needs to own people. He needs for some insane reason to continue owning me."

"What about Anthony?"

"I lied, of course. I told him we wouldn't work out, that the timing was wrong and I would always feel guilty cheating on Jackson."

"But that isn't true."

"No. But that he's gone is best for both of us, even though we would have worked out. I liked him very much and he would have loved you. Still, I couldn't bear the thought of Anthony seeing me as the worst possible whore.

Or his wife who would have destroyed him in court because of me. I would never do that to him."

"Why would Stonewall do such a cruel and heartless thing when he has you whenever he wants anyway? I mean, shit!"

"He's obsessive about cleanliness. He wears condoms even though he's sterile and showers immediately after. He's afraid I'll cheat because Anthony doesn't have the social status Jackson enjoyed, that I won't be clean enough for him. That's why he has me followed. He wants me permanently to himself now that I'm single, while he lures unsuspecting girls into his home for as long as he deems to keep them enthralled, the way he did me."

"That's more than cruel, Murielle. That is truly sadistic."

"We carve our futures, sweetheart, years before we live in them."

"I understand that now. And you'll never...."

Murielle pressed a fingertip to Chloe's lips. She did know, perfectly well.

Chloe put aside her glass. Without asking she squirmed slightly forward before laying back, nestling her head into Murielle's lap. The only warmth she had ever felt from another person was Vance's the times he wanted her before sleep. Murielle's warmth though was different, what Chloe believed must be a loving mother's warmth. "...never know how much I love you."

Part Six
40

Saturday Murielle Belmont woke to her sun curtains
billowing in a warm Caribbean breeze and a much bigger
problem than Stonewall. She was forty-five, and would
keep the unwelcome event to herself.

Chloe Beaudoin didn't wake. She hadn't slept a wink.
She spent the entire night in bed, in the dark, hugging her
knees to her chest and staring past her open doors into
oblivion as a myriad of feelings melded with plausible
strategies in a determined young mind.

Murielle was not a whore. She didn't deserve being
treated as worse than one. The whores she did know were
often beaten and always scared, though seldom coerced or
threatened. Each night was a conscious choice between
money and self-worth, the dollar always trumping self-
loathing. They were the whores, not Murielle.

She had an idea, which was all she had. She was
nineteen and although she didn't exactly epitomize the
essence of youthful innocence and purity, she needed help.
The plan was simple: Get the videos and the pictures. What
she couldn't quite figure out was the how, confident she
would because she owed her life to Murielle.
*

They spent the morning at the pool and strolling along the
shore holding hands, scarcely talking. Murielle was

enjoying her day, at once strangely relieved that at long last she was able to share her disgrace, while deeply dismayed that she had placed her deplorable burden onto such young shoulders.

From a distance they were exquisite twins. To any passerby accustomed to admiring them, they were mother and daughter content with each other's company. Murielle never understood the need to engage with strangers merely because they chose the same resort or flew in on the same plane, while Chloe was sufficiently preoccupied throughout the week dealing with the girl she was seeing in mirrors and windows and the eyes of those strangers each day. That morning in particular she was preoccupied with Murielle, relishing the peaceful mood.

They stepped cool and refreshed into their limousine at noon, while others stood with plastic cups of beer in a confused herd waiting for the bus. They flew out at 2:00, landing at Louis Armstrong at 8:00 PM local time, Chloe conceding that she might possibly fly again. Maybe.

Dinner would have been a functional anticlimax to the week, Murielle suggesting an evening together at her place the following Saturday. Waiting by her car until Chloe was safe and sound inside her condo and waving goodbye from her balcony, she blew a kiss into the air and drove off.
*

Sunday Murielle regretted not taking ten days. She called her friends to meet her for a luncheon, during which 'that girl' was an obvious topic. Their memory of the stripper was simply too vivid to ignore, Cerise good-naturedly pressing Murielle for the details of a previous secret life.

She let that one go. Instead she recounted her vacation, confessing to them that she did meet somebody, someone who made her vacation the best since losing Jackson. Which was fresh fodder for Cerise who went home

421

disappointed, eager to meet Murielle's mysterious someone at dinner the following Saturday.

Sunday Chloe spent her day doing the wash and buying groceries for the week. She bought wine for her cellar better suited to Murielle's discerning palate, a bottle of Rèmy Martin and Jean-Marc XO that wasn't for her. For her own taste whenever she might entertain Murielle, she brought home a bottle of Cîroc that she learned from Murielle to enhance with a splash.

For dinner on Saturday she selected an expensive Pauillac for the table and a set of green and yellow table linen for her hostess. She was becoming a lady.

More importantly, she had to free her mind. Dwelling on her plan, being overly creative, making imprudent changes, would cause her to fail. She would lose focus, which was not an option. She prepared an initial to-do list, revisiting each point each day through to Saturday morning. Satisfied, she decided the next morning and Monday could not come soon enough and went shopping.

Saturday evening she arrived on time at 6:00 dressed in low-heeled pumps, nylons, a linen skirt that was pleasingly short, and a silk blouse that gave to life the silk camisole beneath.

Her hostess was honestly surprised by the wine and her gift, hugging her, kissing her cheek.

"Thank you, sweetheart. I'll use both this evening for our dinner with Charlee and Cerise."

The silence lasted mere seconds. "What! No!"

"Yes, sweetheart."

"Do they know I'm here?"

"They do not. That would not be fair, would it?"

She took Chloe's hand, leading her onto the terrace. The spring evening was delightfully pleasant, Chloe very tempted to gulp her Cîroc with a splash. Even more so moments before 7:00 when, peering over the railing, Murielle pointed out bright red and purple forms hurrying across the parking lot.

Chloe didn't hear the reassuring "they'll love you." She was nervous. The women knew about her, the strangers during her vacation and her neighbours did not. Shit! What she did hear was "Stay here a moment, sweetheart."

At the door Charlee followed Cerise in with wine and a small box, shaking her head. Cerise spent the entire week on a high, excited for her friend. She needed to see this special guy. She needed to cross-examine him.

"Where is he, Mur? Where did you put him?"

"Truthfully, Cerise, he's not here yet. However while we're all waiting for him I do have another surprise for you. After I serve cocktails, ladies. Please go into the living room." Murielle went into the dining room, returning with crystal old-fashioneds filled two-fingers deep with malted scotch. She suggested they swallow a good amount, a really good amount before sitting with their eyes closed. And they were not to cheat, Cerise.

Then, "Ladies, please meet Tulane's next brilliant graduate who one day soon will be the state's finest architect, our Ms. Chloe Beaudoin."

Chloe stood with Murielle's arm around her, feeling like a lamb waiting for slaughter. Cerise and Charlee sat stunned, exchanging blank stares, their minds racing to make sense of what they were seeing. The metamorphosis was no less incredible than the women's uncanny resemblance.

A drawn out "No shit!" flowed from between Cerise's crimson lips, Murielle instantly feeling Chloe's imperceptible flinch.

Charlee said, "Mur what have you done?" She stood, hugging the girl who was staring at Cerise. "An architect,

423

Chloe. Good for you. And Mur, no one will ever believe this gorgeous girl is not your daughter. No one."

Cerise was up next, smiling, cupping the girl's warm cheeks. "Don't get all stiff and panicky on us, kid. I meant 'No shit' in a good way. We like you. We just thought you were a man." She turned to Murielle. "Anything else we should hear about your vacation, Mur, other than you met somebody and 'we' had a very nice time?"

The women put Chloe between them, Cerise needed lots of answers.

She told them about the Prytania condo and the car, about Tulane's forgotten disappointment and her approaching first semester, about her makeover and her vacation. Not the money. Nor did she mention the cabaret and they didn't ask.

Then came dinner and Chloe's turn to hear about Jackson Belmont and Murielle de la Sorbonne, Charlee Boyette and Cerise Quinterre. Though Chloe remained the centre of attention throughout the evening. She was amazed by how level the three women were, by how sincerely interested Cerise and Charlee were in her choice of studies and post-graduation dreams and desires, Cerise emphasizing that ambition would get her to her desires much faster than dreams.

Near eleven Murielle watched from her terrace as her friends and Chloe hugged goodbye at their cars. The evening was a complete success and Charlee was perfectly right. She did have a daughter.

Her phone ringing Sunday morning came as no big surprise, listening for an hour as Chloe gave her a detailed account of the previous evening as though she might have missed something. Then Cerise called, disconnecting an hour later with a fuller understanding of the girl's heartrending childhood and subsequent bad choices that

424

came to an abrupt end with dinner and a clean face.

*

Mid-May was a good time to live in New Orleans. The spring air was fresh, not yet oppressive with summer's wet heat and all things colourful were in bloom.

The moment Chloe woke she poured a juice and pressed the MOM that she put on her speed-dial before going to bed. Disconnecting after a fleeting sixty minutes she showered and coated her body with SPF, dressing for a run in sneakers and white leg warmers, a white microfibre tee and matching low-rise boy shorts that would enhance her golden tan.

She did not need the address. She needed a three-story building overlooking the park with a midnight blue Bentley on the avenue, and hopefully Stonewall standing on the balcony as was his Sunday morning custom. She would simply be exhausted at the end of a breathless run and walk from one end of the street to the other. If she saw him she would happen to notice him and smile. If not she would retrace her steps, halting occasionally to stabilize her heart rate and drink her water.

Leaving her home near 10:30 she wasn't the least bit tense. She was focused, and she was resolute.

She didn't jog through the park, stopping at the far edge to compensate for her lack of effort. She drizzled water between her breasts, palming the tee for effect before daubing her face, arms and thighs with water that clung appealingly to her tan.

Springing onto the sidewalk bordering a practically deserted avenue she jogged in place for a few minutes, gradually slowing her rhythm. She took time to stretch out her legs and arms, touching her toes to stretch out her back. Checking her pulse and her watch, she paused to drink from her bottle before walking in three wide circles to begin her cool-down without bouncing or striding along the avenue. Instead she meandered leisurely, tuned into her iPhone, giving herself ample time.

Several balconies accommodated couples standing or sitting, relaxing with their morning coffees, enjoying the park, enjoying her and other pretty girls who were bouncing along with their ponytails swishing hectically from side to side.

Stonewall certainly was a creature of habit who lived his life by the clock. Either she was on time or he was, her heart skipping a beat that very instant at seeing the gleaming blue symbol of vanity and arrogance parked in the driveway, Chloe stopping at once to stretch out her muscle groups for the man on the balcony not 100 feet from her.

*

Kenneth Stonewall was indeed standing on his balcony, contemplating his next suitable woman. He wasn't worried. Except for Murielle's successor many years earlier he had not once failed to achieve his July 01st mandate in a timely manner, never once failing to honour his year-long commitment to them per the agreement.

A year of luxury and travel culminating with a substantial financial reward would be and was irresistible to any appealing and single woman, particularly since his current choices and those going forward were and would be a decade older than in Murielle's era of enchantment.

The one in his bed was thirty-two, never married. In addition to possessing the prerequisite qualities of intelligence and enviable good-looks she was athletic, conversant with world events, a good lover and companion. In a way he preferred them, the older ones. They didn't whimper and cry a day before his cleaning service changed the sheets. They left with their bonuses and got on with life.

He saw the girl coming, walking in a dream state.

426

Though not as oblivious to the world as she appeared, he believed, most certainly stretching and bending more for the benefit of onlookers than her own. They were all the same, the young ones. All of them teases until dragged behind a tall bush or into a cluster of convenient trees, Stonewall paying no more attention to her than he might any girl prancing around as though meticulously dressed in a thin coat of paint. Then he lurched forward, straining to see more of her as she came even closer.

She looked up, noticing him, slowing again to a stop as a thin smile formed on her lips. She raised a hand in a discreet wave and meandered on her way.

"Murielle," he whispered loudly, his heart suddenly racing.

He didn't take his eyes from her, his breathing laboured when she stopped at the far corner to bend and stretch. When she turned, walking toward him, he sucked in air practically stumbling backward. Within moments he was on the sidewalk, unhurriedly crossing the avenue when every part of him wanted to run toward her.

Stepping onto the opposite sidewalk he returned the girl's smile.

"Hi."

"Hello, and please excuse me. Realizing as you turned in the distance that you would delight my eyes once more I felt compelled to speak with you, to hear your voice which is as soft and sweet as you are lovely."

"Well thank you." Murielle had described him perfectly. He did come across as late forties, with clear eyes and sun-tinted skin that was too smooth even for his sad lie. He was slim and fit, his dark hair full and precisely combed. "I'm Patricia."

"Patricia, how lovely a name. I'm Kenneth. Kenneth Stonewall. Without sounding trite may I state the obvious, that you are exceptionally and delightfully attractive?"

Her bright smile that she practiced and the glint in her eyes were real. "Yes, you may. That definitely makes all this effort worthwhile." Asshole.

"Patricia, I am completely intrigued. If you do not at this very moment enjoy the attentions of an undeserving beau, or a suitor who must certainly regard you as an angel, would you afford me the great pleasure of joining me for a light lunch?"

She furrowed her brow. "I don't even know you."

"I humbly beg to differ. You know my name and you know where I live. I am also the CEO of Southeast Industries whose intentions for lunch are entirely honourable." He pointed casually to the luxury sedan. "I would be honoured to collect you at whatever time and address you choose. Unless of course I have misjudged your age in your favour."

She gawked at the sedan. "That's yours?"

He nodded. "More to satisfy the expectations of others than my own need, I assure you."

"Nice ride. Anyway, I'm twenty-three in my final year at Tulane and I've put boyfriends on hold. My degree comes before faded memories." She checked her watch. "Lunch does sound good, Kenneth. Not exactly what I was expecting when I left home. But yeah, why not? I have to admit, now I'm intrigued. However isn't eleven a little early, wouldn't midafternoon be better? Besides which I am a little damp at the moment."

"A much better suggestion, of course. However, in the meantime, may I offer you a ride home?"

"Thanks." She glanced at the third-floor condo. "But I've got a ten-speed parked on the other side." She pointed to the main walkway into the park. "Why don't we meet over there, say at one?"

"Agreed. A lifetime of minutes and worth every breath. I will see you at one, Patricia."

He stood motionless, completely awestruck watching her saunter from view. If not for the voice and the summer hue of her skin, she was Murielle. That she didn't glance over her shoulder or wave was indicative of nothing. Eyes were the ruination of liars; hers were innocent and clear.

In his condo he changed into dress slacks, a crisp shirt and blazer, advising the woman he had an afternoon meeting. He apologized for not spending the entire day with her, suggesting with a 500-dollar incentive that she might go shopping for an ensemble to wear at dinner the following weekend.

When she was gone he went to the safe in his study where he kept his highly cherished Murielle Collection, bringing her to HD life on his flat screen. The resemblance was exact, Stonewall zooming in to examine every inch of her body, at that moment desperate to have both of them. He could not believe his good fortune, that in his lifetime he would be the one and only to induct two untried Murielles into womanhood.

Patricia would willingly succumb to the good life, his life. She was first to notice him, the first to smile and wave. What he wasn't certain about, what he would very soon discover, was whether she was naïve or naturally uninhibited, which would have no bearing whatsoever on the impending outcome. Either characteristic suited his purpose; the sole aspect of their relationship that would change of necessity would be the manner of his enticement into it.

41

At 1:00 on a picture-perfect afternoon Stonewall stood waiting, casually leaning against the Bentley with his arms and legs crossed. Not a minute late or early, Patricia stepped into sunlight from the shadows of tall trees.

She wasn't cute or girlish; she was trendy and desirable, striding toward him in open-toed green sandals and white high-waisted flared shorts highlighted with a short-sleeve white silk blouse that was sheer enough to enhance her white three-quarter bra while the satin buttons were selectively ignored to enhance the shimmering swell of her breasts.

He loved her instantly, the thought of her and the certainty of having her. He had no need to envision the rest of her, he knew every fine detail. Patricia Someone was his incoming reprieve from the loneliness that accompanies wealth and power. He could see the hope shining in her eyes as she came closer.

Reading her mind as he held the door for her was a simple matter: She was stepping into his life. Body language was nonsense, a factoid, while the eyes would always accurately and reliably reveal truths and lies, envy and lust. What else mattered? Eyes were the windows of the mind, by no means whatsoever tied to an obsolete human soul. He didn't care whether she was warm-hearted or tender, forgiving or sympathetic. He cared about wanting and needing her, about reliving his past with her.

She was entering her fourth year of Sociology, figuring a brief five-year debt load and better wardrobe if she landed her dream job with the government. Until then she was working two jobs because she couldn't afford to work as an unpaid intern. She needed the money. She owned two extra nice outfits and was wearing one of them. She lived with three other girls, eager for her own place and privacy. Studying was difficult with constant parties and sleepovers, not to mention different guys every weekend digging into her personal food supply.

At the intimate garden setting lunch was a huge success. They talked and they laughed. She was a true joy. She was intelligent, well-read and well-mannered, possessing an agreeable blend of correctness and youthful vivacity. Whatever she might lack in her life's education he would soon infuse with luxury and travel that would compel her to stay with him.

As he slowed the car to a stop at the main entrance to the park he invited her to a late lunch on Wednesday, containing his delight when she accepted without excessive eagerness or surprise.
*

Monday morning she lay in bed pondering her summer, mildly annoyed with Murielle for letting her birthday go unnoticed, for Chloe not having her own gift to offer when Charlee and Cerise gave theirs.

She had sixteen weeks before the commencement of her higher education, three weeks before registration, and six before moving in with Stonewall. She figured possibly a third lunch before an elaborate dinner or two when he would suggest a weekend getaway to Biloxi in early June, which gave her two weeks to figure out what the hell she was doing or would do.

She left home near 11:00, arriving at the cabaret thirty minutes later after parking the BMW one block over. She wore jeans, boots and a sweater, nothing provocative or expensive. Inside she explained to the bouncer why she had come. He nodded and left her, telling her to stay put.

The girls seldom danced before midafternoon. Any cabaret was a dark and sombre place most days until then, when cheap beer and health-risk daily specials were more inviting than any girl du jour.

One was practicing her routine on the chrome pole, the others were sitting at the bar drinking sodas. She wasn't surprised and didn't care when they didn't crowd around to ask about her or why she had come back. No longer the victims of her popularity they were all working more, doing more dances, which would often lead them with clients into the more lucrative privacy of the salons. Ungrateful bitches.

The bouncer called her name, signalling her closer, stepping aside as she walked into the office. Closing the door he walked away and forgot her.

"This is a real surprise, Chloe." The man said in a flat voice. "Run out of money, kid? Maybe missin' the admiration in Lafayette?"

"Neither, Bobby-Joe. I'm doing really fine…because of this place actually. Being in the right place at the right time." She went straight to the man's desk, sitting. "I want to do something I'm not very sure about. Something I'm hoping you can help me with."

"A favour?"

"No. More like a solution."

"To what? You bein' bothered, Chloe?"

"Not me. Someone I care about, a woman."

"A friend, a girlfriend?"

"Yes, a good friend. A widow who was coerced into a situation years ago that she didn't understand. She did nothing wrong, Bobby-Joe. But the past won't go away. He won't go away. He's threatened her and abused her for over twenty years."

"This guy, what's the connection? An ex-lover, a bad debt? What?"

"Not a lover, an opportunist. Not a bad debt, a bad man. He's really bad."

"This guy, the woman, they got names?"

"I can't tell you. Except they're both very important, very high-end."

"She's high-end and she needs *your* help? How's that happen?"

"Honestly, I'm working on that. So will you help me, Bobby-Joe?"

He stared into her eyes. "No. I won't. Least ways not till I hear more. And these solutions, they come at a price. You got to know that, kid. You ready to pay up front?"

She didn't hesitate. "Yes."

"Then I'm listenin'." He checked his watch. "You got five minutes."

She told Bobby-Joe about her friend's long ago infatuation with an older man, about how he lured her from her family. She explained the hidden cameras, the explicit videos and damaging photographs, how he misled her, keeping her as his mistress for an entire year before leaving her pregnant and without means. She told him about the abortion and the woman's determined struggle into a better life, about the woman's wedding, the first threat, her life-long abuse, about the husband's death and an even crueller threat.

"Can you imagine, Bobby-Joe, forced to cheat on her husband all those years in order to save her marriage? How cruel is that? And since his death never knowing when he might any day ruin her career and her life?"

"What do you want, Chloe? You want me to hurt the guy, get him killed? What?"

"Yes, but no. I want the pictures and the videos. I know where he lives and where to find them. What I need is the combination to his safe when he's not around. Then I want to turn the tables on him. I want to video and photograph him. He deserves something very bad to happen."

Bobby-Joe chuckled. "Don't we all?"

"No. Not her."

"When's all this happenin'? You got a timeframe, kid, and a key to his place? And if he's not around, how you plan to get nasty with him? Seems to me you got a bit of thinkin' to do."

Chloe shifted in her seat, pausing. "Six weeks, July 01st, and I will have a key. He does this every year to a different woman, then he trashes them. I can be the next one. Bobby-Joe. He wants me. That's my plan and he fell for it."

"You met this guy?"

"I had lunch with him yesterday, and will again on Wednesday. That's his MO. Then he'll take me to dinner; he'll invite me to Biloxi for a weekend, convincing me to live with him, to share his glamorous life for a year, to let him spoil me with travel and luxury while keeping me hopeful that he wants more than my body. Then he'll throw me out."

"I'm missin' somethin' here, kid. You want to spend a weekend with this guy, move in, put out a couple more times, somehow get the videos and get out. You, New Orleans' frigid teenage nude beauty. Is that about right?"

"Yes."

He leaned forward. "No."

"No, you're not going to help me?"

"Your plan sucks big time, kid. Likely as not he wouldn't trust his mother with the combo. So good luck with that."

Her expression spoke volumes. "You won't help me."

"I didn't say that. I meant get out of my office." He snorted, grinning. "Always did like you, Chloe, the short while you were here. Truth is, when you quit I was glad for you. The ones out there, they're goin' nowhere they can't get to on their backs. That's not you. You're different, you're better. You're goin' places, somewhere good." He pointed a firm finger at her, the grin disappearing. "Now you listen. You are a kid. You think strippin' on a stool and hearin' things makes you streetwise. Truth is, you don't know shit. So get your sweet ass out of my office. You go to lunch with this guy on Wednesday, then you get yourself back here. You give me time to think on this."

"You're going to help me, Bobby-Joe? I can pay."

"I said I would think on it." He nodded toward the door. "Go."

*

Bobby-Joe was a relatively decent man. He was honest, married with three kids. His clubs and his work were simply that, though over the years he had met people whose job descriptions were even less conventional. Chloe suspected he was acquainted with certain elements of New Orleans' darker business world, not to would be naïve. Nevertheless, like all the other dancers, she never saw anything and never heard anything.

Leaving the club she forced herself not to feel overly confident, or needlessly disheartened. She knew that somehow he would come through for her, that something good would happen. Otherwise Bobby-Joe would have told her outright.

She went shopping for Murielle's belated birthday gift after calling Cerise with a crazy idea. She was giving Murielle a family ring with four glittering birthstones mounted on a titanium band.

When the gift was ready she called Murielle next, suggesting they meet for cocktails since she was nearby. Murielle suggested Angelo's at 4:00, ending her day uncharacteristically early. They kissed and they hugged, Chloe getting right to the matter at hand with a slightly superior air.

"This is for you, Murielle. Happy Birthday. And please don't embarrass me like that again. I felt terrible not having something for you on Saturday, Mrs. Belmont."

"You gave me a lovely ring, sweetheart. That was my gift."

Chloe scrunched her face. "Twenty dollars from an artisan table. Are you serious?"

"Thank you, sweetheart. And I apologize. I do." Murielle delicately separated the ribbon from the wrapping, studying the velvet box. Raising the lid, seeing the ring, she was genuinely taken aback.

"It's your birthstone and mine, with Charlee's and Cerise's who thought the idea was pretty cool since the three of you are like sisters and I'm sort of adopted. That's what Charlee said."

Murielle was stunned into silence, pressing a palm over her heart. "I am truly speechless, sweetheart. This is incredibly special and thoughtful. I cannot express how much."

"You just did." She raised her glass, looking pleased and a tad smug without smiling. "I love you. And, you know, if you're wondering…July 21st."
*

Tuesday Chloe took Murielle's advice, or rather she obeyed the motherly command of no more tanning beds. She spent the day reading and reviewing Tulane's syllabus on her private balcony. She went to bed early and woke early, not for a moment feeling lonely. She had too much on her mind, too much to plan and implement. Not yet feeling the slightest twinge of regret or fear.

Wednesday she dressed down for lunch since Patricia only had two nice outfits and was saving the other for her first dinner with him, meeting him outside his condo building in the boots, jeans and the sweater she wore Monday.

She reminded him that she didn't have much time since she was either writing her finals or studying for them. Stonewall agreed. His schedule was also particularly demanding, which did not obviate his repugnance of fast-food or those who saw fit to gnaw and masticate their po'boys and other questionable fare while promenading or loitering in public. They would simply not linger over a second glass of wine.

Stonewall took pride in his charm and eloquence, in his natural ability to guide others toward his opinions and resolutions, with his last sip of wine proposing that Patricia be his dinner companion Saturday evening. Nothing pretentious, he assured her, a simple dinner that would keep his heart beating until then. He was enchanted with her, with her intellect and vitality. He wanted to hear more about her, about her future plans. And she agreed.
*

He dropped her off on the corner of Bourbon and Canal. As the chauffeur opened her door she didn't say why and he didn't ask.

She would meet him at the restaurant Saturday, she insisted. She didn't want her roomies pestering her with questions about him. She didn't need the grief and when the corporate limo that she was suitably impressed with disappeared in midday traffic she turned into the Quarter and went directly to the cabaret, through the black doors and through the club ignoring the girls. She was expected.

In the office Bobby-Joe waited silently until she was seated.

"You sure about this, kid? I mean, are you absolutely certain?"

"Yes. I am absolutely certain."

"Okay." He rubbed his face hard. "Chloe, ever wonder why I hired you to dance?"

"My body. What else?"

"That's right, your body. Places like these, we don't care about résumés or accomplishments. Truth is, I was hopin' you wouldn't stay, believin' you were serious about Tulane. Not a bit surprised you pullin' in more than them without gettin' squeezed and pinched in a salon. What I'm sayin' is, we've got us a solution. I just don't want you to mess up and get yourself hurt. You've got to listen real good to me, kid. Real good. Can you do that?"

"You are going to help me?"

"I'm givin' you the means and the know-how, nothin' more. That is the good news. The bad news is you owin' me two grand whether you listen or not. Or givin' me a day of private dances and somethin' I don't think you want."

"I'll give you the cash this afternoon."

"Somehow I thought you might." He grinned, raising an eyebrow. "You sayin' that tells me you might just get this thing done."

She reached inside her purse for pen and paper. "I'm listening. Tell me what to do, Bobby-Joe."

"For starters, put that away. This is not Tulane." He reached into a desk drawer. "I have to believe, kid, had I been your pa, I would have killed that boy for leavin' you high and dry, for drivin' you to this place. No different from your lady friend, seems to me, which is why I'm suggestin' you get things done before July 01st." He put up a hand.

"You go to dinner with this shitbag and when he's talkin' about Biloxi you make certain you get yourself there. You want to do this thing far away. Do not ever shit in your own backyard. And, kid, you do not have to sleep with this guy, not in Biloxi, not here. Do you understand that? You do and I will be sorely pissed."

"I already told him I would. He always puts them in bed first, like a final interview. That's why the dinners and lunches, Bobby-Joe. He's pretty much interviewing me."

"Not this time." He slid a tiny cellophane package towards her, an open palm halting her. He spoke slowly and calmly. "First off, kid, you make damn sure you are covered from head to toe walking through the lobby. Wear a wide hat, dark glasses and gloves. Do not look up, do not look around, and do not smile, which is not a big thing for you anyway. Those casinos, they're loaded with cameras. In other words, kid, you be a lady. Which is clearly already happenin', I'm supposin' because of your lady friend and I am happy for you."

"My friend *is* helping me?"

"And she's goin' to help you even more. She'll be with you, waitin' outside and a good ways off."

Chloe didn't want that. She didn't want Murielle involved, though she understood to remain quiet. Bobby-Joe was her one chance.

"When the concierge brings your bags, you'll be in the washroom with your purse. In that purse you will have silicone gloves, a cotton surgical mask and a plastic shower cap bought here. Not theirs. You will get yourself completely naked; you will put your clothes far from the door and put on those three things in the time it takes to do whatever women do. You'll run a shower and touch nothin' with your bare hands. Nothin'. Then you'll invite him in and he'll be done. He won't see the protection, kid. He'll

439

see you, nothin' else, which will make this thing work."

Chloe wasn't getting it. "Protection from what?"

He pointed to the package. "That there is a gram of scopolamine. The Colombianos call it Devil's Breath. The stuff is very bad and very scary shit, Chloe. So you will treat it with the *utmost* respect. When he comes through the door you will throw all that into his face from your gloved hand and you will get your pretty ass promptly into the shower. Do you understand me?"

"No, Bobby-Joe. Why me naked and why the shower? What is that stuff?"

"A zombie drug that will turn him quick as a blink into a defenseless child with zero free will. In a word, he'll be yours to play with. Want to kill him? He'll do that for you. Tell him to jump from a window, he'll do that. Ask for his combination? He'll jot the numbers for you. Need cash? He'll write a cheque, which I strongly suggest you do not do. Naked because you do not want this shit on your clothes; the shower because you do not want contact with the little you are wearin'. You make damn sure everythin's clean includin' you before you get yourself dressed because he's goin' nowhere you don't want him to. Tell him to sit and be still, he will do that."

"How long do the effects last, and what do I do with him when I do have the code to the safe?"

"With a gram, a couple of days. Want to take him for a walk? He'll seem perfectly fine and lucid, when he's actually one fucked-up mess. Personally I would take serious advantage of the situation. You want payback, some of your own photos? This is your time. Whatever you and the lady consider appropriate given his longstandin' disrespect of her. Thing is, in the mornin' he won't remember shit. Not how he got to where he'll be or why. He won't remember you, your body or the Devil's Breath.

Never. He likely won't remember his name, let alone yours. What he will have is one fucked-up life of nightmares he can't explain to himself or anyone else."

"He doesn't know my real name."

"Then you are set, kid. Just don't do anythin' stupid. Nothin' more than what you know. What you're doin' makes him the victim, not you or your lady friend. You got that? When you're finished you walk away. You get out and when you're back here, when you've got those videos, you get yourself into a hotel ladies' room and change before takin' a walk and losin' everythin' you're wearin' in trash cans and dumpsters. Necessary insurance in case you mess up. Then go home and have a peaceful sleep."

Thirty minutes after leaving with the drug Chloe returned with the cash, Bobby-Joe making her repeat every phase of his instructions verbatim. Satisfied, he wished her success and nicely told her to never come back. She had better things to do with her life.
*

Friday Murielle phoned, inviting Chloe to dinner Saturday.

"I can't, and please don't ask me why. It's kind of a surprise. Is that okay…mom?" Dead silence followed. "Mur isn't my name for you. And I can't really call you Darling, can I?"

Murielle giggled. "No, sweetheart. I suppose not. That would certainly be a little weird. So how about Sunday? You and me, because next week I've got late-day meetings through to a department dinner on Saturday."

"Sunday definitely works. I really do love you, you know."

Her mom loved her too, with wet kisses through their phones.
*

Saturday evening Stonewall was at his table when Patricia

441

walked in to the dining room precisely on time in an outfit that an upcoming college grad could afford with certain sacrifices. She was in deep green mid-thigh suede boots, a bright yellow and nicely short suede skirt, a green silk blouse and yellow suede bolero jacket. To Stonewall she was Murielle de la Sorbonne reborn.

He stood, kissing her cheek, letting the waiter pull out her seat.

"You are incomparably ravishing, Patricia. Words fail me when I most need them."

"Thank you, Kenneth. And you are very handsome this evening. Very elegant." Of course he was elegant, she thought. Everything he was wearing screamed Belmont. "Thank you so much for inviting me."

"It is I who must thank you, for accepting. I also took the liberty of ordering you a Cîroc with soda."

"You remembered. Thank you."

As the evening and dinner came to an end, Stonewall asked for the pleasure of Patricia's gracious company the following Saturday. And she agreed. How could she not? He epitomized the Southern gentleman and she enjoyed his company immensely. In fact she confessed that she thought of him quite often, looking forward to their time together.

He wanted to drive her home, understanding she wanted that part of her life kept personal, Patricia commenting that once graduated her single most important priority would be a decent place of her very own where she would gladly invite him to dinner because she really liked his company. Instead he put her in a taxi content to have the number of the untraceable and disposable phone he did not know Bobby-Joe had given her as a parting gift.

With Patricia fresh in his mind he called Murielle, realizing an entire month had flown by since he last savoured her charms. He was surprised to discover that she had sold her Prytania address, disappointed he wouldn't experience both women the same evening, putting a younger face to a familiar body, reluctantly agreeing to meet her at the Maison Dupuy the next evening.

Disconnecting, she sat despondent despite expecting the call with only a week remaining in May. She wondered how much longer he would live, how many more years he would torment her before tiring of her, dismissing him with a mournful sigh to ponder those she did love and want in her life. She wondered why Chloe had come to her when and where she did, as though sent to save, if not her life, her sanity. Or had she somehow been guided to find and save Chloe from moral destitution?

She wondered about Anthony and Karine, eager to take the woman's place on Monday, pondering what she would do and say on their final day together. Or at fifty would she even care? A ridiculously rhetorical question at best.

42

Sunday Chloe arrived at the penthouse minutes before 1:00. They spoke about each other's week and Chloe's course choices, Murielle assuring her that the following summer she would have an internship position at a leading firm. The mom seldom called in favours, but what better use of her many contacts than helping her daughter? Once in, however, subsequent summer jobs would be hers to ensure.

She left at 8:00. Mom wanted her at home before dark and moments later Murielle stood in her shower making herself clean for Stonewall, sparing herself the indignity of showering in the hotel room while he ogled her. Or worse, showering with him.

She went to the hotel dressed in slacks and a sweater, seeing no need to excite him with lingerie, stockings and garters. Those days were long gone, those titillating moments kept special for Anthony. The faster she got into bed with him, the sooner she would be in her own bath cleaning his residue from her.

She strode through the lobby unnoticed, carrying a briefcase like any other businesswoman with an urgent purpose. In the room she went directly to the minibar, emptying a passable vodka into an old-fashioned. She asked how he wanted her, kicking away her sandals and stripping off the pants and sweater without the slightest hesitation. She downed her drink and crawled to the centre of the bed

444

where she stayed on her hands with her knees wide apart.

"Who would believe, Murielle, that after all our years together you continue to fascinate me with your beauty? You are indeed the loveliest of women."

"Who you choose to threaten and fuck on her knees like a common whore."

"How else might I since you come to me devoid of emotion, without a single accoutrement to enhance the experience other than your exquisite nudity? What you believe is appropriate to our situation, not I. You see, I view myself as simply taking pleasure in you while moderating my compulsion for you…if you will. Not unlike you moderating your compulsive feelings for me by way of your Boston gentleman, I dare say."

"My sole compulsion is loathing you, Stonewall. Tell me, have you started fucking your live-in whore this way? You were never satisfied with the ordinary, you were also never demeaning and cruel. What kind of man does this to a woman?"

"One with leverage, of course. As an average man I suppose I might have penalized you financially through the years. Unfortunately for you I am well beyond average. Being with you this way is the one way I can chastise you, Murielle. Lifting the puppy's paws from the floor as it were."

He crawled onto the bed behind her, gliding his hands across her buttocks, pressing against her to reach for her shoulders. He guided her backward until she was straddling his lap, keeping her pressed tightly against him with hands cupped to her breasts, freeing one indifferent breast to explore the warm curves of her belly and the delicate flesh between her thighs.

He guided her forward onto her hands, neither cruelly nor tenderly, caressing her back, her buttocks and thighs.

He tested for moisture deeming her ready, pushing his way into her, not rushing the moment.

Murielle's body rocked inertly to and fro in sync with his thrusts, ignoring the occasional pressure on her breasts, ignoring him without a single murmur of arousal. When he finished he pushed himself backward from the bed. He went to the bathroom were he flushed his protection against Vincent, returning to her wrapped in a towel. He poured two miniature scotch bottles into an old-fashioned and stood studying her. She was lying face down with her head resting on folded arms, her dry eyes staring blankly into another time and place.

"I wonder where we would be, you and I, had we never met."

She snorted. "I'd be at Gilmore, Stonewall. You'd be in bed with a whore."

"Whores by definition, of course. By which my mother was a willing whore, given a lavish life without toil by my father in exchange for a schedule of physical encounters. You, Murielle, gave willingly of yourself in exchange for an exciting year of novelty, a paid-in-full student loan and a tidy bonus for what you now call cruelty. Whatever you might have imagined in your delirious mind was and is of no consequence. So yes, you are by definition a whore. In fact I very much doubt that without me you would have met Belmont since you undeniably travelled in different circles. Yet you call me cruel for all I have done."

"You are cruel. How many of me exist out there, Stonewall? Forty, fifty? When was your first whore?"

He drained half the scotch into his throat. "I can't recall any woman who wasn't. You all want something. What men of wealth must assume and adapt to, I suppose. The one I currently favour, I must say, came to me fully understanding the contract. She is fully cognizant that she

446

will leave me in five weeks. In her case with a thousand in cash for each week and the pleasant memories of a fully funded year such as the one you enjoyed."

"I've seen her. She's older. Poor you. That doesn't mean you're not a predator, Stonewall. You are a predator."

"I am no such thing. You came to me after a few meals and a weekend. What does that say of you? Have you no clue whatsoever of who and what you are? You are the predator, Murielle. You are the whore. The pizza kid years ago, Vincent throughout your marriage to Belmont, me while Vincent cheats on his wife. You are the whore lying naked on a hotel bed without the slightest shame, who until this evening would greet me at your secret home fully naked without the slightest attempt at cordiality or pleasantries. Those are the actions of a whore, in your mind making the best of a situation you created. You are the whore, Murielle. Can you not see that?"

She turned her head. "Reduced to fucking thirty-somethings. Knowing you can no longer buy the really young ones must really sicken you." She snorted. "Imagine when you're seventy. You are not that wealthy, Stonewall."

"In point of fact I am, notwithstanding the fact that I have as recently as this past week come to understand that the quality of companionship at my age might well be far superior and longer lasting, given the right choice and appropriate contractual agreement. Which naturally does not affect my eternal desire for you, Murielle. Her name is Patricia, who came to me as a godsend with beauty and an agreeable age difference. We're quite enchanted with each other, evolving very nicely toward something more rewarding. Not to marry, of course, rather to keep by my side as an amorous motivation to remain youthful."

Murielle propped herself onto her elbows, glaring at him. "When I see her, and I will see her, I will tell her everything about me, everything about you and your whores."

He chortled, draining the glass. "Then tell her this very minute, Murielle. Search for your reflection and tell her because she is you reborn, from your eyes to your fingertips, from your lips to your breasts to the sensual curve of your hips. She is you in every way, gifted with a sweeter voice if not the exotic hue of your skin. She is that exact a replica of you. My excitation at finding her surpassed solely by the expectation of our first union."

An ice-cold chill coursed through her body. "What did you say?"

"I'm saying that I have somehow recaptured what you and I once shared many years ago. I'm saying that Murielle de la Sorbonne exists in two worlds, both of them mine." He put down the glass, checking his watch. "I would like you once more, my dear, before I send you home."
*

By the time Stonewall finished in the bathroom Murielle was retracing her steps through the lobby, her denigration for the month of May completed in under thirty minutes.

Inside her penthouse, buried in the deep heat of her steaming bathwater, she sat crying and shivering with no one to talk to. Stonewall's Patricia was Chloe. What other explanation was possible? None.

She didn't care about Anthony or that she lied to Chloe about him. She loved him, believing that cheating on him with Stonewall was no worse than what he was doing to Karine. She cared about Chloe. Her entire adult life was a never-ending nightmare because of Stonewall, tarnishing what was good in her life. The first of the month or the last, or anytime in-between. She never knew when. She was no more than a wealthy and successful puppet on a string.

He would not do that to Chloe. No way was that girl

getting involved with him. On her life he would never infect the girl with his body or his corrupted mind. Monday she and Chloe would seriously talk woman to woman without the bullshit.

*

Early Monday morning she phoned Chloe from her office.

"Good morning, sweetheart. I wanted to say how pleasant you made my Sunday. You are such fun to be with."

"I got home safely and locked the door. No boogieman."

"That's good, sweetheart. I worry because I'm not accustomed to having someone to worry about. It's kind of nice."

"I worry about you too. You know that. Hey, can we maybe have lunch sometime? My treat."

"I would love to do lunch, sweetheart. In fact, why don't you invite Patricia to join us? I would love to meet her. From what I understand she looks very much like you, practically a twin." Silence. "Is that your surprise for me, sweetheart? Are you Patricia? Were you with him Saturday?"

"Yes."

"He is a very dangerous man, Chloe. What are you thinking?"

"I'm getting your videos and photos, mom."

"No, you are not. Stonewall is debauched and immoral. How often have you met with him?"

"Two lunches and Saturday. That's all and he doesn't know where I live."

"Yes. That is all because very soon he'll know everything about you including me and you do not want that. He's expecting you to move in with him July 01st, to become his live-in whore and that will not happen."

"When were you with him, mom? Why didn't we have

this conversation yesterday?" Silence. "Darkness isn't the reason you sent me home early. He is."

"I met him in the Quarter shortly after and he will never know to be grateful that I had no suitable weapon with which to kill him when he began talking about Patricia. Had I, he would be dead now."

"He hurt you again."

"He's irrelevant. You are not."

"I can do this. I have a plan."

"What you'll do is be a teenager. You deserve being a teenager. That's my plan, not you stepping out of your league, sweetheart. Very soon he'll invite you to another dinner, then to Biloxi where he'll fascinate you with luxury and money and ruin your life. You have not thought this through. You will never get the combination to the safe, you will never outsmart him, and if you're thinking to catch him with his pants down, that won't happen either. So you *will* stay far away from him, Chloe. He's my dark secret, not yours."

"I won't see him again, mom," not after Saturday.

"Promise me."

"I promise. Does that mean we're on for a lunch, let's say next Sunday?"
*

Murielle hurried home to dress for Anthony in a long silk slip and robe. He arrived near 6:30 feeling strange at dragging his suitcase behind him. Stranger still was when he stepped from a private elevator into her living room.

When he asked glibly where the maid and chef were…

"She's a sweet little thing and comes Tuesdays and Fridays. As for the chef, he just walked in. Let me show you your kitchen, darling."

What she called a kitchen with gleaming pots and an arsenal of knives belonged in a fine restaurant. What she

450

called an en suite was a personal spa and the walk-in seemed more like a small boutique with his Prytania wardrobe hung neatly and looking as though he needed to do some serious shopping.

He was aware that she had money, though he never thought to imagine how she lived beyond her Prytania home. What he was seeing, walking through, was beyond anything he might have conjured in his working man's mind.

After dinner they sat on the terrace watching the sun set over the Mississippi, Murielle telling him to deal with it. She was rich. So what? She continued putting in ten-hour days at Gilmore and twenty-hour weeks at Belmont. She got cramps, had periods, and swore like a frigging trooper whenever she ruined a twenty-dollar stocking.

When the sun was down, the night air pleasantly cool, Murielle pressed a button on a remote to set the alarm. Pressing a fingertip to a second button she darkened the windows and doors, a third dimmed the lights. A fourth filled the penthouse with music and the fifth set the fireplace aglow, Murielle explaining how she could also warm her bed and toilet seat in a city where summer's heat index would soon reach 125° F and higher, prompting Anthony to ask where he could get one.

They made love and slept in a bed set to body temperature, once Murielle assured him he wouldn't get fried in his sleep.

In the morning they drove into separate careers, Anthony with a key and code to the elevator. Each evening throughout the week he felt more at ease, more comfortable with her extravagant lifestyle and amenities, calling Karine while Murielle prepared dinner. He loved her and missed her more each evening, apologizing for the Saturday seminar he had no control over. He would be with her midafternoon Sunday and was taking her to a fancy dinner, all the while wondering how much longer he would or could last with Murielle.

He had a good job, a good career. Still, he flew First-Class with complimentary upgrades; she went First-Class because there was nothing better. He could never afford a Belmont suit, or explain one to Karine. He drank American thirty-dollar wine, hers came with labels he couldn't pronounce. He had a key to his front door in the Boston suburbs, she owned an elevator and time wasn't standing still. The inevitable was coming closer and seemingly faster with each visit.

What would he possibly tell her in five years after then loving her for twenty-eight, half his lifetime? Whatever the words, envisioning their last evening, their final dinner, the final melding of their heated bodies was beyond the scope of his imagination. Loving her was as natural as loving Karine with equal intensity and devotion, as she once loved Jackson Belmont. When he was with one he never thought of the other, never imagining what Murielle might do to survive her lonely weeks.

Friday evening, disconnecting from Karine and forgetting her, he spent another evening at home with Murielle. Saturday he took her to dinner, later strolling hand in hand amongst an aimless mob of tourists and window gazers.

At home she went into the bedroom to change, deciding there was no harm in telling him; he went onto the terrace to call Karine. When he joined Murielle on a sofa to end their week with cognacs, Murielle put aside her tablet.

Without any preamble, "It seems I have a daughter, darling."

"Excuse me. You have a what?"

"Her name is Chloe. She's nineteen and she's adorable."

452

"I'm not getting this." He was stunned. "You what, adopted her?"

"Figuratively, yes. She needed help and I was able to do that? When you see her you'll understand why. She's living on Prytania, attending college in the fall." Murielle sipped her cognac. "She knows about you, in part. I gave her a teenage version. I ran into you some months ago after years apart and we go to dinner when you're in town? Or we did."

"When do I meet this kid?"

"You won't, for a very good reason. I simply felt the need to tell you." Murielle reached for the tablet. "We went on vacation a while ago. This is a collage of our week together. You might notice one thing missing."

Anthony stared into the screen, at the faces and bodies fading from one frame into another.

"I don't believe this."

"You see why I'm helping her?"

"This isn't some sort of scam, like copying the rich lady?"

"Absolutely not."

"She looks like she's going to the dentist, not the beach."

"She's working on that and taking me to lunch tomorrow."

"Then I see one woman having a good time, and another who's trying. So what's missing, a smile?"

"No. You are. You're the reason you won't meet her."
*

The weather Saturday evening was ideal for dinner in an intimate garden setting. Stonewall wore a Belmont blazer with an open collar and slacks; Patricia wore a tube dress, a shawl and three-inch stilettos that would blow her food budget for the coming semester. She wanted to look appealing for Kenneth who saw her as desirable, while most others in the garden saw her as a lovely granddaughter sitting across from a devoted parent.

Midway through their meal Stonewall sat pensively. He liked the girl very much. He wanted more time with her, uncertain how to best broach the sensitive subject, uncertain how she would react. He didn't want to shock her or frighten her away.

"Patricia, you are enchanting this evening. These candles do nothing to enhance your natural glow."

She had practiced the entire day smiling demurely. "Thank you, Kenneth."

He raised his glass. "I propose a toast...to youthful beauty and endless vivacity." The rims of their glasses touched. "You've been on my mind the entire week, Patricia. I have a proposition of sorts that I wish to put forth for your consideration."

"I've thought about you all week too, Kenneth, so looking forward to this evening."

"I've grown deeply fond of you these past four encounters, Patricia. Dare I say infatuated? And I see in your eyes a genuine feeling toward me. What I therefore propose is that we enjoy a weekend together, to spend time together and test those feelings without the slightest expectation of anything more. Separate accommodations, that sort of thing. A pleasant drive along the coast to Biloxi, exquisite dining and possibly a modest degree of good fortune at the gaming tables."

She was openly surprised. "Kenneth. I would love to go with you. What a fantastic idea, and remember I'm twenty-three. I'm an adult. We don't need separate rooms because we do have expectations, don't we?"

"Truth be told, yes. We do indeed. To say otherwise would be a discernible misrepresentation of our growing feelings."

"Then we're on?" Concern washed across her face, prefacing a mournful sigh. "I've already worn my nicest clothes for you. I'm a little wardrobe poor at the moment."

He reached into his slacks for his billfold, counting out five hundreds. "This should get you there, I'm sure. Once we arrive you will outfit yourself with exclusive fashions for our evenings together, and do so without needless frugality."

"Kenneth, really?"

"You must always feel as lovely as I see you this very moment. The entire weekend must be the most memorable for both of us. I can only hope not our last."

"I think my heart's going to burst. This will be my first time away with a man. I think the last year at college is going to seem pretty juvenile after all this. Those guys can be really jerky." Not all assholes wear Belmont suits.

"Which brings me, Patricia, to another reason, a selfish reason for our weekend of discovery. If you believe we can be more to each other, if you sincerely believe that, I would like you to consider sharing my home throughout your final year at college. I would naturally give you a substantial weekly allowance to free you from the woes of menial work and financial worry and with my many weeks of travel you would have ample privacy and quiet to study. However I would also expect that you would vacation with me in the islands and Europe…according to your study schedule, naturally."

"God, Kenneth. Can this be real? Can this actually be happening to me?" Can you imagine for a second the shitstorm coming your way?

"This is happening to us. I've been single too long. I don't want that life anymore. I want this happening to me as well. I want you happening to me, Patricia. I want to show you the world."

"You're making me really nervous here, Kenneth. I'll be a wreck all week wanting our special weekend to be the most perfect ever." She smiled a perfect smile. "The most special ever," one that you will never remember. "All I ask is that you're gentle and patient with me, Kenneth. Because I have never…Well, you know."

43

With dinner over Stonewall put Patricia in a taxi and drove to his suburban estate deliriously happy. He didn't care where she lived, he cared about where she would live in five weeks. He cared about the weekend; he cared about seeing her naked at last, about caressing Murielle's young and nubile warm flesh once again.

She would not spend her final year with her three roommates, she would live in the Garden District condo where she would stay with him for a year and longer.
*

Chloe arrived home near 11:00 and went to bed pleased with her success, eager for the coming weekend. She had done it; she had Stonewall by the proverbial balls. She was six nights from freeing the most beautiful woman ever from a torment she never deserved. However she was not quite as eager for her own fierce shitstorm that she would walk into the next afternoon. Mom was going to be righteously pissed with her.
*

That Chloe woke June 01st to a warm, sunny and clear day didn't matter. That she lay on her chaise-longue throughout the morning tanning and debating with herself in whispers didn't matter. What mattered was Murielle. What mattered was believing in herself and convincing her mom.

She left home at 1:30 in a cute yet sophisticated summer

dress and sandals with her lustrous auburn hair scrunched into flighty curls which she realized wouldn't mean shit once she opened her mouth. She didn't care; she was resolute. What mattered was her workable plan.

Murielle was waiting outside by a fountain as the European convertible turned in to the private tree-lined driveway fifteen minutes later.

Chloe was on her own at Angelo's. Lunch was her treat, she was the hostess. Murielle wasn't helping or suggesting. She ordered Jean-Marc XO and Cîroc, both with a splash. She waited for Murielle to make her course selections before ordering an appropriate wine, before moistening her dry mouth with her second sip of French vodka.

"Mom, do you remember when Cerise told me not to get all stiff and panicky on you guys?"

"I remember perfectly, sweetheart. You were a little tense. She does have that effect on people."

"Yeah, well, I really need for you not to get all stiff and panicky on me now, and please don't make a scene."

"Excuse me?"

"Promise me."

"Just get to it, sweetheart. Were you with Stonewall again?"

"Last night for dinner which is why you have to listen." She raised both her palms. "I also went to the club to speak with a guy, to speak with him, nothing else. His name's Bobby-Joe. He's a good guy, mom. A really good guy. And I really need you to listen because I went to him for help and I'm going to tell you what he said."

"I'm listening, Chloe. I'm having a stroke, but I am listening."

"He's glad I left the club. He's happy for me and never wants to see me again. Anyway, without names I told him about you and Stonewall. I explained my entire plan to get your videos and pictures."

"And?"

"He told me the plan sucks. He told me to go, to get out, that he had to think about it. And he did, mom. He told me to get things done before July 01st, to go to Biloxi with Stonewall this Friday. He also said I don't have to sleep with Stonewall the way I planned. He called me a lady, mom. You know, and he was serious."

"You are a lady."

"He told me how to dress because of cameras and to keep my head low. He said I should drive to Biloxi the day before, to park my car and take a bus back here. He made me commit everything to memory. He said, when the concierge brings our bags I'll be in the washroom with silicone gloves, a mask and shower cap hidden in my purse. He told me to undress quickly, to put those things on, to put my clothes in a safe place and to run a shower. He said Stonewall won't see me protected when he comes in. He'll see me naked. He'll see *you* naked, mom. That is not a big deal for me. I can do this because he won't remember me. You know dancers, they never see faces. I won't see his face. I promise, mom. And he won't remember mine."

The "No. You will not do this" was firm.

The "Yes, I will" was firmer.

"You said you would listen. You gave me a better life that is still a dream for me. Bobby-Joe, he gave me something that will give you a better life, something bad and scary. Something I cannot touch or breathe. Undressing will give me time, the shower will clean me and keep me safe."

"Safe from what? What have you done, Chloe?"

The determined girl took a third sip, the waiter understanding without being told that he should come back.

"Please do not freak out, because I am doing this. I am.

I'm talking about scopolamine. One gram. Bobby-Joe called it Devil's Breath, a zombie drug. When Stonewall comes into the bathroom I'll throw it in his face and he'll be finished. Bobby-Joe promised that will happen and I trust him."

"Dead? You're killing Stonewall? Do you really believe I'm letting you do that?"

"No, not dead. Useless, while I'm showering and dressing without him. He won't have any free will. He'll be like a baby. If I tell him, he will actually kill himself for me. He'll jump from a window or do whatever I say. More importantly, mom, he will willingly give me the numbers to the safe and the keys to his condo and wherever else he lives. He will do whatever I say. Then in the morning he will have no memory of me, the night, or whatever. And I'll be gone. The other thing Bobby-Joe said was, if you want payback, photos of Stonewall, this is our time. Yours and mine. You saved me, I'm saving you. So yeah, I'm taking a disposable camera to really nail this bastard." The foreign giggle was almost wicked, shocking Murielle even more. "Maybe I'll put him a tutu, but I do know to be careful. Bobby-Joe told me a hundred times to not be stupid. You are free, mom."

"What you've done with this Bobby-Joe is reckless. What you're thinking of doing with Stonewall is even worse. The man has no soul. So believe me when I say you are not doing this. End of conversation."

"No, it's not." Chloe stood her ground. "I never wanted my parents. They were cruel and they never loved me. And too late I realized I never wanted Vance; he was my escape from them. I got away and he got me. Then dancing was my one escape from him because stripping was all I could do. I never wanted to strip. I did because I had no choice. However in this I do have a choice and I am doing this,

Murielle."

Chloe nodded to the waiter, which did not terminate the conversation. When he left after serving the wine Murielle asked an obvious question, betraying no shock at hearing the answer.

"Two thousand, that Stonewall will happily repay me in cash. He will also call his girlfriend and tell her to go somewhere. I'm thinking Miami or Vegas."

"And I'm thinking not. Did your Bobby-Joe say what to do if something goes wrong, like the possibility of Stonewall dying? Did he tell you what to do with a dead body?"

"Twenty years of debauchery and fear, mom. Are you kidding me? I mean really, what is your point? And yes, Bobby-Joe did tell me. I have to trash my clothes and go to bed because this thing is over."

"My point is you living with that guilt. He's not worth it."

"But you are."

The waiter brought their meals and left. When the table was cleared Murielle ordered coffee, Chloe ordered sorbet.

When they left the mood was several shades darker than two hours earlier. The drive to the high-rise Shangri-La was quiet, Murielle amazed at how composed Chloe was. She had intended for the girl to stay over, to spend the evening together watching movies, which was clearly not going to happen.

At the main entrance, signalling the doorman to wait, she simply said, "How do I stop you, sweetheart? What can I say or do to stop you?"

"Believe me, mom. This will not ruin me. Stripping was much worse, and he deserves much worse. He's getting off easy." She smiled. "I'm not coming up because this conversation won't end until I leave." She leaned over, kissing Murielle's cheek. "I love you. I'll see you Saturday, early."

Murielle nodded blankly. She thanked Chloe for lunch and took the doorman's gloved hand.

*

Once inside the penthouse she went directly onto the terrace with a notebook and pen. She wrote a sequential list of Chloe's instructions and studied them, deciding something was very wrong.

First was that Stonewall wasn't being killed, which was truly unfortunate. His absolute power over her was merely being eradicated with his induced cooperation. Bobby-Joe knew about her, about what Stonewall was doing to her. So why was she being excluded, deprived of living her recurring dream? Why was she not the one throwing the devil's shit into the devil's face? Why was she not the one to savour his instant degradation, to make him strip and dress in a tutu?

Chloe driving to Biloxi the day before made no sense whatsoever because the girl was lying and that would have to stop, despite wanting her mom far away in the event something would go wrong. Which would not happen because neither did her empty protests make sense. She did want Stonewall hurt in a meaningful and lasting way.

Using Bobby-Joe's instructions as a template Murielle created her own chronology of how June 06th would play out, examining and critiquing each detail, searching for flaws that would make her dream an even worse nightmare. Satisfied, believing she was good to go, she called Chloe.

"Hi, and I am not talking about it."

"You lied to me, sweetheart. Your Bobby-Joe did not tell you to leave your car in Biloxi on Thursday. That is your invention. He wants me there with you. He wants us doing this together."

"He does not. I swear."

"Yes, he does. I've worked a lot of years in lobbying, sweetheart. I know everything possible about bullshit and this afternoon you were full of it. So you get your ass over here with a suitcase. You're mine for the week because I cannot trust you and you are not doing this alone."

Silence.

"You're upset with me."

"No, sweetheart. I'm not. What I am is royally pissed with you for not being honest with me, which stops today. Ladies do not lie, we persuade."

"I lied for a reason, because I love you."

"That's right and you're staying with me until Friday because I love you. I want you here in an hour."

"He's going down, mom? We're doing this together?"

"Oh, yeah. He is definitely going down."

44

When Chloe arrived she sat and listened, not entirely pleased, grudgingly agreeing that mom had a much better strategy in place.

Monday Murielle went to her Gilmore office as usual, Chloe went to the bank to deposit two-thousand dollars. She spent her afternoon on the terrace studying the updated plan, committing each phase to memory, reciting the details to Murielle several times later that evening.

Tuesday she went shopping for a twenty-something outfit with her 500 dollars, modelling the green strapless chiffon mini-dress, green cotton lace gloves, yellow open-toed stilettos and yellow wide-brimmed bowknot hat accented with a long green ribbon for mom that she would wear to Biloxi. She was Murielle de la Sorbonne through and through. The green sunglasses she found on sale at a drugstore for 9.99.

Wednesday Murielle left work early, driving the ninety miles along the I-10 to Biloxi with Chloe for an early dinner. She was familiar with the casino hotel, remembering several romantic weekends with Jackson, though dinner was secondary. She needed Chloe to put a physical dimension to when and where she would be doing her part.

Thursday Chloe went to a spa for a full menu of treatments. Mom wanted her relaxed and looking even more like twenty-three, an hour after dinner listening dispassionately as Patricia spoke with Kenneth Stonewall. She was to arrive at his condo the next day at 2:00. He was eager to see her, to share their weekend.

Friday Murielle would work from home. She and Chloe ate breakfast on the terrace, lounging under a pleasantly warm sun until noon talking girl-talk. At 12:00 they went in to shower and dress, removing their jewellery, Chloe emerging from her room as an elegant and irresistible young lady. Mom was no less disarming, leaving Chloe at 1:00 after a tight embrace.

Chloe left thirty minutes later, arriving at Stonewall's condo minutes before 2:00 that would put them at the hotel an hour behind Murielle. She didn't give the attractive woman standing on the balcony more than a casual glance as she sauntered from the cab to the Bentley. She imagined what the woman was thinking, that she was her successor, that she was someone much younger and prettier.

Empathy wasn't Chloe's strongest trait, though what she did know was that the woman was entirely wrong.

The ride along the I-10 was made all the more pleasurable with her mostly bare thighs and bare shoulders. Arriving on time at the twelve-story Beach Boulevard complex Chloe's whispered "Wow!" might have been real weeks earlier, though not after the luxury of Murielle's penthouse, her own home, and their Martinique vacation.

Inside, the sprawling pristine lobby screamed money and sophistication. Guests weren't showing off their best jeans and sneakers; men were dressed in slacks and blazers, the women in dresses or upscale slacks and chic blouses. Tees, shorts and flip-flops were strictly prohibited.

"Wow, Kenneth. This is fantastic."

"I'm glad you approve, Patricia. At the same time aptly describing our weekend. I assure you."

He left her to her amazement while he checked-in,

practically gloating at his success in winning her over with so little effort. Going to her, leading her toward the elevators, she was an instant sensation with passersby, Stonewall wondering how he would possibly endure the many hours until his nighttime alone with her in their twelfth-floor parlour suite. Though for the greater good he would endure because rushing her into his bed would not be a good thing.

Once inside Chloe scurried to the wall of windows, staring out over the Gulf. She peeked into drawers, pulling out brochures; she looked into the closets and went into the bedroom when she heard a knock at the door. When the concierge was gone she came out.

"I didn't bring many clothes."

"All that you require you will discover in the hotel boutiques, which you will assign to the room." He opened a small carrying case he'd brought to the room himself. "I thought to bring our preferred refreshments. In-room bars, inclusive of the finest hotels, are invariably stocked with pedestrian selections." He poured a Cîroc adding soda from the in-room fridge for her, passing her the glass, choosing not to tamper with the purity of his Glenmorangie vintage malt.

"We should unpack, my dear, and decide what we should do first."

"You unpack, Kenneth. I'm too excited. Besides, I didn't bring much. I would rather finish our drinks and see the place. I want to see the pool. I brought a little bikini."

"The mere thought of which quickens my pulse, my dear." His sipped his scotch. "An excellent suggestion. Allow me a few moments to arrange my wardrobe and I shall give you the grand tour. I believe a leisurely cocktail by the pool before dinner would also be an appropriate commencement to our weekend."

She nodded enthusiastically, beaming a perfected smile, turning to face the Gulf as he wheeled his suitcase into the bedroom.

When he was finished he came in, putting aside his empty old-fashioned. She swayed past him reaching for her hat, her flared dress dancing at her thighs, telling him how happy she was that they had come into each other's lives. Stepping from the elevator into the lobby she was again an instant sensation. Heads turned and eyes gawked. A fact of life she ignored. She was young and she was beautiful, which isn't what they were thinking. Because she had learned to smile didn't mean she would for no reason.

"Kenneth, please. Do you mind waiting? I need the ladies' room."

"By all means, Patricia. I'll meander along the boutique windows."

She turned and left him, disappearing into the restroom and a vacant stall. Waiting a short while she flushed and walked out, complimenting another woman on how absolutely lovely her dress was. When the woman returned the compliment and left, Murielle came out from her stall.

"Hi, mom. He's in suite 1205 and has a bottle of Cîroc." She gave Murielle the key card. "We're going for cocktails at the pool. I'll keep him preoccupied until five. Are you really sure about this?"

She gave Chloe the keys to her Jaguar that she would find some distance away on Beach Boulevard's westbound parking lane, in lieu of an answer. "Do you have the other woman's name, sweetheart?"

"She's Cheryl DeMoine."|

"Thank you. When he leaves you go for a walk on the beach until you see the car, then go somewhere for dinner further on. Do not come back here. I'll call you when I'm ready." She kissed Chloe's forehead and hugged her. "Go."

Murielle waited five minutes longer before walking out.

In suite 1205 she put her handbag by the bathroom door with her hat. Then she waited, using her time to examine the rooms.

At 4:30 she undressed matter-of-factly, putting on her surgical mask, headgear and gloves. Then she went into the bathroom to wait for the call, opening the scopolamine in the shower with steady hands the moment her phone buzzed. She didn't answer. Chloe was calling from the ladies' room, having told Stonewall she had to pee and that he shouldn't wait for her. He was on his way, walking into the suite unwittingly on time.

She heard him preparing drinks, booze gurgling into the crystal glasses. She heard him put on the flat screen, expelling a loud breath as he dropped into an armchair that she knew was facing away from the door. Chancing to prove herself right she glanced past the door, feeling no reaction at seeing the back of head.

She padded from the bathroom to the doorway of the sitting room remarkably calm, as though she wasn't completely naked and carrying the world's most frightening drug. A single directive filled her mind, the last thing Bobby-Joe had told Chloe: Do Not Fuck Up!

When practically at his side, at the precipice of her long-awaited freedom, "Hello, Stonewall, and goodbye."

He lurched sideways, away from her, his smooth face distorted with shock. He didn't understand what he was seeing, that he was seeing Murielle naked, or why she was wearing a ridiculous costume. What was she doing there?

Her aim was exceptional, a mere few specks missing his face, instantaneous oblivion filling his eyes, the scotch falling from his limp hand. Leaving him wasn't easy, placing her faith and her life in the words of a strip club owner.

Ordering him to remain as he was, she went to the bathroom where she first flushed the powder-covered packet. She ran a shower, washing her costume thoroughly with shampoo before her hair and her body.

Walking into the sitting room, slipping her hands into fashion gloves and drip-drying to avoid using a towel, she breathed a sigh of relief. He hadn't budged an inch. She gulped the vodka in a single swallow, putting the bottle into Chloe's suitcase and returning a clean crystal old-fashioned to Stonewall's portable travel bar. Returning to the bathroom she scooped her costume into a facecloth and put that into the suitcase that she placed by her handbag and hat.

No time like the present, she told herself, as though she had a choice. "Stonewall, call your whore Cheryl DeMoine. Tell her to book a hotel in the Quarter. You want a romantic weekend with her. You should be with her by midnight, latest. And she is not to worry if you're late. You have something special to tell her. You love her."

He shrugged. "I can do that for you, Murielle. Of course." He pushed his weight from the seat, reaching into his jacket for his cell. Three rings later...

"It's Kenneth, my dear. Would you do something for me? Would book a suitable suite for us this weekend in the Quarter. I have something special to tell you which I believe merits a more romantic venue than our home." He listened. "Simply put, I love you. I shall be by your side close to midnight and you are not to worry should I not arrive precisely on time." He listened. "Yes. I do indeed love you."

Murielle swept a hand across her throat, ending the call. She left him standing and went to her purse for an envelope.

"Stonewall, write Cheryl DeMoine a cheque for 100 thousand. The money you owe her plus a bonus she

469

deserves for wasting a year of her life with you."

"I do owe her that money, Murielle. And such a bonus is certainly due her as well." He went into his jacket for his chequebook and Montblanc. Sitting at the desk he happily did as he was instructed, passing the cheque to Murielle's gloved hand.

"Now write her a note. Tell her this: My dearest Cheryl. I did mean what I said. Sadly I was unable to be with you for our romantic interlude, for which I do apologize. I trust this, my final gift to you, somehow lessens the pain of our lost weekend and what I can now never tell you. Yours most affectionately, Kenneth Stonewall."

He did, writing as she dictated, adding the woman's name and address to the pre-stamped envelope, giving both to Murielle, waiting as she once again disappeared into the bathroom. When she came out at 5:40 he hadn't moved. Her body was dry, though her hair was damp and she was not finished with him. This time she handed him a proper envelope and writing paper, dictating an address and sorrowful note of confession and regret that she put into her handbag to mail in the coming weeks.

She had one thing left to do: to give herself freedom. She ordered him into the bathroom, to strip, to take a shower and shampoo his hair. She wanted all obvious traces of the scopolamine washed from his head. When he was finished, wrapped in a towel, she told him to put his tainted shirt in Patricia's suitcase. With that done she ordered him to put on a fresh Belmont shirt, tucking the card that got her into the suite into the pocket.

She was strangely disappointed that her dream was going too quickly. She was having a good time, the first with him in over two unbearable decades.

"Stonewall, how much money is in your billfold?"

"Three thousand, Murielle. Would you like some?"

"I would. Two thousand, thank you. I also need the key to your Garden District whorehouse and the combination to your safe. That is where you keep the photos and videos of me? There are no other copies?"

"Correct, my dear. I have no other copies."

He went to his pants, digging into a pocket, counting twenty bills and passing her the money.

Then to his jacket, removing the key from its chain before sitting at the desk to scribble the combination without the slightest concern. Murielle, nearing the end of her time with him went again to her handbag, suddenly realizing she was still naked.

She put the handbag, her hat and suitcase by the door, ordering Stonewall to guzzle all that he could of his precious scotch while she dressed and did a final check of the rooms before leaving him. When she was certain no trace remained of her or Chloe, that she had done everything right, she ordered him to look into her eyes.

"Stonewall, add your shirt to what's on the floor."

He did, his chin and chest glistening with premium scotch.

"All things come to an end Stonewall. This is our final goodbye."

He didn't seem surprised. "Well then, goodbye Murielle."

"However before I go I do need you to do one thing for me. I need you to take that lamp on the desk. I need you to smash out that window. And I need you to crawl through that window. I need you to fly, Stonewall, to float in the air and think of me one last time. Can you do that for me? Can you make me very happy? Can you think of me as you're soaring toward the ground?"

"I can, Murielle, with the greatest pleasure. I will fly for you and soar toward the ground thinking of you."

471

"Thank you. Then we're done here."

Murielle stood by the door ready to leave. She watched as Stonewall smashed the glass without a care in the world, watching incredulously as he scrambled in his towel onto the sill to please her, to fulfill her long-awaited dream. He looked ridiculous, pathetic. He was completely insensible to the blood dripping from his hands and his legs, to the frantic screams below, to Murielle's throaty and gleeful "Bye-bye" a second before he disappeared from the twelfth floor.

In the lobby she strode unnoticed to the main entrance. Stepping into a warm summer evening she dropped the envelope addressed to Cheryl DeMoine into a mailbox, continuing straight to the Boulevard to call Chloe, not at all interested in the mounting confusion and the mess she left behind.

*

Murielle was familiar with the restaurant, sitting with Chloe after a pleasant fifteen-minute stroll. She needed the fresh air, she needed for the girl not to see the parade of police cruisers and ambulances coming from the east.

"Was he surprised, mom? Did that stuff really work the way Bobby-Joe said?"

"He did turn into a zombie before he could blink, sweetheart. I actually do believe he will not remember either of us in the morning. He called the DeMoine woman for me, telling her to meet him here this evening. Then he gave me exactly what I wanted. I have the key and the combination. I also have indelicate photos of him that I never care to see again, as insurance. Thank you, Chloe. I would not be rid of him without you, which does not mean you were not extremely foolhardy putting yourself in danger for me."

"The means justify the end, mom. That is true."

"Yes, this time. Because everything worked in our

favour."

Okay, change the subject. "She'll freak when she sees him, Cheryl DeMoine."

"There is that distinct possibility. She may even profit from his current condition. More importantly, we have the condo to ourselves this evening."

Near ten o'clock Murielle parked the Jaguar a block from Stonewall's condo. They left their designer handbags in the trunk, taking their wide-brimmed summer hats and dark glasses, the key, the combination, and an empty tote bag. Once inside they went directly to his study, the steel door of the safe clicking open with the sixth character of the alpha-numeric code.

Inside the most prominent feature was the shelf dedicated to the Murielle Collection, several DVDs and a four-inch thick photo album that Murielle verified with a lump in her throat as Chloe counted out 1000 crisp hundred-dollar bills. It all went into the bag along with the DVD depicting the love she shared with Anthony.

Murielle also put into the bag the forty-four DVDs and flash drives with names of other girls, now women, which she would review at her leisure and discard.

The folders and files detailing his off-shore accounts they left in the closed safe for the cops to discover whenever the dots connected. Nothing else mattered, particularly Stonewall. Of greater importance was that she had safeguarded Chloe Beaudoin's revived innocence.

45

At the penthouse minutes before midnight mother and daughter showered and put their clothes, hats and dark glasses into plastic grocery bags. Murielle soaked the contaminated shirt in her tub wearing rubber gloves, adding that with the clothes in the suitcase and vodka bottle into a third bag. Then they left wearing jeans and sweaters and drove into the crowded French Quarter where the bags and suitcase were tossed irreverently into separate dark alleys at about the same time Murielle assumed Cheryl DeMoine might be calling Stonewall, surprised if not devastated that she was speaking with a cop.

Chloe spent the night with her mom who put her to bed and tucked her in without much to-do. For Murielle, however, sleep was impossible. She poured a generously deep XO and went into her office to spend hours viewing and shredding videos and photos that made her sick to her stomach. Her one regret was that he wasn't at all terrified when he went through the window.

Too curious to wait, too on a high to sleep, she scanned through the year-long histories of his other forty-four naïve and blind sycophants. The sonofabitch had seduced and kept girls on contract since he was twenty, all of them young and beautiful, all of them degraded for posterity, until then, until that very evening. The one satisfaction any of them might truly glean from their years was that none was anywhere near as tarnished in the minds of so many as the naked and mangled CEO of Southeast Industries whose broken and bloodied body would become the next day's televised breaking news. If they would ever know.

The DVDs she shredded, the flash drives she twisted apart before falling asleep at her desk as the sun came up.

Late Saturday morning she woke to gentle hands clasping her cheeks, to a warm kiss pressing into her lustrous hair. Breakfast was being served on the terrace, a breakfast that ended in Chloe sobbing warm tears.

Saturday evening, after a day lounging in the sun like mother and daughter, they watched the six o'clock news, at once exchanging quizzical glances. The very well-known and respected Kenneth Stonewall was dead at age sixty-five, the tragic victim of an apparent suicide possibly triggered by substance abuse. An autopsy was being performed as police from both cities were interviewing hotel staff, his distraught live-in girlfriend and stunned Southeast Industries executives.

Murielle sat speechless, wanting to laugh long and hard, while Chloe blurted an emphatic "Good!"

They never spoke of him again.

The week passed quickly, as did the entire month of June. One week following the suicide not only was Stonewall dead, he was buried and yesterday's news apart from his illicit business practices. That Friday Chloe Beaudoin fulfilled her own special dream; she enrolled at Tulane, celebrating the event at dinner with her mom who was leaving the next day for a well-deserved vacation in Mexico.

The following morning Murielle departed Louis Armstrong International for a week at a singles club in French Martinique believing it might well be her final opportunity to fulfill the ephemeral fantasies and dreams of those she deemed most deserving of her, the most capable of pleasing her. Though what she truly wanted and what might actually occur during his next trip to the Swamp were such diametrically different realities that she refused to ponder the outcome or to even think of him.

She had no intention of marrying anyone, if not Anthony by some twist of fate. However, if losing him meant more frequent and pleasingly lustful vacations, she could think of much worse things in life. His loss.

Arriving home on the 21st tanned and satiated, the bright wide smile on her daughter's face spoke colourful volumes. Miss Chloe Belmont came running from the terrace waving the official court document that for the first time in her life gave her a real mother who would always love and cherish her.

The following Friday, three weeks after Stonewall's fall from grace, Murielle went to the post office with Stonewall's second letter to finalize arrangements for her coming week with Anthony Vincent who called earlier in the day to say he loved her and that he had changed his flight to Sunday. Karine had an opportune faculty meeting that would last into the evening, giving them more time to be with each other.

Their Sunday and Monday evenings together were romantic and wonderful.

Early Sunday he had come to her with roses and wine, Monday he took her to a romantic setting for dinner where whispers and couples holding hands were the norm.

Tuesday, July 01st, twenty-four years after closing her parents' door, she woke passionately wrapped in his arms, succumbing to the moment until reluctantly beginning their separate days.

Tuesday evening, returning from her day of lectures, Karine Vincent arrived home to a mailbox stuffed with a

padded envelope. Opening the package she put aside the DVD to read the letter. The first few lines stole her breath.
*

Dear Mrs. Vincent, my name is Kenneth Stonewall. We are unknown to each other of course. However we do share a common interest. I have discovered by way of the enclosed DVD and conclusive information recently sent to me by persons unknown that for the past twenty-three years your husband, Charles Anthony, has been delighting in a romantic dalliance with my de facto wife throughout his many trips to New Orleans.

Her name is Murielle Belmont whose charm and beauty are the envy of women everywhere. She is also extremely wealthy, which may or may not be an enticement to him. Though who's to say?

My purpose in writing this correspondence is not to cause you distress, for which I sincerely apologize. Nor am I able to guide your heart, regrettably. I can merely and selfishly do that which is best for me, which is to walk away with a heart that is broken beyond repair.

Best regards, and sincerest regrets,

Kenneth Stonewall.
*

Karine collapsed into the closest chair, horrified, dropping the letter to the floor from trembling hands. She stared at the DVD for several minutes, at once curious and afraid. Finally, lost in time, she pushed herself to her feet. She took the thing and went to the loft to view a beautiful girl and the handsome young man she had once met on a plane evolve into a cheating whore and deceitful sonofabitch.

One stiff drink was nowhere good enough, neither were two or three. Though the fourth did seem to calm her and she reached for her phone.

When Anthony answered her voice was even, clear and

articulate; she was after all an accomplished speaker. They spoke about their respective days. She loved him and he loved her. She missed him, hating that she would spend another night without him. She knew how much he hated being in the Swamp. He missed her as much. He hated being away from her and would be home soon, late Friday.

Then, "Oh, Anthony, one thing more before I finally let you go. Would you mind very much if I have a few words with your swamp slut...Murielle Belmont?"

Pariah In the Mirror

Other Mystery – Suspense - Thriller Novels
By Doug Booth:

The Viewing Room
The 4th Man
The Madam
Family Lies
Mother's Pearl Dagger
From Inside Her Bedroom
The Feast of Tombola
Deferred Prejudice
The Hunt for Gilligan Rose
The Fatal Diners' Club
Silent Conviction
A Christmas Killer, Comfort and Joy
Pariah In the Mirror
***
No One to Tell (Creative Non-fiction)

www.ingramcontent.com/pod-product-compliance
Lightning Source LLC
Chambersburg PA
CBHW030910050726
47498CB00003BA/677

9 780099 213575 1